Praise for Rita Rudner's
TICKLED PINK—A National Bestseller!

"Lots of great punch lines and lots of great wisecracks."

—*People*

"A witty, droll foray into fiction for Rudner."

—*Kirkus Reviews*

"In a story that is both funny and touching, Rudner has handsomely made the transition from nonfiction to fiction."

—*Library Journal*

"Rudner's own background as a comic brings genuinely funny lines and situations to a novel that is not only entertaining, but also a warm study of friendship in an insincere world. Clever and witty."

—*Sunday Mirror* (UK)

"A wonderful, funny book containing a great story and everything that's ever needed to be said about show business. I had a ball from beginning to end. It's terrific."

—Emma Thompson

"I laughed, I cried, I cried some more, I read *Tickled Pink* and I laughed."

—Dennis Miller

"Once again, Rita Rudner proves there is intelligent life in entertainment, thank goodness!"

—Whoopi Goldberg

"*Tickled Pink* is really two books in one. The first is the one you laugh at and the second is the one you laugh at all over again, only crying this time because it's even funnier the second time around."

—Hugh Laurie

Also by Rita Rudner

Naked Beneath My Clothes
Rita Rudner's Guide to Men

Tickled Pink

a comic novel

Rita Rudner

WASHINGTON SQUARE PRESS

New York   London   Toronto   Sydney   Singapore

This book is a work of fiction. Names, characters, places and incidents are products of the author's imagination or are used fictitiously. Any resemblance to actual events or locales or persons, living or dead, is entirely coincidental.

Copyright © 2001 by Rita Rudner

Originally published in hardcover in 2001 by Pocket Books

All rights reserved, including the right to reproduce this book or portions thereof in any form whatsoever. For information address Pocket Books, 1230 Avenue of the Americas, New York, NY 10020

ISBN: 0-7434-4262-8

First Washington Square Press trade paperback printing November 2002

10 9 8 7 6 5 4 3 2 1

WASHINGTON SQUARE PRESS and colophon are registered trademarks of Simon & Schuster, Inc.

For information regarding special discounts for bulk purchases, please contact Simon & Schuster Special Sales at 1-800-456-6798 or business@simonandschuster.com

Cover design by Anna Dorfman

Printed in the U.S.A.

For my Dad

Part I

Youth is something very new—twenty years ago
no one mentioned it.

—*Coco Chanel*

North by Northeast

Mindy Solomon harbored a trust issue from an early age.

"You always have to give people the benefit of the doubt," Mindy's mother used to advise.

"Why?" Mindy would ask. "Isn't it safer to assume people are going to let you down?"

This was a complicated question for a child to ask, but Mindy had always been full of complicated questions: How do families who live in mobile homes get their mail? Where did moths gather before the lightbulb was invented? Why do you never see a baby pigeon? And, most important, how could someone as nice as her mother, who never had a bad word to say about anybody and whom everybody loved, be stricken with a terrible disease? That was a question that defied any answer. *Fish banana.* That's what Mindy's mother would say when things happened that made no sense.

Before her mother's illness, Mindy's biggest concern had been how she would get to ballet class seven times a week. Mindy adored ballet lessons. She reveled in the discipline and the fact that there was always something definite to strive for. One pirouette was achieved, then two. The methodical progression of physical achievement was both satisfying and tangible to her.

Her mother first brought her to a Russian émigré who had

trained with the Kirov. His studio was located above a fish restaurant in Coral Gables. ALEXANDER MISCHINOFF'S SCHOOL OF CLASSICAL DANCE and THE FRIENDLY LOBSTER were both featured on the same sign. Once, an unattended batch of live lobsters made its way up the stairs to the ballet school. Little girls can scream, but they scream louder than anyone can imagine when confronted with live lobsters. Mindy liked to remember the lobsters voluntarily returning to the restaurant, their claws clamped tightly over where their ears should have been.

"You must tuck your tush under so no one will know it's there," Mr. Mischinoff would say to Mindy while tapping her derrière with his stick, thereby creating a fixation that would remain with her for the rest of her life.

One muggy Miami day in September, Mindy sat calmly in the living room on the sofa and listened for her father's car in the driveway. Before he had even opened the garage door, Mindy ran out of the house and said in a voice containing none of the emotion a television movie about the subject would demand, "Dad, mom died."

"Okay," her father replied.

They opened the door that had remained closed so much of the last year, as if to keep the cancer from metastasizing to other parts of the house, and entered the bedroom. Neither Mindy nor her father wept. They stood there quietly for a few minutes, saying final, silent good-byes, then made their way into the kitchen. Her father picked up the red phone receiver that had never quite matched the café curtains in the way his wife had intended. He opened the address book and began the task that had to be performed.

"Harriet, Rose passed away."

"Miriam, Rose passed away."

Mindy watched in silent witness as her remaining parent methodically notified all the people who would be angry if they failed to hear the news directly from him. Mindy realized the term *passed away* was much easier on the people left behind.

The word *died,* with its book-ending consonants, was too final. *Passed away* somehow implied the person now lived in another universe. Mindy, however, was unable to even get to *passed away.* She invented her own personal euphemism: *floated up.* Mindy preferred to think her mother was hovering above her, perched on a Posturepedic cloud, watching the show.

Mindy was thirteen when her mother floated up. She had never been a gregarious child, and her maternal predicament had made sustaining friendships even harder. So much of a child's social calendar is created by reciprocal invitation, and Mindy's mother's long illness had made hosting play days, birthday parties, and sleepovers impossible. Her mother's death further ostracized Mindy. Fellow students were sympathetic to her plight—"There goes poor Mindy" was a refrain she often heard whispered behind her in the school corridors. However, nobody actively attempted to engage the glum, sallow teenager in a meaningful relationship. For her part, Mindy felt neither able to experience nor to understand the carefree hysteria enjoyed by her contemporaries.

She was still happiest in ballet school, lost in the individual complexities of new moves that her growing body struggled to master. It was here Mindy developed her plan: Too young to either consider or fear failure, she would graduate from high school, move to New York City, and become a professional dancer. She had no doubt she would land a job in a Broadway show. Other possibilities never occurred to her, like ending up a murder victim, a drug addict, or, even worse, one of those people who bounce around on street corners, wearing a giant hand pointing to the new condominiums.

And so it was, a few years further on, that seventeen-year-old Mindy stood in the foyer of her Florida home, framed by the midpriced luggage she had requested as her high school graduation present, waiting for a dented taxi with questionable suspension to shake her to the airport.

It was the summer of 1980: Ronald Reagan was running for

president, Elizabeth Taylor was in rehab, and Sting had hair. Nobody was on the Internet, the ozone layer was thicker, and the Spice Girls were not yet potty-trained. It was not an innocent time, but, as with any year, it was more innocent than the times that would follow.

"Why are you going to New York? What have I done? Is it Smila?" her father asked, as beads of sweat serpentined guiltily down his forehead.

"Dad, it's not you, and it's not even Smila."

Actually, it was partly Smila. A mere year after Mindy's mother had died, her father had married a Swedish masseuse. Hal Solomon, possessing no psychological means by which to deal with his wife's tragic passing, had thought the best course of action for both his motherless child and himself was quite simply to replace one wife with another as swiftly as possible. Smila had not been difficult to find, Mindy had noticed bitterly, because Jewish widowers in Florida get snapped up faster than free samples of mouthwash at a garlic convention.

Smila possessed cheekbones that could slice salami and toes the length of fingers. Mindy marveled how, at six feet two inches, Smila could dust the tops of things that average-size women didn't even know were dusty. Mindy did not begrudge her father whatever happiness he could find. She realized how much he deserved a new life. However, his plan had backfired. Rather than providing Mindy with a replacement mother, his marriage caused Mindy to feel even more disconnected. When Mindy was sixteen her father and Smila unexpectedly produced a baby daughter who had a name that no one could pronounce, and now the three of them were a new family unit. Mindy felt it was time for her, part of her father's old life that had ended badly, to vacate the building.

"I have to go. There's nothing for me to do here," explained Mindy.

"You could go to college. That's why Grandpa left you that money."

"That's not what he said to me before he died."

"What did he say?"

"He asked me if he was in Canada."

"He was senile. I know he wanted you to go to college. He wanted you to get a teaching degree so you'd have something to fall back on."

"Well, all he said to me was that he felt there was a possibility he might be in Canada. I took it to mean 'Go to New York, be a dancer, and once in a while, face north.'"

It was a family trait to be glib in serious situations. Mindy remembered her mother, bald from chemotherapy, referring to her wig as a fur coat for her head. And in those final weeks, when Rose was too weak to watch television or to read, she had still managed to teach the family parrot, Rover, to moo. Years later, when asked to supply her religious upbringing, Mindy often told people she was "Glibbish."

The cabdriver honked outside. Mindy hugged her dad tightly and her stepmother loosely. The baby, Vendetta or whatever it was called, cried in the background.

Mindy took one last look at the living room. There was the expensive covered candy dish she had knocked over when she was three that became an ashtray in a house where nobody smoked. Nearby was the beige armchair with the cushion that must never be turned over because of the "barbecue sauce incident." And there on the wall was the too-perfectly-skin-toned family portrait of the happy three of them, precancer. The old furniture her mother had chosen was grouped into one corner of the room to make way for Smila's new modern sectional pieces. Mindy expected the old stuff would soon make its way to the garage, after which the Swedish masseuse would probably set fire to it.

Picking up her suitcase, containing mostly leotards and tights, and her shoulder bag, containing her grandfather's five thousand dollars and a tiny pink rose her mother had once made for her out of satin ribbon, Mindy made her way toward the front door. Her father followed closely.

"You can come home whenever you want to—you can change your mind—please be careful—call me when you get to the hotel."

He ran his sentences together to make sure he got everything in before Mindy closed the brutalized taxi door. As the vehicle pulled away, Mindy lowered her head, hoping the driver was unable to see her crying in the backseat.

A Room with No View

Mindy stood in front of the East Side Hotel for Women. As she stared up at the dirty, red-brick building that had seemed so much grander in the brochure, an ancient doorman appeared at her side. Mindy watched one hand touch the brim of the worn cap that concealed his gray, thinning hair, as the other extended toward the handle of her biggest bag, exposing a thin wrist below the sleeve of a once-green, wrinkled uniform.

"Hello. I'm Ralphie. Take your bags, miss?" the man inquired.

"Yes, thank you," Mindy replied, wondering whether someday he would call her madam and himself Ralph.

Decrepit, dilapidated, and possibly *diseased* could all be used to describe not only the lobby of the hotel but also the women in it. Mindy took in a white-haired woman in a shawl crocheting something long and meaningless in one corner of the room and the woman's companion, sleeping opposite, her arms, legs, and mouth all wide open. To their left Mindy noticed two other crones playing slow-motion checkers, while to their right a bridge foursome appeared permanently frozen either by indecision or rigor mortis. This was not what Mindy had expected. She had imagined something along the lines of the movie *Stage Door,* in which the young Katharine Hepburn and Ginger Rogers were constantly and giddily bounding up and down the polished staircase of a boarding house for ingénue actresses.

The women of the East Side Hotel could be in a movie, Mindy resolved, but it would have to be called *Stage Coffin*.

"Hi. Mindy Solomon. I have a reservation for a single room."

Standing in front of Mindy behind a battered front desk was the type of woman who refuses to admit that time has moved on. Her hair, her makeup, and her clothing had simultaneously achieved what she had considered to be optimum effectiveness, and she had tried to freeze that time. The results unsettled Mindy—eyeliner can enhance, but not when it is allowed to seep; black hair should be a shade of black that is possible in nature, not just in furniture; and surely ruffles after sixty-five were always a mistake. The antique receptionist put down her yellow-paged paperback book and began searching for the reservation.

"When did you make it?"

"May twelfth," Mindy replied. Mindy had not made a lot of reservations in her life, so the date was engraved in her mind.

"I have nothing here."

All the blood rushed to Mindy's head. Luckily, her skull was on duty and kept it inside. She was in a strange city, knew nobody, and was now facing the prospect of sleeping on the street.

"Who did you make it with?"

"A woman who had a voice that sounded exactly like yours," Mindy replied.

"I wonder who that could have been? I wasn't on duty May tenth. I went to see my sister in Syracuse."

Mindy corrected her. "May *twelfth*."

"Oh, May *twelfth*. You said May *tenth*. Oh, now you see, May twelfth, that *was* me. Here it is. You're on the fifth floor," the woman confirmed. "There are no men allowed anywhere upstairs at any time. If a man is found in your room, you will be evicted from the establishment. If you see a man upstairs, you are to report it immediately. There is an evening meal served in the dining room from six to eight. No men are allowed to attend. Any questions?"

"Where's the elevator?"

The receptionist pointed to a dark cage behind a sleeping woman. "It's broken. The stairs are to the right."

"Ahem." Ralphie the antique doorman cleared his throat. He was still holding Mindy's suitcases.

"Not allowed upstairs, miss, so if you'd like to take care of me now . . ." Ralphie stood with one hand extended, palm facing up. Mindy realized she was expected to tip. If anything signaled adulthood, it was this. She reached into her shoulder bag and handed Ralphie two dollars.

"Thank you," said Mindy.

Thanking people as you handed them money seemed to her excessive, but she was sure that was the way she had seen other people do it.

Five floors and two hundred burned calories later, Mindy opened the door to her room. She quickly closed it and opened it again, hoping she had opened it incorrectly and this time it would be bigger. It wasn't. It began with a stained sink, middled with a murky window, and closed with a single bed. Mindy felt confident she would not have to do much to keep men out of this room; even men who had recently been to prison would deem it confining. A cockroach wandered up the wall. Mindy wondered whether it was a male cockroach, or whether the bug kingdom had been notified of the East Side Hotel for Women's all-female policy.

As her face crumpled in disappointment at the thought of living here, Mindy noticed another door on the left side of the room. Her hopes soared. This wasn't the entire apartment. There was another whole room attached. She had prejudged. She opened the door and discovered the smallest closet she had ever seen. Mindy took a brief inventory; the bathroom was down the hall, the phones were downstairs, and her spirits were in the basement. After unpacking her meager possessions, Mindy went downstairs and called home.

"Hi, Dad. I'm here." *(Are you all right?)* "Yes." *(Do you want to come home?)* "No." *(What's your phone number?)* "There's no room for a phone, but you can leave a message with the front desk. I'll call you soon."

Mindy hung up quickly so she wouldn't start crying and went to survey the dining room. It was an orchestra of osteoporosis. Assorted hunched-over women gummed assorted curious meats. Mindy stood a little straighter so as not to catch the hunch.

"You're not seriously considering eating with this bunch of mummies, are you?" a voice behind her asked.

"Well . . . I . . . um . . . I . . .," Mindy stammered.

Mindy turned to see who had made the comment. Behind her stood a willowy girl, perhaps only a year or two older than Mindy in actual age, but light-years ahead of her in all the ways that really count. Ursula Duran was the kind of beautiful all young girls dream of being. Her legs were long and tan, her hair was straight and blond, and her teeth were game-show-host white and miniblind even.

"There's a place 'round the corner that's much better. C'mon—I'll show you."

The place around the corner was a far cheerier cafeteria serving tasty and unfussy food at sensible prices. As Mindy shuffled her tray alongside Ursula's, pulling a salad and a vanilla yogurt out of Plexiglas prison, the girls talked. And talked. And talked.

On the surface, Mindy and Ursula appeared to be total opposites: Ursula grew up freezing in Minneapolis; Mindy grew up frizzing in Miami. Ursula was a Lutheran; Mindy was a Jew. Ursula could not gain weight; Mindy could. For both, however, impossible situations at home had led them to the East Side Hotel for Women.

Ursula's story involved a mother too.

Staying Too Long at the Affair

🌿

Eva, Ursula's mother, had modeled briefly in her native Germany, which was how she had met Ursula's handsome, advertising executive father, Brandon Holmes.

When Brandon opened the door to his chic hotel suite, Eva was in heaven. She stood on the balcony, gasping at the beauty of the city lights twinkling below. The couple sipped champagne from cut-glass goblets while reclining in the Jacuzzi. They made love three times, then once more in the morning right before Brandon's flight.

Brandon checked the closet, the drawers, and the bathroom one last time.

"What for are you looking for?" Eva asked, glad that she had studied English at school and unaware that she should have studied harder.

"I'm just making sure I haven't left anything here that I'm going to miss when I'm back in New York."

"What about me?"

Brandon took Ursula's mother-to-be in his arms and assured her, "I'm never going to miss you. I'm sending you a ticket to New York next week. I've checked out, but you can stay in the room 'til eleven."

He kissed her passionately and disappeared down the hall-way. Eva flopped down on the sofa and planned her new life in America as Mrs. Brandon Holmes. Three weeks later the ticket had not arrived and neither had her period. She left numerous messages for her paramour at his New York advertising agency, but none was returned. Eva, however, was a determined woman.

"I need seeing Mr. Holmes," Eva told the receptionist as she stood in the waiting room at Benton and Burton in New York.

"Mr. Holmes, there is an Eva Rossler here to see you."

Brandon arrived instantly.

"Eva, good to see you." He threw his arms around her in a friendly fashion. "What can I do for you?"

"What can you do for me? You leave me in hotel room in Germany and I never hear again from you and you are asking me, 'What can I do for you?'"

The receptionist smiled as she pretended not to listen.

"Why don't you come into my office?" a panicked Brandon suggested.

Unlike its occupant, Brandon's office was sterile. With a plank for a desk, a stick for a lamp, and a brush stroke for a painting, the office could have been entitled *Portrait into the Psyche of the Uninvolved.*

Eva sat down on the backless sofa that was too low and demanded an explanation. "Why I did not hear from you?"

"You didn't really expect to, did you?"

"Yes. I did."

"But surely you knew it was a one-night stand?"

"You said you would never miss me because you were send-ing me ticket to New York."

"And when I didn't, what did that tell you?"

Eva's eyes began to well up with tears. "That you were lying. That you never want to see me or the baby."

Brandon's eyes opened wide. "What? But . . . ? Surely you were using something?"

"It did not work."

Brandon did some quick arithmetic. It had been only six weeks since the Munich shoot. He sat back down on his ergonomically correct chair and breathed a little easier.

"I know a doctor who will take care of you. Don't worry; I'll pay the bills. I'll pay your way back to Germany. This little episode is over."

"No, this little episode is not over. You will marry me, and I will be staying in America."

"Eva, you're a beautiful young girl, and believe me, if I wasn't already married, this would all go completely differently."

This time it was Eva's turn to expose her eye whites. "You are married?"

"Very," said Brandon, as he wrote out a check for a thousand dollars and handed it to Eva. "This should take care of everything. I'm sorry. I thought you knew the ropes a little better. I have to get back to work."

Eva took the check. Then she took off her dress. Her body was still sensational.

Their affair continued until Eva's pregnancy started to show. Brandon begged her to have an abortion, but Eva knew that the baby was her trump card. Once that was gone, there would be no chance he would ever leave his wife. Brandon wrote Eva a final check for five thousand dollars, demanding that she obtain an abortion and return to Germany. He would no longer see her or accept her phone calls, he told her firmly.

Eva felt she had no choice but to reveal her existence to Brandon's wife. On a windy winter's night, she confronted the rather plain, slightly overweight woman on the doorstep of a mock-Tudor mansion somewhere in New Jersey. In a grand gesture, she flung her coat open, held out her belly that housed Ursula the fetus and announced, "This is your husband's baby."

The maid said, "One second—I'll get Mrs. Holmes."

Instead of Mrs. Holmes, Brandon appeared at the door and wordlessly slammed it in her face. A few weeks later Eva admitted defeat and married Ted Duran, a junior executive at another ad agency. She had met Ted at a party launching the slogan for a new shape of potato chip: "Square, but that doesn't mean *you* are." Brandon had abandoned Eva that evening when some clients appeared who knew his wife. Eva had turned to Ted for emotional support.

"When will he leave her?" she asked Ted repeatedly.

"He won't." Ted replied. "Eventually you'll realize you should be with me."

Eva didn't think Ted was serious, but five months pregnant and with her visitor's visa about to expire, she accepted when yet again he offered to marry her and raise her baby as his own. They married quietly at a courthouse, and Eva continued to obsess about Brandon. When the opportunity came for Ted to be transferred to Minneapolis, he was sure things would change for the better. He was wrong. Now, not only were Eva's Brandon dreams over but Eva's modeling career had departed as well.

At eight and a half months pregnant, the body that was once Eva's greatest asset was now a waddling watermelon. She hated Ted for making her move out of New York, she hated the baby for ruining her body, and she hated herself for losing the battle for Brandon.

"Things will get better after the baby's born," Ted reasoned, and for a while he was right.

Although Eva's drinking increased, her English improved and she appeared content. She was fascinated with Ursula, at first.

"Look at her," she would say. "She's a little me."

She named her daughter Ursula Duran, determined to keep the exact nature of Ursula's father a hazy inconsequence.

Eva brought six-month-old Ursula and her touched-up baby modeling pictures into Henderson's Modeling Kingdom for Children and Young Adults and demanded a contract.

"Look at this exquisite child. Look at this face," she said, as she cupped Ursula's drooling baby chin in her hand.

"She *is* a beautiful baby," conceded Henny Henderson, as he sat behind his rented desk and scratched his hairpiece. "I think we can do something with her."

"She's got good genes," Eva said, deep-sea fishing for a compliment.

"She certainly has," agreed Henny, ever mindful of potential ten percent commissions.

When Ursula was six months old, her perfect face was featured on billboards all over Minneapolis, advertising Minnesotan milk. Eva used the money to get away from Ted, whom she soon replaced with someone else who also disappointed her.

As Ursula grew into a beautiful young woman, Eva began to resent her. When Ursula won the local teen modeling pageant and was the top junior model at the largest downtown department store fashion show, Eva refused to attend. Ursula could do nothing to please her conflicted mother.

Matters came to a head, Ursula confided to Mindy, when Eva's latest husband visited Ursula in her bedroom late one night. Mindy sat in the cafeteria listening wide-eyed, finding it difficult to believe what she was hearing, completely intrigued by Ursula's racy tale. Did things like this really go on?

"What did you do?" Mindy asked, licking the last dollop of cafeteria yogurt off her spoon.

"I kicked him in the groin."

"What did *he* do?"

"He doubled over and made a croaking noise."

"Then what?"

"Then my mom came into the room, and I told her what had happened."

"And she kicked him out of the house!" Mindy exclaimed.

"Close. She kicked *me* out of the house."

"Why?"

"She blamed me. She blamed me for making up a story about Sig."

"But you didn't."

"Do you think she wants to believe that? Do you think any-one wants to believe she married someone who tried to screw her daughter?"

"Wow . . . You really were caught in a shit storm without a paddle."

Ursula laughed. "I think the expression you're looking for is 'up shit creek without a paddle,'" she corrected.

"I don't think so," Mindy responded defensively.

"I do," said Ursula.

"That's how we say it in Florida," countered Mindy stub-bornly. "Maybe it's different in Minnesota."

"Maybe. Anyway, I like your version best. You're right. I was caught in a shit storm without a paddle."

Ursula stood up, and one of her elegant long arms sent the plate that had contained her Caesar salad flying. "There I go again," she said. "I am such a klutz."

Previously Ursula had dropped her tray when they had approached the cashier to tally up the cost of their meals. Mindy found Ursula's awkwardness delightful; somehow it made her even more attractive.

The two women returned to the hotel, sat in a corner of the lobby, and talked until late in the night. Ursula had been in the hotel for a month and was relieved to have found someone of her own generation to talk with. When Mindy finally went up to bed, she was exhausted but content.

For the first time in her life she felt she had truly connected with a female contemporary.

Falsie Advertising

The following evening, Mindy found herself waiting for Ursula and Ursula's new boyfriend Craig in a small bar on Lexington Avenue. She had been disappointed but not surprised to discover that Ursula had a boyfriend. Selfishly, she had hoped to keep Ursula all to herself. Craig's existence also further delineated the difference in maturity level between the two women. Not only had undeveloped Mindy never had a boyfriend, she had never even been in a bar before.

Mindy surveyed her surroundings, nursing the Tab she had ordered. Above the bar, a small television was tuned to a baseball game. Two stools away, a woman was talking to an imaginary neighbor.

"Son of a bitch," she said. "You lying, scumbag son of a bitch. Who the fuck do you think you are, you stinking bag of shit?"

Mindy was appalled and fascinated by the woman and her vehement anger. Suddenly the woman arose from the stool and walked toward Mindy.

"You see that son of a bitch? You see that lying, scumbag son of a bitch?"

As the woman pointed to the empty chair. Mindy froze. What would make a crazy lady less angry: to see her imaginary person or not?

"Yes," Mindy said opting for the former.

"Well, you stay away from him. He's mine. I don't want any sluts like you hanging around him, giving him ideas."

"Yes, ma'am," a frightened Mindy agreed.

The woman returned to her seat. "Mike, another scotch and soda."

"Sure thing, Gert," the bartender replied.

Mindy hoped that Ursula and her boyfriend would arrive before Gert accused her of having an affair with her invisible companion. She kept her eyes rooted to the television as Brooke Shields, looking like a thirty-year-old version of a twelve-year-old, whispered in a sophisticated innuendo, "Nothing comes between me and my Calvins."

Mindy wondered what it would be like to be beautiful, rich, famous, sexy, and twelve. Gert had a different reaction. She stood up and shouted at the television.

"Slut. You're a slut. You're a hairy whore-bag."

Where were Ursula and Craig? Mindy looked at her watch. They had gone to see *The Rose* and were due out at five. It was now six-thirty. Mindy started to worry, hoping her new friend had not been involved in any kind of accident. She had yet to learn that when people are late for an appointment, they are never dead. They will arrive eventually and blame traffic.

"Sorry," Ursula said breathlessly as she and Craig entered the bar. "The crosstown bus was a nightmare."

Ursula leaned into Mindy and whispered, "So? What do you think of him?"

Mindy looked over at Craig, leaning on the bar waiting for Mike the bartender to take his order. Craig was twenty-one and as unfairly handsome as Ursula was gorgeous.

"Cute, isn't he?"

Ursula needed no reply. She knew the answer.

"He's nice too," she continued. "He's the kind of guy you can really trust."

"How long have you known him?" Mindy asked, ready to

make a mental note of how long it would take her, once she found a boyfriend, to attain this special feeling.

"Almost a week. We met at a commercial audition, and that was it."

"That was it?"

"Uh-huh. I'm not coming back to the hotel tonight," Ursula smiled.

"Oh," replied Mindy, wanting more information.

"If you want to sleep in my room, you can. It's much nicer."

"What?"

"They gave me your room at first, but I said, 'Forget it, I'm checking out,' and they came up with this great corner room. I have my own bathtub."

Craig arrived at their table carrying two wine coolers and another Tab for Mindy. Gert looked on, admiring Craig's physique. Ursula reached for her drink but instead knocked it out of Craig's hand.

"Sorry. I'm so clumsy."

Mindy sneaked another look at Craig as they gathered together things that were absorbent. A person never feels quite as alone as when sitting opposite two people who think they are in love. Craig held both of Ursula's hands. Mindy was unsure whether this was a gesture of affection or whether he was just trying to stop her from knocking anything else over, but she suspected the former.

Mindy whispered to them all about her experience with the crazy lady at the bar, and Craig laughed heartily and justifiably at Mindy's curious turn of phrase and look of wide-eyed innocence. She was an unusual raconteur, which left Ursula confused. Not particularly funny herself, it had never occurred to Ursula that being funny was an attribute worth owning. Indeed, she had been schooled that being funny was somehow unfeminine.

"The man is always the funny one," Eva had always told her.

"The woman is the listener and the laugher; she is there to make the man feel important. The more important a man feels, the more he will give you, in bed and out."

Ursula had seen Eva laugh at all of her husbands. She had seen her wait on them hand and foot, and she had seen her grow to hate them when they failed to achieve the wealth and position she had envisioned. The ad agency executive, the lawyer, the podiatrist, the souvenir salesman, and now the restaurateur; Ursula referred to them by profession rather than by name. Craig would be a famous actor. Ursula was sure of it. Even if he were not, the strength of her love for him would be completely unaffected. Ursula handed Mindy the key to her room and left the bar draped around her man.

Mindy was amazed to find that Ursula's room had new wall-to-wall carpeting, freshly painted walls, and bathroom tile seams filled with young grout. Mindy settled into the sofa (yes, Ursula had a sofa) and slept better than she did in the bed in her own room. It was the first night of many she spent on Ursula's couch. Ursula started seeing Craig so much that she slept in her room only a few nights a month.

Mindy and Ursula's friendship deepened quickly during their long talks about love and men and relationships. Ursula admitted she had first had sex at fourteen, whereas Mindy admitted she was a reluctant virgin. However, seeing how swiftly Ursula's focus had shifted from her career goals to obsessing about her relationship with Craig, Mindy decided to put on hold any search for a person interested in deflowering her. She put her total focus on her dancing career.

Every week Mindy bought the trade papers and scoured them for open calls. Her first audition happened two weeks after she arrived in New York. It was held, rather suspiciously, in a hotel room on 57th Street. As Mindy rode up in the creaky elevator she thought to herself, "This is it; this is the way I'll be killed."

She searched for room 625, while her hand scoured her dance bag, feeling for anything that might serve as a weapon. Mindy's fingers curled around a particularly lethal roll of Wint-O-Green Life Savers just as the door opened, revealing four girls in leotards and tights sitting in a waiting room.

"Is this the place for the audition?" Mindy asked.

"Yes," replied one of the girls. "Armando will be out in a minute. Just change in there and sign in here."

The girl handed Mindy a clipboard and pointed to a makeshift dressing room in the corner. Mindy signed in and then stepped behind the curtain to pretend she was changing. In reality, she had her dance clothes on underneath her street clothes, since she could think of no circumstance under which being naked in a strange place might be deemed a good idea.

Mindy came out of the dressing room after an appropriate time lapse and took her place among the jobless dancers. She had chosen what she considered to be her sexiest leotard: fire-engine red with high-cut legs and a low-cut front. Though it was sexier than the baggy black T-shirt worn by the girl at the end who was at least forty pounds overweight, it was no match for the see-through crocheted number worn by Contestant Number Two.

Just do your best. What else can you do? That's what her mother used to say. *If they don't like you, fish banana.*

The door at the end of the waiting room opened and Armando and a small blond dancer appeared.

"Thank you very much for coming in," Armando said to the girl in an nonspecific European accent. "Next."

One by one, the girls were called into the room. The door was closed behind them, and ten minutes later they were excused. The door opened once more, and the girl in the crocheted leotard came out.

"Could you wait a second please, Suzie?" asked Armando.

"Sure," Suzie replied excitedly.

Mindy, the last to audition, was now summoned into the room. Shaking on the outside but sure of her talent on the inside, she listened to the instructions. The dark, attractive Armando taught her an adagio. This was Mindy's specialty. It was a slow routine that showed off her leg extensions and her balance.

"Very good," Armando proclaimed. "You are very good dancer."

"Thank you."

"How long have you been in New York?"

"Two weeks," Mindy replied.

"And you do not have a husband?"

Uh-oh. Warning signal ahead. "No."

"Good. Then you will be free to be on the cruise ship for six months."

Cruise ship? Six months? The audition in the paper had failed to mention anything about a cruise ship.

"Yes," Mindy heard herself saying.

"Excellent. Just wait here." Armando stuck his head into the waiting room. "Suzie, come in here, please."

A freshly powdered and lipsticked Suzie made her way into the room.

"You are both very nice dancers. You do the routine well. Now I have to see it without the top."

"You want to see it from the middle?" Mindy asked stupidly.

"No, I want to see it with no top. I am not trying anything funny. This is topless adagio act. I have to make sure they are right. They don't jiggle."

Suzie and Mindy looked at each other to see what would happen next.

"The ad in the paper didn't say 'topless,'" Mindy protested.

"Look, I don't have time for this babyness! If you don't want to do it, you leave."

"How much is it a week?" asked Suzie.

"Five hundred dollars. You get your own room on the ship and meals are free."

As Suzie lowered her leotard, Mindy excused herself.

Back at the East Side Hotel, Ursula was sympathetic, but only to a point.

"I don't see what the big deal's about," Ursula told Mindy casually as she sketched. "They're just breasts."

Ursula had been sketching a lot lately, saying it relaxed her. She was good at it, although she didn't consider it a talent. "Doodling," her mother had always called it, dismissing Ursula's drawing as a waste of time.

"I felt cheap," Mindy complained.

Ursula tore the page out of her sketchpad and stuck it to the wall with a dozen others. "Mindy, you're selling the way you move your body. That's what a dancer does. That's why show-girls wear skimpy outfits and nuns wear habits."

"Maybe that's what I should do. Become a Jewish nun," said Mindy, examining the drawing. "This is really good, Ursula. It looks just like me."

"Pfft." Ursula waved off the compliment. "It's cheaper than buying posters."

Mindy decided that Ursula was right about the audition. She had to toughen up and be less inhibited. This could have been her big break. It never occurred to her, and certainly not to Ursula, to blame Armando for failing to advertise in the paper that it was an audition for a topless act.

The next day was Mindy's eighteenth birthday, and Ursula and Craig took her out to celebrate. Ursula gave her Blondie's "Autoamerican," and Craig gave her a Rubik's Cube. Craig could solve it in under sixty seconds, but Mindy thought it looked prettiest all mixed up.

Mindy was grateful for her friends, but she couldn't stop thinking about the audition. She went back to her room to practice dancing topless in front of the mirror. If other potential employers wanted to see her breasts, she would be ready. Unfortunately, they did not. Mindy was cut early on in the next four auditions she attended. Winter was closing in and her money was dwindling.

Spirits sagging, Mindy began ever so slightly to panic.

Ursula began to panic as well when a few weeks later she found herself lying naked in a garage in Brooklyn. She had recently landed her first TV commercial. She was to be the Mattress Maiden for a new brand of bedding purported to be so advanced it could actually improve the purchaser's life. At the start of the commercial, Ursula would be discovered sleeping deeply on a mattress featuring foam rubber–coated smart springs designed to respond on an individual basis to various body parts. Seconds in, she was to be levitated over this magnificent engineering feat, visually underscoring the company slogan, "It's like sleeping on air."

To facilitate this heavenly image, it was first necessary to build a plaster body cast that Ursula would wear under her flimsy nightgown.

"Don't wiggle, or I'll have to start over," warned Elliot, the elderly plaster-casting specialist.

"Everything itches," complained Ursula.

"Good. That means it's almost ready."

The timer chimed, indicating that the casting was cooked. Elliot carefully lifted Ursula out of the tub by her shoulders and guided her on to a thick sheet of plastic. He produced a small but sturdy chisel.

"Lay very still so I won't gouge you."

Ursula cast her mind back to when she had auditioned for the commercial. She was certain the word *gouge* had never come up. She would have remembered it. It had been such an easy audition. All she'd had to do was lie on a mattress in front of a bunch of executives. She didn't believe it when her agent called to inform her she had booked the job. Of all the girls who had lain on the mattress, Ursula had apparently looked the most comfortable. This was a national commercial, and the residuals could keep coming in for years. It was worth a bit of gouging.

Elliot peeled Ursula out of her plaster girdle.

"Shit, this hurts," complained Ursula, as her pubic hairs were ripped out of her inner thighs.

Ursula showered in Elliot's small, grungy bathroom located in the back of the garage, dressed, and made her way back to Manhattan. As she sat on the plastic subway chair covered with angry graffiti messages, she contemplated whether to share her good career news with her mother.

"I think I should tell her," Ursula concluded to Mindy.

"Of course. She'll be proud of you. You've only been here a month and you have a boyfriend, an agent, and a job. All I have is a complex. I'm surprised you still talk to me."

Ursula stared at the phone, reached for the receiver, and knocked it out of its cradle. She turned to Mindy. "That's an omen."

Ursula carefully dialed her mother's number. "Hi, Mom—me. Hey, guess what? I have some great news. I got a TV commercial. . . . Well, my modeling agent sent me on the audition, and I got it. . . . I know I'm not in a magazine but . . . no, I'm not getting sidetracked. They needed a model to lay on the mattress. . . . No, I'm sorry, Mom. I'm going to do it. . . . No, I'm not giving the public the wrong idea. I'm just lying on the mattress. I'm not fucking on the mattress. Oh, fuck you."

Ursula hung up on her mother and started to cry.

"She's such a fucking nightmare."

"She doesn't mean anything," Mindy said, administering verbal aspirin and secretly admiring how well Ursula said *fuck*. "She loves you. She just doesn't know how to show it."

"Why does she rip me apart whenever anything good happens to me? Aren't mothers supposed to be happy when good things happen to their children?"

Mindy thought about her own mother and how ecstatic she had been when Mindy had won the role of the cowardly lion in her summer camp production of *The Wizard of Oz.*

"Your mother lives and my mother dies," Mindy said to Ursula. "If there is a God, he definitely isn't paying attention."

Ursula's makeup call time was six in the morning. Mindy woke up with Ursula at five and held ice packs to her friend's swollen eyes. A flamboyantly gay makeup artist painted Ursula until she was a goddess, then a quietly gay hairdresser piled Ursula's beautiful blond hair up on top of her head, pulling down a few tendrils and carefully arranging them with a curling iron until she was an angel. The account executive that Ursula remembered smiling at her during the audition poked his head in the makeup room and gave her two thumbs up. Ursula reveled in the attention. As always, it helped take away the sting of her mother's behavior.

A lot of work went into floating on air, Ursula noticed. Elliot carefully fitted his plaster creation onto her body. Ursula then slipped her nightgown over the body cast that extended from her shoulders to just under her buttocks. As she lay on the bed, the cast was attached to the hydraulic lift that would rise unseen behind her. The set for the commercial contained a bed placed in front of a light blue cyclorama with cotton clouds dangling on clear wire from the high ceiling in between. The hot, bright lights that pointed at Ursula and the mattress were jiggled, positioned, repositioned and re-repositioned for almost two hours while Ursula did her best to stay perfectly still and not sweat. Finally the lighting director shouted, "Beautiful."

"Thank you," replied Ursula.

"I was talking about the mattress," he responded.

Ursula had already learned that in the world of commercials, nothing is more important than the product. The product must always be presented at the zenith of its appeal, because it represents food on the table for the families of the people who make it, market it, and sell it. This was presumably the reason, Ursula concluded, why everybody involved in a commercial shoot always looked so worried.

The director resecured his backward baseball cap that hid his bald spot and yelled, "Action." A supervisor read the copy aloud, carefully keeping one eye on her stopwatch. All Ursula had to do was relax. She smiled in her pretend sleep.

"Cut," shouted the director, whose name was John, although he spelled it *Johann.*

He walked over to Ursula and leaned in, careful not to touch the bed. "Why are you smiling? Is something funny?"

"No, I just thought I should sleep happy."

"Well, don't. Just sleep. All you have to do is sleep. Enjoy your sleep, but we don't have to see it."

"Okay," replied a slightly shaken Ursula.

The commercial director, who was certain he should really be a movie director, returned to the chair bearing his name. A minion handed him a glass of water, and Ursula watched him take a self-important sip.

"Action," he bellowed.

The camera rolled and Ursula slept, this time internalizing her happy thoughts. Twelve seconds into the spot, the hydraulic lift was activated. Ursula began to rise. Her eyes opened wider than if she had seen a ghost.

"Cut," the director yelled. He walked over to Ursula. "Lover, the idea here is that you remain asleep. This mattress is so comfortable that you're sleeping on air."

"I know, but it's scary."

"That's why we're paying you," he said, his smile not reaching his dead eyes.

"I'm sorry. I'll be better next time, I promise."

Ursula smiled back at the director and wiggled her eyelashes, a technique that had neutralized men who had been annoyed by her in the past. This time it had no effect.

"Could I talk to you for a second, please?" the mattress executive said to the director and the guy from the agency. They huddled in a corner for an impromptu meeting.

"Can we fire her?" the mattress executive asked.

"Elliot, can we talk to you for a second?"

Elliot appeared quickly and joined the three in the power corner. The advertising executive put his hand on Elliot's shoulder to give the impression of casual camaraderie.

"Elliot, how long would it take you to make a new body cast?"

"A day."

The advertising executive turned to the mattress executive. "He'll take a day to make the cast, we'll take two days to find a new girl, then we'll have to rebook the studio and the technicians."

He turned to the director. "Johann, are you available?"

"I can juggle," Johann replied.

"Ballpark, the whole change will cost you around an extra hundred thousand," the executive concluded.

"Let's stick with this girl," the mattress executive decided quickly.

The director returned to his chair. "Okay, Ursula, you're doing great. And . . . action!"

The copy was read, the hydraulic lift was activated, and Ursula was raised elegantly into the air. Ursula concentrated on keeping her legs the same level as her body for a full thirty seconds. This took her just over three hours to achieve. A further approved take "for safety" took another three hours because the hydraulic lift became temperamental and started to vibrate. Ursula kept her eyes closed and her legs level, but the shaking seemed uncontrollable. At eight o'clock it was all over, and Ursula never wanted to see another mattress again. In fact, she had already decided tonight to sleep on the floor. Ursula had changed into her street clothes and was on her way out when the advertising executive approached her.

"Great job."

"Thanks, I'm sorry it took me a while to get my legs the right level."

"You were terrific. Do you have time for a drink?"

Ursula paused. She was meeting Craig at eight-thirty. "Another time, maybe."

The executive handed her a business card. "Call me. I'd like to take you to dinner."

"Sure."

He's old but cute, considered Ursula as she continued out the door, unaware she had just been hit on by her father.

The Happy Hoofer

Mindy spent New Year's Eve alone, making resolutions, while Ursula and Craig went to Times Square to watch the ball drop. The second week of 1981 gave Mindy a chance to fulfill the first resolution on her list: "Get into a show."

Mindy hoped fervently that the audition for a replacement dancer in the new hit musical *Heavens to Betsy* was the opportunity she had been waiting for. The advertisement in the paper had requested a young dancer strong in ballet, tap, jazz, and acrobatics, and between five foot six and five foot eight. This was uncanny. She was perfect for this job. The paper might as well have included the phrase *named Mindy*.

However, her previous audition experiences had made Mindy a little wiser regarding the ways of the theatrical world, and when she arrived at the stage door of the Landers Theater, she was not surprised to find over five hundred other young women who also fit the description.

Along with all the other auditioners, Mindy filled out a numbered card and handed it to a tall bald man wearing shorts and a T-shirt reading SO MANY MEN, SO LITTLE TIME. She pinned her number—227—to her leotard and joined one of the groups of twenty that the women had been divided into. She was taught a simple ballet combination by an impressive dancer who was the choreographer's assistant. Mindy made the first cut.

Now her chances were one in two hundred fifty.

The next combination was a jazz routine that showed off Mindy's turning ability and extension. Again, she escaped elimination. Only one hundred women remained, and Mindy felt her heart muscle tighten. Tap was not her strong point, but she got over the next hurdle and through to the final group of thirty. Four hours and twenty minutes into the audition, Mindy felt she had run an emotional marathon. Now the final thirty were asked to get out their sheet music and sing. *Sing?* Mindy panicked. The advertisement had made no mention of singing. What was it with these people? Why could they not include all the relevant information in the paper? Maybe she was going to have to sing topless.

One by one, women handed their sheet music to the pianist in the corner, walked out onto the empty stage, and warbled familiar songs to the invisible judges seated in the pitch-black theater. The good news, Mindy quickly realized, was that none of the women seemed in immediate danger of being offered a recording contract. The bad news was that Mindy had no sheet music, and she had never sung anywhere before, unless the shower counted. Her mind raced. She had to pick a song. It had to be a song that she knew well enough to muddle through. It had to be a song that the pianist knew, and it had to be a song she had sung enough times to be confident of the lyrics. It had to be a song entitled "Happy Birthday."

Mindy whispered into the pianist's ear. "Happy Birthday."

"Thank you, but it's not 'til June," the pianist replied.

"No, I want to sing 'Happy Birthday,'" Mindy explained.

"Oh. What key?"

"I don't know. A good key."

"Okay. Best of luck."

As Mindy walked out onto the stage, she realized that her hands had gone numb, as had her feet. Her upper lip began to twitch uncontrollably. The pianist started with a flourish, then carefully plucked out a starting note that Mindy managed to find. She sang "Happy Birthday" very loudly and clearly and, most importantly, on pitch. She then retreated to the wings of the stage and attempted recuperation while anticipating rejection.

"I didn't know they were going to ask me to sing," she moaned to Auditionee Number Nineteen, whom Mindy had heard abuse "Oklahoma."

"They always ask you to sing. I do fine until they fucking ask me to sing. Do you know how much singing lessons cost? I can't keep them up. My neighbor won't let me practice anymore, anyway. I start a scale, and she's on the fucking phone, complaining. Do I complain when she has parties and plays the fucking Bee Gees all night long?"

The tall bald man arrived in the wings holding five cards in his hand.

"Numbers Ten, Three-Eighty-Eight, Fifty-Eight, One-Seventy-Two, and Twenty-Seven—no, I mean Two-Twenty-Seven—please stay. The others, thank you very much for coming."

Mindy couldn't believe what she had heard. She was in the final five. She looked over and saw that Number Twenty-Seven was crying. This was not a business for the faint of heart.

They repeated all of the routines that they had learned that day, this time one by one.

"How much longer can this go on?" Mindy wondered, as she waited with the four other nervous dancers.

The tall bald man ambled over and said laconically, "You're all terrific. We have your phone numbers. We have things to discuss before we can make our final decision. We'll call you."

Mindy had arrived at the theater at two in the afternoon and was leaving at nightfall. She had used every muscle in her body, including some she had never met, and all she had achieved was hearing an indifferent bald guy saying, "We'll call you."

She had given them Ursula's number, and as Mindy entered Ursula's room, she noticed her friend was on the phone.

"Ursula, can you call them back?" she pleaded. "I might be getting a call."

"It's for you," Ursula told her, handing the receiver to Mindy. "It's someone from the Landers Theatre."

This could be rejection. She had to handle it like an adult, Mindy warned herself as she took the receiver.

"Hello. Yes. No. Yes."

Mindy hung up and turned to her friend. Her eyes filled with tears.

"I got the job," she screamed, as she and Ursula jumped up and down with excitement and relief.

Three days later Mindy arrived early for her first day of rehearsal. She felt a surge of pride as she walked down the dank, smelly alley, past the homeless person sleeping in the refrigerator box, and arrived at the stage door. No longer a civilian—a theater-loving, ticket-buying, seat-sitting ordinary Joe—she now had the right to enter a theater from the back. She paused to enjoy the moment she had worked so hard to achieve, then attempted to pull open the heavy iron door. It was locked.

I'm in the wrong place. I didn't really get the job. My watch has stopped, and I'm late. All these thoughts raced through Mindy's mind. She pulled the iron door again. Nothing moved. The homeless person stirred in the alley. He said one word that radically changed Mindy's immediate future forever. He said, "Push."

Mindy pushed open the door.

"Thank you," she mumbled.

"You're welcome," the man replied, wrapping the folds of his box a little tighter around himself.

Mindy entered the backstage area and looked around. Inside a partitioned cubicle sat a grubby old man on a grubby chair chewing a grubby, unsanitary cigar and reading a grubby copy of the *New York Post*.

REAGAN INAUGURATION MOST EXPENSIVE ON RECORD announced the front page. The stage doorman desultorily looked up from his paper.

"Yeah?"

"Hi. Mindy Solomon. I'm the new dancer," Mindy gushed.

"Downstairs," he barked, his cigar waggling in his mouth with each syllable.

Mindy descended the stairs worn shiny by years of eager feet and ventured into the large dressing room reserved for the female chorus. Racks of costumes took up most of the floor space, all grouped together in order of musical number. The headpieces, some feathered, some sequined, some strangely hairy, were placed on a shelf six feet from the floor that ran around the room's entire circumference. Above that, costumes deemed too large for floor level were suspended from the ceiling.

Against one wall Mindy saw five dressing tables facing a series of mirrors, all framed by bare lightbulbs. Each area clearly reflected a personality. The first exclusively featured Chanel products carefully placed upon a dark green towel. A picture of a handsome man whom Mindy recognized as the newscaster from *Live at Five* adorned this table's mirror. A half-burned candle was the focal point of the next table. All of the products here were labeled "natural" or "organic," and there was a picture of a friendly black dog wedged in this mirror's corner. A book entitled *Being Is Believing* was balanced on top of another paperback called *Chanting for a Better Everything*.

The third dressing area was sparse. A cardboard box half filled with beauty products sat beside a dying, potted plant. This, Mindy assumed, was to be her place. She sat down at the table and looked at her reflection in the mirror. *Heavens to Betsy* had been running for almost a year, and Mindy was the first replacement dancer to enter the show. She contemplated how proud her mother would have been of her as she pulled the pink satin rose she had brought with her from Miami out of her dance bag and hung it on the dressing table mirror.

"Look, Mom. I did it," Mindy whispered.

Of course you did, baby. You can do anything, her mother whispered back inside her head.

A rotund woman capped with bright orange hair and a pronounced overbite entered the dressing room. When the woman introduced herself as Bunny, Mindy was hardly surprised. The top front teeth in Bunny's mouth were at such an angle that they acted as an umbrella for her chin. It was strange to think that they had never met the rest of Bunny's chewing team, Mindy thought. So close and yet so far away; living in the same area but destined to keep missing each other by only half an inch. The woman reached for a long black dress on the first rack.

"Let's start with Black Tango," she sprayed.

Mindy tried on the silk haltered tango dress. It was beautiful. There was one problem. Correction, there were two problems. Margo, the woman who was leaving the show, was flat chested. Mindy, who was replacing her, was not. The two strips of black material provided in the dress's current form covered Mindy's nipples and not much else.

"Bunny, I have cleavage coming out the side. That can't be right," complained Mindy.

"Honey, it's sexy. This is the sexy dance in the show. It looks great. I wish everybody looked like that in Black Tango. Honey, if you fall out, I'll add strips to the sides to make you comfortable. Now try Red Tap Tux."

Bunny reached over to the rack of red satin tuxedos. Mindy was relieved that this costume fitted her a little better on the top, although was dismayed that the seams were tested in the hip department.

"Can you let this out about an inch?" Mindy requested in a soft, timid voice.

"Baby doll, it fits you like a glove. Here's Winter in New York," said Bunny, handing Mindy a long wool coat with a fur collar.

"This fits perfectly," Mindy said with relief.

"I'm not happy with that length. Two—no, two and a half—inches shorter. Stay there; I'll pin you."

Kathy, the dance captain, was businesslike and distant as she drilled Mindy repeatedly in routine after routine. Mindy danced and sweated and even grunted, which was unusual for her, and at the finish, all Kathy would say was, "Again." Ed, the pianist who had played "Happy Birthday" for her at the audition, was a welcoming, friendly face. At the end of the grueling eight-hour day, Mindy's head was spinning with dance steps she thought she would never remember. Overwhelmed but exhilarated, she just had time to dash home, take a shower, turn around, and rush back to the theater to watch the show.

Later that night, Mindy knocked on Ursula's door, hoping to share the adventures of her day. There was no answer.

"Strange," thought Mindy. She knew Craig had acting class on Monday nights, and Ursula had said she'd be home by seven.

Mindy searched in her oversize handbag that so effectively obscured whatever the item was that she was looking for and finally emerged with Ursula's key. The room was more of a disgrace than usual. Abandoned stockings and shoes littered the floor as if tossed from a moving car, and almost all of Ursula's clothes and costume jewelry decorated the furniture. Mindy was sorry she had missed the show. "Better like this? Or better like this?" was one of their favorite games. The two friends would take turns standing on the bed to get the best view of their creations in the small, blurry mirror over the bureau, endlessly attempting to assemble outfits that would be the envy of women they did not know. As Mindy hung up Ursula's New Wave black leather miniskirt next to a Laura Ashley lace blouse, she spotted a note in the rubble:

"M—gone out on a date. Tell you all about it later. U."

Ursula's on a date, and Craig's at class. Interesting, thought Mindy, standing on the bed and admiring one of Ursula's necklaces in the mirror.

Blond Date

Ursula had to give the advertising executive top marks for persistence. She had sweetly but firmly turned down his several requests for dinner, explaining she was in a committed relationship. However, his last call, in which he had offered to take her to any restaurant of her choosing, no strings attached, had weakened her resolve. Ursula had always wanted to go to Le Cirque. Eva had been taken there once, and it had remained a highlight of her life, representing as it did the style of opulence that Eva desired her days to be filled with.

Ursula had bought a tight, deep brown micromini suede skirt and an even tighter light blue sweater at the after-Christmas designer sale at Bergdorf's. Even on sale, the clothes were more expensive than a major appliance, and she had been forced to put them on the charge card that the smitten man in the credit department had been stupid enough to give her.

"No one else has been able to zip up that skirt," the bosomy saleswoman with the penciled-in eyebrows had commented approvingly. "Three of us tried to get it on a woman yesterday. I held the top together, Mona worked the zipper, and Elise watched to warn us if the side seams started to split under the stress. We got it up, but the woman couldn't walk. Look at that fit. It was made for you."

There in a nutshell was the dichotomy of fashion. Women

who can afford lofty prices usually have hips. Women who are young enough to have boy-style hips usually have no money. Ursula and Mindy had discussed this irony, and Mindy had suggested inflatable hips; blow them up if you want to have children, let the air out if you're going to a party. Ursula giggled as she remembered the concept.

Brandon was waiting for her as she walked up to the restaurant.

"Good evening," he purred. "You look lovely."

Brandon had remained devoutly single since his divorce fifteen years earlier, but had recently been considering getting himself a new Mrs. Holmes. After all, he didn't want to be alone in his golden years. He wondered whether this girl was a potential candidate for the vacancy. Brandon did the math as she walked toward him.

I'm fifty, but I look forty, he reasoned to himself. *She's twenty, so when I'm seventy, she'll be forty. That'll be about right, because I'll look fifty.*

God, he's old, thought Ursula. *He's got to be at least fifty. When I'm thirty, he'll be in his sixties. We'd look ridiculous together. For this to work out, he'd have to get a face-lift. Either that, or I'd have to get my face loosened.*

"This is bad," Ursula said as Brandon kissed her on the cheek. "My boyfriend would be very upset."

"Then we won't tell him," Brandon said, flirting, holding the door to the restaurant open for her and ogling her legs and behind as she made her way inside.

The interior of the restaurant was still exactly as her mother had described it so many times when Ursula was a child. Huge bouquets of fresh flowers stood regally on every available surface. Ursula wondered whether it was like this every night or whether someone connected with the restaurant had either died or won something. The Upper East Side clientele fascinated Ursula.

"Wow, look at that ring!" she whispered to Brandon. The woman seated at the table directly opposite was wearing a diamond that seemed the size of a baseball.

"She has to wear that ring so you won't look at her face. She'd happily give it up to look like you for just a day."

"Yeah, right. My turquoise necklace looks a little crummy compared to that. Do you think I should take it off?"

"No. You should leave it on, but you should take off everything else."

So there it was. His first thrust, so to speak.

"You're not shy," Ursula retorted.

"There's very little point to being shy. As you get to know me better, you'll see . . . with Brandon Holmes, what you see is what you get."

"The question is, am I going to want it?"

"Eventually," Brandon said confidently.

He perused the wine list in a commanding fashion, eventually settling on a '62 Burgundy. After Ursula confessed she had no idea what to order from the complicated French dishes staring at her from the menu, he ordered the food that best accompanied the wine.

"Delicious," Ursula enthused, after swallowing a piece of whatever it was. She knew she had to be careful. In addition to knocking things over, she had a tendency to talk with her mouth full, and occasionally, bits of food could travel onto unsuspecting dinner partners.

"Should I order us another bottle of expensive wine that I'm sure your unemployed actor boyfriend could never afford?"

"I don't think so."

Ursula had been feeling a little queasy all day. Craig had the flu and she hoped she wasn't catching it. The last thing she wanted to do was to throw up in the beautiful bathroom at Le Cirque. She had already knocked over a pepper mill the size of a small child on her way to the table.

"It does not matter. It was just an antique for show," the maître d' explained sadly as an army of French men with brooms appeared to erase the evidence of Ursula's clumsiness.

"I can't believe that was your first commercial. You seemed like an old pro."

Chew, chew, chew, and swallow.

"Thank you. I was really nervous. I thought you were all getting mad at me when I couldn't keep my legs the same level."

"Don't be silly. You were fantastic. And you'll never guess what I have in my apartment."

"Let me guess . . . a wall-to-wall bed?"

"A copy of our commercial. It's the director's uncut version. It runs about an hour and twenty."

"Really? Oh God, I'd love to see it, but I don't go to strange men's apartments on first dates."

"Well, this is a terrible situation," Brandon replied in mock horror. "What do you think we should do about it?"

"I don't know. Maybe I'll stand on the sidewalk, and I can watch through the window."

"I'm on the twenty-ninth floor. You might pull a neck muscle."

"That's true."

"How about if I promise not to touch you unless you want me to? I told you . . . with me, what you see is what you get. We'll take this as slow or as fast as you want it to go."

Ursula looked at him doubtfully.

He stared back deeply, suddenly serious. "Honey, I'm that old-fashioned thing your generation makes fun of. I'm a gentleman."

Ursula noticed he looked a little younger when he opened his eyes like that, particularly if she squinted.

A wealthy older man is like a little black dress, she remembered her mother counseling. *It may fray a little around the edges, but it never goes out of style.*

• • •

It was the kind of apartment that divorced men covet: perfect for affairs, a game of poker, or an autopsy. A black leather sofa was centered in the sunken living room behind a midnight lacquered coffee table. A huge aquarium full of brightly colored fish dominated one wall. If James Bond and Jacques Cousteau had married and had a bachelor son, Ursula decided, he would live here. A huge picture window provided a magnificent view of the guy in the building across the street. Brandon quickly lowered the shade as soon as they entered the apartment.

"And we say *bon nuit* to my good neighbor, Bill. A nightcap?" he asked, slipping behind the corner bar and taking two glasses from the mirrored shelf.

"Brandy, please," ordered Ursula.

Although she had never tasted brandy before, she recalled her mother, a firm believer in the medicinal properties of alcohol, recommending brandy as a sure-fire remedy for a bad stomach.

"Good girl. I'll have one too."

As Ursula collapsed into the luxurious sofa, Brandon sat down next to her, placing the drinks on the black lacquer coasters that lived on the black lacquer coffee table. Before Ursula could fully sense what was happening, Brandon took her in his arms and kissed her. Ursula was too shocked to do anything but kiss him back.

"Hey, what happened to 'as slow or as fast as you want to go'?" she said, her eyes opening wider than a cash register after a robbery.

"I was testing you. I can't know the speed until I drive the boat."

Suddenly it was happening, and there was nothing Ursula could do to stop it. She did not want it to happen in the worst way. She was not that type of girl.

However, she looked at Brandon, he looked at her, and there, right on the sofa, Ursula threw up.

Show Too Much Business

Mindy sat paralyzed at her dressing table, staring at the good-luck presents that sat unopened in front of her. It was a tradition for the gypsies in the show to give the new dancer token gifts to make her feel welcome.

"Open them already. It's almost half-hour," commanded Becca, the cute Asian dancer lying on the floor, stretching her leg above her head.

"Ming, ming, ming, ming, ming, ming, ming, ming, ming," Nicole vocalized up the scale, disturbing Fredlyn, who was in a crucial stage of false eyelash application.

"Nicole, you're not allowed to vocalize after half-hour," said Fredlyn, holding the lashes that her eyelids had already rejected twice that evening.

"It's not half-hour yet," snapped Nicole.

"Hey, girls. It's Mindy's opening night. Could we keep the atmosphere in here level for her?" Heather pleaded, her eyes closed as she meditated in front of her scented candle.

"Half-hour, company. It is now half-hour," the stage manager's voice boomed over the loud speaker.

"*Now* it's half-hour, and *now,* I will stop vocalizing," Nicole announced snottily, beginning to apply her Chanel makeup.

It was seven-thirty, and Mindy had been rehearsing at the theater since ten A.M. The union-sanctioned two-hour full dress rehearsal had occurred at five P.M., and it had not gone well. Mindy knew the routines perfectly when alone with Ed the pianist and Kathy the sour dance captain, but once the sets, orchestra, costumes, and cast had been included, her head had emptied faster than an embassy following a bomb threat.

"It's perfectly normal," said Ed, consoling a distraught Mindy. "Bad dress rehearsal, good show."

Mindy attempted to distract herself by opening her presents. Incense from Heather, a makeup organizer from Becca, a scarf from Nicole, and cookies in the shape of penises from Fredlyn. The last envelope she slit open contained a card that read "I know you'll be great. Love, Ed."

Mindy's father and Smila the Swedish masseuse had flown up from Miami for Mindy's debut. The only person missing was Ursula, still feeling too weak to venture out after her abortion.

Four days before, an emotionally distraught Ursula had knocked on Mindy's door. She had just been phoned with the results of her pregnancy test.

"Do you have a paddle?" she sniffed tearfully.

"Why?" Mindy asked.

"Because I think I just hit a shit storm."

Ursula had already made the decision to terminate the pregnancy. Mindy helped her friend find a clinic, accompanied her and her overnight bag there early one morning, and then brought a paler and emptier Ursula home the next day. Mindy felt guilty. As she was having the best week of her young life, Ursula was having the worst.

Mindy's first night in *Heavens to Betsy* was a blur, although one thing was opaquely clear; Bunny was going to have to add those two panels to the bosom area in the Black Tango gown. As Mindy bent over and held her position stoically for the required sixteen beats, an unruly breast popped out to say hello. Her gay dance partner, Shane, was too afraid to coax the offender back indoors, never having touched one before.

Otherwise, Mindy's wig fell off only once, and the drummer was able to toss it back onstage almost immediately. There are many lessons that can be learned only through that cruel friend and enemy, experience: How to secure a wig to a scalp and bosoms to a skimpy costume were two of them.

After the show, Mindy's fellow cast members were kind in that way people affect when they don't know what else to say.

"You were fine," Fredlyn said in a high, lying voice. "I fell and needed twelve stitches in my forehead my opening night in my first Broadway show."

"It was an amazing performance."

"So much enthusiasm!"

"Wow. You did it, didn't you?"

The cast members' words were arranged more carefully than Elton John's hair. There was a knock at the dressing room door.

"Mindy, could I talk to you for a second?"

Mindy stepped outside the dressing room and into the dimly lit hallway. Kathy, the enthusiasm vacuum, was sucking her lips together even harder than usual.

"Belinda wants to see you."

Mindy's entire body froze.

"Why would Belinda want to see me?"

Kathy shrugged. "All I know is she didn't sound happy."

As Kathy led Mindy down the stairs to the star's dressing room, Mindy mentally replayed anything she had done that could have offended Belinda Mason, the star of *Heavens to Betsy*. She'd had no contact with her onstage and had met her just once briefly before the show.

"Welcome to the family," Belinda had cooed in her trademark deep voice. She had squeezed Mindy's hand and smiled sincerely and was already walking away as Mindy replied, "Thank you."

Belinda Mason was that aging bundle of energy that exists only in the world of Broadway theater. Mindy knew the multi-talented Belinda had seen her three smash Broadway hits go to the big screen starring actresses who could neither sing nor dance but whose features pleased the camera in a way that, even after her extensive plastic surgery, Belinda's never could. When Mindy entered the Number One dressing room, Belinda was seated at her dressing table wearing her robe and an attitude.

"Come in. Sit down."

Belinda ushered Mindy to her crushed-velvet sofa and plopped down next to her.

"How old are you?"

"Eighteen."

"Oh, my God."

Belinda turned her head away so the words would not hit her directly.

"Well, I just wanted to tell you the little bosom show you put on tonight was not appreciated. If you want to expose yourself to live audiences, I suggest you move over to 42nd Street. There are plenty of theaters there that would be happy to accommodate you."

"But it wasn't on purpose. I asked Bunny to redo the top of that costume, and she wouldn't."

"I see. Blaming the costume mistress for your own devious ploy for attention. Your wig falling off—was that Bunny's fault too?"

"No, ma'am. I didn't know how to pin it."

"Yeah, right. Do you think I'm stupid?"

Belinda's surgically altered eyes stared accusingly at Mindy.

"No, ma'am," Mindy replied, her eyes welling up with tears.

"Don't call me 'ma'am.' Just don't do it again! And for God's sake, get older."

Kathy escorted Mindy out of the room.

"I didn't do anything on purpose. Honestly," Mindy protested.

"Belinda's a little insecure. You would be too if you were three times the age of the rest of the cast."

"Three times? How old *is* she?"

"Nobody knows. Rumor has it she even gets her X rays touched up."

An hour later, Mindy, her father, and Smila were seated at a window table in a revolving restaurant overlooking Times Square. Mindy's father raised his glass of champagne.

"To my daughter, a new Broadway star."

He and Smila sipped their champagne while Mindy worried.

"I don't think they'll fire me, do you?"

"What do you mean? You were great. The others were garbage."

"Hal, a person can always be fired."

Smila reached into the small bowl on the table and picked out a mystery snack that seemed a cross between a cracker, a nut, and a dried pea.

"It was only my first night. I'll get better, Smila."

"Honey, she didn't mean it. Did you, Smila?"

"Mean what?" Smila challenged.

"What you said. That they might fire Mindy."

"Hal, I don't think you and your daughter should gang up on me like this."

"We're not ganging up on you. It's Mindy's first show, and she's a star. Anybody can see it."

"Well, Belinda Mason certainly didn't," Smila said.

"It's my opening night in my first Broadway show. Why are you being so mean?" Mindy asked, a little too forcefully.

"Hal, are you going to let your daughter talk to me like that?"

Mindy wondered which way her father would lean.

"Now, now, Mindy. There's no need to raise your voice. Apologize to Smila. This is her first time in New York, and we want to have a good time. We don't want to argue."

"I don't want to argue either. Have a nice time sightseeing tomorrow and a nice trip home." Mindy stood up to leave.

"Mindy, sit down. Please don't ruin our evening," Smila ordered, confident that she had won Hal's support.

"It's not your evening. It's my evening, and I'm leaving," Mindy said, picking up her dance bag. She attempted to locate the exit, which, when one has been sitting in a revolving restaurant for over an hour, is more difficult than it at first appears.

Ursula was asleep when Mindy got back to the hotel, but there was a note stuck to the mirror: "Sorry I couldn't wait up. Hope it was great. Love, Urs. P.S. Ed called. Who's Ed?"

Ursula, Get Your Gun

Every time Ursula looked at Craig all she could think about was the lost little person she'd removed from her body. There was only one solution to this problem, she decided. She had to stop looking at Craig.

Unaware of her pregnancy complication, Brandon thought Ursula had been made sick by something she had eaten in the restaurant and felt somewhat responsible. He had called her repeatedly since the unfortunate regurgitation, asking when he could see her.

"Hey, we have to go out again. Nothing's ever going to happen that's worse than that."

"No. Thank you, but no," was all Ursula would say before putting the phone down.

She knew she could not look at Brandon either. Ursula had been careful not to mention anything about her predicament in her weekly phone call to her mother, and Eva was too busy talking about herself and her impending divorce to notice any tinge of sadness in her daughter's voice.

"I can't believe I did it again. What a loser," Eva whined into the receiver. "Career. You concentrate on your career. Forget about a man taking care of you. They're all big, hairy losers."

Ursula could hear the ice rattling in Eva's tumbler of Scotch.

"How are you doing? Any jobs coming up?"

"Three."

"*Three?* You have *three?*"

"Yes, two prints and a runway job for Daniel G."

"I might come up to visit you. I've got to get out of stinking Minneapolis. It's still so cold here, I'm peeing ice cubes."

"You're going to come visit me? My room is really small. Are you sure?" Ursula started to panic.

"Maybe I'll stay for a while. Maybe we'll get an apartment. Why don't you start looking for something on the East Side? I don't want to live on the West. They're not civilized over there."

Eva hung up the phone. She was wired. If an electric plug had been fitted up her nostrils, she could have powered a small appliance. The tips of her fingers tingled as she tossed her suitcases on the bed and began speed-packing and speed-fantasizing. Eva had read how Brooke Shields had recently segued from model to movie star and was being managed by her mother. If her daughter's career was starting to take off, Eva rationalized, Ursula too would need a manager. *Brooke* was a great name. Eva wondered if she should have named Ursula after a body of water. *Lake. River. Puddle.* No, *Brooke* was the best water name and it had been taken.

Ursula had been a lousy choice, she realized. It sounded so serious. The *Ur* was the problem. It was too guttural and stern. An *Ursula* would smack your knuckles with a ruler if you talked out of turn, thought Eva. An *Ursula* would neglect to give a thirsty dog water. An *Ursula* would wear her hair in a bun and purse her colorless lips in an expression of permanent disapproval. There had to be other names that were sexy, unusual, and fun. What about weather, Eva wondered. *Windy, Stormy, Balmy.* Those were great names, but most of them had been adopted by strippers. Eva kept thinking.

Ursula was not going to be just another model, she decided. Eva would turn her into an industry. The opportunities were endless. Eva could produce the movies that Ursula would star in. The perfumes, the skin creams, the hair products. Eva's nose began to twitch. She could actually smell the money. Fuck men. Fuck everyone except her and her daughter. They would live in a penthouse so high they would look down at the Empire State Building. Maybe she would fail to tell people that she was Ursula's mother right away. If she lost a little weight, people would think they were sisters. Ursula had better be careful not to introduce her dates to her, Eva considered wryly, as she closed a bag and caught a bit of lace from her best pair of panties in the zipper.

Normally this would have devastated Eva. Tweezers would have appeared and a detailed operation rivaling the separation of Siamese twins would have ensued. Instead, Eva ripped the lace out of the zipper with abandon and tossed the underwear to the floor. In a few months she could afford to buy an entire underwear store, she rationalized. *Who cares about a little bit of lace? Lace. No. Lacey. That's a good name. Feminine. Sexy. See-through. This is my daughter, Lacey.* Yes, that sounded good. Eva considered calling Ursula right then and telling her to make an immediate change but then decided she would tell her tomorrow when she saw her.

Ursula awoke the next morning unaware that her name had been changed and her life was no longer her own. She looked over at Mindy sleeping so peacefully on the sofa and debated whether to wake her up to tell her about Eva's new plan. No, Ursula considered. She knew her mother too well. Eva would meet a new man tomorrow and not give another thought to moving to New York. Ursula slipped out of the room, taking care not to wake her friend.

Some time later, Mindy was dreaming about termites. They were tapping, tapping. They wouldn't stop tapping. She wrapped the pillow around her ears. The termites continued to tap. They were getting bigger. These were sumo termites. She opened her eyes and realized that someone was knocking on the door. Blearily reasoning that Ursula had forgotten her key again, Mindy staggered to the door in her oversize T-shirt.

"Maybe I have the wrong room." Eva looked at the number on the door. "No, this is it. Who are you?"

"Mindy Solomon. I'm a friend of Ursula's. Who are you?"

"I'm Ursula's mother."

Eva began the cumbersome process of pushing her substantial suitcases into the already-filled-to-capacity room.

"They don't even let a man help you with the luggage in this place. Ridiculous."

As often as Ursula had described Eva, Mindy still was unprepared for the bleached-blond presence that stood before her. The bright red, too tight, low-cut dress at ten in the morning was more suitable for a hooker than a mother. A large fake diamond pendant was being molested between Eva's substantial breasts, and the cinch belt that was nestled in what Eva perceived to be her waist was barely visible. As Eva pulled her sequined cigarette case from her fake fur leopard handbag and plopped herself down on what used to be Mindy's bed, Mindy watched her produce a lighter in the shape of a muscled man in a Speedo. Eva flicked the lighter; the man bent over, and a flame appeared out of his behind.

"Isn't that cute?" remarked Eva, noticing Mindy staring at her boy-toy.

Eva sucked in some primo tar and nicotine, crossed her large, shapely legs, and removed her spiked-heel shoes. Mindy had never seen such tortured toes. They were piled on top of each other like a Chinese circus act.

"So where is my daughter?" asked Eva, rubbing her high arches with the hand not in charge of the nicotine fixes.

"I think she had a print job today."

Mindy was torn about how much information to give Ursula's mother. Maybe she shouldn't have said "print job."

Maybe she shouldn't have even said she was Ursula's friend. The last thing Mindy wanted to do was create further friction between her best friend and her maniac mother.

"Where?" Eva demanded.

"I don't know, but she's usually back by seven."

Mindy started to collect her personal items and attempted a quick exit before any more questions could be launched in her direction.

"Who's her agent? He'll know where she is."

"Ursula doesn't really tell me these things. I have a ballet class at eleven and I'm a little late. Very nice to meet you. I hope you have a great time in New York. 'Bye."

Mindy closed the door behind her and scuttled back to her own horrible room that was suddenly looking really good. So were, for that matter, her father and the wretched Smila.

Eva was already on the phone when Mindy closed the door. The address book on the nightstand had provided her with Ursula's agent's number.

"I'm her mother, and today is her birthday, and I want to surprise her," Eva said, fabricating.

"I didn't know it was her birthday."

Brittany Klein was suspicious. Her fingers tap-danced through her file drawer as she plucked out a bright blue folder and looked up Ursula's details.

"My records show that Ursula is going to be twenty on May twenty-third. Today is the thirteenth."

"I think I know when I screamed for drugs. She's lying. She was born on May thirteenth at five o'clock in the morning, and she is not turning twenty. She's turning eighteen."

"Well, if that's the case, we need your signature on her papers," Brittany replied in a sunny voice that masked her panic. Her client was just starting to blossom. A pushy mother would ruin everything. She tried to make nice-nice. "I'm really looking forward to meeting you. Ursula has said so many lovely things about you," she lied through her clenched, capped teeth.

Eva would have none of it. "I'll need to review whatever papers my daughter has signed with you. When can I see them?"

"I can assure you they're just the normal papers that all clients sign with their agents."

"Look, sweetheart, you might take my daughter for a patsy, but you haven't met me. Where's she working today?" Eva demanded, standing up and unhooking her belt in the event a louder tone of voice might be required.

"I don't think you should bother her at work. Why don't we all meet later in the day?"

"If you don't tell me the whereabouts of my daughter immediately, I'm going to have you investigated for employing a minor without parental consent. I don't think that will be especially good for your business, do you?" threatened Eva.

"Noon at six-two-six Eighth Avenue. Studio nine."

Brittany hung up the phone and shook two aspirin out of the almost-empty economy-size bottle she kept on her desk. She washed them down with warm Diet Coke and wondered why she had ever became an agent; things had been so much less complicated when she was an exotic dancer.

Eva had been in New York City for less than an hour and was already furious at her daughter. What was Ursula doing telling her real age? Had she learned nothing from her mother? Eva knew it was a good thing she was here now to handle these important details before Ursula could screw up anything else.

"You're mixing the brownies, but at the same time you're smiling at your son," the photographer directed as he adjusted his camera tripod.

Ursula was wearing a housedress covered by an apron and standing in a pretend kitchen. Her eight-year-old son for a day was staring up at her, adorably perfect and costumed in jeans and a baseball cap worn backward. Advertising being advertising, a twenty-year-old beautiful young woman who had never baked a brownie, worn an apron, or was even physically capable of having an eight-year-old child had been chosen to sell this product to middle-aged housewives across America.

"That's it. Hold it. Smile. I love it. Perfect."

Eva looked at her piece of paper, then looked at the sign on the heavy iron door that said STAGE NINE. She pushed it open and stepped inside. All heads turned as Eva screamed, "Oh my God in fucking heaven."

Seeing her daughter cooking in an apron had not been the image she had been anticipating.

"Mother!"

Ursula accidentally dropped the brownie-battered spatula on top of her pretend son's head.

"What's going on? You're a fashion model. What are you doing wearing a rag in a kitchen?"

The client was already on the phone to the police. "She's creating a disturbance. I don't know who she is, but she's crazy. She could have a gun."

Ursula ran off the set. "Mother, stop it. I'm working."

"Not anymore. This is a disgrace." Eva pulled her daughter into a corner. Casper, the photographer, came to Ursula's rescue, wrestling Eva's hand from Ursula's arm.

"Hey, leave her alone."

Eva slapped him. "Don't touch me and don't tell me what to do. Ursula, get dressed. We're going."

"No, Mother. Get out. Now."

Brittany Klein had thought it might be wise to show up a little early on the set to warn Ursula about what was heading her way. She tipped the cabdriver and made her way toward the building slowly, because the car accident that had ended her exotic-dancing career had left her with a pronounced limp.

Brittany assumed the squad cars parked in front of the building were there for just another routine Manhattan robbery or murder. She had no way of knowing that they were surrounding Eva on stage nine.

In a strange way, Eva was enjoying the attention as the beefy men in navy blue pulled her away from her daughter and cuffed her hands behind her back.

"Calm down. You're going to have to calm down now," the officer commanded, sitting Eva down on the sofa.

Eva reverted to the little-girl voice she brought out for special occasions.

"Yes, officer. I didn't mean to cause a problem. I just haven't seen my daughter in over six months, and I got so excited I wanted to hug her, and then all these people started screaming and trying to hurt me."

Big tears welled up in Eva's eyes as she raised her shoulders and squished her bosoms together to great effect. The cop turned to Ursula.

"Is this your mother?"

"Yes," Ursula answered.

Casper, the brave photographer whose face was still stinging from Eva's slap, spoke up.

"Hey, she totally disrupted my shoot. She hit me, and she manhandled her daughter."

"This is the man who grabbed my arm and hurt me. I was so afraid. Thank you for being here," Eva whimpered, lowering her head and beginning to sob.

"I think we've had a misunderstanding here. I'm going to let her go."

The cop uncuffed Eva's hands, and his fellow officers began to retreat. He addressed the stunned onlookers who had been going about their work so peacefully before Eva's arrival.

"I don't want to hear that any one of you has upset this lady again. Am I making myself clear?"

As the officers left, Brittany took control of the situation. "It's almost twelve now. Let's break for lunch and start out fresh at one."

"You give my daughter only one hour for lunch? Where is she supposed to eat? McDonald's?"

"One-thirty," Brittany revised.

"Two," Eva commanded.

As Eva sipped her martini at Sardi's beneath a caricature of Danny Kaye, she perused the contract that Brittany had handed her.

"Mother, what are you doing?" Ursula wailed as Eva tore out an entire page of the document and crumpled it into a ball. "Brittany is my agent. You just can't barge into my life like this."

"Oh, so I'm barging into your life? Well, it's a good thing too, missy. I come to New York and find you posing for a picture dressed like a slob in a kitchen. You are a fashion model. You can't be seen like that."

"I have to defend myself here," Brittany interrupted. "Eva, that is what's known as a print job. There are jobs that models have that pay the rent before they get famous."

Brittany was close to extricating herself from this painful situation and leaving her spinach salad to wilt in the bowl it called home.

"Not my daughter. I have a plan for her, and as of now I'm taking over her career. I'll leave Ursula with you under two conditions: I approve every job she takes, and you reduce your commission to five percent."

Brittany stood up as quickly as her bad hip would allow. She could take the abuse, she could take the humiliation, but the words *five percent* caused her to lose control of her fork.

"I wish you and Ursula all the best," she proclaimed tersely, and left the bustling restaurant, lopsidedly weaving through the waiters.

Ursula was stunned. Brittany had taken her on as a client when Ursula had nothing. She had set her up with new photographers and built up her book until she had landed her first job.

"Jesus! I can't believe you just did that. Do you know how hard it is to get an agent in New York?"

"She was a limpy, nothing lady. From now on you'll listen to me. Finish your lunch. We're going shopping."

"I have to go back to finish the shoot."

"Over my dead body."

If only that were possible, thought Ursula.

Mother and daughter arrived back at the East Side Hotel loaded with shopping bags and fresh debt. Eva considered Bloomingdale's a little slice of heaven on earth. It had everything she wanted at prices she was confident she would eventually be able to afford.

"I've never spent so much money in my life," Ursula noted, kicking off her shoes and flopping down on her bed.

"We haven't spent as much as you think." Eva went through each bag and carefully gathered the receipts. "We wear everything once, and the things we feel we can live without, we return the next day."

"I don't think that's legal."

"What kind of daughter did I raise? Are you a parole officer or a model? Beautiful women can get away with anything."

The phone rang, and Ursula reached for it. Eva stopped her.

"Never, ever answer the phone on the first ring. You are always busy doing something more important."

Eva waited another ring and a half. "Now."

Ursula picked up the receiver and considered throwing it at her mother. "Hello?"

"Ursula. It's Brandon. I'm inviting you to dinner, and I'm not taking no for an answer."

The idea of getting away from her mother for a few hours, even with Brandon, was suddenly appealing to Ursula.

"Are you busy tonight?" he persisted.

"No."

"Then I'm not even letting you talk. I'm meeting you in an hour at La Caravelle."

"I can't. I have my—"

"One hour. La Caravelle."

"What is it. What's going on?" Eva interrupted.

"Who's that?" asked Brandon.

"My mother," Ursula replied.

"Bring her too," said Brandon.

"But—"

"One hour. La Caravelle."

Brandon put down the phone. The mother thing was a pain, but maybe he could use it to his advantage. He knew if you impressed the parent, you impressed the girl. Perhaps he could get into Ursula's pants through the mother.

"Who was that?" Eva inquired, miffed that she did not already know.

"This guy who keeps asking me out. He wouldn't let me say no. He invited you too." As Ursula heard the words escape from her mouth, she considered biting through her tongue.

"Where's he taking us?" Eva asked.

Ursula knew she was defeated.

"La Caravelle," she whispered softly.

"La Caravelle! I've always wanted to go there. Thank God I got us something to wear." Eva began to admire her new purchases in the tiny mirror.

"Maybe your boyfriend has a friend for me," she said hopefully.

"Sure. Maybe he'll even like you better than he likes me," said Ursula sarcastically.

"Stranger things have happened, my dear. Stranger things have happened."

Fish Banana

As Mindy walked to the theater, she checked to make sure her diaphragm was in the secret pocket of her handbag. Last week she had finally put her cervical yarmulke to practical use for the very first time with Ed, the piano player. Ed had taken her out after the show every evening last week. They had dined together between shows on matinee days, and last Sunday night she had stayed over at his place.

In truth, Mindy knew the experience had not been earth-shattering. Ed was nervous and out of practice, and Mindy was too young to know how to put him at ease. But it had happened. Mindy had confided in Ursula the next morning, and Ursula had told her that her first time had been much the same but that it had gotten much better after that. As Mindy turned into the alley that housed the stage door, she hoped Ed was free that evening so they could try it again.

In only a few weeks, he had begun to completely monopolize her mind. What would Ed think about this? What would Ed think about that? *I have to tell Ed* was the first thing Mindy thought when anything occurred. Mindy wondered whether she would marry Ed. It didn't bother her at all that he was divorced, was twelve years her senior, and already had two kids. Love conquers everything, she believed, having yet to learn that not only does love not conquer everything, there are in actuality many things capable of conquering love.

An hour later, Mindy was seated on the dressing-room floor stretching Fredlyn's leg over her head.

"Ow! Oh my God, that hurts. Keep pushing."

Mindy obeyed, continuing the torture until Fredlyn's leg touched the floor.

"Excruciating. Now the other one." Fredlyn raised her other leg. "How's Ed?" Fredlyn asked between groans.

"Eddish," Mindy replied.

Fredlyn was her favorite in the dressing room. At twenty-two she was the closest to Mindy's own age, plus she was the only one who really went out of her way to talk to Mindy and to make her feel at home.

"You know he's got a crazy ex-wife and two kids, don't you?" Fredlyn inquired carefully.

"I knew everything except the crazy part."

"Those darn men. They leave one word out, and it changes everything."

"By 'crazy' do you mean a little weird or certifiable?"

"Let me put it this way: If you're planning on having an affair with him, learn karate."

"But they're divorced."

"Just because she can't have him doesn't mean anyone else can."

"Places, please," the stage manager's voice crackled over the intercom.

"Tell me more about this man. Who is he?" Eva asked, as she tightened her gold belt another notch around her new white gauze cocktail dress.

"I worked for him, we went out to dinner once, and he keeps asking me out," Ursula replied, determined to keep all embarrassing details to herself.

Eva proceeded to ask questions in rapid fire.

"Money?"

"Yes."

"Married?"

"No."

"How old?"

"I think fifties."

"Too old for you. Just right for me. Hurry up—I can't wait to meet him."

They scurried out the door for what promised to be a memorable evening.

All through the first act, Mindy was a little distracted, to say the least. There was a very real possibility that a crazy ex-wife was out there trying to kill her. Who was that woman staring at her in the wings? Had she seen her before? What was she holding? It was Kathy, and she was holding a can of Diet Coke. False alarm. Mindy had to concentrate. She almost missed an entrance, and she hated herself when she made mistakes.

In Eva's eagerness, they arrived at the restaurant a few minutes early and sat at the bar.

"I'm Lacey's older sister," Eva explained to the bartender, stuffing peanuts into her mouth. "I'm visiting her from Connecticut."

"Who's Lacey?" Ursula wanted to know.

"I'll tell you tomorrow."

Just then, someone tapped Ursula on the shoulder.

"Hi there, beautiful," Brandon said softly.

Ursula turned around. "Brandon, hi. This is my mother. Mom, this is Brandon."

As Eva turned, a small whimper of disbelief escaped from her lips.

Mindy was afraid to jump. It was only a distance of four feet, but she was afraid. It was not her first time jumping. She had done it before. However, on this occasion an inner voice, a premonition, an intuitive impulse of some kind caused her to hesitate.

Kathy had visited Mindy at intermission to alert her to the fact that she was aware of the missed entrance. As Mindy stood on the table and stared at Hancock and Christopher, she knew she had to jump. Belinda would have a fit if the show were disrupted because of Mindy's stupid premonition. Hancock and Christopher had caught her before. They would catch her again. Just because they weren't looking at her didn't mean they were unaware of their duty.

Although they were positioned at their usual stations, it appeared to Mindy that for the first time they were looking at each other rather than at her. She cleared her throat loudly in an attempt to capture their attention. This proved to be as effective as vacuuming a beach. Mindy bent her knees and tensed her calf muscles. Perspiration appeared beneath her armpits and began to blacken the top of her crimson bustier. The orchestra swelled, the audience watched, and Mindy stood frozen in indecision on the table she was supposed to vacate vertically, wondering whether or not she should trust these men to catch her.

"Have you fucked her?"

The restaurant fell silent.

"Mother!"

Ursula was mortified. This was the worst. Her mother had finally completely lost her mind.

"Have you fucked her?" Eva screamed.

"Do I know you?" asked Brandon.

Something about this crazy, plump, bleached creature seemed oddly familiar.

"Brandon, have you fucked her? Please say you haven't fucked her," Eva whimpered.

"If you say that again, Mother, I am going to slap you. And no, he hasn't fucked me."

"Thank God," Eva sighed with relief.

"Eva? Eva Rossler?"

"Exactly."

Brandon turned and looked at Ursula. "Then, you mean . . . ?"

"I mean."

"Oh my God!" Brandon leaned against a barstool for support. "I nearly fucked her."

"Would someone please tell me what the hell is going on," Ursula pleaded.

Eva took a deep breath. "Ursula. This is your father."

Ursula could not believe it was happening again. But it was. The first projectile of vomit landed directly on Brandon's three-hundred-dollar Ferragamo shoes and began to soak through his Calvin Klein socks.

"This can't be happening," moaned Ursula.

Hancock could not believe this had happened to him. He had never had any homosexual experience of any kind. But last night with Christopher had been a revelation. He finally knew who he was, and it was a glorious release. He looked over and smiled at the charming, handsome man who had changed his life forever.

Mindy jumped and landed on the stage in a position that closely resembled a swastika. She was sure everything would have been fine and the audience would never have known that this was not part of the choreography, except for the fact that she could no longer move.

Hancock and Christopher picked Mindy up and gently moved her into the wings. The other dancers continued with the number as best as they could while Mindy lay on the floor backstage waiting for the ambulance to arrive.

"This can't be happening," moaned Mindy.

Life.

If you knew what was waiting for you around the corner, you'd stand perfectly still, but even then someone might spit on you.

Fish banana.

Part II

By indirection find direction out.

— *William Shakespeare*

One-Night Stand Up

"You'll risk permanent movement limitation," the orthopedist pronounced, "culminating in increased discomfort that will escalate incrementally as you advance in years."

"You mean it's going to hurt?" Mindy wondered if doctors wouldn't keep patients waiting so long if they just employed more economic phrasing.

For six months Mindy had been searching for a physician who would pronounce her fit to dance again, sitting long hours in white rooms that contained too many fishing magazines. It was all to no avail. Second, third, and fourth opinions all supported the original diagnosis: Her professional dancing days were over.

She knew her choices were few. Behind door number one: return home to Miami and apply to college. Behind door number two: suicide. Behind door number three: find a new way to make a living. Too cowardly even to dare think about doors one and two, Mindy cowered in front of door number three as it challenged her to step toward it. *When the going gets tough, the tough change direction,* she misremembered.

Mindy reflected how the same advice might well be applied to her relationship with Ed, as she picked mystery lint off the shoulder-padded angora sweater with leg-of-mutton sleeves she had chosen to wear on their date that evening. She had been harboring secret second thoughts about Ed's paramour potential for a while now. The frisson of an older man paying attention to her had begun to cool, and she was certain sex should last longer than it took to microwave oatmeal. However, today was her nineteenth birthday and tonight she was determined to enjoy the beginning of her final teenth. Even though she knew Ed was more attracted to her than she was to him, she would postpone dealing with that conundrum until a later, more propitious time.

"I'm going back to my wife," Ed blurted out as they were leaving the restaurant. "I still want to be friends."

Mindy bit her lip. "I still want to be friends" was verbal litter. Mindy felt any person who uttered it should be ticketed and ordered to pay a fine.

"It doesn't mean we can't see each other anymore," Ed pleaded.

They were standing in front of a nightclub on Lexington and 55th. Mindy looked back a hundred yards to where the actual dumping had occurred and noticed that unknowing pedestrians were stepping right in it.

"Just come inside," Ed urged. "I have to play for only one singer tonight, and then I'll take you out for more birthday dessert. Frozen hot chocolate at Serendipity's?"

Mindy stiffened. "I don't need anything frozen and hot right now. I'm confused enough."

Mindy turned to leave, but Ed grabbed her hand.

"You're young. You'll meet someone who isn't as messed up as me. I have to give my marriage another chance. For the kids!"

"When we started dating, you knew you had kids," Mindy replied icily. "It's not like they've just recently appeared. And why choose my birthday to tell me? Why not choose somebody else's birthday? Your birthday, for instance?"

"I couldn't hide it. I like you too much. You're a nice girl. You deserve better than a beat-up piano player who feels guilty about his ex-wife and kids."

Despite her secret agreement with Ed's prognosis, Mindy was determined not to let the piano player off lightly. She glanced up at the sign outside the nightclub.

"Tars of Tomorrow? What type of loser works at a place called Tars of Tomorrow?" she demanded.

"It's supposed to be Stars of Tomorrow. They've got the *S* on order," Ed explained. "I play late-night piano here three nights a week. Come inside. Please."

Ed opened the door to the bustling, dingy dive, and a curious Mindy begrudgingly let herself be led into the interior. A cocktail of stale liquor odor and cigarette smoke assaulted her nostrils and stung her eyes. Mindy looked on the bright side; she was smoking and drinking, and it hadn't cost her a cent. To her immediate left a bartender behind a perfunctory bar skillfully mixed watered-down drinks, then passed them on to harried waitresses waiting at the end of the counter. A collection of disheveled young men sat on stools at the bar, each studying a wrinkled sheet of paper. A square, bald man was planted on the final red vinyl stool. His rear end hung over either side like a pillow on a fence post. He spotted Ed's reflection in the mirror behind the bar and swiveled around.

"Eddie, how ya doin'?"

The man extended a massive paw in Ed's direction. Mindy stood transfixed by the sight of the ring that encircled the fat man's sausage index finger. Mindy was sure she must be mistaken; nobody would wear an embossed human eye, would they? As she stared at the bright, blue ring, it stared back.

"Mindy, this is Moe. Moe, Mindy."

Noticing her fascination with his finger, Moe held up the organ jewelry for her closer inspection. "It's a human eye. A little souvenir from a short stay at Riker's Island."

Mindy failed to understand the implication. "Were you on vacation?"

"Yeah," he chuckled. "For five years."

"He didn't do it. They just found him with the body," Ed chimed in.

"Yeah, right. And *I'm* doing a movie with Pacino," the bartender added sarcastically.

Unsure as to how she should react, Mindy turned to her right and saw a cramped coat checkroom. A diminutive, fine-boned woman perched her elbows on the half-door that was badly in need of a new coat of varnish. This pose displayed to their optimum advantage the woman's modest but pert bosoms nestled in their low-cut spandex top. Although she was pretty, Mindy suspected the young woman's size rather than her looks had gotten her the job. Surely no larger woman could possibly hope to fit in so restricted a space?

"Ed, ten thirty-six . . . white rabbit," the woman said.

"Gotcha, Lizzie."

Ed knew exactly what the woman was talking about. Mindy remained mystified. As close as she could decipher, at exactly ten thirty-six Ed had to walk Lizzie's white rabbit. Mindy decided she would wait a while to see whether she was to be invited on the walk or whether the brief exchange was some sort of code and meant something entirely different.

In front of Mindy was a red velvet rope. Mindy had noticed during her time in New York that there was something about a red velvet rope that commanded people to stand behind it. Indeed, Mindy had already considered that maybe, when she finally had her own apartment, she might forfeit a door with a lock and just guard her possessions with a velvet rope. This particular velvet rope had been handled so often the majority of its fuzz had disappeared. Although badly in need of a velvet transplant, the rope still contained the magical properties necessary to cause several couples to line up behind it. Beyond the rope, a thick purple curtain, possibly on loan from a New Orleans bordello, muffled the waves of laughter that erupted from the mystery room beyond.

A black leather jacket wearing a red-haired man unclipped

the rope and allowed two more couples into the club. A curious Mindy tried to sneak a peek at the entertainment behind the curtain, but she was denied even a glimpse. The owner of a receding hairline pushed through the curtain, consulted a clipboard, then spoke.

"Alvin, you're on."

"I am? How'm I doin'?" a man at the bar replied, as thin as licorice and as pale as a communion wafer.

The thin man got up, folded his wrinkled sheet of paper, tucked it in his rear pocket, then edged past the crowd and vanished behind the curtain. Mindy regarded the people left on the stools. They were all the color of wet newspaper.

Don't these people ever see the sun? she thought to herself.

Even the black man studying his notebook at the side of the bar looked like he could do with a session under a tanning lamp, Mindy mused as ex-Ed tapped her on her arm.

"Follow me. Lizzie's on next."

Mindy followed Ed into the smoke-filled showroom, where about a hundred people were crammed together along rows of tables, craning and twisting their necks to face a six-foot-square raised platform that contained reedy Alvin. The thin young man's eyes were cast downward as he played with the microphone cord tangled in his fingers.

"This is only my job at night. I have another job during the day. . . . I'm a golf club."

The crowd burst into laughter.

"You think I'm skinny now, you should see me after I sneeze. I disappear."

Behind Alvin, a piano and a set of drums sat waiting their turn in the spotlight. Ed found a single seat for Mindy toward the back of the room as Alvin was coming to a close.

"Thank you very much, and before I go, I'd just like to say— and I mean this sincerely—to the guy right here in the front row, your pants are on fire."

Mindy laughed along with the appreciative audience as Alvin slowly shuffled off the stage amid generous applause.

He's pretty funny, Mindy thought. *I wonder how he does that.*

There was an energy in this nightclub that Mindy had never experienced before. It was different from the excitement she felt being in a show. On Broadway, Mindy was used to waiting until eight o'clock, when the curtain rose and a controlled, rehearsed, repeated performance began. Here, something could happen spontaneously. These were the "Tars of Tomorrow," and they could be discovered at any minute.

The shiny-domed man who had poked his head through the curtain now leaped onto the stage.

"Alvin Stone, everybody—let's keep it going for Speedy Alvin, as we call him here at the club. He ran the New York Marathon in record time: four years and sixty-two minutes."

The audience continued its applause. Mindy watched Ed and a drummer drift onstage and take their places behind their instruments as the master of ceremonies continued.

"Now, please give a warm welcome to a singer who is as at home on this stage as she is in the coatroom. . . . Put your hands together for Miss Lizzie Carmelina."

Ed and the drummer began a driving musical introduction as Lizzie strutted onto the stage. The high-heeled shoes at the bottom of her black-tighted legs gave her an extra six inches, but she still had to lower the microphone for it to find her mouth. The audience watched and waited as Lizzie momentarily fought with the release mechanism. With the device finally at an acceptable level, she launched into "White Rabbit" by Jefferson Airplane. Mindy silently thanked God that she had not asked Ed if she could accompany them on the walk with the white rabbit. She marveled at how Lizzie's deep, rich vibrato filled the room. The audience was transfixed, except for the couple in front of Mindy who were making out.

"Feed your head. . . . Feed your head. . . . Feed your head," Lizzie belted out from the bottom of her shoes.

As the song ended, Ed left the piano and made his way over to Mindy.

"Serendipity time?" he inquired.

Another comedian had just taken the stage. This one had a tougher demeanor.

"So how are you? Like I give a fuck," he barked at the audience in a thick, Brooklyn accent. "So, I'm balling this chick. . . . Excuse me—I don't mean to shock the women in the audience. . . . I'm balling this lady . . ."

Mindy and Ed ducked out of the dark showroom. As they passed through the crowd in the bar area, Mindy spotted Alvin arguing heatedly with a man whose face was the color of borscht.

" 'Pants on fire' is a generic closing. You don't own 'pants on fire.' Nobody owns 'pants on fire.'"

Mindy watched Alvin's hands swoop animatedly in the air as he defended his closing bit.

"I did it first in this club," his opponent retorted. "The person who does it first in the club owns the bit."

"I'm sorry. I wasn't taught that in Comedy College," Alvin shot back. "I guess they chose not to explain that at the University of Punch Lines."

While Ed went to retrieve her coat, Mindy eavesdropped on another conversation. A freckle-faced woman hiding behind oversize round eyeglasses was talking to a heavily mustached, older man, who stroked his chin pensively, as if he were trying to solve a complicated math problem.

"I have the setup," Freckles was saying to Mustache. "It's 'My father isn't into strenuous exercise. He took up bird watching.' That's it. That's the setup. I know there's something there."

Mindy watched as Mustache thought for a moment.

"Bird watching," he mumbled. "Yeah you're right. There's something in bird watching. *Exercise* is the wrong word. Maybe . . . *strenuous activities.*"

Freckles repeated the setup: "'My father isn't into strenuous activities. He took up bird watching.' Yeah, I think that's getting better."

"Is your father really into bird watching?" Mustache asked.

"Yes," the woman replied. "He went out and bought binoculars."

"And a bird," the man added.

Mindy stifled a laugh. That was funny.

"Yes," cried the woman. "That's it. Thank you, Ronnie. 'My father isn't into strenuous activities. He took up bird watching. He went out and bought binoculars . . . and a bird.' I'm trying it out tonight."

"I don't think you need 'went out,'" said Mindy, much to her own surprise. " 'He bought binoculars . . . and a bird.' I think that has a better rhythm."

"She's right," said Mustache.

Mindy declined Ed's dessert invitation. She had some thinking to do. As she lay alone in her birthday bed, her mind raced around in her head like a sparrow caught in a bathroom. *What is a joke? Why do people laugh? Could I ever do anything like that?*

That night Mindy made the decision to steer her obsessive personality toward comedy. At first glance it appeared a bizarre choice of profession. Mindy the introvert surely did not belong in a section of show business that appeared to attract extroverts. However, if Ed's friends in the club were any example, the stand-up comedy world was peopled with outcasts. Among outcasts Mindy could fit right in.

Over the next few weeks, Ursula became Mindy's main comedic sounding board. Mindy would clutch a broom instead of a microphone and stand in the middle of her room. Ursula would hold a drink and sit on the bed.

"Don't laugh if it's not funny," Mindy begged.

"It's already funny. You're talking into a broom."

Ursula would then proceed to laugh at everything Mindy said. She was prejudiced. She already liked her. Mindy knew the

only real way to find out whether she was funny was to perform for strangers. People who had no emotional investment in
her feelings were the only people she could trust.

A month after her birthday breakup with Ed, Mindy sat on the
sidewalk outside the club at six o'clock in the morning. The sun
was just daring to peek through the New York attitude, and
Mindy wondered whether the sun ever got bored doing the
same job every day. Perhaps gloomy days were just days the sun
called in sick. Mindy decided that was an interesting thought,
but not a joke. She wrote the observation down in her notebook
under the "maybes."

Every Monday Stars, as Mindy now called it, let novices
onstage between the real comedians and singers. Mindy learned
there was no way to know how many audition numbers would
be given out on any given Monday. It depended on the audience
and the circumstances in the club that night. The previous week
Mindy arrived at eight A.M., and when the numbers were
passed out at noon, they had stopped at fifteen. She stood help-
lessly in the sixteenth slot as the unsympathetic club representative muttered a perfunctory apology. Mindy and the ten
potential auditioners lined up behind her temporarily abandoned their hopes of being discovered that particular night and
returned to their lives. Mindy retreated to the park, disappointed but a little relieved that she had another week to pre-
pare her five minutes of comic repartee.

This particular morning Mindy arrived at a time she considered fisherman early. To her dismay, five people were already
ahead of her in the audition line. Two more people joined the
line behind Mindy as the sun that moments earlier had boldly
frolicked in the morning sky now disappeared behind a cloud
the color of exhaust fumes. Mindy looked down at her notebook and watched tiny droplets of water begin to dot the pages.
She had at least six hours to wait until the numbers were issued.

The auditioner in front of Mindy, who had already caught her attention because he had a face that looked like a foot, reached into his battered briefcase to retrieve a compact umbrella. The man held up his black umbrella with two broken spokes as though it were treasure and gazed down at Mindy.

"Would you like to come under?"

"Sure."

"Twenty bucks."

Mindy was uncertain whether he was kidding. She reached into her handbag. He did not tell her to stop. Twenty dollars was half of Mindy's food budget for the week. She pulled out a stick of Trident.

"Gum?" she asked.

"Sure."

"Twenty bucks."

As the man took the stick of gum, Mindy shimmied closer, protecting her notebook first and her person second.

"I love umbrellas. I don't go anywhere without them," the man noted. "They're protection against potential disaster. They're rain condoms."

"That's funny," said Mindy.

"It's mine," he shot back proprietorially. "I said it."

Mindy was hurt. "I wasn't going to say it. I just wanted to tell you I thought it was funny."

"Sorry. Last time I said something to someone on line, he used it in his act. I'm just being careful." He pulled out a miniature tape recorder and talked into its side. "Umbrella, rain condom. October fifth, 1980." He flicked the machine off and placed it back in his pocket.

Mindy corrected him. "It's 1981."

"I like to pre-date things. Just in case. How many times have you auditioned?"

"This is my first time. You?"

"Thirty-seven."

"You're kidding."

"No. That's how I knew to bring an umbrella. I have a portable fan I bring in the summer. My favorite time to be on line is April. Mid-sixties, slight breeze—beautiful."

Mindy continued to chat with the man, and the two of them exchanged the Cliff's Notes of their lives until the authority figure with the numbers arrived. He handed the bits of paper down the line. One, two, three, four; as he handed number five to Mindy's neighbor, he said, "Dan! Back again?"

"Yep. This time I'm passing. I can feel it."

"Good luck," replied the numbers man, unconvinced.

Mindy's heart rate accelerated as he turned his attention to her. His eyebrow flickered, and the sides of his mouth descended. She had seen this body language before. It preceded rejection.

"Sorry. We have an important talent booker coming in tonight so we're only taking five auditioners."

Mindy protested. "You can't. I got here at six A.M. and sat in the rain and I'm only number six. Last week you gave out fifteen numbers."

"Last Monday was slow. This Monday—different story."

A frustrated Mindy was determined to get something out of the situation.

"Can I at least sit in the back, and maybe if you have time you can squeeze me in at the end?"

"Yeah, all right," the man said, relenting. "Be here tonight at eight."

"Don't I get a number?"

"No, just tell the emcee that Tony said it was all right."

"Tony who?" the emcee demanded, as Mindy stood in front of him eight hours later at the designated time.

"Tony—the guy who gives out the numbers. He said, 'Just say that Tony said it was all right.'"

"What was all right?"

"If I sat at the back and watched, and maybe if you had time at the end you could fit me in."

"He said that, did he? Fucking Tony. I told him we had time for only five. We have comedians auditioning for *Letterman* tonight."

Suddenly, a hand wearing a blue eye ring landed on the emcee's shoulder. Mindy looked up and saw Moe smiling down at her.

"This is Ed's friend. Let her sit in the back," Moe ordered firmly.

"Sit over there. Not at the back, on the side," the emcee offered grudgingly, confident that his power base remained intact so long as he still possessed the ability to dictate Mindy's precise location.

Mindy did as she was told and found herself seated at the comics' table. She recognized Alvin and Ronnie. They were intently studying the members of the audience as they filed in and were shown to their tables.

"I think they're going to be stupid tonight," a frowning Ronnie remarked.

"Of course they are." Alvin agreed. "Why do they have to have these *Letterman* auditions on Mondays? The crowds are always stupid on Mondays."

Ronnie continued the rant. "I know. Who goes out on a Monday night? People who have no jobs and people who have just been fired."

Penelope, the freckled woman with the big glasses, joined the table. "How do they look?"

"Stupid," Ronnie and Alvin replied in unison.

"Oh, no." Penelope sat down dejectedly. "I hate stupid. I'd rather belligerent than stupid."

Mindy wondered how these people could look at an entire audience and characterize it. *She* was there on a Monday night . . . but then she hadn't been to college and she was unemployed. Maybe there was something to Ronnie's theory.

The drummer and the Monday-night pianist took the stage. Mindy scanned the club, making sure there were no familiar faces in the audience. Ed, who had distanced himself from Mindy after deciding to remarry his ex-wife, knew nothing about Mindy's new endeavor. Ursula was the only person to whom Mindy had confided, and it was under the strict condition she would not attend.

"Why aren't they seating people at the front?" moaned Ronnie. "Why seat them at the back?"

"Is the back bad?" asked Mindy.

Alvin explained. "If you get the front table laughing, it's contagious. It spreads to the whole room. Plus you have to group people together so they feel like they're at a party."

"These people are tucked away in corners like they're hiding from the law," moaned Ronnie.

"I don't care where they are. I can make 'em laugh if they're sitting in the restaurant next door," another comedian announced cockily as he plonked himself down at their table.

Mindy recognized him as the borscht-faced comedian she had seen arguing with Alvin about "pants on fire."

"Fuck you, Mendel. You don't care because you didn't get to audition."

"It's pointless for me to audition. They know I'll only do *Letterman* as a guest host."

Ronnie stood up. "I can't stand it," he wailed.

As a member of the public passed the comics' table heading for the back of the room, Ronnie grabbed him by the arm. "Sit in the front," he growled.

The frightened man hurried to occupy a forward table. Penelope turned her attention to Mindy.

"Who are you?"

"Nobody. Mindy Solomon. I may be auditioning later."

"For the *Letterman* show? Where have you worked out? I haven't seen you before."

Mindy noticed Penelope was immediately threatened by another female presence.

"No, I'm just a person auditioning for the club. I'm a friend of Ed's," Mindy added, desperately grasping for a conversational limb.

"Oh."

An indifferent Penelope opened a notebook full of illegible scribbles and began studying.

A waitress bent down and whispered to the table, "He's here."

The comics sat a little straighter, glancing up at the purple curtain and attempting nonchalance.

"There he is," Ronnie whispered. "There's Walter."

A well-groomed man wearing a crisp light brown suit entered the club and headed for a table directly in front of the stage. Just before sitting down, he turned in the direction of the comics' table and acknowledged them with a curt nod of his head. Before the motion could be returned, the comedians were looking at the television executive's back.

"Oh, shit. Not right in front," said Alvin, livid.

"I thought the front was good," a confused Mindy commented.

"Not for him. He makes us nervous. Better he should be at the back."

"Why's he come dressed like a grocery bag?" Penelope asked.

"He's too neat. I bet he irons his socks," Ronnie noted. "Nobody neat can ever know anything about comedy."

"That's true," Penelope confirmed.

"Laurel and Hardy—funny," continued Ronnie, warming to his theme. "The Third Reich—not funny."

A waitress delivered a glass of ice water to the executive's table.

"He's ordering water. Not a good sign," Alvin mentioned.

"This club is so cheap they water down the water," Penelope quipped.

Mindy laughed. All attention was suddenly focused in her direction.

"I'm sorry. That was funny."

"It was?" Penelope asked Ronnie. "Should I say it tonight?"

"Stick with your set," advised Ronnie, leaning into Penelope. "Who is she? Is she a comic or a regular person?"

"She's a regular person. Cindy. A friend of Ed's."

Ronnie extended his hand. "Hi, Cindy. This is Penelope, that's Alvin, and I'm Ronnie. We're auditioning for the *Letterman* show tonight and you have a good laugh. When we get onstage, whatever we say, laugh, Cindy, laugh."

"I'll try," Mindy replied, deciding that this was not the appropriate time to correct the name confusion.

The lights dimmed. The drummer and pianist began a credible version of the Stones' "Start Me Up" that crescendoed as the emcee bounded onto the stage. However, despite the energy exhibited on stage, the atmosphere felt entirely different from the last time Mindy had been in the club. The aura in the room that night had been crisp and exciting. The audience had been attentive, alert, and ready to be entertained. The aura in the room tonight was soggy and unfocused. The customers were talking among themselves and barely noticed the show beginning.

"So, my name is Marty, and I'll be the captain of this comedic ship tonight. If the jokes get choppy and you feel a little queasy, feel free to throw up on the person next to you."

There was a slight titter in the back of the otherwise silent room. Mindy was confused. She wanted to laugh but couldn't. She thought the emcee was funny, but something about this setting was forcing her to remain silent, forcing her to be a spectator rather than a participant.

Marty the emcee, who had been so relaxed and easy with the audience when Mindy had seen him previously, was now tense and tight. The *Letterman* talent scout that he was attempting so hard to impress stared intently at his glass of water as if trying to contact it spiritually. Marty finally had to mention it.

"Excuse me, sir. Why did you come to a comedy club tonight when you're obviously happiest staring at a glass of water?"

Alvin put his head in his hands. "I'm going to kill myself. Now, not only is he humorless, he's angry."

"Well, I'm not going to mince words here," Marty continued. "I'd rather perform to plankton. And now please welcome to the stage, the comedy of . . . Alvin Stone."

Mindy couldn't believe the same jokes that had an audience exploding with laughter a few weeks before were now landing flatter than a Calvin Klein model. Penelope and Ronnie befell the same fate. They were telling funny jokes, but there was no energy in the crowd. Mindy watched the talent scout leave the club without saying a word to any of the comedians that had worked so hard to attract his attention.

"Let me be the first to say it," Alvin dejectedly spewed later. "He should get stomach cancer."

"He could say, 'Good job. Not exactly what I'm looking for. Thank you anyway.' Why does he have to treat us like nonpeople? Like we're comedy lepers. Why does he have to be such a pig?" whined Penelope.

Mindy was realizing stand-up comedy was more fragile than she had first thought. Rather than a casserole dish that turned out the same every time, it was a soufflé. Even if you were skillful and used nothing but the finest ingredients, you still needed a lucky oven to keep it all from collapsing. Monday's comedic oven was so erratic Mindy was relieved she wasn't being allowed to perform that night. She relaxed and watched the show, no longer sure that becoming a stand-up comedian was a good idea at all.

Some time after the *Letterman* representative left, the five amateurs who had been waiting on line in front of Mindy that morning were allowed onto the stage. They were interspersed with regular comedians, and one by one they performed their five minutes. It was not pretty.

Marty the emcee was in charge of passing the amateurs. He stood on the side of the room with his head tilted up and his eyes narrowed in judgment. Ten sleepy people were left in the audience at one in the morning when Mindy's umbrella companion Dan took the stage. Everything about him screamed uncomfortable. His face angled downward and his tense grip of the mike made everyone in the audience wish he and they were somewhere else. Dan began to mumble into the sound system.

"I don't want to forget my act, so I've written myself a little note."

He reached into his pocket and produced a small white sheet of paper. He began to read.

"Dear Mom and Dad. These are the reasons I have decided to take my own life. . . ."

He returned the piece of paper to his pocket.

"Wrong note. . . . They say dogs look like their owners. My dog is dead. . . . My dad always wanted me to follow in his footsteps. . . . He was killed by a train."

Something about Dan began to click with the smattering of people who were left in the club. One person started to laugh, then the laughter started to spread around the room. The continuous jokes, culminating in his own death, stacked one on top of another and became funnier and funnier right up to Dan's closing line.

"Thank you very much. I have to go now. You don't want to keep an embalmer waiting."

Dan left the stage to the most noise ten people could make. Mindy overheard Marty crossing him on his way back to the stage.

"Wait in the bar, please," Marty whispered.

Mindy could see the excitement on Dan's face. He had done it. On his thirty-eighth try, he had passed the audition. Mindy looked around. There were now only two couples left in the audience. She had decided to find Dan and congratulate him when Marty leaned down and whispered into her ear, "You're on."

"I can't be on. There's nobody left in the audience."

"I count five people."

For the first time, Mindy noticed a lone person seated in the shadows of a gloomy corner of the club. The person knocked over a drink and the glass crashed to the floor. *Great* thought Mindy. A drunk in the audience was all she needed on her first night of stand-up.

Marty was brusque. "Do you want to go on or not? You've been waiting here all night. I thought I was doing you a favor."

"Yes."

Mindy stood up and moved toward the stage. Lots of things raced through her mind, but nothing from her act. What was her act? What had she written down, and more importantly where had she written it? It was somewhere in her handbag. She noticed she was still carrying her handbag. Where do female comedians put their handbags when they go onstage? It was too late to ask. She heard Marty announce, "And now please welcome to the stage Mindy Solomon."

Mindy's body shook harder than a Buddha made of Jell-O. As she walked across the uneven floor toward the stage, still holding her handbag containing her act and her mother's pink rose, all she could think was *I can't get any more frightened than this, and I'm still alive. I might as well do it.*

Being on that stage at nearly two o'clock in the morning in front of those few people felt to Mindy as dangerous as standing on the edge of the Empire State Building in a hurricane. Too afraid to take the microphone out of the stand, Mindy stood rooted to the spot, as stiff as a banker at a party, with a frozen smile plastered across her face.

"Hello, my name is Mindy Solomon, and this is my first time doing this, and I have no idea where to put my handbag, so if I put it over here . . ." Mindy placed her handbag on the side of the stage and picked out what she considered to be a friendly face in the audience. " . . . will you watch it for me?"

The audience tittered.

"Sure," the man replied, leaning back in his chair. "Hey, I have to ask you a question: Whatd'ya do for a living?"

The audience giggled. Mindy was terrified. She was being heckled. Nobody else the entire evening had been heckled and now, her first time at bat, she was hit squarely between the eyes with a verbal fastball.

"I'm very sorry," she said. "As I mentioned, this is my first time on stage, so I've never been heckled before and I have no idea how to deal with it. Could you please come back and heckle me when I'm more experienced?"

There was laughter in the room.

"My first laugh. It was good for me. Was it good for you?"

Another laugh followed.

"I'd do my act, but I can't remember it. Wait a second. I think I'm remembering it now. . . . No, that's not it. Let's see. . . . I know this is an unorthodox method of doing stand-up comedy, but . . . does anyone out there know any jokes?"

More laughter, but Mindy knew she was in trouble. Her mind that had thought of nothing else but her act for the past few weeks was now emptier than Audrey Hepburn's refrigerator. She was desperately trying to remember even one thing she had written in her notebook.

A voice in the back of the club yelled, "Have you ever done any commercials?"

A fresh syringeful of embarrassment shot through Mindy's veins as it dawned on her that the klutz in the back of the room was Ursula. As angry as Mindy was with Ursula disobeying her strict edict of nonattendance, she was also grateful. Ursula knew her act.

"That's my best friend, Ursula, who promised not to come tonight. Okay, here's the thing. . . . My parents didn't want me to be a comedian. They wanted me to do something in show business that had culture, so I did a yogurt commercial."

There was a collective audience groan.

"I guess that wasn't funny. . . . Ursula told me it was, but then, as we've already established . . . she lies."

Strangely, people were laughing, but they were laughing between the jokes Mindy had written.

"Okay, here's one, and I really think this is a good one. . . . Why do people press elevator buttons that have already been pressed?"

Mindy waited for the laugh that would never come.

"I guess that joke wasn't finished yet."

Again they laughed. Mindy began trying to figure out how to get off the stage. She looked directly across the room and for the first time noticed a huge mirror attached to the back wall that directly faced the performing area.

"Well, I can tell it's time for me to finish because I just looked in that mirror, and my reflection has already gone home."

Mindy heard a few titters, grabbed her handbag, and flew off the podium. Ursula followed her as Marty took the microphone.

"Let's have a hand for Mindy Solomon. A work in progress."

Dan was waiting for her in the empty bar as Mindy flung herself at the counter and buried her head in her arms.

"I was so horrible. How could I be so horrible?"

"You were horrible?" Dan asked. "I heard people laughing."

Ursula was right behind her. "She wasn't horrible. She was funny."

Dan was now through talking about Mindy. "I passed.

Everything worked. I don't know why. I think it was the gum you gave me."

Mindy raised her head. "Congratulations. I saw your set. You were great."

"Yeah, you were really funny," Ursula added.

"I was, wasn't I? Is it too soon to ask you to marry me?"

Dan was beaming. Mindy guessed he had never had a woman as beautiful as Ursula even look at him, let alone award him a compliment. Mindy spotted Marty the emcee coming toward her and decided to leave before he could personally relay his disbelief at her lack of talent.

"Let's go, Ursula. That is, if you still want to be friends with a big loser."

Mindy hustled her friend toward the exit, but Marty called after them as they opened the door.

"Wait a second. I want to talk to you."

Mindy half turned, embarrassed.

"You don't have to. Thank you for putting me on," she mumbled. "I know I was terrible."

"Well, I have to be honest. You weren't very good."

Ursula came to Mindy's defense. "Yes, she was."

"I'm not gonna listen to you. You're a liar." He turned to Mindy. "You could be funny. Your material isn't there yet, but you have a good presence on stage. You're likable. If you want, you can hang out at the club. I can only put you on late right now, but come early and watch the acts, especially Ronnie Braverman. He's the best joke writer in the club."

Mindy could not quite grasp what Marty was saying. "Are you saying I passed?"

"Yes."

Mindy hugged Marty. Marty gestured toward Ursula.

"Is it all right if she hugs me too?" he asked.

The Grim Weeper

Eva waited nervously in Ursula's room, casually leafing through her daughter's appointment book to see what her offspring had been up to in the six months since they had last spoken. The book was full of modeling assignments, which came as no surprise to Eva. Hardly a month had gone by without a photo of Ursula gracing the pages of one of the fashion magazines Eva stole from a neighborhood newsstand.

Eva slumped down onto Ursula's bed and glanced at her watch. It was almost two in the morning. It didn't matter. Eva was determined to stay there until her daughter appeared, restraining order or no restraining order. Eva was feeling unbelievably sorry for herself. Once again she felt the events in her life had done a handstand as the forces of the universe had collaborated in whipping up a cosmic cocktail designed with the single and solitary intention of fucking her up.

At first Ursula's shock at discovering that Brandon was her father had frozen the young woman in emotional paralysis. The most she could achieve was to put her parent issue to one side, like a room she would clean later. However, as days passed and shock was replaced by anger, Ursula decided to ban both Brandon and Eva from her life forever. Banning Brandon was easy. She couldn't find him. Her mother, however, posed more of a problem.

Eva had initially refused to accept Ursula's decision, but once her daughter had hired a lawyer and a judge had ordered Eva to stay a hundred yards away from her child at all times, she grudgingly retreated into the background of Ursula's life. After moving into a dilapidated hotel, Eva had eventually exhausted her meager savings and for the past two nights had slept in Grand Central Station.

Ursula and Mindy tottered along the corridor of their hotel. It was three in the morning, and the two of them were still giggling and celebrating Mindy's successful audition at Stars of Tomorrow. Ursula opened her door and screamed at the sight of her mother in her bed.

A bedraggled Eva sat up and began to beg.

"Please. Don't throw me out. I've got nowhere to go. I have to talk to you."

Ursula was shocked at the change in her mother. The woman who usually took more time with her appearance than a female impersonator now looked like a witch from a fairy tale. Her shoulders, her jowls, her eyelids, her spirits—everything was drooping. It was almost as if someone had lit a wick on the top of her head and she had melted.

"Do you want me to stay?" Mindy asked Ursula.

"I'll be good. I promise. I just want to talk to you," whimpered Eva, now standing and futilely attempting to straighten her wrinkled clothing.

"It's okay," Ursula told Mindy softly. "It's my problem. I have to deal with it."

"Call me if you need me. Hello, Mrs. Duran."

As Mindy scuttled down the hallway, Ursula closed the door and asked the question whose answer she knew virtually guaranteed a downward turn in her fortunes and happiness.

"Mother, what do you want?"

Eva could tell by the harshness contained in Ursula's voice that this was going to be a challenge. Staring into her beautiful daughter's eyes she saw resistance. She saw bitterness. She saw hurt. She did not, however, detect hatred, and that was the moment she knew she was in with a chance. She launched into her chosen manipulation du jour. Water balloons of tears cascaded out of obedient eye ducts, then ran down her cheeks onto her grimy blouse.

"I have nothing. Please help me. I have nothing."

She hunched over as her shoulders began the crying shake. In Ursula's entire life she had never seen her mother cry, and it affected her far more deeply than she would have imagined. The feisty, controlling woman who always seemed to come away from any difficult situation with the will to move forward seemed finally to have been beaten. Ursula moved over to comfort the pathetic figure and noticed her mother no longer smelled of cheap perfume. Rather, she needed a shower. Eva grasped Ursula tightly and turned the shaking up a notch to ensure her offspring felt her pain. By the time Eva calmed down, Ursula was the one who was begging.

"What can I do to help you? I can't stand to see you like this."

"That's all right," Eva hiccuped. "I don't want to be a bother."

"Let me help you," Ursula pleaded.

"I don't want money. I just want you to know that. I don't want money," said Eva, wanting money. "I just want to be involved in your life."

Ursula quickly erected a roadblock on the path she felt her mother was traveling down.

"Mother, you know you can't be my agent. Brittany is my agent. I rehired her."

"I know. And she's doing a wonderful job. I've seen your pictures in the magazines. You look so beautiful."

Eva caught a glimpse of herself in the mirror over Ursula's bureau and shuddered involuntarily. To her surprise, she felt real tears well up in her eyes.

"Look at me. How did this happen? How could anyone ever love me again?"

Ursula dabbed at her mother's crinkled eyes with a tissue.
"It'll be all right, Mom. I promise."

"You're nuts," said Mindy, coaxing on blue jeans that used to be
looser.

As far as Mindy was concerned, Ursula's letting Eva back into
her life was like letting a rock band stay in a five-star hotel; the
only question was how extensive the damage would be.

"She's just going to do the things I'm too busy to do. Like find
me an apartment."

Finding Ursula an apartment had been Eva's suggestion. Eva
believed the ploy worked on a variety of levels. One, it showed
that she could be useful to her daughter. Two, it showed, by her
nominating a one-bedroom, that she wasn't planning to move
in with her. Three, it got Ursula away from Mindy, whom Eva
knew to be both disapproving and something of a rival to her
maternal ministrations. Separating the two girls, Eva believed,
would give her the opportunity to replace Mindy as her daughter's confidante. With Ursula out of the hotel, Eva was sure
Mindy was going to struggle to stay within Ursula's radar; the
difference in their earning capacity was simply too immense a
chasm to straddle. Ursula was making a thousand dollars a day
and Mindy was making nothing. That ought to be enough to
torpedo the friendship, Eva was certain.

Ursula moved into a high-rise building on Central Park South
with the promise to Mindy that she would try not to fall out of
the window, whereas Eva took a small apartment on the Upper
West Side. From Ursula's vantage point, Eva had performed a
most impressive about-face. She had done a three-sixty-one.
The previously disgraceful mother was now the perfect assistant, whether picking up dry cleaning, doing the grocery shopping, or setting up cars to go to the airport. In reality, the job
suited Eva's meddlesome personality; she could keep track of
her daughter's every move and get paid at the same time.

When Ursula began traveling around the world on modeling

assignments, Mindy received postcards from places she thought existed only on postcards. As Ursula graced the fronts of more and more fashion magazines, Mindy was careful to put coffee cups only on the non-Ursula covers. Despite their intimate friendship, Mindy chose not to confide in her pal just how desperate her financial situation had become. During the first weeks after her injury, Mindy had once moaned to Ursula about the costs of her treatments. The very next day an envelope had appeared in Mindy's mailbox at the hotel. It had contained an anonymous three thousand dollars in cash. Mindy had confronted Ursula about it, but her friend had denied all knowledge of the gift. However, a grateful but embarrassed Mindy had no doubt that the money had come from Ursula and had determined to be more circumspect about her financial state when around her generous friend.

Just as her bank balance was dwindling toward zero, Mindy caught a break. When Ed left his wife yet again to run to the West Coast with Lizzie the singer, Mindy managed to grab the coat-check job. There was no salary, just tips. Some people left dimes, some dollars, and some mints. It was certainly not a lot of money, but it was enough to get by, and the job did have ancillary benefits, Mindy rationalized: The coatroom was so small it made her room at the hotel feel spacious. Plus she could work on her material all night, getting input from the other comedians.

Every night Mindy squeezed into the coatroom and pondered the same question that had preoccupied her brain for these past few months: *Why would anyone laugh when she stopped talking?* The art of writing a joke was so mysterious and frightening to her that whenever she attempted the task, her eyes would glaze over and her brain would lock like a water waiter's being asked about the special of the day.

Ronnie was the most helpful source of advice: "Start with the truth, ask yourself questions, and then fuck around with it."

Mindy's goal was to find an opening line that worked consistently. She had noticed that once a comedian put the audience at ease with an unforced opening joke, the set had a chance to click. Starting off badly meant that even if the rest of your act was funny, you had a mountain to climb until the audience trusted you again. Mindy saw that many comedians based their first line on the way they looked. Alvin was skinny. The golf club line was good because it was a funny visual that pertained specifically to him.

Mindy stared at herself in the mirror, trying to pinpoint what an audience might see when they looked at her . . . the face that was a little too long; the nose that inspired the question "When did you break it?"; the front tooth that had been chipped on the bottom of a swimming pool. It all spelled "unpopular." Mindy started with the truth: "I never had a date."

Then she fucked around with it: "In high school I was voted the girl most likely to become a nun."

When she tried the line on stage the audience tittered but the sentence failed to achieve an actual laugh. She knew it still needed a punch line. It needed a twist. It needed to be a thought that made sense in a nonsensical way. She asked herself a question: *What kind of school was it?* And that was how she came up with the punch line.

"That may not be very impressive to you now, but it was quite an accomplishment at the Hebrew Academy."

When Mindy put all the parts together and said it like she meant it, she was delighted to discover the audience laughed. Mindy felt immense satisfaction whenever she created a funny idea that had yet to exist in the universe until she thought of it. She had gone from being someone capable of moving her body a specific way when so ordered to being someone capable of thought. She almost wanted to write Hancock and Christopher a thank-you note for dropping her and ending her dancing career. She realized that sometimes the things that happen to you that make no sense turn out to be the things that open up new opportunities.

Fish banana fish.

Mindy enjoyed the camaraderie of the club. Nobody noticed if someone was black or white, Jew or Gentile, old or young. Here, there were only two possible social groups to belong to: the comedians and the public. It wasn't a utopia. On the contrary, there was a definite undercurrent of jealousy fueled by ambition. However, in a world in which regular people worried about keeping their jobs and feeding their families, these people worried about one thing and one thing only: being funny. Creating comedy material was more intoxicating than snorting cocaine, which, incidentally, Mindy had heard was happening on a regular basis in the club's basement.

Mindy was sad that Dan never went over again as well as he had that magic audition night. There were some comedians who could click into any crowd's wavelength and turn them around. Mindy knew Dan was not one of them. He was a comedic orchid, a fragile act that needed the perfect environment to flourish. Time after time he would get onstage, repeat the exact same act that had convulsed the late night stragglers that perfect Monday night, and be met with only disapproving stares.

"I can't put you on unless you start coming up with new material," Marty had warned him after his last set.

As the regular emcee, Marty was in charge of the nightly parade of comedians, and he wielded his scheduling power like a sadistic air traffic controller. Every performer was allotted a certain number of stage minutes. If that special number was not strictly adhered to, Marty would pull out his flashlight and blind the comic with its beam until the stage was vacated.

The pressure was mounting on Dan. He was living at home in Brooklyn, where he cared for ailing and demanding parents. His stage time was the ice cream of his existence. Experiencing severe joke block, he suggested he and Mindy meet in the park with their notebooks. Dan and Mindy were not an especially inspired joke-writing partnership. Tossing ideas around with Dan always resulted in his writing a joke about death.

"I have a setup," Mindy said, sitting on a bench and hoping the small animal with the borderline tail she had just seen scurry under a rock was a squirrel and not a rat. "It's 'You can tell a lot about a baby while it's still inside of you. My friend had some tests done, and it seems the baby is normal and it's a boy . . .'"

"What about 'and it's dead'?" Dan offered.

"I don't think so. What about ' . . . and it's a lawyer'?"

"I like 'and it's dead' better. I have one. 'My car wouldn't start, so I checked the battery . . .'"

" 'And it was dead'?" guessed Mindy.

"No, you're totally wrong. It wasn't dead. It wasn't even there. Someone had stolen it. And you know what was there in its place?"

Mindy thought for a second. "Something dead?"

"You've heard this one already?"

Opting to return to writing alone, Mindy spent her days listening to comedy albums she had borrowed from the Lincoln Center Library. She would then attempt to formulate a thought that could develop into a setup that would eventually be a joke. The four walls of her tiny room seemed to shackle her mentally. Very often she found herself thinking, *What's funny about a wall?*

So, one beautiful, spring day, Mindy decided to attempt joke fertility in a Manhattan office park. Sitting in a metal chair that was specifically designed to deter the homeless from sleeping in it, Mindy stared at the vertical concrete waterfall, watching the clear, unsafe-to-drink, recycled liquid plummet and swirl. She watched for an hour. She could think of absolutely nothing. She needed someone to talk to. She realized how much she missed Ursula. When Ursula had been around more often, Mindy had been free to toss out an idea and play around with it. Although Ursula could never think of punch lines, just verbalizing a thought could open up a new compartment of creativity. Mindy felt if she could just start up a conversation with a stranger it might help. Looking to her left she saw, in another, uncomfortable metal chair, a sleeping, homeless woman, surrounded by shopping bags. Directly past her in the corner, huddled with her knees up to her chest like a folded garment bag, was a woman Mindy recognized. It was Penelope.

Mindy greatly admired Penelope's joke-writing skills. So it was a relief to discover her fellow comic exhibiting the same tortured appearance that all comedians adopt when trying to write. The two women had not had much contact in the club. Before Mindy's arrival Penelope had enjoyed solo female status there, and Mindy had felt a definite coolness from the other comedian. Onstage Penelope had a presence that Mindy loved to watch. She was confident, smart, and slightly cranky. Habitually wearing an oversized denim jacket, a white shirt, and khaki pants, she would linger behind the mike stand and utter slowly, "I'd take the mike out of the stand, but I'm really lazy. My whole family's lazy. On our family picnics, we don't even get together. Wherever we all are, we eat outside."

Mindy decided to risk rejection and to say hello. Penelope looked up as Mindy approached. It was too late for Mindy to turn back and too rude for Penelope to leave. Mindy sat in the chair next to the cranky comedian.

"I came to watch the waterfall for inspiration, and it's only reminding me I have to do laundry."

Mindy knew Penelope's smile was a comedian's equivalent of a laugh.

Penelope said, "I like that. The only problem is you're going to have to bring an entire audience to this park before you say it."

"Well, by bus it wouldn't be that expensive."

• • •

The budding comedians spent every day that spring and summer strolling and exchanging ideas for material. Mindy was in awe of the way Penelope's mind worked. While Mindy was methodical and ordered, Penelope was free-associative and chaotic. On some days she would come up with nothing, and then on others the most wonderful, abstract thoughts would make Mindy laugh with Saturday-night-audience abandon.

"You know what must be a difficult job?" Penelope said one day, lying on a park bench gazing at the sky. "To be a skywriter in Japan."

This began a succession of riffs on terrible careers that struck them as so funny that park strollers moved to the other side of the path as they passed by.

"I had an awful airline job too. It was so boring."

"What was it?" Penelope asked, poised to laugh.

"I was a stewardess. On a helicopter. I'd say, 'Do you want something to drink?' They'd say, 'Yes.' I'd say, 'Then we're going to have to land.'"

Penelope shared her terrible office job.

"I used to clean the windows . . . on the envelopes."

Mindy was a waitress in a revolving restaurant and she had a bad memory for faces. "Most times I'd just say, 'Shut up and eat it.'"

The Ties That Loosen

Mindy noticed her friendship with Penelope was entirely different from the friendship she shared with Ursula. Penelope revealed nothing about her background or her family, and Mindy knew she would feel uncomfortable revealing hers. This was a business relationship. Mindy had the discipline to harness Penelope into a work ethic, and Penelope had the free-associating imagination from which Mindy could learn.

Their writing partnership was the envy of other comedians. Both of their acts took giant leaps forward. Penelope began to work paying jobs in clubs in Philadelphia and Washington, not just New York City, and Mindy was offered her first job for the sum of fifty dollars by a talent buyer from New Jersey. Waiting out in front of the club for her ride to the gig, Mindy saw Moe approaching her. His constant presence in the bar area always puzzled Mindy. She had asked Ronnie to explain what Moe's exact function was.

"Nobody knows," he replied. "He looks so tough nobody wants to ask."

"Mindy, how's it goin'? I heard you got your first gig."

"Yeah. I really hope I don't bomb."

"Naw. I saw you the other night. You've got potential."

To have potential in show business is a terrible thing, Mindy had decided. How do you know if you really have it or if you are just wasting your time? Does ambition combined with talent equal potential? Or does talent thwart ambition because it invites self-doubt? Self-doubt was definitely a killer of potential, Mindy had concluded, but people who have ambition without self-doubt usually go into politics.

"Hey, you know something stupid?" said Moe, laughing in anticipation of his pending hilarious remark. "I was gonna to ask you out. I didn't know you were a lesbian."

Mindy stood very still.

"What? What are you talking about?"

"You and Penelope. Don't get me wrong. I'm not putting you down or anything. I think you two make a cute couple. I just didn't know."

Mindy's ride pulled up, and she quietly got into the car, wondering whether her friend Penelope really was a lesbian. If she was, why hadn't she mentioned it? But then why should she? What did it matter anyway? Maybe Moe was just jumping to a conclusion because Penelope never wore dresses or makeup. Mindy wondered whether she should tell Penelope that people thought she was a lesbian. She then wondered whether she should make some sort of announcement regarding the fact that she herself was not of that persuasion. Mindy eventually concluded that the assumption she was gay had probably saved her life. It had deterred Moe the murderer from asking her out.

The mystery of Penelope's sexual orientation was solved on the day Penelope visited Mindy's brand-new studio apartment on West 66th Street. Never one for social formalities, Penelope had brought Mindy a bran muffin as a house-warming present and was sitting on Mindy's beanbag chair eating it when she saw the stack of fashion magazines piled on the floor. Leafing through the stack, she noticed the similarity in covers. She eyed Mindy cautiously, then opted to take the plunge.

"You've got a thing for Ursula Duran too?"

"She's a friend," Mindy replied.

"Oh."

Mindy saw how Penelope was slightly embarrassed at her faux pas but simultaneously thrilled that she was friends with someone who was friends with someone of whom Penelope had photographs stuck to her refrigerator.

"You know her? What's she like?"

"Terrific."

"Is she gay? I heard she's gay."

"No, she's not."

"How do you know?" Penelope said in challenge.

"Well, I lived with her for a while, and the only time we ever had physical contact was when she stepped on my foot."

"Maybe that's because you're not gay. Maybe it would be different if she met a gay woman."

This was the closest the women had ever come to a personal discussion, and it was not going well.

"Penelope," Mindy said gently, trying not to hurt her friend's feelings. "I don't think so."

"Oh." Penelope stared glumly at a picture of Ursula in a bikini on a yacht.

"She's in town this week," said Mindy. "She's doing a shoot for *NYC Magazine*. I'll introduce you."

"Really?"

Penelope began rearranging her hair in anticipation.

NYC Magazine had decided to name Ursula one of the five new faces of 1982. Together with a playwright, a sculptor, a chef, and a comedian, Ursula was that very day posed at a fountain in Central Park. The photographer of the moment was urging the group to move together a little closer when Ursula fell into the water. The photographer kept clicking as Tommy Marsico, the comedian with the new face, jumped in after the model with the new face.

"I'm good in water up to two feet," said Tommy, lifting Ursula out of the shallow fountain.

Ursula's now transparent clothing clung to her bare skin and dripped dramatically. The other three new faces looked on help-lessly as the couple stood in the middle of the cascading waters and stole focus.

Tommy Marsico was the comedian all other male comics envied. Tall, dark, and almost handsome, he had been perform-ing at Stars on the night a big-time film director had decided to drop by. Tommy had subsequently been tapped as the co-lead in the director's next project: a buddy cop movie called *Two to Tangle*. The advance word from the rough cut was that Tommy stole the picture. The comic was in town doing some advance advance prepublicity publicity, aware that this film was his big chance to ascend to a far higher career plateau.

Ursula had not had a serious boyfriend since Craig. Under-standably cautious about getting involved again, she had dated but said good-bye to a variety of men who had begun to get too close. Since the photo shoot was near her apartment, she invited Tommy back while she changed into dry clothing. When Ursula came out of the bedroom, Tommy was sitting on the couch reading a magazine. He was wearing his shoes and socks but otherwise was totally naked.

"I didn't want to be too forward, so I've left my feet covered," he said.

There was a momentary silence, broken by Ursula's genuine roar of laughter. Tommy's fashion risk had paid off. He thought it would. He had used it before. Tommy's wiseguy sarcasm, cut with a generous pinch of self-deprecation, was a winning com-bination that made women want to bed him and take care of him simultaneously. Two hours later the model and the come-dian were lying in bed, exhausted but exhilarated, when the phone rang.

"I'll get it. It's probably your neighbors. I'll tell them it's a new relationship. . . . We'll be quieter next time."

Tommy picked up the phone, but Ursula snatched it away.

"Hello? Mindy? Hi. It's so great you called. I wanted to ask you something. . . . Do you know a comedian named Tommy Marsico?"

Mindy had heard of Tommy Marsico, but he had already made the move to Los Angeles by the time she had started performing at the club. She was uncertain what to tell Ursula. Maybe the cocaine rumors were untrue.

"I've never met him," Mindy said cautiously.

When Tommy and Ursula entered the club that night, almost everybody in the bar momentarily froze and stared at the personification of dating perfection. A noticeable exception was Penelope, who had combed her hair and was wearing her precious Beatles pin on her jeans jacket lapel in preparation for her Ursula meeting. The normally self-assured and cocky comedian was a nervous mess.

"Penelope, this is my friend Ursula," Mindy said.

As Penelope extended a vibrating hand, Mindy looked forward to hearing the sparkling, polished aphorism she was certain her strange friend had readied for the occasion.

"Hi."

"Nice to meet you," replied Ursula, smiling, then moving on.

"How do you think it went? I think it went well. I think it was good," Penelope postmortemed.

Tommy ushered Ursula to a seat inside the club, then excused himself and disappeared into the drugstore/basement. The bar moved back to normal speed as everyone readjusted to the fact that the extraordinary people were gone and only the ordinary folk remained. Mindy was amazed at the effect Ursula could have just walking through the bar. The last time Ursula had been in the club was the night Mindy had passed the audition. At that time Ursula was just a pretty girl whom men noticed; now she was a famous model whom women, as well as men, were awestruck by. Mindy, in stark contrast, had only just recently felt secure enough in her comedy career to quit her coatroom job. Plus, her fellow comedians all thought she was a lesbian. When she considered how equal she and Ursula were when they first met at the women's hotel, Mindy could not deny feeling a nagging twinge of jealousy.

The house band launched into a deafening version of "Born to be Wild," and Tommy exploded onto the stage. The audience became unhinged. This was someone they recognized from television. This was extraordinary. This was a privilege. Tommy's stage charm allowed him to insult members of the audience while making them feel special at the same time. He singled out a man wearing a tie featuring red dots.

"What's your name, sir?"

"Pete," the man replied cautiously.

"Pete. That's a nice tie. What's that pattern called, babe? 'Pap smear'?"

The man was not in the least offended. He was proud to be christened "Pap-Smear Pete" by this future superstar. Similarly, the woman in the front row whose handbag Tommy began to dismantle was equally charmed, even when he held up its more intimate contents and showed them to the rest of the audience.

Tommy appeared not to have anything so mundane as actual material. Rather he seemingly improvised, riffing on whatever subject happened to pop into his obviously oversize brain. It was an impressive technique, not because the material was improvised but because in reality it was highly rehearsed. Tommy performed virtually the same set every time he took to a stage. He always opened with "Pap smear" and "handbag." His gift was his ability to appear spontaneous. Indeed, a less charitable critic might point out that had an audience known that Tommy's jokes were prewritten rather than created on the spot, they might have been more judgmental, especially if they knew a lot of them had been prewritten by other comedians from whose acts Tommy stole.

Tommy completed his ten-minute set to wild applause, and

Ursula said a quick good-bye to Mindy as the golden couple hailed a lucky cabdriver to take them to one of the places special people go. Although they seemed the epitome of contentment, surely nobody would have predicted that early the next morning, munching on her muesli, Mindy would answer the phone and receive such startling news.

"But you've only known him two days."

"I know, but it just feels so right. He's the one, Mindy. I'm sure."

Mindy was the opposite of sure. Tommy Marsico? Marriage? This could end faster than a new network comedy series.

"Congratulations. I'm so happy for you," she said, concealing her reservations.

Ursula had not flown to Las Vegas with the intention of getting married, although she had happily agreed to Tommy's midnight whim of flying to Las Vegas from New York for an extravagant getaway. Tommy had been singing in the oversize marble shower of Caesar's Palace's most opulent suite when Ursula took it on herself to unpack his suitcase. She discovered the square black velvet box almost immediately. Ursula tried not to open the package, but jungle instinct defeated her. It was like trying to keep a starving tiger away from a dead deer. Just a peek, she promised herself; just a peek to determine what part of her anatomy Tommy was intending to decorate. She could feign total surprise when he gave it to her later that evening. Although not an actress, and hopeless at dissembling, Ursula knew even she could manage that charade. However, when she clicked the tiny jewelry coffin open and the vision of the sparkling diamond ring passed through her optic nerves and entered her bloodstream, she forgot her master plan and began to cry. Tommy emerged from the bathroom wearing a towel and stood perfectly still.

"I'm sorry. I opened it."

Tommy retied his towel, walked over, and got down on one knee.

"Marry me?"

The chapel downstairs had time to marry them at 5:46 and offered a variety of services. With Cleopatra acting as her maid of honor, Ursula was married to Tommy by Octavius Caesar himself, Emperor of the Entire Roman Empire, just three or four minutes before the commencement of happy hour.

"What's your real name?" Ursula asked Caesar as she prepared to give him an autograph after the ceremony.

"Sam," the emperor replied.

Ursula felt complete. With her mother in line and her career blossoming, a man she could trust had been the only thing missing in her life. Tommy appeared equally content. He had not stopped grinning since he had proposed, although a more experienced woman might have noticed that there was something disquietingly fixed about the grin. Alone it probably meant nothing, but when added to the unfocused quality in his eyes and the sweat glistening on his forehead, it possibly augured potential problems lying ahead. Sam the emperor noticed it. He had seen the expression when serving in Vietnam. All the prisoners of war had it.

As a wedding present to Ursula, Mindy agreed to break the news to Eva. At first Ursula's mother was shocked and blamed Mindy for not better policing her daughter's relationship.

"You're her friend, and you let her go off and ruin her career without even mentioning it to her mother?"

"I was as surprised as you are, Mrs. Duran."

Eva felt threatened. At forty-five she had finally achieved an existence that was predicated on her own abilities rather than a husband's. Her newly parametered relationship with Ursula had settled into a mutually beneficial partnership. Indeed, to celebrate her mother's recent birthday, Ursula had given her a dream present. Eva's suitcase stood ready in the corner, about to be taken on the special birthday trip. So Eva was understandably nervous of anything that might disturb the hard-fought equilibrium that mother and daughter had finally achieved.

"Who is he? I've never heard of Tommy Marsico," Eva barked, pouring a midmorning Scotch.

Mindy explained that Tommy was a successful comedian who was about to become a movie star. Eva reevaluated. Rather than signaling the end of Ursula's career, this new union might in reality be a career opportunity. Modeling was fine for now, but Eva knew career longevity and incalculable financial reward could only come if her daughter became a movie star.

"I brought you a photo of him from the club."

Mindy offered up a glossy eight-by-ten as sacrifice to the angry goddess. Eva grudgingly admitted he looked appealing.

"Hmmm . . . the model and the comedian . . . maybe that has potential," she mused, throwing the Scotch to the back of her throat.

Back in her apartment, Mindy tried hard not to be jealous.

"Never be envious of other people," Mindy's mother used to say. "Just live your life the best you can and let them live theirs."

It was difficult when the luckiest woman in the world, who seemingly had everything, was your best friend. Mindy had never seen anyone so in love.

"I've never fallen in love," Mindy told an audience at the club much later that day. "I've stepped in it a few times."

The audience laughed. Mindy had a new joke, but even that depressed her. She had written several new jokes that all worked well, but nobody seemed to care. Something was happening that Mindy had not anticipated. Whenever talent scouts came to the club in search of comedians, they invariably were looking for funny young men. Both she and Penelope were finding it difficult to get stage time.

Oh to be a beautiful blonde. They definitely had more fun, Mindy reasoned. They must. How many brunettes did you see walking down the street with blond roots?

Mindy was upset but not surprised when Ursula gave up her

apartment to move to Los Angeles to be with Tommy full time.

"I'll call you constantly," Ursula promised, trying to close her overstuffed suitcase.

"No, you won't. You'll forget all about me."

Ursula stopped what she was doing.

"Mindy, you're my bestest friend in the whole wide world. We're never going to lose touch 'til the day one of us dies. Promise me that."

Mindy and Ursula hugged tightly.

"I promise," gulped Mindy.

"We're always going to be there for each other," continued Ursula. "Whenever one of us hits a shit storm, the other one's gonna turn up with a paddle."

Mindy laughed, remembering her slipup during their very first conversation.

"How old was I then?" asked Mindy.

"About nine," smirked Ursula.

"Late. We're late," Tommy yelled impatiently from the living room.

As Ursula and Mindy successfully pushed the enormous suitcase through the doorway, Tommy attempted to lift it.

"I didn't know you were taking the furniture."

"When your husband complains that the suitcase is too heavy, that's when you know you're officially married," Mindy remarked.

Ursula hugged her again. "Love you."

"Love you too."

Standing on the sidewalk watching the two speed away in their chauffeured limousine, Mindy hoped she and Ursula would remain friends forever. However, for the time being she, for one, was prepared to accept the glaringly obvious. Her friend Ursula had outgrown her.

All About Eva

Eva was frightened. Four-thirty in the morning is not a happy time of day. Only disc jockeys and surgeons are operating at that hour, and Eva was certainly not scheduled to appear on any radio program. She stared at the ceiling above the single bed on which she lay and questioned her sanity.

She reminded herself that of all the plastic surgeons she had interviewed, Dr. Kramer had been the most impressive. Her second choice, Dr. Applegate, was equally qualified, and the rumor was he had done Jackie O. However, the Picasso prints he chose to feature on the walls of his waiting room had made Eva wonder whether he possessed a full understanding of the symmetrical.

Dr. Kramer's outer office was deliberately baroque, specifically designed to negate all things medical. The expensive furnishings were also intended to imbue in the waiting the idea that the care lavished on the surroundings exactly mirrored the care that Dr. Kramer and his staff would lavish on the bodies about to be placed within their charge. In the center of the room, a tiered fountain mesmerically trickled water down into sculptured basins. Velvet draping decorated the mahogany walls and was held in place by golden tassels that perfectly matched in color the filigree highlights contained within the Louis XV sofas that peppered the room. The entire effect suggested a turn-of-the-century Viennese whorehouse.

Seated on the ornate velvet sofa, the backs of her knees pressed against a golden cherub blowing a trumpet, Eva perused the scrapbook prominently positioned on the antique escritoire. The book featured photos of patients before Dr. Kramer had applied his facial sculpting skills and then photos of their transformations. Eva considered the women in the notebook who'd allowed the before photographs to remain in existence to be braver than foot soldiers. After her surgery, she intended to have a bonfire on her tiny terrace and watch all evidence of the old Eva disappear into anonymous ashes.

Another woman, Chanel-suited and -shoed, entered the outer office and reported her arrival to the smoothed receptionist. Eva studied the new patient's face, trying to determine what work had been done to it. The only lines on this woman's face were her stenciled-on eyebrows. The woman looked at Eva and smiled carefully.

"You'll like him. He's very good," she murmured, attempting to allay any fears Eva might be having but in fact only confirming to Eva her obvious need for immediate surgical attention.

"If you don't mind me asking," Eva inquired, "what have you had done?"

"Last time? Eyebrow lift and cheek implants. I have some sort of plastic surgery every year as a birthday gift to myself."

"Did it hurt?"

"Which time?"

"Any time."

"A little. But it's worth it. I'm just having him look at this little sag here. I want to see what he recommends."

Pointing to her chin line, the woman's eyes glazed over as she disappeared into an antiseptic dreamworld in which skilled fingers cut into her aging flesh. "He's a genius," she announced, snapping out of her reverie.

The genius was a saggy man in his sixties, the proud owner of a nose so big and bumpy it looked like a knee. At two hundred dollars a consultation, Eva hung on Dr. Kramer's every word during the assessment process. He sat Eva down in front of a three-way mirror and stared at her as if she were a car he was considering purchasing.

"Your cheekbones are good, but so long as you're going to be under, for a nominal additional charge I can do your eyes and your chin. I can laser the crow's feet and zap a little collagen into those laugh lines. Are you happy with your body?"

In late-twentieth-century America, that was a question only a Barbie doll would answer in the affirmative. And Barbie cannot talk. That's part of her allure. Eva had adopted an exercise and diet regimen that, although offering a money-back guarantee if excess pounds and inches were not shed, had failed to mention anything about loose skin. Six months of zero booze, tasteless milk shakes, and aerobic exercise had resulted in thirty lost pounds that had caused Eva's previously puffy rear end to deflate and her stomach to pouch. When a naked Eva looked backward into a mirror, it looked to her as though she'd recently sat in gravel. Eva lifted up her skirt, and Dr. Kramer inspected the offending derrière.

"I'll just suck that cellulite out and take a tuck right here. The scar will be in the folds of your buttocks. Easy."

Eva also sanctioned the breast lift, tummy tuck, and thigh-tightening combo. Because she'd also opted for the face-, eye-, and neck-lift, accompanied by the laser peel and the collagen injections, Dr. Kramer gave her two thousand dollars off the regular price. He had used computer imagery to show Eva what her face would look like after the procedures, and she'd begun to cry. To look as she did twenty years ago, to know what she knew now, and to be making a deal with only a doctor and not the devil himself was quite simply a miracle.

"Wear loose clothing that you can slip over your head and flat shoes because you're liable to be dizzy."

That was the last thing that the doctor had said after Eva had handed him a check for ten thousand dollars.

• • •

Eva's remodeling was taking place in the operating room at the back of Dr. Kramer's office. There, among state-of-the-art machinery and with the help of two able nurses, Kramer performed two face-lifts a day. Eva had deliberated whether to be the first lift of the day when the doctor was fresh, or the second when he had warmed up. Lying on the operating table while Dr. Kramer marked her body and her face with a red Magic Marker as if she were a side of beef about to be hacked apart, Eva hoped that early morning had been the correct decision.

The last thing Eva remembered was the needle containing the powerful sedative being inserted into her vein. When she awoke some hours later, a barrelful of sand appeared to be lodged in her larynx.

"Don't cough," the nurse instructed. "You'll rip the blood vessels in your throat."

"Wadda," Eva croaked.

The nurse held a cup with a straw to Eva's lips.

"Here. Suck carefully. Place the straw between your teeth, not your lips. Don't move your head. You'll pull the stitches."

"Dotta Kanar?"

"Doctor Kramer? He said everything went well. He had a luncheon. We'll help you get to your car whenever you feel ready, so long as it's not longer than twenty minutes."

As her bleeding, bandaged frame was transported by wheelchair into the Lincoln Continental waiting for her in the office's underground garage, Eva realized the surgery she regretted the most was the buttock lift. She'd previously had no idea how underappreciated the buttock was as a working body part.

The freshly carved Eva carefully balanced her wounded posterior on the edge of the leather seat. She selected the position that caused her the least discomfort, then turned her bandaged head away from the dark tinted window to avoid anyone catching a glimpse of the mummy inside. The Chanel woman in the waiting room had certainly undersold the searing pain that accompanied the quest for physical perfection. Plastic surgery must be like childbirth without the child, Eva reasoned. After a while, if you're satisfied with the results, you forget the pain and want to do it again.

Because she lived alone and Ursula was at present ensconced in Los Angeles with her new husband, Eva had booked herself into The Willows, a hotel-hospital on the Upper East Side that administered postoperative care to the rich and tightened. The Willows specialized in privacy; at no point during her entire stay did Eva catch even a glimpse of another patient. Once she was inside The Willows' underground entrance, a waiting nurse shifted Eva onto a pillowed wheelchair. Eva was wheeled into a private elevator, then down a corridor of closed doors and into a cheerful room overlooking a private park. The adjustable bed alleviated the pressure on Eva's sensitive areas, and the pain pill administered by the white-clad nurse transported the broken Eva into a cloud of anesthetized bliss.

There Ain't Nothing Like a Jew

At that very moment, Mindy was also lying in a strange bed overlooking a park. Late one night at the club, a man whom Mindy recognized as someone who had recently frequented Stars had approached her at the bar.

"I like the way your mind works," he'd said.

Mindy had a fan. A man with hair the color of brick and a penchant for blazers, ironed trousers, and shiny loafers liked the way her mind worked. At first, Mindy was deliberately cold to him; she'd decided that a homicidal fan bent on murder would undoubtedly dress like a preppie so as to disguise his intent. Laurence Milford III was not, however, a quitter, and he continued to pursue Mindy throughout the fall. When Mindy saw Moe approaching her suitor one night to put him out of his misery by advising him of the comedian's sexual preference, she intervened and accepted the offer of dinner.

Mindy was not particularly attracted to Laurence. She was attracted to Robert Redford. However, Bob wasn't calling, and Mindy, the lover of order and structure, felt it was time she tried once more to connect with a male. Laurence was Republican to the core. His voice had that twinge of stereotypical nasal snobbery Mindy had noticed was symptomatic of the inherited rich, who always seemed to have something lodged in their adenoidal passage, perhaps coins, that gave their vocal tone a different timbre than that of ordinary folk.

Laurence Milford was polite to a fault. Mindy had never dated a chair-puller before and was slightly confused on their first date as to when, exactly, to sit. Too soon would be a disaster, so she erred on the side of too late, waiting until the second chair noise was complete before she committed herself to the sitting position.

Laurence hailed from a prominent New York banking family. After graduating from Yale's business school, Laurence Milford II's alma mater, Laurence went directly to work for his father's firm, doing the same job his father had done for his father when his father had graduated from Yale's business school. In his late twenties and single, Laurence III was desperately attempting not to turn into Laurences I and II, unaware that he had already done so.

"So why are you hanging around a comedy club?" Mindy asked after they had ordered their aperitifs.

"I'm not just a boring banker like my father," he replied. "I like to do things that are a little crazy. I'm unpredictable."

"I'm a novelty to you, then?"

"No. Like I said, I like the way your mind works. The women I meet all have marriage and children on their mind. I love that you do something that's so unusual. It's piqued my interest."

"That's good. I'll order something expensive."

"Anything you want. But not lobster. My father and I are both allergic to lobster."

"I'm missing something here. If I order lobster, it affects you?"

"Exactly. Even someone eating it at the same table can cause a Milford to swell up."

Not only was Laurence shellfish-delicate, but he also had an irrational fear of touching polyester. However, Mindy found his idiosyncrasies rather endearing, and dating someone with a full wallet transformed New York into an entirely different city than the one in which Mindy had previously lived. Manhattan restaurants that had previously only been awnings to her now had interiors that she could mentally reference.

The interior of Laurence's marble-floored and oriental-rugged Fifth Avenue apartment was sparsely but elegantly furnished.

"I like barren surfaces," he stated proudly, pointing to patinated, empty tabletops. "My father collects antique clocks from around the world. I don't."

Mindy was unable to afford to take her new boyfriend out to the types of restaurants to which he was accustomed, and her culinary expertise ended with eggs any style except fried, poached, or over easy. So the first reciprocal dinner she prepared for Laurence was scrambled eggs and toast.

"What's for breakfast?" he asked. "Boeuf Bourgignon?"

The unlikely couple actually worked well together. Laurence was developing a sense of irony, and Mindy, pleasantly surprised at finding Laurence to be a skilled and selfless lover, was enjoying her second sexual relationship. Laurence was much more excited about sex than Ed had been and seemed genuinely turned on by Mindy. Quitting dancing had caused Mindy to add a few pounds, and it suited her. Unlike Ursula, she had never been conscious of provoking lust before, and she found the attention hugely satisfying.

"I'm thinking of dyeing my hair blond. What do you think?" she asked him one night, as she stretched out lazily and nakedly on his antique Bakshaish rug.

"No," Laurence urged, his eyes taking in her full breasts and dancer legs, topped off with the swirling mass of curly brunette hair. "I love everything about you just the way it is."

The twosome arrived hand in hand one Saturday night at the club. Determined to dispel the lesbian rumor, Mindy was conscious of Moe's gaze as Laurence leaned over and kissed her on the lips. She sat her boyfriend at the comics' table and proceeded to do her allotted twenty minutes of material. Laurence hugged her enthusiastically when she left the stage as her befuddled cohorts looked on incredulously.

"Was that a *guy?*" Ronnie whispered to Alvin after the couple left the club.

"No. I think it was a banker," Alvin whispered back.

Laurence's thirtieth birthday party was held at his father's country club in an exclusive part of Connecticut. His burgundy E-type Jaguar glided Mindy and him up the winding, tree-lined driveway of the rural estate, past the perfectly manicured eighteenth fairway, and pulled to a stop outside the lantern-lit stone clubhouse. Mindy noticed an inquisitive squirrel, perched at the edge of the golf course, examining her as she began to ease herself out of the low sports car. This squirrel had a remarkably bushy tail compared to the squirrels she had seen in Central Park, causing Mindy to wonder whether there was some kind of squirrel salon on the premises where they were blow-dried.

Laurence Milford II, waiting curbside for his offspring, blew expensive cigar smoke into the crisp night air. He was a study in casual cashmere. Mindy calculated that the price of the soft black lintless jacket covering the off-white turtleneck sweater must have reached well into four digits pre–decimal point.

"Happy birthday, son," said the father, shaking hands with Laurence.

"Thanks, Dad. Where's Mumsy?"

"Your mother is inside, complaining about the size of the centerpieces. I'm hiding out here until it blows over."

Mindy was still recovering from *Mumsy* when even more questionable vocabulary assaulted her ears.

"This is my comedy friend. Mindy."

The father smiled perfunctorily, shook Mindy's hand, and murmured a greeting.

• • •

" 'Comedy friend'?" Mindy repeated, as they entered the club-house. "Should I have worn a red nose and funny glasses?"

"It's just that he knows you do comedy."

"He knows I'm a girl too. What about 'girlfriend'?"

As they entered the dining room, a female stick crowned with copper hair moved in their direction. They were about to be greeted by a very large caramel apple. Mindy realized that the color of Laurence Millford III's hair and the color of the hair heading toward her matched perfectly. This had to be Mumsy.

"My baby," she said, throwing her diamond bracelets around Mindy's escort. "How can you be thirty when I'm only twenty-nine? Happy birthday, darling."

"Thank you, Mumsy."

Laurence looked at his date.

"This is Mindy," he said, careful not to repeat his mistake.

"Oh, how wonderful," Mrs. Millford proclaimed, clasping her hands together, which caused her several large but tasteful rings to clunk against their opposite number. "The Jewish come-dienne. Well, I have to check on something. Laurence, all of your friends are here. Don't forget to circulate."

With that, caramel apple Nazi Mumsy moved off to belittle someone in the service industry. Mindy was about to register a complaint about Mumsy's classification of her when a beige woman in a beige dress approached the couple.

"Laurence, I haven't seen you for ages," said the woman in a beige voice.

"Hi. I'm Mindy the Jew," Mindy blurted out. "Are there any matzo balls anywhere, or should I have brought my own?"

"Excuse us," Laurence said, ushering Mindy away from the guest. "What's the matter with you?"

"Is that how you're rebelling against your family? By bringing the comedy Jewess to your party?"

"Mumsy didn't mean anything. She doesn't know many Jews, and she's intrigued. She meant it as a compliment."

"Are Jews allowed in here?"

"Certainly."

"Really?"

He hesitated. "Well, as guests."

"What?"

"Not as members. Look, they have their own club down the road that we're not allowed to join."

" 'They'? Maybe I should go there. Maybe they're doing *Fiddler on the Roof* this evening. It's Friday, isn't it? I think that's Gefilte Fish Night."

Laurence was caught off-balance and was unsure just how seriously to take Mindy's comments.

"You're not really angry, are you? You're joking, aren't you?"

In truth, Mindy herself was doing some mental whirling. Nobody was saying anything false. She *was* Jewish, and she was a comedian. But why had it sounded so condescending when the caramel apple had said it? Mindy decided to take the high road. If she was unable to identify why she was offended, she would try not to be offended. It was his birthday. The last thing she wanted to do was spoil it.

"Yes, I'm joking," she confirmed.

"Good," Laurence said, giving her Semitic hand a squeeze.

The four-piece band massacred Toto's "Rosanna" as Mindy sipped white wine and munched on salmon toast points. Laurence's fraternity brother, Anson, shared a story with her about how he once got drunk and attempted stand-up comedy at a party but didn't really think it was for him.

Mindy noticed a gathering forming at the entrance to the dining room. A muted rendition of "That's Amore," a song far more suited to the talents of the band that Mindy had mentally named The Rented Tuxedos of West Hartford, filled the background as the caramel apple took the microphone and announced the arrival of a very special guest. This guest, even though currently studying renaissance architecture at the

University of Milan, had apparently flown in especially for Laurence's thirtieth birthday party.

Mindy watched her boyfriend's color turn to oatmeal as Mumsy proudly introduced Caroline, Laurence's fiancée. As the crowd parted and a smiling Caroline, straight out of a Ralph Lauren advertisement, stepped forward, Laurence whispered, "I can explain" into Mindy's ear.

"No you can't," Mindy whispered back.

A Star Isn't Born

*H*is drug problem really wasn't a problem at all, Tommy explained to Ursula as he opened up a tiny envelope of white powder in their honeymoon suite.

"I've got so much going on, I just need to do this now to stay on top of things."

Ursula had tried cocaine a few times. She liked it, but it made her twitchy and unable to sleep. Because her entire career depended on looking good, cocaine abuse did not seem a logical activity. However, she gamely joined in, if only temporarily, so as to keep up with her energetic husband.

California suited them. Ursula's mane of blond hair whipped like cotton candy above the Porsche 911 that was guided by Tommy's firm, driving-gloved hands as they drove in from the airport. With the J. Geils Band blasting from the car's stereo, the vehicle dove off Mulholland Drive, burrowed deep into one of the hillsides perched above Beverly Hills, and then pulled up outside Tommy's recently acquired property.

From the front, Tommy's house looked like a giant white box. If there had been a slit at the top, it could have dispensed enormous pieces of Kleenex. Inside, floor-to-ceiling windows overlooked a pool perched precariously on a cliff.

"If we have an earthquake, the guy below me gets my pool, but I get the guy above's tennis court, so it all evens out."

Through the dirty-milk haze, Ursula could see from

Tommy's patio the localized neighborhoods of peaked, clustered modern buildings that interrupted the surprisingly rural view. Sinews of red taillights snaked throughout the vista, contrasting with the hint of blue ocean located in the far right background.

"The view's not great in the daytime," Tommy said, standing out on the deck with his arm around his bride. "See that layer of brown gunk? That's not smog. That's insincerity. But at night, with all the twinkling lights, it's so pretty that for just a few seconds, I might have to stop looking at you."

The house had obviously been furnished by a single guy and needed attention. Exercise equipment cluttered the dining room, and a pool table occupied the living room. When Ursula entered the bedroom, she was relieved to find a bed and not a diving board.

"Buy anything you want," Tommy instructed his wife. "Just make sure it costs a lot of money."

Not only was her husband nice and funny but he was generous as well. Ursula made a mental note to enlist Eva's help with the redecoration. Her newly improved mother was due to relocate to California in two weeks, a month after her surgery.

Ursula had decided to take a break from her career to better acclimatize herself to her new lifestyle. She set up an easel on the patio, began painting Hockneyesque views of the city, and became Californian. Tommy, on the other hand, was constantly on the move. The brink of stardom was a busy place. His phone rang incessantly, and the pressure occasionally precipitated overreaction.

"No," he screamed into the phone. "That's bullshit. Well I'm not doing it. Fuck you."

He slammed down the receiver.

"Who was that?" Ursula asked.

"My mother. She wants me to call my sister."

A manager who wanted Tommy to sign with his company

had arranged to take the couple to dinner at the newest, chic showbiz-frequented eatery. Boccelli's was an Italian restaurant that used to be The Pink Duck, which was a Chinese restaurant that before that used to be Reginald's, which specialized in steak. Restaurants in Los Angeles, Ursula noticed, were not so much dining establishments as they were unstable cuisine regimes destined to be toppled.

Marc Mosley did not conform to Ursula's perceived image of a powerful personal manager. This was no hairy-chested, medallion-wearing con artist. This was a meticulously groomed, well-spoken, college-educated gentleman who wore a tan the color of a perfectly cooked turkey. Marc's hair had not been interrupted by a forced part but had been allowed to listen to its needs and separate according to its feelings. This style allowed for Marc's habit of running his fingers through his hair, which changed the cut's position for a second, then returned it to its original formation, reinforcing just how happy it was with its own arrangement.

Marc Mosley spoke so quietly that Ursula had to stop chewing to hear what he was saying. Although his eyes were focused on Tommy, his ears were so finely tuned to everything that was occurring at other tables in the restaurant that they appeared to rotate.

"I know I don't yet represent you," Marc said, after swallowing a piece of bluefish baked with apples and mustard, "but I've taken the liberty of negotiating a three-picture deal for you. Nothing is in stone. It's all very premature. However, the studio is interested and, on your behalf, I couldn't let that interest go away. I felt it would be wrong . . . and selfish of me."

He raised his finger in a miniwave to a patron passing by, then wiped his mouth with his cloth napkin in triplicate as he did after every bite.

Tommy was intent on following a path of caution. The hefty fifteen percent a manager charged, on top of an agent's ten percent and a lawyer's five percent, combined with the government's and the state's percentages, meant less than half of anything Tommy made would go directly to him. Plus, he had heard horror stories of managerial duplicity, as clients' interests were sacrificed on the altar of the manager's self-interest.

"I'm intrigued. But I need to think about it more."

Marc's manner subtly hardened.

"Don't think about it too long. I know this town. You don't. This is a business about windows of opportunity. Once the windows close, they tend to stick. You're a talented guy. Right now, people who matter care. You can be just as talented tomorrow, and they wouldn't look at you if you had rattlesnake tied to your dick."

He turned to Ursula and said quietly, "Excuse me."

As if noticing her for the first time, he murmured, "Do you have representation?"

Ursula was flustered and spit a tiny particle of chicken pesto onto Marc's suit. Marc quickly flicked it off with a manicured digit.

"I'm a model. I can't act."

"That's what Ali McGraw told me."

"She was right," Tommy added. "Ursula's modeling career is going fine. I don't think she really wants to get involved in the acting thing. Right, honey?"

"Right."

When they returned home that evening, a huge basket of flowers was blocking the front door.

"This guy doesn't quit," Tommy said, exasperated.

He opened the card leaning against the basket.

"It's from a different one," he moaned.

A suited figure appeared out of the darkness.

"One minute of your time. I just need one minute."

The couple hurried indoors.

• • •

The dress Tommy chose for Ursula to wear to the premiere, purchased from an exclusive boutique on Sunset Boulevard, was so delicate that it appeared to have been woven by fairy pixies rather than the quartet of illegal immigrants that had painstakingly put it together. Strategically placed patterns of sequins covered the more intimate areas of Ursula's anatomy, while sparkling, transparent layers of clinging gauze held it all in place so as to prevent arrest for indecent exposure.

"Are you sure it's not too revealing?" Ursula asked Tommy as he sat in the chair reserved for shopping husbands.

"For anyone else, yes."

Ursula's cocaine use had caused her to shed a few pounds, leaving not an inch of her to fold or bulge. Another woman entered the store and was transfixed by the image of female physical perfection standing before her.

"Can I help you?" a saleslady inquired of the woman.

"No. Not right now. Now, I have to go kill myself."

"We'll take it," Tommy said, as the woman turned and left.

Ursula readjusted the skimpy dress one last time as the stretch limousine pulled up in front of the cordoned-off Westwood movie theater for the world premiere of *Two to Tangle*.

"Good luck, baby," offered Ursula supportively.

Tommy took one last snort of cocaine as the driver clicked the door locks to their full, upright position. Before they could get out, one of the passenger doors opened just wide enough to admit a heavily lipsticked, whispering mouth into the rear of the vehicle.

"Stay there another two minutes. Brian and Judy are still on the carpet. I want some separation."

Stella Steen, Tommy's publicist, was determined to create a moment. Brian Shaw, the actor who played the crusty old conservative cop paired with Tommy's young, irreverent, impulsive cop, was still busily being photographed and interviewed by the media. His loyal second wife stood by his side, holding in her stomach and her age as she waved and smiled broadly. As the actor who appealed to the older demographic disappeared into the theater, Tommy heard Stella's voice bark, "Now."

Ursula extended a slender hand to the attendant opening the door and unfolded herself out of one side of the stretch. Tommy followed closely behind. The couple was met with a barrage of flashes as a bank of cameras exploded in front of them.

"Ursula, over here. Ursula, this way. Ursula, just one second. Ursula, where'd you get the dress? Tommy, turn this way," shouted the jostling reporters and photographers as Tommy and Ursula began the ritualized walk along the red carpet.

Although it was an impressive reception, one detail was a little awry. There were four Ursula calls to every one Tommy call. Stella edged closer to Tommy.

"Walk a little in front of her," she suggested. "Ursula, stand back."

"Sure," Ursula replied, eager to oblige.

Stella had inadvertently created a moment for the wrong person. The majority of the cameras remained focused on Ursula as Tommy proceeded down the carpet, waving to nobody in particular. When one of Ursula's sequins caught on her handbag and precipitated the unraveling of her fairy dress, the few lenses that were still aimed toward Tommy were immediately repositioned toward his more photogenic wife as she frantically attempted to keep her already challenged modesty intact.

Tommy backtracked, removed his jacket, and gallantly placed it around Ursula.

"I'll give her my jacket, but I refuse to relinquish my pants," he announced to laughter, figuring that sharing the center of attention with his glamorous partner was the best he was going to do.

Once inside, a walkie-talkie'd, blue-blazered studio employee ushered the pair to the roped-off, red-taped VIP seats toward the back of the theater.

"Red Rose? Red Rose? This is Apple Crumble. I have Timmy Marcenco plus one here. Ten four."

He turned his attention to Tommy and Ursula.

"Can I get you anything? Soda? Popcorn?"

"No. Can we get you anything?" Tommy asked back. "Brain? Real job?"

Ursula admonished Tommy with a kick to the shin.

"He was only trying to do his job," she told him as Apple Crumble disappeared back up the aisle.

"Then he should learn my fucking name. It's outside in big fucking letters," Tommy growled. "I'm going to the john. Just sit there and try not to get your picture taken."

Tommy pushed past Ursula, heading for the bathroom and the inevitable couple of lines of Peruvian marching powder. Meanwhile, outside the theater, celebrities continued to preen for the assembled media. A woman with platinum hair and a figure-hugging Nolan Miller gown stopped and waved at the cameramen as though they should know her. Given her confidence and obvious star quality, the photographers began snapping, until one brave soul asked the question they were all too timid to pose.

"Excuse me, miss, but who are you?"

"I'm with Tommy Marsico. We're related," the mystery woman replied.

"Are you his sister?"

"No."

"His first wife?"

"No. I'm his mother-in-law," Eva said proudly, checking that her hair was still covering the now almost invisible stitch marks. The low-cut gown revealed her perfect, pert bosoms, and her face glowed with the sheen of a laminated driver's license. Eva had finally found the man she was missing in her life. It was Dr. Kramer, and she only needed to see him once every ten years.

Eva displayed her ticket and was led to the VIP section. Her seat was already occupied. The ugliest man she had ever seen had taken up residence in aisle M, seat 3. An usher attempted to guide Eva away.

"I can show you to another seat, equally as good," she said soothingly.

"But that's my seat. I want to sit there," Eva replied, hoping to shame the pretender in her chair into vacating it immediately.

The man ignored her, continuing to munch on fistfuls of popcorn, some of which were going in his mouth.

"That's Leonard Felk," the usher whispered nervously. "He's the head of the studio. I can't ask him to move."

Eva looked over at the messy man whose squashed features made him look as though he were permanently wearing a stocking over his head.

"*I* can," she announced, sauntering over with her ticket prepared as evidence. "Excuse me. You're in my seat."

Leonard Felk turned and smiled at Eva. "There are lots of others. Why don't you take one of them?" he said, attempting polite but achieving rude.

"Because I want this one," Eva announced, plonking her newly lifted derrière onto the studio chief's lap.

Leonard Felk laughed.

"Barry, give me your seat," he told the person sitting in M4.

Barry, a subordinate, happily obliged, and Leonard moved over one.

"You're a messy eater," said Eva, flicking popcorn kernels away with the toes of her high heels.

"You have no idea," he replied suggestively.

Now it was Eva's turn to laugh.

"Who *are* you?" Leonard Felk inquired, intrigued by his brash, beautiful neighbor with the sexy European accent.

"Sssh," said Eva. "The movie's starting."

In the first scene, Tommy was introduced to his begrudging new partner while hanging upside down in a doorway. The test audiences had exploded with laughter at the brash young cop's saying casually to the grizzled veteran, "I used to be a cop in Australia."

It had been a line that Tommy had improvised on the set to end a lengthy production delay. The original line had been "I've always been a little bats," which both the director and Tommy had disliked. The director had asked for the screenwriter to be contacted to see whether he could come up with an alternative. Scott Bentley was eventually located in Japan, where he was directing a lucrative beer commercial after using the writing credit from *Two to Tangle* to segue from screenwriting to directing. Unfortunately, Scott felt, because this was a scene that had survived intact from the original screenplay that he had been brought on board to rewrite, he was morally obligated to suggest that the original screenwriter be contacted. This proved fruitless when it was discovered that the original screenwriter had committed suicide some years earlier, a direct result of being fired from this project that he had originally developed for Steve McQueen and Richard Pryor in 1972. So Tommy had improvised, and the film crew had chuckled.

Tommy, waiting for the guaranteed laugh, was shocked when the line received just a few tentative titters.

"Crowd's dead," Tommy whispered in Ursula's ear. "Completely dead. Dead crowd."

"They'll warm up," Ursula whispered back, kissing him on the cheek.

She was wrong.

The party afterward was held in a tent especially erected over an outdoor parking lot at a busy intersection in the center of Westwood Village. Cars were stopped and traffic was rerouted by red-jacketed valet-parkers waving officious, oversize, glowing flashlights. This was Hollywood and this was a premiere; working stiffs who were trying to get home for dinner would just have to wait.

Because much of the movie took place in prison, the theme of incarceration was employed as the post-premiere party motif. Forbidding black prison bars were projected onto the tent's exterior structure; wardens pretend-frisked guests as they entered; the drinks-waiters were outfitted in penitentiary clothes and, by necessity, traveled in pairs because they were manacled together. At the far end of the tent, partygoers lined up to have their pictures taken sitting in an authentic electric chair that had been shipped in from Alabama.

The general reaction to the film had been "positive." That's what Tommy's agent Lou Feldman had said as he accompanied Tommy and Ursula into the party.

"Don't worry about anything. Premiere audience responses are always muted. I've seen the numbers. You tested through the roof."

"But they didn't laugh," noted a worried Tommy.

"That's good. That means they're jealous. Laughter in a comedy is death. Laughter means it's a stink bomb."

Ursula noted that Lou Feldman could probably have convinced the passengers on the *Titanic* that sinking was a good thing, but she was pleased to see that his words seemed to mollify her husband somewhat.

"So what did you think of the movie?" Eva asked Leonard Felk as he walked her from the theater toward the party marquee.

"It'll do about fifteen million domestically," drawled Leonard. "Nothing internationally. We won't get hurt. We may even make a little. I'd hire him again."

"The comic?"

"No. The director. The comic's crap."

"Really?"

"He's a pounder. Hits every joke too square. Tries too hard. Can't act. Grates."

"It's his first movie."

"It's his last movie for me."

"Oh."

It was only one syllable, but Leonard heard the note of disappointment it contained.

"Who *are* you exactly?"

"Eva Duran. I'm the pounder's mother-in-law."

"Oops. Sorry, Eva, but I like to be direct."

"Me too. Are you married?"

"Yes. Does it matter?"

"No."

Leonard hesitated beside the opening to the tent. "Look, do you want to go somewhere for dinner? If I see another Tommy Tang buffet, I think I'll barf."

"Sure. Let me just say hi to my daughter. She's over there."

Eva hurried over to Ursula, who was fixing a plate of crispy Long Island duck with honey ginger sauce for the pounder as he circulated around the tent, accepting phony congratulations. Eva had arrived in Los Angeles only two days earlier, and Ursula was still finding it difficult to believe how wonderful she looked.

"Hi, Mom. You look great. Did you like the movie?"

"Fifteen mil domestically. Nothing internationally."

"What?"

"I can't stop. The head of the studio's asked me out to dinner. I'll call you tomorrow."

"Okay. Have fun."

Leonard watched Eva talking to her daughter. Only a few years ago, it would have been the hot young model he would be trying to seduce. However, since his surgery he felt more comfortable with women ten years his junior rather than thirty. They were more grateful and therefore more understanding of his peculiarity.

In Ursula and Tommy's limousine on the way home, the air was thick with hostility, resentment, and an overwhelming fear that the acting career he had mapped out for himself was a pipe dream. And that was just the air around the driver. In the back seat, Ursula was doing her best to pull her husband out of his despair.

"The movie opens to the public tomorrow. That's who matters, not these Hollywood types. Once the reviews come out—"

"Let me stop you there," Tommy interrupted. "Lou advised me to avoid reading anything about the movie in any publication. He also told me bad reviews were a good thing."

As the driver opened the door to let the twosome out of the car, Tommy, ever mindful of appearances, handed the chauffeur a fifty-dollar bill.

"Thanks for taking such good care of us."

"You're very welcome," the driver replied. "And it's not that bad. I snuck in the back and saw some of it. It's not what I would have chosen for *my* first vehicle, but it's cute."

Later that night, lying in bed, they both stared silently at the ceiling. Tomorrow Tommy was supposed to be a star. Like a well-meaning spouse, Hollywood often makes promises it finds itself unable to keep. It was 5:00 in the morning when Ursula and Tommy finally closed their bloodshot eyes, went to sleep, and tried not to dream about the reviews.

TOMMY TANKS TANGLE was the headline that most offended Tommy. The reviewer went on to praise Tommy's costar. "Brian Shaw, the veteran actor, battles valiantly to no avail against the twitchy, hyperactive comic."

"Why is it my fucking fault?" Tommy screamed into the phone the next morning at his agent. "You were the one who told me to do that piece of shit."

"I'm late for a staff meeting. Let me get off the phone and start tracking scripts for you, big guy."

Lou hung up on Tommy and glided on to his next call.

"It's the public that decides who's a star," Tommy said. "Let's go check out *real* people's reactions."

He and Ursula, wearing baseball caps and sunglasses, hovered behind a street lamp outside a movie theater, attempting to mingle with the Friday matinee crowd as it exited the 1:30 screening.

"I thought it would be better."

"I didn't believe for one minute that the young guy cared about the other guy. I don't think his character was fully developed."

"I thought he was good . . . that old guy. I've seen him in some other thing and I liked him then too."

"Have you seen that young guy's wife? She's hot, man. What's she doing with that loser?"

Tommy turned slowly toward Ursula.

"I think I need a manager," he said.

Leonard Felk's prediction proved too generous. Three weeks later, *Tangle* had clawed its way slowly to a gross of ten million dollars. Four weeks later it was harder to find than Zsa Zsa Gabor's birth certificate. The phone that had rung incessantly was now continuously being checked by Tommy to see if it was still working.

Meanwhile, the phone line Ursula had installed for herself in their bedroom was ringing off the hook. The photograph of Ursula attempting to cover her bosoms as her dress unraveled around them had been picked up by almost all the various print outlets worldwide. One day Ursula picked up the phone and heard a familiar voice.

"Hi gorgeous, it's me."

"What do you want, Brandon?"

"Well, first, I'd like it if you'd call me Dad."

"Dream. How did you get my number?"

"I have my connections. Listen, I've got a TV commercial for you. A good one. For a soda. I can't divulge the brand until I know if you're interested."

"Brandon, consider me on permanent hiatus."

"From modeling?"

"From you."

Ursula decided to mute the ringer and let an answering machine pick up future calls. This pleased Tommy, who had privately concluded that this was the only way he and the additional phone could cohabit the house.

Tommy had put five calls in to Marc Mosley, whose assistant, Liam, had promised Marc would get back to him.

"He's a little crazy right now" was the unspecific excuse that Liam had used each time Tommy called.

"I don't need a manager. I need a doctor. I have cancer of the career," raved Tommy, off the phone.

"You shouldn't panic. Things will change. There are always new opportunities out there. You just have to be open to them," Ursula, who had taken to reading self-help books, said consolingly as she sat cross-legged on the deck one morning.

"Maybe I should wear a dress that explodes in public," Tommy said sharply. "Maybe a peek at *my* genitalia would generate a few calls."

"You picked out the fucking dress. And anyway, what does that have to do with your movie stiffing? Is that my fault too?" she screamed, throwing her copy of *Winning Is Just the Beginning* at him.

"Sorry," Tommy mumbled.

He needed to blame somebody for his demise, and Ursula was there. The model every man would want in his bed was in his, and Tommy resented every bit of her. She reminded him of who he was *supposed* to be. He had failed. She was proof. What was a girl like her doing with a guy like him? Every time she looked at him, he wanted to evaporate. He was a con artist who had sold her bad land. She had bought a movie star destined for fame and fortune, and when she got him home she had opened the package to find only the scrawny kid with a bad complexion who was unable to get a date. Tommy's self-worth was entirely wrapped up in other people's opinions of him. When people were telling him he was great, he was great. When people failed to return his phone calls, he was a loser.

Ursula had a different problem. If Tommy's self-worth was wrapped up in what other people thought of his talent, Ursula knew that the only reason anybody thought she was special was because of how she looked. Her life was based on a set of genes she had nothing to do with. Indeed, she was fully aware that her looks had been the catalyst that had captivated Tommy in the first place. So Ursula saw Tommy's depression as an opportunity—an opportunity to expand the spiritual side of their relationship and to demonstrate a connection between the two of them that extended beyond the physical. She had seen her mother run out on partners when times got tough, and she was eager not to repeat that pattern. "For better or for worse" was the vow she had taken, not "for better or forget it." She was determined to help Tommy. She just did not know how.

Ursula sat on the floor of the bathroom and talked quietly into the phone receiver to Mindy.

"I don't know what to do. He just sits there, staring at MTV all day. If I see that "Men at Work" video again, I swear I'm going to smash something. We've got bills up the kazoo, and he's not making any money. I'm going to have to go back to work."

Mindy listened intently. There was a little secret joy in the fact the Ursula needed her again.

"Do you still love him?"

"Yes." Ursula said without hesitation.

Mindy had a suggestion. "Why doesn't he start doing stand-up again? That's what got him hot in the first place. Tell him he can't just sit there like a lump and wait for the phone to ring."

"Why don't you start doing stand-up again? That's what got you hot in the first place. You can't just sit there like a lump and wait for the phone to ring." Ursula had so liked the way it sounded when Mindy said it that she had decided to repeat it verbatim.

"Go down to the Comedy Stop? How's that going to help with the bills? They don't pay anything" was Tommy's initial response.

"I can make money. You don't need money. You need to do something constructive instead of destructive," said Ursula, repeating a catchphrase she remembered from that month's *Psychology Today.*

After a few months of stalling, Tommy reluctantly agreed to try a new arrangement. They decided that all bills would be sent to Eva, who would pay them out of one of the many accounts she had set up and was managing for Ursula. Tommy would focus on his comedy material and Ursula would resume modeling until Tommy once again held show business by its testicles.

The Comedy Stop, a sleazier Los Angeles equivalent of New York's Stars of Tomorrow, now became home to Tommy every night from 7:00 in the evening when the chipped black doors were first unlocked until 3:00 in the morning, when they were reshackled. To Tommy's surprise, he loved it. At the club, he was still a star. The younger comedians would ask questions about how he put a set together for the talk shows and whether he wanted to do another movie.

"I might, if the right script comes along. I just don't want to rush it," was his standard reply.

The young hopefuls would fill the back of the club when it was time for Tommy to do his set, watching as he bounded onto the stage, as confident as a professional wrestler who knows the fight is fixed in his favor. Tommy's political jokes needed updating, and his references to current events were no longer current, but when he snatched a woman's handbag in the front row and wittily rummaged through it, the crowd was still his.

Ursula was on the Great Barrier Reef in Australia modeling

for a swimsuit calendar. The time difference made it difficult for Tommy and her to connect. Tommy could never get it straight; she was either twelve hours ahead or behind, and it was either the next day there or the day before. All he was certain of was that at the end of the week, Ursula would be back home. By then, Autumn, the twenty-year-old waitress who had somehow ended up in his bed every night after the club closed and off whose flat stomach he was at this moment snorting two fat lines of cocaine, had better be gone.

"I love this place. It's so awesome," Autumn remarked, sitting naked on an oversize lounge chair at 4:00 in the morning, smoking a cigarette as Tommy massaged his tender, overworked nostrils.

"I feel like I'm in . . . what's one of those places that's right at the top?"

"A penthouse?" sniffed Tommy.

"Yeah, that's it; a penthouse. You're so lucky. Like, I look out there and feel so sorry for all the animals who are living in bushes and don't have a place to stay."

Autumn was young, stupid, unsuccessful, and everything Tommy thought he deserved. Gradually falling asleep to the muzak of her incessant chatter, Tommy almost fell off the lounge chair when the calm of 4:00 in the morning was suddenly disturbed by a car pulling up in his driveway. Even a husband who has been drinking and snorting for thirty-six hours straight sobers up enough to know he has to get rid of a naked, twenty-year-old waitress before his wife comes through the door. As Tommy gathered Autumn's clothes and pushed her through the side gate to her dilapidated Volkswagen, Ursula guided her key into the lock. With the split-second timing of a jewel thief, Tommy wrapped a towel around his waist and feigned a large yawn as he shuffled toward the doorway and his wife.

"Wow. What a coincidence," said Tommy, gathering Ursula in his arms and checking past her left shoulder to make sure the

Volkswagen was maneuvering silently down the canyon hill-side, its handbrake, headlights, and engine all switched off. "You look just like my wife Ursula who's in Australia."

"The shoot wrapped, and I couldn't wait. I took a plane a day early," Ursula replied with a grin.

As they kissed and she felt his heart beating through his shirt, she mistakenly assumed the palpitation was caused by the excitement of seeing her. They made love that night as if they were back on their honeymoon, then slept until 2:00 the next afternoon.

As Ursula happily puttered around in the kitchen, gathering remnants in the refrigerator that might pass for an afternoon breakfast, she was pleased to note that Tommy's persona had reverted to charming, and he appeared to be more content and accepting of his lot.

"Bacon and bananas sound good?"

"Not for me. Just coffee."

"How about a nice butter sandwich?"

"I don't think so."

"We have to get some food in this kitchen. It's positively Third World."

Tommy had already snorted his breakfast and was ready to start his day. Nutrition was not something he gave a lot of thought to these days.

"You should eat something. You're very skinny," Ursula advised.

"Hey, I don't need you to start telling me what I have to do."

Ursula looked at her watch.

"Wow. Eleven hours before we started to fight. Pretty good. Of course, we were asleep for eight of them."

"Sorry," Tommy said, and smiled, eager to avoid an extended argument. "You're right. I haven't been taking care of myself. Now you're back, I'll be better."

• • •

Ursula knew she had to get Tommy to stop abusing cocaine. The book she had read on the plane recommended distraction. Rather than denying someone something that he desired, the book advised distracting him with something else he desired even more. Ursula decided on a romantic dinner by the pool. Caesar salad, spaghetti carbonara, red wine, chocolate soufflé, then her. How could he resist?

With a shopping cart full of calories, Ursula took her place in the checkout line. In front of her, the inevitable coupon lady slowly matched little slips of colored papers with items on the conveyor belt, so Ursula perused the covers of the tabloids. She immediately noticed a photograph of herself in the ripped sequinned dress juxtaposed against a photo of a sultry but sullen brunette. The headline read:

URSULA DURAN STOLE MY FIANCÉ!

Ursula reached for the tabloid. The coupon lady turned around to make sure all of her groceries had been collected off the belt and recognized the supermodel behind the sunglasses.

"You did that to that poor girl? Shame on you," she scolded.

Ignoring her, Ursula opened the magazine and began to devour the story of Diana Lupone's broken heart.

"I was his girlfriend since high school," the item began. "After one photo shoot with Ursula Duran, I never saw him again."

An interview with Tommy's mother, whom Ursula had met only once and with whom she had felt instant mutual antipathy, continued the story.

"Tommy showed me the ring he was planning to give Diana that weekend. I was so thrilled. Diana's a very special person. But Tommy used the ring to propose to that Ursula Duran person instead."

Ursula reviewed the Las Vegas proposal and realized it all made perfect sense. When had Tommy had time to go shopping for an engagement ring? She cringed as she recalled finding the ring in his suitcase while he was in the shower. She realized that his real intention had been to take Ursula on a wild Las Vegas weekend before marrying the girl next door. He had married Ursula to avoid embarrassment.

The groceries stood orphaned in their basket as Ursula tore out of the supermarket to confront Tommy with the article. However, when she arrived home, the only thing present was a note on the kitchen table: "Gone to the club to do a set. Be home at eleven."

Ursula called Mindy. "Please don't let it be her answering machine," she prayed to the telephone gods.

"Hi, this is Mindy. Please leave me a message. I can't come to the phone right now. I'm out eating things that are bad for me." Beeeeeeeep.

Ursula decided to leave a brief message.

"Paddle," she said, then hung up.

Nowadays, Mindy was always on the road somewhere doing her act. It was impossible to get hold of her. Desperate to talk to someone, Ursula called her mother but was grateful when the phone remained unanswered.

Unable to wait until Tommy came home, she drove to the Comedy Stop. She had never been there before and as she wandered through the hallway asking for Tommy, word spread faster than toilet paper rolling down a hill that Ursula Duran was in the club. A friend ran to the door of the bathroom stall Tommy and Autumn were presently occupying.

"Hey, Tommy. Your old lady's here," he warned.

"Shit. Stop it. Get up," a panicked Tommy said, pulling Autumn up off her knees and poking his rapidly deflating penis back into his jeans.

Tommy breathed deeply, attempting to regain his composure. Ursula had undoubtedly seen his note on the kitchen table and had decided to drop by to see his comedy set. Yes, that was it, he reasoned, as he checked the zipper on his fly before leaving the men's room.

She was standing in the main corridor of the club. Her eyes were slits and her lips were pinched and tense. Tommy had seen Ursula angry before, but never like this.

"Have you seen this shit?" Ursula raged, clutching the copy of the tabloid in her fist.

"What do you mean?"

"Why didn't you tell me? Why weren't you honest with me?"

Tommy's mind raced around to the best of its coked-up ability. How could she know about Autumn? How could it be in a paper? Somebody must have had a telescopic, infrared camera trained on them as they lay on the patio.

"I was just giving Autumn a place to stay. That's all there was to it," he threw out experimentally.

Ursula exploded. "Who the fuck is Autumn?"

Aware he had made some kind of misstep, Tommy snatched the paper from Ursula's outstretched hand, deciding to read the article in question before he committed another verbal faux pas. He read it slowly so he could estimate exactly how much trouble he was in. A lot, was his conclusion as he lowered the paper and braced himself for further punishment.

"Is it true?" Ursula demanded.

"Kind of."

"What do you mean 'kind of'?"

"Well, I'd bought the ring for her, but then I accidentally fell in love with you."

"And who is Autumn?"

"Nobody."

"I am not nobody," said the waitress, emerging from the men's room. "I might not be a fancy model, but I'm not nobody."

Ursula departed a day early for the spring Paris fashion shows. She left it to her mother to begin divorce proceedings on her behalf.

TV or Not TV

Mindy paced nervously back and forth in the dressing room, murmuring the same sentences over and over again at double time. An observer could be excused for assuming that the young woman was engaged in either a Catholic or an Eastern praying ritual. Only a fellow comedian who had been booked on *Late Night with David Letterman* for the first time would realize that Mindy was going over her act.

Disparate thoughts jumbled around in Mindy's head. What if she forgot her jokes? What if she stood perfectly still on national television with her mouth hanging open like a wet Cheerio and just stared into space? She hoped her dream the night before had not been prophetic; tap-dancing in a clown suit while drowning in vomit would hardly be a good career move.

"I can do this," she told herself. "I've told jokes in impossible situations to people who were barely conscious. I can certainly make a sober audience that is facing forward laugh."

This was Mindy's third time waiting backstage to be summoned onto the NBC studio floor. The first two occasions had resulted in earlier, higher-profile guests running over their allotted segment time and Mindy's returning to her apartment to make apologetic phone calls to friends pumped up with caffeine and late-night anticipation. This time she had only told her father, who since his divorce from Smila was finding it difficult to sleep, and Ursula, who was back in Los Angeles, living without Tommy. Ursula woke up every morning at the crack of noon anyway, so to her, a late night was a habit rather than an imposition.

It had taken her over two years to get here. Mindy thought back to her first fifty-dollar gig in New Jersey. When she'd initially heard the club was called Nutty's, Mindy had failed to envision the barrels of peanuts scattered throughout the venue. After the first few nuts were thrown at her she'd politely thanked the customers for the free food but informed them that the management's policy was "not to feed the comedians." This quip did not have the desired effect. An avalanche of nuts made their way onto the stage as Mindy stood awash in horror, humiliation, and monkey food.

She shivered as she remembered those out-of-town gigs. Such bookings almost always consisted of three comedians: an opener, a middle, and a headliner. The headliner was usually a high-energy guy who had been on television a few times. The middle act was someone who had a strong twenty minutes and who was of sufficient skill not to ruin the audience for the headliner by being either too good or too bad. The opening act was usually an inexperienced comic who owned a car and so could drive the other two to the gig.

One Saturday night Mindy found herself in the back of a vehicle she suspected was held together by gaffer tape. A man named Milos with a face the texture and color of Parmesan cheese was at the wheel of this jalopy. Ronnie, the mustached comedian from Stars of Tomorrow, was in the front seat, nervously looking at the speedometer.

"Milos, tell me, why does the speedometer say zero when we're obviously moving forward quite quickly?" Ronnie asked.

"I don't need a speedometer to tell me how fast I'm going. I know."

"And the gas tank?" asked Mindy. "Same thing? It says empty, but you know how much is in it?"

"No, that's empty," Milos said as the car slowed down and pulled onto the side of the road. "Don't worry. I always carry some in the trunk," he said reassuringly.

Mindy and Ronnie watched from the sidewalk as Milos funneled gasoline from the can in the trunk into the tank.

"Isn't that illegal? To carry gasoline in the back of the car?" Ronnie inquired.

"Yes," Milos answered, as the trio climbed back in the deathmobile.

Mindy leaned forward and tried to make conversation with the strange person. "So, Milos, what kind of an act do you do?"

"Fire."

"I need more than that."

"I set my forearms on fire."

"That's good. What's the trick?"

"There's no trick."

Milos pushed up the sleeve of the jacket covering his right arm and revealed his fleshy scars.

"Impressive," Mindy said. "Do you also swallow fire?"

"I tried once. Too hot."

Except for the consumptive engine, the car remained silent until they arrived at Valentino's, which turned out to be an Italian restaurant in Queens that had invented a comedy night to increase its low Tuesday attendances. Mindy and Ronnie never did get to do their sets that evening. After Milos performed the place was evacuated. One of his arms had refused to go out and had accidentally brushed against the back curtain. The fire department came quickly, but not quickly enough to save the front six tables.

"Does that happen often?" Mindy asked Milos on the way back to Manhattan.

"Yes," he replied.

Mindy's musings about dues paid were interrupted by a knock at the dressing-room door, followed by just the head and left hand of Walter, the talent booker, entering the room.

"Do you want makeup?"

"More than anyone could possibly imagine," Mindy replied.

"I'll be back when they're ready for you. Don't look so nervous. It's television, not a firing squad. Dave's gonna love you. Are you going to wear that?"

Mindy looked down at her black Norma Kamali jumpsuit.

"Yeah, I'm going for a kind of comedian–cat burglar look."

After a brief visit to makeup, Mindy followed Walter to the back of the studio, where she stood quietly.

"We're in a commercial break," Walter whispered. "Just wait here 'til Dave introduces you, find the red X on the floor, and tell those jokes. We're running a little long tonight. Cut about a minute."

Cut about a minute? Mindy thought quickly. Her last line was a callback to the first line, so the cut would have to be in the middle. Her childhood. She had three jokes about her childhood and she was running at about three jokes a minute. Yes, the childhood hunk would have to go.

"Welcome back. We have some fine entertainment for you folks now. A young lady making her television debut . . . it's her debut, ladies and gentlemen, and you know what that means . . . she might not know how to behave. Please make very welcome Mandy . . . no. Wait a second. I've made a horrible mistake . . . Mindy Solomon."

Mindy walked out onto the stage, planted herself on the red X and began moving her mouth. The first laugh came. It wasn't as big as she had hoped but not as small as she had feared. She pushed ahead. Two minutes in and Mindy's hands and feet began to prickle. She told herself to keep going. Two more minutes of telling jokes to the little red light on the camera and she'd be home free. With the final joke out, Mindy crossed to the host desk on numb feet and sat herself down in the large blue guest chair. The seat was harder than it looked on television, and instead of relaxing into it, she sat at attention.

David Letterman shook her hand. "Good job. My God, your hands are freezing. What's your blood pressure? Ninety over nothing?"

Mindy didn't know what to say. She had prepared four minutes of panel material, which was material that was not funny enough to include in a set but funny enough to get big laughs if it appeared spontaneous. However, she had no retort for the blood-pressure quip.

"Thank you for pointing out to America my lack of circulation." Mindy heard a titter. "It's not my fault, though. It's freezing in here. What's the thermostat turned down to? Häagen-Dazs?"

The audience's laughter allowed her to take a much-needed breath.

"I like my audiences like I like my women . . . frigid," replied Letterman. A huge laugh ensued. It was going well, thought Mindy, although she was finding the whole experience of sitting and conversing with someone whom she had admired from a distance immensely surreal.

"So, I understand you didn't start out to be a comedian," Letterman said, after nonchalantly glancing at his note card.

Mindy snapped into her prepared response. "No, originally I studied ballet. But I wasn't very good. In *Swan Lake* I was the lifeguard."

"And you're single?"

"Very. I had a boyfriend for a while, but he took me to his country club and something happened that was very embarrassing."

"And what might that have been?" asked Letterman, setting Mindy up for her punch line.

"Well, I walked through the front door of the clubhouse and I accidentally set off the Jew detector."

Mindy chose to close her appearance with the story of Milos and his fiery forearms and had to hurry the ending of the tale as the show was running out of time.

"Is that it? Is that the end of the story?" Letterman asked.

"Yes."

Letterman turned to the audience. "Good night. See you tomorrow."

The late-night host pulled off his tie and exited rapidly. He was back inside his dressing room before the band had completed the show's theme tune. Walter stepped over to Mindy.

"Good set."

"Really?" said Mindy unconvinced.

"Absolutely. Dave loved it. When the corners of his mouth almost go up, that's the sign he loves it."

Mindy retreated to her dressing room to reassess her performance. Now that it was over, she was sure she could have done it better. Because the show taped between 5:00 and 6:00 in the evening she had at least seven hours to obsess over how it had gone until her image was actually broadcast into the living rooms of insomniacs across the country. She went home and called Ursula.

"How'd it go?"

"I think okay. I'm not sure Letterman liked me, but I don't think he hated me. I think that's the best you can hope for with him."

"Who cares about him. What about the audience?"

"They were good. Not like a club crowd. They're behind cameras and there are only about a hundred of them. It's freezing in there."

"I can't wait. I bet it's awesome. I am majorly psyched." Ursula had just returned home from an aerobics class and was awash in positive Los Angeles lingo.

Dan and Penelope arrived at Mindy's apartment to watch her television debut, armed with a mushroom-and-pepperoni pizza and a bottle of white wine.

"No. Wait a second," they heard Letterman say. "I've made a horrible mistake . . . Mindy Solomon."

"Oh, my God. That's me," Mindy shrieked, pointing to her television set. "Why do I look like that?" Mindy's mental image of herself in her black jumpsuit was infinitely superior to the reality. "Why aren't I taller and thinner?"

"Because you're funny," Penelope volunteered, dribbling melted cheese onto Mindy's carpet. "There's nothing funny about good-looking people."

"Except for me. I'm funny, but I'm also devilishly handsome," Dan said smoothing back his few remaining strands of hair with the palm of his hand.

Mindy thought she moved her head a little too much and noticed her mouth twitch nervously on her applause breaks, but it was definitely a debut she could be proud of. Her father was the first to call.

"You were tremendous. That guy you were on with. He's nothin'."

"David Letterman?"

"Yeah. That guy. You should have his job."

"I'll tell him if I'm ever on again."

The phone rang nearly continuously for the next hour, as Mindy's friends called to congratulate her. She finally got to sleep at 3:00, but woke again at 4:30 to the phone ringing. It was Ursula, and she was crying.

"I know it's late, but I had to call. I am so proud of you." Her friend sniffled. "I can't believe I saw this happen from the very beginning. From that first night when you were terrible."

"You said I was good."

"I was lying. You were awesome tonight, Mindy, really awesome. You did it, babe. You really did it."

Mindy started to cry as well.

"I did, didn't I?" sobbed Mindy, the full impact of her journey from Miami through her injury to her new career hitting her with an emotional thump. "I wish my mom could have seen me."

"She did, Mindy," said Ursula. "I'm sure she did."

Mindy could hear in Ursula's voice how genuinely happy her friend was for her success. Ursula was sounding so much better—still emotionally on edge but a little more together—than when Mindy had rushed to California after Tommy's affair with Autumn.

Ursula had been hit hard by Tommy's deception. She had cried from the time Mindy arrived at the airport until the time Mindy left. Ursula was convinced she was a failure. The one thing she had never wanted to be was divorced, and there she was with a huge, imaginary D stamped on her forehead. She was just like her mother, unable to keep a marriage together. Tommy had blown a huge hole in Ursula's self-confidence. She felt neither interesting nor smart nor talented enough to deserve the attention of a man. Who would ever believe that the smiling, carefree beauty gracing the pages of fashion magazines around the world was on the edge of a nervous breakdown?

"Ursula, you're nuts. You were just too good for him," Mindy had told her friend.

"Yeah, right. That's why he cheated on me. I was too good for him."

They had talked about the breakup from morning until night and back to morning again. They had talked about it until Mindy could swear she had seen a plant in Ursula's living room turn the other way in disgust.

Ursula had decided to stay in Los Angeles but to throw herself back into work. Marc Mosley, the manager, had finally returned Tommy's call and Ursula had answered the phone. Marc had no interest in trying to salvage Tommy's career as it nosedived toward oblivion, but he reiterated how he felt Ursula had potential. Ursula had signed with the manager, and he had enrolled her in an acting class and begun sending her on movie auditions.

Movie audition offers were not exactly what Mindy expected

when she awoke the morning after her TV debut, but she did expect her life to have been altered in some way. She had, after all, been on national television. Something had to occur. Deciding she needed to venture outside for the occurrence to take place, she dressed and made her way down to the corner to enjoy a bagel and a cup of coffee. Prepared for recognition, she ordered from the heavyset man behind the counter.

"A plain bagel with cream cheese, please."

"Right away," the man replied, fetching the circular carbohydrate.

Nothing was different. She was Mindy ordering a bagel.

Mindy lowered her new Ray-Bans while putting her money in the bus change machine, then glanced at the passengers, carefully allowing them to see her face. Again, nothing.

Finally, standing in the checkout line at the grocery store, Lila the cashier squinted at Mindy. Lila had followed Madonna's example and tied a piece of black mesh in her hair to make herself look hot. Instead, she looked like a supermarket cashier who had tied black mesh in her hair.

"Weren't you on the *Letterman* show last night?" Lila asked.

"Yes. Yes, I was," Mindy replied, proudly.

"You look much better in person," Lila opined.

Mindy tried to resist questioning further but failed. "Was I funny?"

"I think so. I was half asleep."

As she entered the club that night, Marty the emcee gave Mindy a hug.

"I have a cancellation. Do you want to go on at eight forty-five?"

Mindy suddenly understood what her television appearance meant in terms of her immediate career. Not fame, not fortune—just better time slots at the club. Quite a few members of the audience had seen her debut and clapped heartily as she stepped onto the stage. She launched into the set that had killed on *Letterman* the night before, but the laughs were muted. Mindy realized there was something else that had changed since last night. Members of the audience now knew her best jokes. She needed fresh material.

Getting a second appearance on the *Letterman* show proved even more difficult than getting the first. After she'd spent months working on new material, Walter deemed Mindy's new set "not Dave's cup of tea," so Mindy was now attempting to find that rare blend of steeped herbs the talk-show host might enjoy. Over Christmas, Mindy and Penelope had written a film script together about Cinderella, Sleeping Beauty, and Snow White finding out they had all married the same polygamous Prince Charming. They peddled their story from agency to agency, but to no avail. Mindy's career prospects seemed bleak until one cold February night a man approached her at the club's bar.

"Mitch Putnam," he said. "I think you're very funny. I'd love to talk to you about a sitcom."

Mindy was sure it was a pickup line.

"Which one? I like *Cheers*. I like *Family Ties* too, except for the last five minutes when they try to teach you something."

"I don't have a business card or anything, but I'm represented by William Morris. You can check. Ask to speak to my agent Todd Allen, and he'll happily put you on hold."

Mindy laughed as Mitch sidled onto the bar stool next to her. He smelled nice, Mindy noticed, and he had an engaging, lop-sided smile that involved every part of his face. His ears, though tiny, were tilted at an angle that demanded they be noticed. He looked friendly, she concluded, and rather attractive.

"I have a deal with ABC to create a sitcom, and I'd love to write one around your persona. I can't promise you it will get anywhere. It might not even get made. But I have to hand in a script in three months, and you've tickled my fancy, and I usually don't let anyone near my fancy. . . . It's noisy in here. Can we go somewhere quieter?"

Mindy and Mitch went to the coffee shop next door, and Mitch spent the next three hours explaining the world of TV comedy to her and making her laugh a lot. Mindy was flattered by his attention. This was a professional show business person who thought she was special.

Over the next few days, Mindy and Mitch were inseparable. He watched her act every night; he studied her habits; he wrote down her likes and dislikes.

"It's as though he's studying for a degree in Mindy Solomon," Mindy told Ursula over the phone.

"Sounds great," said Ursula. "Have you slept with him yet?"

"Ursula!" Mindy retorted, shocked. "This is a professional relationship."

"Does he watch your handbag while you're up on stage?" Ursula asked.

"Yes."

"Case closed," said Ursula. "You're going to sleep with him."

"I bet you I'm not."

Ursula declined to take the wager that Mindy lost ten days later. Everything felt right to Mindy. She knew this was a guy she could really be with, even though Mitch was still nervous that the mix of business and pleasure might be combustible.

"These sitcom things are a crap shoot," he told her as they lay naked in bed one night watching a midnight movie and eating Chinese food leftovers. "I don't want our relationship affected by the outcome of the project."

Mindy told him not to worry. She knew herself to be level-headed enough to prioritize. The comedians at the club noticed a change in Mindy. She was happier and more confident. She took fashion risks. She studied her joke notebook less often. She occasionally swore. Mitch had become the light in Mindy's refrigerator; he illuminated everything she had inside. She was no longer a hundred percent Mindy. She was fifty percent of Mindy 'n' Mitch.

Gradually the comedy script took shape, centering around a bouncy brunette named Mindy who worked in her family's dry-cleaning store in Brooklyn. After completing the first draft of *Mindy,* Mitch was summoned to Los Angeles at the end of March for notes. Mindy waited anxiously for the Hollywood verdict. Mitch called the next day.

"Do you want the good news or the bad news?"

"The good news. If it's really good, then maybe I'll hang up before you tell me the bad news."

"The project's still alive, only now you're the feisty daughter of a building superintendent in Queens."

"What?"

"The network thought dry cleaning was too upscale. They're looking to appeal to a more urban demographic. They want me to stay out here and work on it. Should take me two or three days tops."

Four weeks later, Mindy had become, in turn, a police-woman, a driving instructor, and a social worker. The powers that be finally settled on the character of a feisty daughter who wanted to be a social worker but who worked in her family's dry-cleaning store in Queens, part-timing as a driving instructor for the police.

Mindy knew only about ten of the more than one hundred scripts the network had ordered would actually be filmed. Mitch's was not one of the initial batch picked by the network, but it had not yet been discarded. It was, in TV parlance, "on the bubble."

Mitch dared not leave Los Angeles, as that would send the wrong message to the network. He called Mindy every night to give her an update, or, as he called it, "a downdate." He explained how *Mindy,* because it had no children in it, was labeled a "nine-o'clock show." That hour of TV time was the most coveted time slot of all, and other nine-o'clock projects had more senior writers attached. This was all fascinating information to Mindy, who had previously and wrongly presumed that decisions were predicated on whether a show was funny. At least there was a cutoff date for Mitch's pain. No pilots would be made after April thirtieth. When he heard nothing from ABC the day after the deadline, a defeated Mitch packed up his Century Plaza hotel room and returned to New York and the welcoming arms of his sympathetic girlfriend.

"It doesn't matter if nobody does *Mindy,*" she said. "I have another name. You can write a different show called *Solomon.*"

In truth, Mindy had desperately wanted the pilot to happen, but she was equally eager to protect her new relationship from the vagaries of her career. Three weeks later, Mitch's phone rang. One of the pilots that ABC had made involving alien mechanics was so awful it was no longer under consideration. *Mindy* was back on track, but with one proviso. The network wanted to return to the first draft, feeling that in later versions of the script Mitch had weakened his original premise. Mitch flew out to California that afternoon and two days later phoned Mindy, hyperventilating the information down the line.

"I got you two first-class tickets, leaving tomorrow. You can bring Penelope to keep you company."

Mitch went on to explain that as a formality the network would have to see two other actresses for the part of Mindy. It was standard practice for a network to be offered three casting choices. However, the network president, the vice president, and the head of casting had all seen Mindy's *Letterman* tape, had all loved it, and were all looking forward to meeting her.

"Don't worry about the audition," Mitch promised. "It's just a formality. I can't pick you up at the airport because they want a quick polish before the auditions, but a car will pick you up from the airport and take you directly to the hotel. The script will be waiting for you in an envelope at the front desk. Your meeting is at noon."

"You're not kidding?" Mindy asked. "This is really happening?"

"Hey, I'm a comedy writer. I don't kid."

Mindy hung up and immediately phoned Ursula. Ursula was out, but her answering machine, being far less popular, had remained home. Mindy decided not to leave a message. Knowing Ursula, she would call back in the middle of the night, and Mindy had to try to get some sleep. She decided to call her friend from Los Angeles and surprise her with the news of her new job. Mindy's whole body was palpitating with anticipation. She had seen Alvin, the skinny comic, parlay a shot on the *Tonight Show* into a second lead in a sitcom, but to participate in an eponymous show was a coup she had never dared dream for herself.

How much should she pack? She had forgotten to ask Mitch. After she got the job, would she have time to come back to New York to get her things? Maybe ABC had people who came back and packed for you? She chose three outfits that could be mixed and matched in case she needed to be chic for a week.

Eighteen hours later, Penelope was misbehaving in the first-class cabin.

"Penelope, put your feet down."

Penelope had made herself a little too comfortable. Her dirty Reeboks were perched on top of the seat directly in front of her.

"It's first class. You can do whatever you want. I looked at my ticket; it cost twenty-five hundred dollars. If I want to shit in my seat, for that kind of money they have to clean it up."

"Could you please take your feet off the seat," the flight attendant requested.

Penelope reluctantly obliged. "I should have made a deal. I'll take my feet off the seat, if she'll chip off eight layers of foundation." Penelope took a swig of her complimentary beverage. She spat it out. "Eeerrgghhh!"

The flight attendant hurried over.

"This Coke is hideous," Penelope complained.

"It's New Coke."

"Well, I have old mouth. Do you have any old Coke?"

"They've discontinued it."

"Brilliant idea. Well, can I have a glass of water, or has someone fucked with that too?"

Five hours and two thousand miles later, Mindy and Penelope were met by a black-suited, peak-capped driver holding up a cardboard sign that read MINDY SOLOMON. ABC.

"If this is a practical joke, it's a good one," Mindy said to Penelope as they played with the television in the back of the lengthy car.

It was Penelope's first visit to Los Angeles, and she was busily absorbing every detail. The car turned off Santa Monica Boulevard and onto a street called Avenue of the Stars.

"I wonder if there's a side street called Avenue of the Costars?" Penelope quipped.

As they stepped out of the stretch limousine, a bellman wearing a forest green suede vest whisked their bags away.

Penelope leaned into Mindy. "I don't think he works here. He's taking our bags because he needs better clothes. If I open my suitcase and find a fungus-colored vest in there, I'm going to be very upset."

The lobby was aglow in marble floors so shiny Mindy wondered why guests did not continuously slip and sue. A bubbling fountain dominated the center of the lobby as important-looking people carrying briefcases full of moneymaking information scurried by.

When Mindy checked in at the front desk, a clerk handed her a large manila envelope that read "ATTN: Mindy Solomon. PERSONAL."

Mindy tore open the envelope and pulled out a copy of the script. Phew. It was still called *Mindy*. Mitch had included a note inside: "Hi. Welcome. You're going to be terrific. I'm still doing changes, but this is the script so far. I hate execs. I miss you. I'll be in the room in the back, laughing loudly. Big kiss, Mitch."

It was 11:00 A.M. Mindy had half an hour to read the script, change into what she considered the type of outfit the daughter of a dry cleaner in Brooklyn might wear, and run across the street to the sixteenth floor of the Century City building containing the network offices.

"I didn't hear you laughing when you were reading the script," Penelope said as Mindy struggled into her denim dress. "Is it funny?"

"I don't know. I've read so many incarnations, I can't tell anymore. But I know I can play a spacey brunette in her twenties named Mindy whose boyfriend wrote the script. How do I look?"

Penelope looked at her friend. "Great." The normally stoic Penelope's top lip began to tremble as she hugged Mindy tightly and wished her good luck. The gravity of the next couple of hours was weighing on both of them.

"Will you still be my friend after you're a big television star?" Penelope asked.

"Are you kidding? I've already shown Mitch our film script. He wants to hire you on the show."

"In that case, it's not enough money. I need a raise."

At 11:45 Mindy walked across Avenue of the Stars, holding the latest draft of the script tightly to her chest. When the elevator stopped at the sixteenth floor, she took a deep breath, stood up a little straighter, and walked to the reception desk.

"Hi. Mindy Solomon. I have an audition for *Mindy* at noon."

A woman wearing a telephone headset told Mindy to take a seat. At 12:30, Mindy started to worry. She stood up and reintroduced herself to the woman at the reception desk.

"Hi, I'm still Mindy Solomon, and I still have a meeting thirty minutes ago."

"They're aware that you're here."

Just then, a door to the inner offices opened and closed and Mitch appeared. Mindy smiled with relief as they hugged.

"First audition just finished. Just as I predicted, she stank. You're next."

The door opened again, and a woman Mindy had seen a few times on various shows emerged and pushed the elevator button. Mindy quickly sized her up as being too old for the part.

"Melanie, you were great," said Mitch the politician. "Very funny."

"When will I hear something?" the actress asked pointedly.

"Check back with your agent later this afternoon," Mitch said, with a smooth smile. "I know they're going to make a quick decision."

As the elevator doors closed, Mitch whispered to Mindy, "I don't see why I should tell her she didn't get it. That's her agent's job. I know him. He'll enjoy it."

"Who else is auditioning?" asked Mindy.

"The other woman is going to be even worse. Someone called in a favor, so she got the audition. It's a lock. Don't worry," counseled Mitch, squeezing her hand supportively.

"They're ready for you now," announced the receptionist.

Mindy and Mitch walked down a corridor and into a room that turned out to be a minitheater-cum–screening room.

"Knock 'em dead," whispered Mitch, leaving Mindy to wander out onto the stage alone as he took his place at the rear of the tiered seats where five people sat staring at her.

"Hello, Mindy. I'm Perry Strauss, the president of ABC. Welcome."

"Hello to all of you. It looks very comfortable over there, but if you don't mind, I'll audition here in this lonely pit," said Mindy.

They laughed. She relaxed.

A meek woman who could have done something with her hair introduced herself to Mindy.

"I'm Roz, I'm the casting director on the project. I'll be reading with you today."

Roz pointed to the folding chair next to Mindy. "Would you like to sit or stand?" she asked.

"I don't know. Which burns more calories?" Mindy asked.

Mindy stood as Roz, in her thin soprano voice, began to read the part of Mindy's sixty-year-old overbearing father. The room was certainly not conducive to comedy. The cold, silent ambience, coupled with the tension and the seriousness of it all, was more like an execution than a comedy audition. Yet somehow, Mindy got laughs. Her befuddled quality, combined with her experienced timing, came through for her. As she left the stage Mitch gave her a surreptitious thumbs up.

Her heart thumped loudly as she made her way back to the reception area. It hadn't been a ten. But Mindy never gave tens. It had been an eight. Maybe even a nine. She opened the door to the waiting area and was shocked to see who was sitting there.

"Ursula? Did Penelope tell you I was here?"

"Mindy! No. I'm here for an audition. Oh my God!"

"You're here for an audition?"

"My manager called me this morning and told me to get over here. Apparently someone saw me on the cover of something. I was just reading the sides they sent me."

"Remember the project I told you I wouldn't tell you about unless it happened so I wouldn't curse it?" Mindy said. "This is it. My new boyfriend wrote the script. It's based on me. I just auditioned."

Ursula's mouth fell open. "No!"

"Yes!"

"As I was reading it, I was thinking how perfect *you* were for it."

"And now you know the reason," Mindy giggled.

"Well, I'm completely wrong for it," said Ursula. "Could I have worn anything less appropriate?"

Mindy permitted herself a moment of selfish, smug satisfaction as she regarded the tight, hot-pink spandex dress and high heels Ursula had chosen to wear. Good for the part of a hooker, perhaps, but not for the part of the daffy, uncertain brunette dry cleaner from Queens.

"Ursula Duran. They're ready for you now," the receptionist announced.

"Where do I go?" Ursula asked.

"I'll show her," Mindy offered. "We're friends."

As Mindy pushed her friend out onto the stage, she could not resist hovering near to the closed door and listening to the muffled voices of Ursula and Roz beyond. She was unable to hear precise words, but knew she heard no laughs. She was not surprised. She loved Ursula like a sister, but funny was not her forte. Rather disquietingly, there was suddenly an enormous laugh, then nothing. Ten minutes later, Ursula emerged.

"Well, that was embarrassing," she noted, as they walked back together.

"Why?" Mindy asked.

"I fell on the floor."

"What?"

"Uh-huh. Tripped over a chair and landed right on my tush. Maybe they didn't notice. Maybe they think I improvised it," she laughed. "Oh well, *c'est la vie.*"

The two women returned to the reception area.

"Which one was your boyfriend?"

"The one at the back."

"He looks nice."

"He is."

Ursula looked at her watch. "I've got to get over to the Valley. I have another one of these things over at NBC. Where are you staying?"

"Across the street at the Century Plaza."

"It's one-thirty now. What if I come by and meet you at four?"

"Sounds great."

They hugged again.

"I cannot believe I fell over," Ursula said, and moaned, mortified at the memory.

"I can," Mindy giggled as her beautiful but awkward best friend disappeared behind the elevator doors.

Mindy returned to the hotel, as Mitch had instructed, and waited for news. Penelope was munching her way through the entire contents of the minibar. She was down to the individual Edam cheeses. The two friends opened up the miniature bottles of wine and dissected the audition. Penelope agreed that Ursula was in there to just make up the numbers. She was gorgeous, but NF. Not Funny. The professional actress worried Penelope.

"These network guys think acting is hard. They don't think stand-ups can do it. I've seen it before," she warned.

"Mitch said it's a lock."

"I hope so."

They stared at the phone. It finally rang. It was Mitch.

"What room are you in?"

"Two thousand five. Did I get it?"

"I'm coming up."

Mindy knew then. But she still held on to a little shred of hope as she waited for Mitch to ascend the twenty floors and grimly enter the room.

"I really fought for you. But they'd made up their minds. Morons."

"They gave it to the actress, then? Melanie Whatsit?" said Penelope. "I was afraid of that. When Mindy told me she had auditioned, I was afraid of that."

Mindy could not speak. Her legs buckled as she collapsed onto the edge of the bed, her face ashen, her mouth dry, and her stomach knotted. A woman named Melanie was going to play her on television. It made no sense.

"No. They gave it to the blonde. The model wearing the fuck-me dress. What's that bit you do in your act about blondes getting all the breaks? Well, it's certainly fucking true," Mitch spat bitterly.

"Ursula?" croaked Mindy hoarsely. "They gave it to Ursula?"

"Yeah. Didn't you say you knew her?"

"Yes," said Mindy. "I know her."

"They've decided she's a brilliant physical comedian. The new Lucy. She improvised a bit of business with a chair that made them laugh."

At that moment, Ursula appeared at the door.

"Knock, knock. Hi. The guy at the desk gave me your room number. They're not supposed to do that, but . . ."—Ursula shrugged naughtily—". . . he did it for me. Hi, Penelope. I didn't know you were here. Hi, Mitch. We met across the street. Can I use your phone, Mindy? I promised my manager I'd call him."

"She doesn't know," said Penelope. "She doesn't fucking know."

"Know what?" said Ursula, sensing the gloomy atmosphere. "Did somebody die?"

"Congratulations," said Mindy. "You got the part."

"What?" said Ursula incredulously. "Let me phone Marc."

She phoned, and the news was confirmed.

"Yes, I know it's a big break for me, Marc. Yes, I am happy about it. Did we hear anything from NBC? Oh. I didn't get that one."

"Wow. An audition Ursula didn't get. Stop the presses," said Mindy sarcastically.

"No, I am thrilled, Marc. Believe me. It's great news. I'll call you later. Bye."

She put down the receiver, and turned to Mindy.

"I'm so sorry, Mindy. I know you really wanted it. But there'll be other parts. It's just television."

Mindy exploded. "Other parts for a girl named Mindy based on me? I don't think so."

"They've already made me change the name," Mitch chimed

in. "She's called Cindy now. And they want rewrites. They want her blond, not brunette, and really good-looking. I'm going to make her entirely different than you. Sorry—that didn't come out right."

"You're staying on the project?" said Mindy in disbelief.

"I can't walk away from this project now, not after all the work I've done. I'll have a big hit with this, and then I'll have more clout when I write *Solomon.*"

"What?" spat Mindy.

"Look," said Mitch hurriedly. "It's not all bad news. I can hire you and Penelope as writers on the show."

"Really?" said Penelope, sitting up.

"You think we'd write on the show after I've been treated like this?" said Mindy disparagingly.

"I'm in," said Penelope. "With or without her, I'm in."

"What?!"

"Mindy, I'm not as good a stand-up as you. My material's good, but the audiences don't like me. I'm a writer, not a performer. I need to get off the road."

"Me too," said Ursula. "I'm getting too old to be a model. I go on these jobs, and the girls are sixteen. I'm sick of traveling and smiling, traveling and smiling. I want to stay in one place for a while."

"Get out. *Get out. All of you get out!*" screamed Mindy.

Two hours later, Mindy was on a plane back to New York. She had lost her boyfriend, her best friend, and her writing partner.

It had not been a good day.

Fish banana, banana fish.

Part III

Experience is the name everyone gives
to their mistakes.

—*Oscar Wilde*

Architectural Indigestion

Eva was happier in Hollywood than a germ in a jacuzzi. Sitting on Leonard Felk's lap had turned out to be a brilliant flex of her knees. On leaving Tommy's movie premiere, which coincidentally was also his movie closiere, the studio head had taken Eva to Le Dome for dinner, then whisked her back to his mansion in Bel Air.

It was Eva's first time in a Rolls Royce. She marveled at the quiet engine, as undetectable as the raw egg in a Caesar salad. She thrilled at the handmade interior, especially the extra-soft leather seats and the burnished walnut trimmings. This wasn't a car. This was a living room that moved.

"We won't be disturbed. My wife is on a buying trip in Rome," Leonard explained.

"Oh really? What's she buying?" Eva inquired.

"Rome."

Winding up Stone Canyon Road from Sunset Boulevard, Eva was disappointed to find none of the neighborhood's homes visible from the street. All she could see were gates. At Halloween, the trick-or-treaters must have to be lowered in by helicopter, she surmised. Eva assumed a direct correlation between the size of the gates and the size of the mansion being guarded and was therefore delighted to discover that Leonard's gates were huge. They were also smart. When Leonard's car pulled up in front of them, the gates somehow recognized their master and quickly parted for him.

The Corniche cruised up the weeping willow–lined driveway, past the immaculately kept, if rarely used, north–south tennis court, past the orangery, past one of the estate's two swimming pools, and then slowed and paused. The driveway concluded in a cul-de-sac, edged by a perfectly uniform hedge interrupted at regular intervals by four-foot-high stone pedestals on which were balanced various, cast-stone statues of Cupids.

There before Eva lay a Jacobean-style English manor house, the largest and grandest private structure she had ever seen. Eva took in the ostentatious opulence and experienced a mental orgasm.

"Ohhhhhh," she said.

"Do you like it?" Leonard asked, confident of the answer.

"Ohhhhhh," Eva repeated, still unable to form words.

"I had it moved over here piece by piece."

"From England?"

"From Pasadena. I found this lot, then the house, and I brought the two things together. That's what a movie executive does. He puts the pieces of the puzzle together until it costs ten times the amount it should, then he makes someone else pay for it."

Eva was intrigued. "So who paid for it?"

"Hey, the Japanese fucked us in World War II. I fucked them back."

Eva glanced over at Leonard; her attraction to this genetically challenged man was growing like compound interest. Leonard returned her glance, taking in Eva's perfect profile, then continuing down deep into her cleavage. On the boob meter, he rated her a nine and a half. Money had made Leonard handsome, and Dr. Kramer had made Eva beautiful. They saw what they liked, and they liked what they saw. Sometimes you just have to give it up for superficiality.

For the first time, Eva noticed a miniature version of the house to the right of the main structure. It was a perfect replica down to the smallest detail but was a tenth of the size.

"What's that?" she asked.

"Watch," Leonard replied, pressing a button on the polished dashboard.

Silently, two of the hedge sections and one of the pedestals suddenly disappeared into the ground. At the same time the front of the miniature house rose magically up into the air in one entire piece. Leonard pulled the Rolls Royce through the space and headed for what was evidently the garage, because a 1956 Cadillac, a brand-new Maserati Quattroporte, a 1969 Morgan convertible, and an antique motorbike were already asleep inside the structure.

"I got the idea from the *Batman* TV series. Remember how the Batmobile came out of the Batcave? That's where I got the idea."

"Ooooh," said Eva, as another shot of materialistic pleasure quivered through her body.

The Rolls snuggled into the space next to the motorbike.

"See this bike?" said Leonard, helping Eva out of the car. "This was D. H. Lawrence of Arabia's bike. The one he was killed on."

Leonard looked around his garage fondly.

"I love my cars," he said. "They're like children who can be controlled."

"Do you have any children?" asked Eva.

"Two. Twin maniacs. They don't live here. They live on a mountain and they meditate with a guru. They eat only brown rice, wear sheets, and have to sleep facing west. What are you gonna do?" said Leonard.

His eyes glazed over as he momentarily contemplated the horror and disappointment of his offsprings' lives.

"At least they're not on drugs," said Eva, trying to make him feel better.

"Well, one of them isn't," said Leonard.

He shook off his momentary depression and beckoned Eva forward.

"Let me show you the house."

The door leading into the house from the garage opened into a small, bare, spotless alcove. The tiled floor of this room slanted toward a central, grated drain. Other than a sink containing an extendable hose attachment secured to a tap, the room was bare.

"This is the mudroom," said Leonard.

Eva looked confused.

"You take your boots off in here when they're muddy," he explained.

Eva said nothing.

"It's a stupid fucking idea," continued Leonard. "Makes sense in England, where it's always fucking raining, but here in Southern California it makes sense once every ten years. My wife thought it was classy. Come through here."

He opened a door at the far end of the mudroom and led Eva into a kitchen large enough to support a medium-size restaurant. Even though the room contained two enormous subzero refrigerators, a ten-burner stove, a pizza oven, three dishwashers, six separate sinks, and a limestone center-island above which were racked an extended family of shiny, dangling copper pots, the room was still spacious. Indeed, at the farthest end of the kitchen there had been space enough to include a cozy sitting area containing two large sofas, a fireplace, a built-in TV, and a pine table that sat eight.

"Your wife must be quite a cook."

"She doesn't cook; she poisons. We had a gourmet chef, but she fired him for cooking food that had flavor. Now we just eat out."

They continued into the main hallway of this castle. The modern appliances and cozy feel of the kitchen area were now replaced by an interior that better matched the house's faux-Jacobean exterior. The hallway's tiled flooring was boldly checkerboarded and its ceiling heavily beamed, both characteristics copied from a Tudor estate that one of the seventeen designers employed by Mrs. Felk had used as his muse. Various antique paintings and items of furniture decorated the hallway. Eva was particularly taken with a towering carved Carpathian walnut armoire and a set of ornate muskets crisscrossed above a doorway.

"Where are they from?" Eva asked, pointing at the weapons.

"Bloomingdale's," Leonard replied.

The central wooden stairway, with its ornate, stained-glass window illuminating the landing at the stairwell's midway point, reminded Eva of Tara. She mentioned it.

"Very observant. It's copied from the movie," confirmed Leonard. "Hey, you really have an eye for this sort of thing. Come in here. You'll love this."

He opened up a pair of heavy wooden doors to reveal his favorite room.

"This is the library."

Eva marveled at the double-story walnut-paneled room, suffused throughout with the glow of the leather book bindings that occupied all of the surrounding shelves. In the center of the room, three oversize leather chesterfields were positioned around a giant, low coffee table that had been fashioned out of a Bavarian castle portcullis. Leonard picked up the remote control laying on the table and pressed a button. The bookshelves at one end of the room spun around, converting the wall into a full-size cinema screen. A projector glided upward from a trapdoor located behind the largest of the sofas.

"Same guy that built the garage did this," reported Leonard.

The dining room featured a painted ceiling imported from a sixteenth-century chateau in Toulouse, a Baccarat crystal chandelier, and a cherrywood dining table that comfortably sat sixteen.

"See that table?" Leonard said proudly. "Harry Cohn fucked Joan Crawford on that table. I love things that have history."

The living room contained several major works of art that were displayed against a jacquard wall covering. Eva's eyes darted around the room as she tried to recall famous artists' names, hoping to match one against a painting and thereby impress Leonard with her cultural depth. Eva spotted a rendering of lilies in a stream on the far wall. Surely it was either a Monet or a Manet. Which one, though? She decided to blur the vowel.

"Is that a Menet?" Eva inquired.

"I don't know. Denise bought it. See that piano? Liberace is said to have fucked Rock Hudson on that piano," he said, opening a bottle of Dom Perignon. "Isn't that great?"

Eva raised the paper-thin, cut-glass flute to her lips and felt the bubbly liquid jitterbugging on her tongue. It tasted like carbonated money. She was finally where she belonged. The memory of sleeping in Grand Central Station could be erased forever. That was the old Eva. She could not believe her good fortune. She had achieved something even Shirley MacLaine would envy: She had managed to be reincarnated while she was still alive.

Leonard moved the tour upstairs.

"More champagne?" he asked, as they stood in the doorway of the master bedroom.

"Why not?" replied Eva, flute extended.

Leonard refilled her glass and noticed her staring at the room.

"Unusual, huh? Denise has always had a thing for the Orient, ever since we visited the owners of the studio in Tokyo."

Unlike the rest of the house, the master bedroom was decorated entirely in a somewhat playful interpretation of *wafu*. The wide, low bed, its sides inlaid with mother-of-pearl decoration, dominated the lantern-lit room. A collection of wall-mounted seventeenth- and eighteenth-century Noh masks also fought for attention. Eva decided that, following Leonard's divorce, she would not be one of those new wives who demanded that everything the last wife had chosen be banished. She would keep the house exactly the way it was. Except for this bedroom, which would have to go.

Eva could hardly believe it. When she had examined her reflection in the mirror pre-premiere, she had known she looked good. However, even she could not have predicted that on her very first public outing she would end up in a mansion with a multimillionaire. Of course, she knew what was expected of her. But could she deliver? As she tilted her head back and coaxed the last whisper of champagne from her glass, Eva wondered whether she should or could force Leonard to postpone sex until a later rendezvous. Eva knew her gown masked a multitude of telltale scars. Her stitches had dissolved and her wounds had closed, but angry red marks remained beneath her bosoms and buttocks. To add to her complications, her right breast felt ever so slightly on fire.

When Eva had gone for her postoperative interview, Dr. Kramer had explained that the sensation was perfectly normal and nothing to worry about.

"The nerve endings are like stepchildren. They take time to adjust to their new environment."

"Why doesn't my left breast hurt?" Eva had asked.

"No two children are alike," the doctor retorted.

Eva was weighing the different merits of possible scar explanations she could offer Leonard. A bizarre car accident that demanded specific areas of surgical attention was the best she could devise.

While Eva fretted over her scars, Leonard was internally debating the best way to introduce Eva to his device. Leonard loved fucking. It was his third favorite activity, after having a hit movie and buying a car. He had known from an early age that he was homely and had dealt with it by trying to bed every woman in the world. Tall ones, tiny ones, black ones, yellow ones, white ones, old ones, young ones, fat ones, thin ones—

Leonard had fucked them all. He had been very excited when he was promoted from head of production to the head of the studio at the age of fifty. In Hollywood, men of fifty are like women of twenty; just entering their prime. Given his rarified job, Leonard was now assured of prime vaginal real estate. Imagine his disappointment, then, when Leonard's doctor told him to brace himself for some serious news.

It was supposed to be just a minor checkup. Leonard had been having problems peeing recently. He seemed to hover in his private office bathroom for minutes at a time before a thin dribble would finally deign to appear, then drop lethargically into the porcelain bowl. The doctor had insisted on further tests and two weeks later had delivered the depressing biopsy results to Leonard.

"It's your prostate," said the doctor. "There's a malignancy."

Leonard gasped. This was worse than *Howard the Duck*.

"What are my options?"

"Removal."

"Or . . . ?"

"Or . . . could be 'Good-bye, Leonard.'"

"What happens if it's removed? Do I need it?"

"Not really. A man can live a long, active life without a prostate. There will, though, be a significant lessening of sexual function."

"Impotence?"

"I prefer the term *erectile dysfunction.*"

The doctor kept his expression rigid. He was eager not to reveal how much he was enjoying himself. He knew for a fact, despite her denials, that Leonard Felk had bedded the doctor's attractive second wife Jackie the weekend he had attended that medical conference in Boston. Maybe universal justice did exist after all.

"Perhaps you would like to discuss the matter with your wife?" said the doctor.

"Why?"

Leonard and Denise's marriage had transmuted into a mere business relationship years before. The only inconvenient effect Leonard's potential impotence and curtailed dating would have on Denise was that he might be home more often.

Leonard had refused to believe the prognosis. The prostate problem, he accepted incontrovertibly. However, he refused to acknowledge the possibility that Mr. Naughty would not stand to immediate attention the moment it saw a naked woman.

The operation was tougher than Leonard expected. He woke up in considerable pain, and it took several days for him to even be able to totter out of his hospital bed. After three weeks, though, he was feeling better, and five hundred dollars convinced his buxom nurse how therapeutic he would find the removal of her uniform. The starched white outfit dropped to the floor, followed by the nurse's underwear. Leonard stared at the woman's large breasts topped with nipples like walnuts, then looked down at his groin. Nothing. Zero. Zilch. Nada.

Leonard began to research his problem exhaustively. He sat in his library for hours, poring over medical encyclopedias and manuals. The two methods used to defeat impotence both appeared to him terribly rudimentary. Injection was one possibility. A doctor injected the equivalent of quick-hardening cement into the member of the patient who then rushed from the clinic, hoping to find the erection's proposed recipient both at home and in a receptive mood. A pump was the other alternative. This at least seemed more adaptable. Leonard read how an implanted device could be inflated and deflated at will via a valve imbedded at the base of the scrotal sac.

The CEO commissioned the studio's special-effects department to build a top-secret, state-of-the-art pumping device, fashioned from a titanium compound for sturdiness but thin as the wing of a hummingbird for minimal intrusion. Leonard returned to the hospital and had this metallic balloon inserted, making sure that the valve was small enough to hide within a scrotal fold.

It had been five months since this operation. Leonard had practiced with the device often but had not yet found a mature, worldly partner with whom he felt comfortable enough to reveal his secret. He had thought over dinner that maybe Eva was the one. Now he was not so sure. What if she screamed? What if she laughed? What if she sued? Leonard decided to adapt his plan. He dimmed the lights to virtual darkness and attempted concealment.

Eva breathed a sigh of relief as the lights lowered. Maybe, if it were dark enough, the scars would remain invisible. She would endure the pain of Leonard touching her right breast as long as she could. If and when it became unbearable, she would simply steer him along to the breast that was behaving. She groped in the dark for the low bed, tripped over it, and then flopped down onto the silken coverlet crafted from antique kimonos. Leonard followed.

Eva was impressed with Leonard's body. His personal trainer had been concentrating on his abs, so his stomach had never been tighter. His pecs were bulging and his glutes were firm. Little did she know how much Leonard wished Wade, his trainer, had an exercise that could strengthen genitalia.

Leonard was equally impressed with Eva's anatomy. He knew her breasts were fake, and that was fine with him. Leonard preferred fake. He found them more manageable. He noticed that when he caressed Eva's right breast, he got more of a reaction than when he caressed the left, so he concentrated on the right. He touched her nipple, and she moaned. He tweaked it, and she squealed. He bit it, and she yelled, "Oh, my God in heaven."

Leonard was careful to keep Eva's eager fingers away from his problem area. He had decided to delay the air insertion until approximately ten minutes in. He had no way of knowing how long the air would hold, given that this was the device's maiden voyage under battle conditions. When he felt the time was appropriate, he excused himself and made his way into the bathroom. Eva used this time to try to recover from the searing pain in her right breast.

Once inside the bathroom, Leonard removed the pump from the medical cabinet. He ejected the tiny plug that was lodged underneath his penis and quickly attached the rubber hose. As he pumped furiously, his penis began to rise, until there it was; his old screwing partner had returned for another bout of bumpy-bumpy.

Leaving the bathroom, he found Eva curled up on the bed, moaning softly. Leonard was impressed that his foreplay had been so effective that minutes later she was still enjoying the sensations. As if on a tightrope, he carefully walked toward the bed, trying not to disturb his manliness. Eva took him in her arms and steered him underneath her. She was determined to be on top. There was no way he was even getting close to her right breast again. Leonard was equally determined to occupy the upper bunk. With himself on top there was no way she could detect the rubber screw holding everything in place. They jostled back and forth until it was no longer lovemaking; it was a wrestling match. Finally, Eva positioned herself on top of the exhausted movie mogul and began to guide his erection into its vaginal destination. That's when she felt the rubber screw.

She quickly reviewed all the things it could be. Tick was the worst and mole was the best. She went with mole and was happily bouncing up and down when a small, black object flew across the room, accompanied by the sound of something deflating.

"What was that?" Eva asked.

Leonard pushed Eva off him and went in search of the vital piece of equipment, but to no avail. With his dick flopping around like a slinky, he had no option but to confess all.

Crawling on their hands and knees, searching for the tiny rubber screw, Eva divulged to Leonard the condition currently bothering her flaming right breast. They agreed to attempt sex again only once Leonard had obtained a spare part and Eva's jangling nerve endings had subsided.

Some weeks later, after she had mastered the pump and the pain in her right breast had substantially decreased, Eva checked out of the shabbily chic or chicly shabby apartment she had been renting by the week on Franklin Avenue in Hollywood. She moved into the small house Leonard had rented for her in the San Fernando Valley. The house was quaint, a euphemism for "small and in need of paint and a new roof," but was conveniently located, at least for Leonard. Directly situated between his office and his home, it afforded an hour of Eva pleasure in each direction without his ever having to go out of his way.

Leonard also employed his new girlfriend as a studio reader. Eva's job was to read and report on scripts that had been submitted to the studio for consideration. This allowed the studio chief to slip his entire Eva outlay through the company accounts. Leonard was the master of the dubious expense claim. Standing in the corner of a desolate graveyard, holding a hastily convened and brief meeting with four junior executives, Leonard had even managed to write off his mother's funeral.

Eva approached her new endeavor with maniacal zest. Despite the fact she had never previously read a movie script nor knew anything about character development, plotting, pace, or dialogue, Eva was savagely opinionated. She tore through the detailed stories experienced writers had sweated over, either crossing out entire pages with a thick black Magic Marker or, where she felt the dialogue needed expansion, scrawling in the margin "MORE HERE!!!" Had the writers seen their scripts after annotation by the ex-model for whom English was a second language, they would probably have carried their typewriters over to her San Fernando Valley location and beaten Eva to death with them.

Fortunately, nobody saw anything Eva wrote. The scripts she covered for Leonard were previously rejected offerings that were over thirty years old. Leonard would nod sagely and intently as Eva gave him a précis of her opinions. He would then take the pile of examined scripts, carefully arranged and numbered in the exact order Eva had decided the studio should film them in, and place them in the trunk of his car. The next day Leonard's secretary would send them over to the studio's recycling center.

Eva's real job for Leonard was to keep Mr. Naughty standing to attention. Ironically, the very thing Leonard thought would prove a sexual minus had turned out to be a plus. Eva liked the pump for the same reason Leonard liked silicone breasts; the degree of control the artificiality provided was a boon. No more stroking and praying that the moody male member would respond and hold; inflation was such a certainty, Eva believed it was something even men without prostate complications should consider. She became so adept with the pump she could erect Leonard at different degrees and angles, depending on her needs. And, of course, there was no chance of her boyfriend ever cheating on her, because Eva kept the pump tightly secure in her medicine cabinet, in between her Tylenol and Ban roll-on.

Alone at night, Eva dreamed of gates: gigantic, inflatable gates so tall they touched the sky. The gates in her dream would creak open slowly to reveal a curving, winding road that was so long that the magnificent castle at its top appeared as but a speck in the distance. On her hands and knees Eva would begin her journey up the winding road. She would fight wind, rain, snakes, and a dozen skinny, warted witches all named Denise until at last she would push open the castle doors and claim the extravagant splendor lying beyond as her own.

At first, Eva was unsure which approach to adopt to facilitate her dream's becoming reality; should she delicately pick away at Leonard like an elegant harpist, or should she beat him into submission like a two-year-old with a drum? Leonard was a worthy opponent. He was honest with her from the beginning. He had disclosed the exact nature of his marital situation, making sure Eva fully understood it and her position before continuing their relationship. He even had it put in writing: "I hereby testify that I, Eva Duran, understand that Leonard Felk will never leave his wife, and I, Eva Duran, am entitled to absolutely nothing if and when our affair is terminated."

It had been Leonard's lawyer, Davis Elliot, who had presented her with the pre-affair agreement. Davis had smoothly explained to Eva why divorce for Leonard was impossible. When he was but a puppy, Leonard had made a horribly foolish mistake. At the time of his marriage, possessing very little except potential, he had neglected to have Denise sign a prenuptial. Under California law, in a divorce Denise would get half of everything Leonard owned and had earned, a turn of events that, the lawyer confidently predicted, would quite simply cause Leonard to die. Eva had exchanged her signature for the keys to the house in the valley and had decided to bide her time. An opportunity would present itself and then she would strike. Her only enemy was impatience.

Impressed by Leonard's legal assassin, Eva decided to employ Davis Elliot to represent Ursula in her divorce from Tommy Marsico. Eva was not disappointed when informed of Ursula's decision to dissolve her marriage. If Tommy's film had been a surprise hit, Eva's reaction would have been different. Had all the studios been dangling ludicrous amounts of money in front of Tommy to secure his next picture, then, as Ursula's business manager, she might have advised her daughter to hang in until the millions were in place and then go for half. However, Leonard assured Eva that, at least for now, ludicrous millions were not in Tommy's future.

"You can never count anybody out in this business. I've seen actors with careers deader than my mother's brisket come back to life and win Academy Awards. But they always have to do a small movie, and they usually have to play a character with a debilitating disease."

Leonard loved to analyze the entertainment industry, and Eva loved to listen. After sex she would put the pump away and then lie beside him to absorb the lesson of the day. Leonard explained to Eva where Tommy had gone wrong.

"You always have to have at least two more in the pipeline."

"What do you mean?"

"You have to increase your odds. Tommy was so sure this movie was a hit, he waited 'til it came out before he made his next move. Everything's a hit before it opens. The second you finish a movie, you should ride the hype and do two more. You wanna make sure that if the first one comes out and stinks up America, you've got two more chances before you have to sell your house in L.A. and tell *Variety* you're moving to New York because you can't wait to get back to theater."

In the settlement, Ursula not only retained all of her money but also took over the payments on Tommy's house once it was transferred to her name. As for Tommy, he entered a drug clinic somewhere in northern California. He was not even famous enough to be accepted into the Betty Ford Clinic. Eva was happy to be rid of a son-in-law like that.

She was less happy with Ursula's decision to employ a manager. She felt the deal stank. Eva understood Marc Mosley's taking fifteen percent of any money he procured, but the moment Ursula had signed his management contract, he had started to demand fifteen percent commission on all of Ursula's modeling fees as well.

"Why do you think you deserve fifteen percent of a part of her career that existed before she even met you?" Eva asked, trying to renegotiate.

"That fifteen percent gives her the opportunity to know me. Do you think I would represent someone who was earning nothing? I have to be compensated for my time."

"Can I ask you exactly what you're doing for her?"

"Certainly. I'm talking about her."

"What do you mean?"

"I mention her. Whenever I feel it's appropriate, I mention her."

"And then what?"

"What do you mean, 'and then what'?"

"I mean what happens then?"

"Gradually, people know I'm representing her," Marc replied.

"And what does that do?"

"It makes people think more highly of her. That she knows me."

"Why don't you call casting directors and get her auditions?"

"That's her agent's job." Marc was becoming irked. "Mrs. Duran, I know you've just arrived in Hollywood, so let me give you some guidelines. Agents secure auditions and agents negotiate contracts."

"So what do you do?"

"I refuse any auditions and contracts I feel are beneath a client represented by me."

"You turn down jobs? And for that you think you're worth fifteen percent of all her earnings?"

Marc was angry. "Hey, she's paying for my personal relationships. Unlike you, I know the important players in town."

Eva was angrier. There she was, operating the penis pump of the head of a major studio and being told she knew no important people in town.

"Leonard Felk is one of my closest friends," she spat.

Marc was impressed. "Really? Could you introduce me?"

"What?"

"You could set up a dinner party."

Eva could not believe what she was hearing. "You want me to set up a dinner party for you so I can introduce you to my friend Leonard Felk?"

"Sure. It would be an excellent opportunity for me to mention Ursula."

Eva hung up the phone. Surprisingly, her conversation with Marc did seem to galvanize the manager into galvanizing Ursula's agent. Soon after their debate, Ursula began auditioning for acting roles almost daily. However, when Ursula called her mother to tell her she had secured the lead in a television pilot, Eva was uncertain how to react.

Having spent so much time searching for the perfect screenplay that was right for her daughter and humping the person who could get it made, Eva was nervous that Marc Mosley had potentially screwed everything up by sending her daughter toward the lesser medium of television. However, unless she had a better, concrete alternative to offer, she knew the best reaction was to congratulate and fawn. Age had taught her the value of dissembling.

After blowing a kiss and hanging up with Ursula, Eva busily rifled through the new scripts Leonard had given her, searching for a potential Ursula project that could be greenlit once television had made her progeny a household name. One particular script caught her eye. It was called *A Girl's Best Friend.* Eva glanced at the plot summary attached to the front of the manuscript. The story involved a mother and daughter who teamed up to steal the world's largest diamond. Eva snuggled into a cushion, turned the first page, and began to read, wondering whether the project was one she and Ursula could perhaps star in together.

South By Southwest

Mindy would have never believed it was possible for someone to be this unhappy in first class. On the red-eye back to New York, she huddled into the corner of her oversize seat by the window and cried silently behind her sunglasses.

She continued to relive the disaster. How could Ursula have betrayed her like this? How could the network executives think that Ursula had improvised comedy business with a chair? Ursula had been tripping over things daily since Mindy first met her. She was a klutz, not a comedian. The left side of Mindy's brain tried to be rational. It wasn't Ursula's fault. Mindy had told her nothing about the project. How was Ursula supposed to know it was Mindy's show written for Mindy around Mindy's act by Mindy's boyfriend?

The right side of Mindy's brain refused to collaborate. Ursula knew exactly what she was doing, showing up in a tight, short dress with no stockings and high heels. Women men want to sleep with always win when men are making the decisions. Nobody could have worked harder at her craft than Mindy, and it simply had not mattered. She would have been better off bleaching her hair blond, getting plastic surgery, and learning how to trip over furniture.

The jealousy Mindy had managed for years to keep a lid on had finally boiled over. Why was Ursula always the subject of intense admiration when, in reality, she could do absolutely nothing? Why did Mindy always feel fat, ugly, and inconsequential standing next to her? Well, that would no longer be a problem.

Then the fantasies kicked in: Maybe the network chiefs would realize they had made a mistake and call Mindy back. That thought was quickly erased as a new one demanded room to fester: Mitch and Ursula. Now that Ursula had Mindy's job, what was stopping her from taking her boyfriend too? And what kind of skunk boyfriend was he, anyway? He saw how upset she was, and he hadn't stood up for her at all. He was probably screwing Ursula right now. And let's not forget Penelope, that opportunistic backstabber. What had she done to deserve a nightmare like this, thought the self-pitying Mindy, already missing the three people whom she hated. The only thing she was certain of was that things could not get any worse.

A few hours later Mindy stood in the hallway of her building and surveyed the lock on her apartment in disbelief. The wood surrounding the lock had been chiseled away and the deadbolt had been hacked off. She pushed open the door she had left tightly closed and flicked on the overhead light. Mindy's bloodshot eyes roamed over the scene of destruction. She began a mental inventory. Television—gone; stereo—gone; lamps—gone. Mindy tiptoed through the detritus scattered across her floor and picked up her phone to notify the police of her misfortune. Her answering machine was gone as well, she noticed.

She stood alone in the middle of her raped apartment and looked over to the window. Bright sunlight might have helped lighten her mood, but the depressing vista of rain falling onto this unseasonably cold, gray, wet morning only contributed to her depression. The sudden end to her dancing career was appearing inconsequential compared to this. She started to cry.

• • •

Back in balmy L.A., Mindy's friends sat drinking breakfast coffee in a diner, debating what to do. Ursula had decided to turn the show down. There would be other jobs, but there would never be another friend like Mindy.

"Ursula, if you turn it down, they won't hire Mindy," Mitch explained.

"Why not?"

"They've decided she's wrong for the part. They won't backtrack. They'll put the project on hold and audition new people for a possible shot at midseason."

"Well, I'm still going to turn it down."

"Mindy's overreacting. She'll reconsider and come back to write on the show with me. She's not stupid," Penelope commented.

"She'll cool down and call me. I know she will," Mitch said, attempting to convince himself.

Ursula used the phone at the diner to check her home answering machine for the fifth time. Mindy had not returned any of the messages she had left on her friend's machine last night. Ursula was now becoming annoyed. Her friend was being selfish and unreasonable. She returned to the booth. Penelope, who could see her future as a professional comedy writer unraveling in front of her, decided it was time to beg.

"Ursula, listen to me. Mindy's best chance is if Mitch's show is a hit. Then he can write his own ticket for his next one. Mindy'll get another shot and then she'll have a hit, and we can all retire at thirty-five. But if you don't do the show, all of our futures stop right here."

Ursula hesitated. There was a certain logic to Penelope's argument. By not doing the show, she might be harming Mindy further.

The locksmiths drilled away at Mindy's door, installing a new, improved lock that would someday be tampered with by a new, improved burglar, as Mindy sifted through what remained of her belongings. Suddenly she realized she had not seen her mother's pink satin rose anywhere.

She had kept it in a jewelry box on top of her bureau. The box was no longer there. The burglars probably thought it contained real jewelry and had picked it up without checking. Still, Mindy frantically ran into her bedroom and began a thorough search. With her heart pounding and her head aching, Mindy somehow managed to find more tears as she tore through the clothing and drawers that had been tossed around the room by the hurried criminals. Discovering she had been stripped of an item that could mean nothing to anybody else and everything to her was simply too much to bear. Mindy's silent crying gave way to enormous shudders of pain as she collapsed on her bed, gathered her knees in a fetal position, and wailed violently.

That evening, without any electronic images or recorded sounds in her living room to keep her company, Mindy dressed and headed toward the club, hoping that hanging around there might lift her spirits somewhat. Moe was the first to greet her as she walked through the doorway.

"I'm so sorry," he said. "There'll be other shows."

Dan approached her with his arms spread wide, like a plane coming in for a landing, and hugged her tightly.

"They're idiots. They don't know what they're doing. Ursula Duran in a porno, I understand. But in a comedy? It's ridiculous."

"How do you know? Who told you?"

"Penelope. She called Marty."

"Poor Mindy." That's what everyone in the club was whispering to each other. It had been ten years since her mother had died, ten years since she had heard "poor Mindy" murmured behind her as she passed by. She sidled up to Ronnie at the bar and tried to ignore the sympathetic stares of her colleagues.

"Hi, kid. Tough break."

"Thanks."

"Show business is full of sorrow," said Ronnie. "That's why I'm getting out."

"What?"

"My dad's sick. He wants me to go back into the family business. He has a really successful medical supply company in Jersey, and he needs my help."

Mindy could hardly believe what she was hearing.

"But you can't. You're too good."

"Mindy, I'm forty-three. I've been doing this for fifteen years. Sometimes you have to face the fact that it's time to move on. You'll get another shot. You have youth on your side. Nobody's going to come in the club and say, 'Let's see the hot new forty-three-year-old.'"

Marty tiptoed up behind her as if he were visiting an invalid in the hospital and softly placed his hand on her shoulder.

"Do you feel like you want to go on?"

"I don't think so. No. Yes. I do. No. Maybe."

"Do you want to get back to me when you've consulted with all of your personalities?"

"No. I'll go on. It'll make me feel better to hear people laughing."

"In that case, you're up next."

Mindy got up from the bar, walked through the velvet curtain, and stepped onto the stage.

"Hi. How are you? My name's Mindy. Let me tell you a little about myself. I wasn't very popular growing up. In high school, I was voted the girl most likely to become a nun. That may not sound very impressive to you now, but believe me, that was quite an accomplishment at the Hebrew Academy."

Nothing. The sure-fire laugh that always followed the rock-solid punch line was absent. Something had gone wrong with Mindy's delivery. Her lightness of touch had disappeared, replaced by an underlying tone of resentful anger that the audience found off-putting and hostile.

A man in the front whispered a few decibels too loudly to his date, "She really sucks."

"Oh, fuck you," spat Mindy. "Fuck you, fuck this shitty club, fuck New York, fuck everything."

Mindy dropped the microphone down onto the floor, ran out through the bar, into the street, and hailed a passing cab.

"Where ya goin', lady?" the cabdriver asked.

"I have no idea," Mindy responded.

She gave what was left of her furniture to the old Russian couple next door and paid her landlord for the two months that were left on her lease. She left no forwarding address and had her phone disconnected.

It had been over five years since Mindy had seen the low white house she had been raised in. Her father had visited her in New York regularly after his divorce, but Mindy had never made the trip back to the place where her mother had died.

The late purchase of her plane ticket guaranteed Mindy the dreaded middle seat on the flight back home. Wedged between two armrest-hoggers, she kept outwardly still while experiencing severe inner turbulence. Was this the right thing to do? Was it cowardly or sensible? Would the move back home restore her inner equilibrium or make her feel worse? What would it feel like being back in her house after it had been Smila'd? Mindy looked down and noticed the red welts that had appeared on her forearms. She positioned her forearms and hands under her thighs in an attempt to conceal from her too-close neighbors this physical manifestation of her frazzled nerves.

Her father met her at the airport wearing a wide grin and an even wider waistline.

"Now that you're home, I'm going on a diet," he quickly volunteered before his disciplined daughter could mention the spread. "I'm joining a gym. I'm gonna look like that Arnold Shwartzameter."

As Hal's Buick LeSabre cruised into the driveway, Mindy's

eyes widened in horror. Smila had painted the house a shade of salmon reminiscent of a cow's tongue. Inside, Smila's fondness for pastels had been allowed to run amok, reaching its zenith in the ubiquitous vinyl wallpaper featuring lavender palm trees topped with silver fronds.

"What do you call this motif?" Mindy asked her father. "Gay jungle?"

"Hey, she wanted the wallpaper. I said okay and tried not to look at it."

As Mindy had predicted, her mother's antique furniture had been banished. In its place, Smila's predilection for Lucite and chrome had been allowed to flourish. However, when Mindy opened the door to her old bedroom, she was delighted to discover that it remained entirely as she remembered it. Her four-poster bed was still covered with its blue flowered quilt and still surrounded by her Ethan Allen furniture. Her oversize spotted, stuffed dog was still comfortably ensconced in the rocking chair, and, most importantly of all, the framed photograph of her mother still stood on the top of her desk.

"I didn't allow Smila to touch anything in your room," her father explained. "If you came back, I wanted it to be just the way you left it."

Mindy smiled gratefully, then heaved her suitcases onto her bed and plopped down beside them.

"Why is it crunchy?" she asked, feeling the top of the quilt.

"I don't know."

Mindy inspected the bedspread more closely and noticed a layer of soot.

"Dad, when was the last time you had this cleaned?"

"What do you mean, 'cleaned'? No one has been in here since you left. It can't be dirty."

Approximately two thousand days of dust covered everything in the room. Unable to renovate the room, Smila had apparently instructed the maid not to bother with Mindy's quarters.

"Hungry?" Hal asked.

"A little," Mindy replied.

Sitting in the breakfast nook of the kitchen where Mindy had made herself two packages of instant oatmeal every morning before school, father and daughter munched on Oreo cookies together. Fruit had been Mindy's first choice of nourishment, but an examination of the refrigerator and pantry had revealed that her father's diet no longer included anything that could spoil.

"Is there any milk?"

"I have powdered milk in the cabinet underneath the stove. Two tablespoons to a glass."

Hal, wifeless for over three years, had adopted the eating habits of a soldier. Canned tuna, canned soup, and canned fruit were neatly stacked on the shelves. Multiple packages of paper plates were piled on the kitchen counter.

"I understand if you want to use paper plates because you don't want to wash stuff," Mindy giggled. "But why did you buy seven thousand of them?"

"That was all they had," her father answered. "These are the good ones. They're the kind I like. I bought the store out in case they never have them again."

"When *was* the last time you went to the store?"

"I just went. I go every April fourteenth. I do two things on that day; I file my taxes, and I go to the grocery store. Everything is fresh. I don't buy anything that expires before the next year."

"And when was the last time this kitchen was cleaned?" Mindy nagged good-naturedly, trying to determine exactly what on the lavender linoleum her shoe was sticking to.

"I clean it every Labor Day. I have a system. I mop in September, and I vacuum in December. I can remember it because it rhymes."

Still smarting over Smila, Hal had erased the possibility of ever inviting another woman into his house. Even Smila's housekeeper had been evicted forever, and the kitchen floor stood testament to that decision.

"Do you hear from Smila and the baby?"

"I don't want to know nothin'."

"Where are they living?"

"Don't know. Gave her a nice settlement. She got married to the guy I found out she was shtupping. Don't want to know."

"You don't even want to see the baby?"

"It's a very nice baby. I want it to have a good life with her and the other guy. I made a mistake. It's over. I move on. No more women. I like television. I can turn it off."

One wife had died, and the other had betrayed him. Mindy wanted to ask her father about her mother. She wanted to ask him whether he thought about her and whether he missed her and why he never brought her up in conversation. She watched him stir the two tablespoons of powdered milk into the glass of water and realized that he no longer wanted anything or anyone in his life that could leave him. Even milk.

Of course, Hal totally supported Mindy in her decision never again to speak to her friends. Indeed, he elaborated.

"You never let anyone know you care. That just leaves you open," he advised.

"So, you're saying I should never fall in love with anyone and never get married?"

"I'm not saying that. But if you do, just don't get too involved."

Living at home with her father was going to be a challenge. However, that night, Mindy felt better as she snuggled into her old bed that smelled of growing up and infinite future possibility. Surrounded by familiar objects, and with somebody who loved her unconditionally asleep in the adjacent room, Mindy felt enveloped by the wave of reassurance she had come to Miami to find. She lifted the covers and peeked down at her forearms. The red welts had vanished.

• • •

Mitch, Ursula, and Penelope flew back east for a day to find Mindy. Nobody at the club had seen her for weeks, and her apartment was empty. Mitch was determined to play detective. He wore a black suit and claimed to be with the FBI.

"I'm looking for a Mindy Solomon," he said, flashing a *Man from U.N.C.L.E.* badge around Mindy's apartment building. "She's disappeared, and it's imperative we find her."

"Why?" asked the freelance artist who lived on the ground floor.

Unprepared with a follow-up line, Mitch improvised. "She's a spy," he said, not too convincingly.

The man sighed. "All I can tell you is I saw her get in a cab with a couple of large suitcases."

"Which way did she go?" asked Mitch, pulling out a small notepad.

"Well, since it's a one way street, I think she went that way," the artist replied, pointing in the direction the traffic was moving.

Mitch's subsequent questioning of other erstwhile neighbors revealed only that she had left wearing a blue sweatsuit and sneakers.

He suspected Florida as a possible Mindy destination and began the challenging task of phoning all the Solomons living in the area. There turned out to be quite a few. Being a Solomon in Miami was almost as common as being a chopstick in Japan. Penelope and Ursula both took turns cold-Solomon-calling, but they came up empty. Mindy's father belonged to the many anti-social Solomons that chose to be unlisted.

Mitch, Ursula, and Penelope finally reached the joint conclusion that Mindy did not wish to be found. Enough time had elapsed for their friend to cool down and discuss the problem in an adult manner. She had chosen not to. The onus of the broken relationships now firmly rested on her shoulders.

Mitch in particular was especially angry that Mindy had let something as mundane as a television show destroy the very special relationship he felt they had shared. He began formulating a revisionist history of Mindy. She had probably never cared for him at all, he reasoned. If he had been an accountant, instead of someone who could advance her career, she would undoubtedly not have given him a second glance. Mitch became convinced that he was lucky he had found this out about Mindy now, rather than later. After they were married, someone else might have come along who could put her in a movie, and Mindy would have traded up and abandoned Mitch without a moment's hesitation. Mitch now felt totally guilt free about participating in a show that, after all, he had single-handedly created.

Mitch decided to focus all of his energies on turning *Cindy* into a big, fat hit.

Mean Sheets

Toward the end of her first week home in Florida, Mindy went exploring her old haunts. The neighborhood had changed while she had been away. The influx of Cubans had made the entire area far more colorful and lively. South Beach, a district Mindy had always considered decrepit and decaying, was slowly coming back to life. Old Art Deco buildings were being renovated, and restaurants and boutiques seemed to be sprouting up on every corner. *Miami Vice* had begun filming there the year before and was pouring a good portion of its sizable production budget into the area. Mindy decided to pay a visit to Alexander Mischinoff's ballet school. It was gone. So was the lobster restaurant. Both had been replaced by a single enterprise.

A glass case was now positioned at the foot of the stairs Mindy had skipped up so often in her youth. Inside, eight-by-ten photographs of people Mindy vaguely recognized sat curled by humidity. A hand-stenciled notice above the photos proclaimed, EVERY TUESDAY NIGHT IS OPEN-MIKE NIGHT. Mindy looked up at the letters stuck to the side of the building that spelled out THE COMEDY OUTLET and smiled at the irony. She could not resist, especially because today was Tuesday. That night, armed with the joke notebook that had been buried at the bottom of her suitcase, Mindy entered the club.

The Comedy Outlet was bigger than Stars and in much better

condition. The premises of the Friendly Lobster had been transformed into a main stage with tables and a bar, whereas upstairs, Mr. Mischinoff's erstwhile establishment now served as a restaurant, serviced by the seafood house's old kitchens. Its policy was completely different from Stars'. Comedians who had TV credits were flown in to perform over the weekends. And they were paid. Substantially. Mindy learned that David Brenner had performed here a while ago, as had Richard Lewis. On the slower nights, like Tuesdays, the club lured customers in with Open Mike Night.

It seemed to be working. Although it was still early, the club was over half full. When Mindy entered the bar area, the club manager, wearing a Hawaiian shirt and a handlebar mustache, greeted her with a friendly smile.

"Do you have a reservation?"

"No, I'm here to audition."

His smile evaporated as he pointed to a checkered-table-clothed, diminutive round table.

"Over there," he pointed. "And you have to order at least two drinks."

Mindy obediently sat down at the wobbly table. *Hardly a glamorous beginning,* she mused, *but better than sitting on the sidewalk for hours in Manhattan.* Mindy looked up to find a large woman wearing a multicolored muumuu heading her way.

"Weren't you on *Letterman* a while ago?" the woman inquired loudly.

Mindy nodded.

"You were really funny. What are you doing here?"

"I'm auditioning."

"Come with me."

The bossy woman took Mindy by the hand and brought her to the club manager.

"Norm, this girl has been on *Letterman.* Treat her with some respect."

Norm's scowl was replaced by a sheepish grin as he offered

Mindy a soda and asked her when she would like to perform.

Loretta, the woman who had recognized Mindy, was the mother of six children and a part-time receptionist at an exterminating company. She acted as the club's emcee. Loretta's plumber husband disapproved of his wife's infatuation with comedy, as did Loretta's mother, who was presently at home taking care of her daughter's children, one of whom had a temperature. Mindy learned all of this in less than three minutes. Loretta liked to talk. Onstage, she took command as if all of the members of the audience were her children.

"You, the skinny one in the back. Finish your food. There are audiences starving in India. Don't make me come over there. I'm warning you—I'll vacuum."

Midway through her opening joke, Mindy sensed that her timing and attitude had returned. She gave the audience her best ten minutes, and it responded enthusiastically, especially to localized material.

"I went to school here in Miami. My first-grade teacher was an illegal alien. She taught the whole year from a crouch behind her desk."

Mindy left the stage to sustained applause.

"Anytime you wanna come by. Anytime," gushed Norm, as Mindy got ready to leave the club.

"Thanks," Mindy replied, suddenly hearing a strange thumping noise behind her. She turned around to see an elderly man manipulating his walker through the crowded nightclub.

"Young lady, could I speak to you a second?"

"Sure, what can I do for you?"

"You're very funny and attractive."

"Thank you." Mindy began to walk away. An octogenarian boyfriend, though being good comedy material, was not high on Mindy's to-do list.

"Good set," Loretta said, appearing from Mindy's left and slapping her on the back.

"She's a funny girl," the old man said. "Slap her again for me. If I let go of this thing, I lose my balance."

Loretta slapped Mindy again. "Here's one from Irv."

Irv turned out to be not a slow stalker but a retired agent. Formerly with ICM in New York, he had moved to Florida after his stroke for a more relaxed way of life.

"But I'm too active," he confided to Mindy, as they sat upstairs in the restaurant drinking coffee. "I can't sit around playing canasta with old people."

Irving Levine could spot a trend. He had begun in vaudeville as a teenager and had quickly discovered that taking a ten-percent booking commission from the people who were moving around the country with their acts was infinitely more sensible than being one of the shmucks with an act. He had mined the big-band era of the '40s, booked the crooners of the '50s, represented the folk singers of the '60s, and scheduled worldwide the behemoth rock acts of the '70s.

Irv had decided that the wheel had come full circle. Now, in the '80s, vaudeville was back. Cable television was exploding and needed affordable product. Low maintenance was a prerequisite. No fancy sound equipment. No staging. No intricate lighting. No musicians. Irv was a pro. He had needed only to watch one funny person standing in front of a faux brick wall to see the potential. Comedians were destined to be the entertainers of the '80s.

"I discovered Loretta, and I've been booking her in clubs around the country. She'll tell you; I'm legitimate. No hanky, no panky. At my age, foreplay is brushing my teeth . . . when I can remember where I put 'em."

Irv laughed at his joke. "I could be a comedian, but I couldn't do stand-up. I'd have to do 'lean-over.'"

Irv had a gig for Mindy the following week, middling in a new club in Tampa. Mindy stocked her father's refrigerator and then headed up the coast for some northern Florida humidity.

The Chuckles comedy club provided a three-bedroom condominium for the comedians while they stayed in town. Mindy opened the condo door to find a table, a lamp, and a sofa. Because she was the first to arrive, Mindy checked each bedroom in an attempt to secure the most lavish. Every room was identical in its minimalism, the club owner having spared every expense.

A taciturn man wearing a Chuckles T-shirt arrived in his dirty Toyota and took Mindy to the club.

"I'd take you through the back," the driver explained as he dropped Mindy in front of the club, "but then you'd have to walk through the garbage."

The club's front door was propped open, and the noisy, expectant chatter of the people inside spilled out into the street. Photographs of the three comedians performing that evening were stapled to the felt bulletin board displayed beside the open door. Mindy paused and looked. Her photo was in the middle. To its left was the photo of the opener, Don Bingham, a black comedian Mindy had never heard of. To the right was the headliner.

Mindy froze in front of the bulletin board. Ursula's ex-friend was middling for Ursula's ex-husband. Did Tommy know about the sitcom pilot? Did he know that Mindy was privy to every intimate detail concerning what had gone wrong in his marriage? Was he still on cocaine? Was he still in love with Ursula, and, most importantly, would he be living in the condo with Mindy for the rest of the week?

The young black comedian on the bill approached Mindy with a big smile and an extended hand.

"Hey, there," he said in a north Floridian accent. "Don Bingham, but you can just call me The Bing."

"Hi," Mindy replied. "Nice to meet you. Have you worked this club before? How is it?"

"Honey, I live in Tampa, and I work here almost every week.

You won't have a problem. These crowds are happier than a buncha black women in a beauty parlor. Tommy's plane's late coming in from L.A., so we're gonna hold a few minutes."

Tommy did not arrive at the club until Mindy was already onstage. She saw Don in the wings imitating a plane landing and knew it was time to close.

"Thank you very much. You've been a wonderful audience. I have to go now, because I have so many exciting things to do. . . . I have some pens I want to test to see if they still write. I've been meaning to clean my phone. Sometimes I just like to take my shoes off and give them a good spray. Thank you again. Good night."

As Mindy walked offstage, she crossed by Tommy Marsico standing in the wings.

"Good set," he said, giving her shoulder a squeeze.

Mindy had not really meant to sleep with Tommy. It just happened.

Sharing a bottle of wine back at the condo, a nervous Mindy drank a little too much. When she emerged from the kitchen with a bag of pretzels and found the naked Tommy reading a magazine and wearing only his socks, she laughed. He smiled. It always worked.

Mindy had attempted to bring up Ursula.

"She had every right to do what she did. I was an asshole," Tommy confessed. "I've been through rehab; I've been through therapy; I've been through Disneyland. I learned the most in Disneyland. The best rides are the hardest to get on and the hardest to stay on, but they're worth it."

Mindy was unsure whether Tommy was talking about his career or his personal life, or whether he was serious or whether it was part of his act, so she smiled politely, accenting her reaction with a slight nod of her head.

"You have to have patience and determination. It'll happen for me again. I know it," Tommy insisted.

This was a totally different Tommy from the one Ursula had described. He seemed focused, sensible, and introspective. This was also the ultimate revenge. Sleeping with Ursula's ex-husband made Mindy feel good in a number of ways. Not only was she hurting Ursula, she was hurting Mitch. Even if they never found out, Mindy felt superior knowing that it had happened.

Mindy was not under the delusion that this was love. She was, however, under the delusion that she would be the only woman Tommy would sleep with that week. The following evening Tommy brought an eager waitress back to the comedy condo. To be fair, he was polite enough to ask Mindy whether she was into threesomes. The rehab clinic Tommy had attended could hardly claim the white-nosed comedian as a success statistic either. The second waitress Tommy slept with hooked him up with a connection in Tampa, and he spent the rest of the week in Tootland. Mindy's sexual foray, intended to hurt people who knew nothing about it, had backfired and turned into a fiesta of self-humiliation.

Fishy, fishy, fish, fish. Banana, banana, banana.

Making the Worst of a Bad Situation

The *Cindy* pilot was moving ahead. A casting director was hired to fill the remaining parts that were still being debated and reworked. A set designer was contracted to build a location that had yet to be agreed on. Mitch was rewriting the script once again, this time for the beautiful daughter of a superintendent of a building in Chicago.

"We have too many pilots set in New York this year," the bespectacled, development executive had explained. "We still want urban, but we don't want to alienate people who don't live in a big city."

"How about Chicago?" Mitch had suggested.

"That's perfect. The network loves Chicago. It's middle America with an edge. But make it a part of Chicago that looks a little like Queens. We don't want you to spoil the original feel."

The development executive also passed along the network's request that there be a love interest for Cindy. Plus, if it was possible, since Ursula had been on the cover of the swimsuit edition of *Sports Illustrated* that year, maybe there was an instance in which Cindy could be in a bikini?

"In Chicago? Why is she wearing a bikini in Chicago?" Mitch demanded.

"Maybe there's a scene in a health club."

"She's a superintendent's daughter! She can't afford to join a health club in the middle of Chicago."

"Nobody said it had to be in the middle," answered the executive huffily before walking away.

Mitch completed the latest rewrite on a Tuesday morning at 8:00, a full two hours before the scheduled network read-through. The assistant to the vice president in charge of network read-throughs busily set up chairs in a drafty rehearsal room. At the far end of the room, the cast assembled behind a cracked Formica table on which were displayed various breakfast pastries and cups of overbrewed coffee.

"God, I'm so nervous. I've never been through one of these things before," Ursula admitted to the veteran actor Joseph Fisco, who had been cast to play her father.

"Nothing to worry about. These things are a breeze. The network suits *have* to like it. They've already bought it. We just have to read it out loud. They'll make a few stupid suggestions and then move on to fuck up someone else's day," Joe said, wiping his mouth free of chocolate doughnut residue.

One by one the executives entered the room and intermingled with the talent over the meager breakfast buffet. Ursula noticed how small talk segued into tiny talk then drifted into teensy eensy beensy talk until there was no talk left at all. One by one the executives snuggled into their seats and stared up at the actors sitting on the dais in front of them, anticipating the show that was about to be spoon-read to them like a bedtime story.

Seated behind a long table were the nine characters featured in the *Cindy* sitcom: five regulars, a guest star, and three day-players. In front of each actor was a copy of the script and a pencil. The actors, having finished their free food, were now leafing through their scripts, obsessing over their lines. An expectant aura hung over the room. Ursula beckoned Mitch over to the table.

"Mitch, what are we waiting for? Why don't we start?"

"See those three empty chairs up front? The head of the network isn't here yet."

Perry Strauss, the head of ABC, and his two assistants meandered into the room some twenty minutes later. Strauss leisurely helped himself to a cup of coffee, took his seat, then nodded curtly in Mitch's direction like a Roman emperor. It was time for the games to begin.

"Good morning to you all," Mitch said in a strained voice behind a forced smile. "I'm Mitch Putnam, the creator of *Cindy,* and I'll be reading the stage directions in the script for you today. Let me introduce everyone to you—"

"Mitch," barked Perry Strauss. "Let's move this along, shall we? I have a lunch at twelve."

All the actors except Ursula sailed through the twenty-two-minute-long teleplay, getting little laughs where bigger laughs would later be electronically installed. They all had experience working in television. Even Kirk, the six-year-old boy who had been added as Cindy's brother to widen demographic appeal, had guested on *Family Ties.*

Inexperienced Ursula, however, with nothing to trip over, was a disaster. Correction: She would have been a disaster had anyone been able to hear what she was saying. So frightened of not being funny, she mumbled most of her lines directly into her cleavage. At the end of the read-through, ten suits and one skirted suit huddled in the back of the rehearsal room, conferring in hushed tones. Mitch was summoned over to hear their thoughts and suggestions.

"We have a big problem," stated Perry Strauss.

"I know," Mitch said, wondering exactly how he was going to fire Ursula.

"The woman who's playing Cindy's mother isn't funny."

"You don't like Catherine Flood? She's been in sitcoms for twenty years. She won an Emmy last year for a guest-starring role on *Kate and Allie.*"

"She's stale and mannered. She's overpowering Ursula. Replace her."

The only woman in the huddle spoke up.

"I think the relationship between Cindy and the guy at the health club needs to be deepened."

"I didn't want to make it too deep because he's a guest star and the following week's storylines don't involve him," Mitch argued politely.

"But it's like they just met. You have to raise the stakes. I'm not going to care that they break up at the end of the show unless you can convince me that they're really in love. Why would I want to watch two people who aren't really committed to each other have an argument? I have other things to do. I don't need to see that."

The female executive reached in her handbag and angrily shook a Tic Tac out of the little Tic Tac door on top of the Tic Tac house.

"I'll look at that," Mitch replied through tightening lips.

Perry Strauss's mouth stretched into the famed Perry Strauss grin.

"Good work. Try to put a little more sex in it. Don't play safe. Push the envelope," he said.

Rehearsals began the next day after Mitch had deepened the relationship between Ursula and a guy she had just met and before a new mother for Ursula could be hired. Brady Schoop, the show's director, was in great demand during pilot season. His ratio of pilots picked up to pilots filmed was extremely high. A former actor himself, he was especially good at putting nervous performers new to television at ease. His positive attitude and his sunny disposition inspired confidence in the direst of situations. Everyone felt fortunate that Brady had squeezed *Cindy* into his busy filming schedule after Perry Strauss had sent him the photo of Ursula in the bikini on the cover of *Sports Illustrated*.

Mitch enlisted Penelope's aid in coaching Ursula on comedic readings.

"Might be an idea, any chance you get during the day, to go to your dressing room with Penelope and work on your lines," Mitch suggested to his lead actress.

Despite Mitch's casual demeanor, Ursula was immediately suspicious.

"Why? Am I no good? Does the network hate me?"

"No, of course not. The network is in love with you. They think you're a natural comedian. I just want to make sure you're completely prepared," Mitch said soft-pedaling.

The Chicago apartment that could have been in Queens was taking shape. The kitchen that was three times the size of a kitchen a family of that income could afford was almost complete. Ditto the living room, Cindy's bedroom, and the bathroom. The most lavish and expensive set was the health club, even though it was a set that would never be used again other than for the pilot episode.

Brady pulled Mitch to one side at the end of the first day of rehearsal. He had not been involved in the development of the script thus far and felt he could be helpful "as a fresh eye."

"I think you're overdoing the whole relationship with Cindy and this guy she just met at a health club," he said. "What's the big deal? They meet, she finds out he used to be a woman, and it's over. It's a sitcom, not Chekhov."

"I'll take a look at that," Mitch said, his jaw tightening with tension.

Under Brady's directorial guidance, the show began to gel. Everybody had a specific comedy beat he or she could play. Everybody except Ursula. In desperation Mitch inserted a moment in the script where Ursula tripped over furniture. She was even unable to accomplish that.

"I can't trip over things on purpose. I have to really not know it's there."

The day before filming the pilot Mitch called an emergency meeting with Brady and Penelope.

"Penelope, I thought you were going to explain the comedy beats to her."

"I tried. You told her the network thinks she's a natural comedian. She won't listen to me."

"Brady, the show tapes tomorrow. How are you going to stop her from trampling over every joke like a unfunny elephant?"

"There's nothing I can do. She's a comedy vampire, and Perry Strauss is in love with her," said Brady.

"God knows why," said Mitch.

"Have you seen his wife he married straight out of high school?" asked Brady. "She's a gorilla. Perry can't believe he's even in the same room with Ursula Duran. Look, we've put funny satellite characters around her and I suggest we make all of her skirts at least two inches shorter. Draw the attention away from what she's saying. Women in sexy clothing test well. There's nothing to worry about."

Marc Mosley made his first appearance twelve minutes before the pilot began filming. He pulled Mitch and Brady aside.

"How's my gal doing?" he asked, chewing something trendy.

"She's fine," Mitch lied.

"Good. I'm glad we could make this happen. Where's her dressing room?"

Mitch pointed in a direction where Marc Mosley could find the person who was about to kill Mitch's career. Eva and Leonard were already in Ursula's dressing room when Marc arrived. An aroma of flowers filled the small space. The twenty-five-dollar director bouquet was being surpassed by the fifty-dollar agent bouquet, which was being dwarfed by the hundred-dollar manager bouquet. Ursula rose to greet Marc.

"Marc, thanks for the flowers. They're beautiful. You know my mother, I believe, and this is her friend, Leonard Felk."

Marc extended his hand to Leonard.

"It is such an honor. I'm a big fan. A huge fan. I'm such a fan."

Marc never again left Leonard Felk's side. Even when wishing

Ursula good luck, he forfeited a hug from his client in exchange for holding the door open for his new best friend.

In the taping studio, a network usher removed red tape from the special seats being held for the VIPs. Marc carefully watched Leonard and Eva sit before he committed himself, making sure of a position next to the studio chief. The warm-up comedian threw candy at the hyped-up studio audience as the reggae band played loudly to keep up the energy in the freezing room.

"I hope this sitcom plays better than it reads," Eva grumbled to Marc.

"You didn't like the script?" asked Marc, shocked.

"No. Did you?"

"It's on my weekend read."

Mitch introduced the cast to the studio audience to tremendous applause, ending with the introduction of swimsuit cover girl Ursula Duran as Cindy. The skirt Ursula was wearing was so short and tight and her high heels so spiked, she could muster only tiny baby steps toward the audience. She took a constricted bow and teetered offstage. The first set was lit up, and the taping began.

The evening was long and tedious. One of the cameras was malfunctioning, and the cast had to repeat scenes so many times it was difficult to tell whether anything was funny or whether everything was just sad. The six-year-old's scene had to be filmed first because of child labor laws. Out of context, the scene made no sense whatsoever to the studio audience, causing people to start talking among themselves. As the filming continued, Mitch stood off to the side of the action, attempting not to burst vital blood vessels as Ursula misread joke after joke.

The skirted suit made her self-important way over to Mitch.

"Perry thinks Ursula needs a stronger line at the end of the new mother scene," she said. "And when did the pilot become about Cindy's relationship with her mother? If you'd deepened the health club scene instead of the mother scene, you would have had a much better shot at getting picked up."

Mitch and Penelope worked out a comeback line for Cindy to say to her mother. Ursula massacred it so badly, they chose to return to her original misreading.

It was all going very slowly. Marc Mosley left his seat to locate Mitch on the studio floor.

"Mitch, I've managed to get Leonard fucking Felk to this taping. Is there anyway you could speed this up?"

Perry Strauss stayed until just after the bikini scene, then had to go home to his gorilla. Leonard stayed until eleven, then had to go home to Denise. Marc left two minutes after Leonard, and three quarters of the audience left before the final scene was filmed. The taping that had begun at 6:00 P.M. ended around midnight. After that, the entire cast stayed another two hours for additional camera angle pickups. Eva fell asleep in the bleachers.

At around two in the morning, the permanently unfazed Brady approached Mitch, who was despondently slumped in a director's chair.

"I think the taping went very well."

Mitch looked at Brady the way a bull looks at a red curtain.

"It always looks like shit before we've cut and sweetened," continued Brady. "I think it's a hit."

Brady was right. Ursula in the bikini tested better than any other character in any other ABC pilot that season. The network was certain that in Ursula Duran they had a new comedy star for the mid-'80s. After firing all of the supporting actors, including six-year-old Kirk, the network ordered the pilot refilmed.

In the new version, Ursula went shopping for a bikini, tried several on, then knocked things over when she tried to put them back on the rack.

Satisfied, the network picked up thirteen episodes of Cindy as a midseason replacement show.

The Stuff Dreams
Aren't Made Of

How ironic was this? Mindy sat in the doctor's reception area, contemplating the situation she found herself in: Miss Goody Two-Shoes waiting for the results of an AIDS test.

She hadn't been feeling well for the past few weeks and had almost canceled her engagement at the Dunes Hotel in Las Vegas. Irv had convinced her otherwise.

"A change of air will do you good. Get out of this humidity. It's dry heat there. Besides, if you do well at the Comedy Corner, maybe I can book you into some of the big rooms as an opening act."

So she packed a lot of Alka-Seltzer and flew to Las Vegas.

The Comedy Corner was a new club that had opened in the Dunes. *Club* was probably too flattering a noun. The Comedy Corner was a small, unused banqueting room a local promoter had convinced the casino to renovate by assuring the management that comedy was the next big thing.

As she waited for the doctor, Mindy saw a strangely familiar face come out of the office.

"Hello, hello. Remember me? 'Butterfingers'?"

Hancock looked so frail Mindy hardly recognized him as the robust young dancer who had dropped her so spectacularly on Broadway.

"Yes, I've got the dreaded," he told her, seeing the fleeting look of concern crease her face as she took in his appearance. "So has everybody. Broken record, broken record, change the subject. Look at you. You're doing so well. Chris and I felt so badly about what happened. How's your back?"

"Fine."

Mindy's back injury now seemed entirely inconsequential in comparison to the obvious death sentence Hancock was facing.

"What are you doing in Las Vegas?" Mindy asked.

"I work backstage at the Follies show at the Stardust. With Belinda Mason. You remember her."

"Oh yes. The most frightening woman in show business."

"In fact, she's a sweetie. She was the one who got Chris and me jobs in the show. And when I couldn't dance anymore, she got me the backstage thing."

"How is Chris?"

"He died. Just over a year ago. Blah, blah, change subject. I can't believe you're a comedian now. You were never funny. Oops. Sorry. Came out wrong."

Mindy smiled. "That's okay."

"Are you married? Seeing anyone?"

"No."

"Well, you be careful out there, missy. They like to say that it's just gays getting it, but I know two girls in New York who have it. This thing's the black fucking plague," Hancock said bitterly.

"I know. I'm so sorry."

"Change subject, change subject. I must tell Belinda all about you. She'll be thrilled."

"Really?" said Mindy unconvinced.

"Absolutely. Well, you take care of yourself, you hear?"

"You take care too, Hancock. Stay well."

"Thanks, honey."

As Hancock left, Mindy's mind raced again. God knows how many people Tommy Marsico had slept with. Maybe in jaded moments when he had exhausted the gamut of all heterosexual possibilities, he had even slept with other men. She had not seen any needles, but given his history, intravenous drugs were also a possibility. Mindy upbraided herself for being stupid enough to have sex with Tommy Marsico and for being stupid enough not to use a condom. This was it. This was why she felt so ill. Tommy Marsico had given her AIDS.

"The doctor will see you now."

Mindy steeled herself and walked into the doctor's office. Seated behind a mahogany desk, surrounded by walls adorned with autographed celebrity photographs, Frank Baroni was the quintessential Vegas doctor. His blow-dried, blue-black hair, lacquered into a perfect bouffant, was entirely complemented by the substantial gold chain around his neck, the matching bracelet, and the pinky ring.

"Hello, Mindy. Take a seat," he said, shining his capped teeth in her direction. "Let's get the most important thing out of the way first. You're not HIV positive."

Thank you, God. Thank you, Jesus. Thank you, Elvis. Thank you. Thank you. Mindy's stomach settled.

"But you are pregnant."

Mindy's stomach once more roller-coastered in an upward direction. "But . . . but . . ." She gulped. "But I can't be. It's a mistake. I always use a diaphragm."

"Really? How long have you had it?"

Mindy used her fingers to calculate.

"Eight years."

The doctor chuckled. "You're supposed to get a new one at least every two."

"But this one's virtually brand-new. I haven't used it all that much. Hardly at all."

"Have you checked it?"

"Yes."

"How long ago?"

"Never mind. Are you sure? Absolutely sure?"

"Oh yes."

"Oh God."

"Not good news?"

"I can't have a baby. I can't. I'm too young. I'm living at home. My career's just starting to come together. This can't happen."

"You're only a few weeks along. You've got plenty of time to make a decision."

"I've made a decision. Make it go away. Now."

The medical man leaned forward paternally. "At least wait 'til you get back home."

"Sure. Good idea. That way my father can drive me to the abortion clinic," ranted Mindy, verging on the hysterical.

The doctor sighed, made a decision, and scribbled something on a pad. "Here's the number of a pro-choice medical center here in Las Vegas. But don't act rashly. Make a careful decision."

Mindy reached out and grabbed the note. "Thank you."

"And look, I know this is a bad time to ask, but if you get a chance, I'd love a photo."

"A what?"

"For my wall." He gestured toward the smiling celebrities.

"Oh. Right." Mindy stood up to leave.

"Just in case you're ever famous."

Back in her hotel room, Mindy held up the diaphragm she thought was her friend and peered through the miniscule hole that had introduced Tommy Marsico's sperm to her egg. How could something so tiny cause a problem so big? Stupid, stupid, stupid. No wonder she was nauseated. No wonder her period had failed to arrive. *Duh. AIDS? Duh. Pregnant, dumbo. Pregnant and single. Okay, rational thought.* The doctor was right. There was no rush. By her calculations, she was only at six weeks. By further calculation, if she brought this baby to term, she would give birth sometime in March '87. Mindy the Mommy! *Oh my God!*

It was an hour before show time. Mindy turned and stared at the phone, desperately trying to think of someone to call. Her father was the only emotional outlet available to her, but this just was not the type of thing you tell your father. This was the type of thing you tell your mother, who then tells your father. God, how she missed her mother! God, how she missed Ursula! Ursula was the one she needed. Paddle. Paddle. Paddle. Paddle red alert. Mindy remembered how she had seen her ex-friend through the very same problem. She also remembered the emotional damage the abortion had caused Ursula, and she winced at the memory.

What was she thinking? Leaving aside the fact that their friendship was in tatters, what would Mindy say to Ursula about the father? "Oh yeah, it's your ex-husband's. I screwed him out of spite to get even with you."

Ursula was not an option. Mindy had no one to help her. She was on her own. Her bottom lip began to quaver. *Can't cry. Not now. Got to do the show. Got to get ready.*

Mindy regurgitated her act on automatic pilot. The audience had no idea of the turmoil going on behind the smiling, happy mask telling them jokes. Back in her dressing room, Mindy collapsed on a chair and let the flood of tears she had dammed up pour out.

"What are you like when it's a *bad* audience?" asked a female voice.

Mindy looked up. Belinda Mason stood in the doorway, inexplicably looking younger than when Mindy had last seen her.

"Hi," snuffled the distraught Mindy.

"Hi. Is this a bad time for you?"

"I'm pregnant."

Belinda Mason wrapped the younger woman in her arms and let her sob.

"There there, sugar. There, there."

And so, with nobody else to confide in, Mindy poured out

her story to Belinda. As they sat in the hotel coffee shop, Belinda lit up yet another Benson & Hedges slim-line cigarette and attempted to recap.

"So the father of your baby is the ex-husband of your ex-best friend, who's working for your ex-boyfriend with your ex-writing partner?"

"Yes. So what should I do?"

Belinda considered, allowing a thin line of smoke to coil upward toward the illuminated keno board above their table.

"Listen, honey. Show business is full of sacrifice and disappointment. They don't tell you that when you're seven years old practicing time steps in a mirror and dreaming of a spotlight. It demands you give things up. Things ordinary people take for granted. It demands you put it first if you want to succeed. Look at you. Show business has already cost you three important relationships."

"Do you think I was wrong?"

"Were you wrong to be angry? No. Were you wrong to expect your friends to all fall on their swords in support? Maybe. It was a rotten situation."

"I feel the worst about Ursula," Mindy admitted. "I was thinking today of how much better I'd feel if I could share all this with her."

"Well, if you do, I'd leave the paternity part out."

"We were always there for each other. When I got hurt in *Heavens to Betsy,* and I couldn't afford the medical bills, Ursula sent me three thousand dollars anonymously to help me through it, and when she and Tommy split up, I dropped everything and went out to L.A. to help her."

Belinda stubbed her cigarette butt out in the ashtray.

"I'm sure Ursula Duran's a lovely woman, but she didn't send you that money."

"How do you know?"

"I just know."

Mindy's eyes narrowed as she weighed the import of what Belinda Mason had just said.

"It was you, wasn't it?"

Belinda waved her hand in the air dismissively. "Well, you were so young, and I know how expensive doctors can be when you don't have insurance. And I'd been mean to you and I felt bad. Please don't tell anyone. I don't need this type of thing getting out, ruining my diva image."

Mindy's eyes welled with tears.

"See?" cautioned Belinda, glancing at Mindy's expression. "This is just the kind of thing I loathe and despise."

She gestured to a passing waitress. "More coffee. And make it hot this time."

Sensing her new friend's discomfort, Mindy changed the subject. "Belinda, if you were me, would you have this baby?"

"I *was* you. How old are you?"

"Almost twenty-six."

"I was twenty-four and dancing in my first Broadway show," Belinda confessed. "I wasn't in love with the father, and I didn't even think about it at the time. I just did it. Like going to the dentist. I figured, I'll have children later. I'll fall in love with someone when I'm in my late thirties, when my dancing career will be coming to an end, and I'll have the time and money then to give a child what it deserves. Well, none of that happened, and when I did fall in love with someone, I was forty-five and my eggs were completely hard-boiled, which turned out to be a good thing, because so was he. I didn't think about the abortion again for years . . . then one day I saw some kids in a limo dressed up for their prom and I realized my child would be eighteen now, and I just started keeping track. I decided it would have been a boy, and last week, can you believe it, he would have been forty."

Belinda's eyes opened wide. "Oh, my God. I've just told you how old I am. Nobody knows how old I am. I'm going to have to kill you now."

"Don't worry. I'm terrible at math. By my calculations, you're thirty-seven. So you think I should have it?"

"I'm not saying that. *You* have to decide. I'm just saying it's a decision a woman never forgets. Never. So you have to be ready to take the consequences either way. For me, it was probably the right decision. I'm like my mother: not the motherly type. I'm vain and shallow. If I go into a hospital, I want to come out looking younger, and I know this isn't a popular opinion, but I don't think women can have it all. I think you have to choose which is more important, and I know I would always choose career. I didn't want my kid to think Mommy was the woman who was home just on Monday nights. My sister has two children, whom I spoil and adore, and that's enough for me. But you have to decide what's right for you."

"But I don't know," whined Mindy.

"You will," said Belinda.

When she returned home from Las Vegas, Mindy sat her father down in the kitchen and poured a generous measure of Scotch into a glass tumbler. She slid it over to him.

"Dad," she said, "I have to tell you something. . . ."

The seriousness of Mindy's tone made her father's eyebrows take on a quizzical, worried tilt, turning up at the tops and down at the ends.

"What's the matter?"

"I'm gay," Mindy said.

"You're kidding?"

"Yes, but I am pregnant."

"You're gay and you're pregnant?" asked her confused parent.

"No. I'm only pregnant."

"So why did you say you were gay?"

"To make it easier to take that I'm pregnant."

"Oh." Mindy's father drank the tumbler of Scotch down in one gulp.

"Are you married? What else don't I know? Jesus, you were only in Las Vegas for a week. What goes on there?"

"It's nothing to do with Las Vegas. It happened a couple months ago. I was stupid and got involved with someone I shouldn't. I don't love the father, and I'm not even going to tell him it happened. I just wanted to tell you. Even if you hate me, I wanted to tell you. I think I want to keep it, and I know that's a decision that affects you, and I want to know what you think."

Mindy watched her father carefully as he tried to digest all the information. He sighed.

"Sweetie, you're my only daughter. Whatever happens, I'll always be there for you. Who knows? Sometimes a mistake turns out to be a good thing. It'll be an adventure. The good news is I don't have to deal with a putzy son-in-law I don't like."

Mindy hugged her father tightly. "Thanks, Dad."

He hugged her back just as tight. "You know what your mother would say if she were still here?"

"What?" asked Mindy, surprised and grateful that her father had finally mentioned her mother.

"Fish banana."

Back at the Comedy Outlet, Mindy found her new friend Loretta to be an encyclopedia of pregnancy knowledge. She even recommended an obstetrician and accompanied Mindy to her first visit.

"I want her to know I referred you. Maybe she'll give me a discount on my next one," Loretta explained.

Mindy counted on telling her octogenarian agent she was pregnant around her sixth month and then taking a leave of absence from spreading mirth around America around her seventh. So when Irv called with the news that he had landed her a slot in the new HBO special *Girls Just Wanna Have Fun,* he was shocked at her lack of enthusiasm.

"When does it film?"

"No set date yet. In a couple of months. January, February, somewhere around there."

"I can't do it."

"What do you mean? I sent them a copy of your *Letterman* spot, plus some tapes of your new material, and they booked you for the special. This is a big break, kid. What's the matter with you?"

"Maybe Loretta can do my spot," Mindy said, remembering Belinda's warning about giving things up and choosing.

"She's on it too. Can you believe it? An old retired Jew in Miami books two gal comedians on a big special. They have another woman they like in Boston, and they're looking for one more. They'll fly you to New York, put you up in a fancy hotel, and pay you five grand. What's the problem?"

"Irv, I'm pregnant."

The other end of the phone went silent.

"Irv . . . ?"

"Mazel tov. You'll stand out from the pack."

"Are you sure?"

"Absolutely. David Brenner has the nose. Phyllis Diller has the laugh. You'll be the pregnant one."

"I can't *stay* pregnant."

"I'm a very good agent. Who knows what I can pull off," said Irv.

Mindy chuckled.

"So that's a 'yes'?"

"I guess so," Mindy said, acquiescing.

"Good. Now let me off the phone so I can try to get the kid billing."

A Yen for Change

Leonard faced the equivalent of a legal firing squad. Five lawyers, leaner and meaner than Doberman pinschers, were shooting mathematical bullets at him.

"A hundred thousand dollars for a swimming pool for your home, Mr. Felk?" barked the lead Doberman.

"I use the pool to relax after meetings. Very often the solutions to studio problems come to me on the float," Leonard explained smoothly.

An assistant Doberman chimed in. "There was already a pool on your property."

"I got no ideas in the first pool. It was too small."

Leonard had smelled a major problem when the team of Japanese accountants had swept onto the lot five days ago, politely demanding access to all the accounts.

"Why was your wife's recent trip to Rome billed as a company expense?"

"She was scouting locations."

"For what?"

"*The Italian Medallion,*" Leonard invented. "I'm talking to Stallone about it."

"Is there a script?"

"It's in development."

"Where?"

Leonard tapped the side of his head. "Up here. In fact, I should be in my pool right now, working on the second act."

"Let's move on. There was an item billed under the budget for the film *Two to Tangle* that particularly concerned Mr. Takashiri: the construction of a penile implant. Why was that considered necessary?"

"Did you see the film?" asked Leonard.

"No. Neither did anyone else, judging by all this red ink," joked the lawyer sarcastically.

"I think time will be very kind to *Two to Tangle,*" said Leonard defensively. "You know, *It's a Wonderful Life* bombed when it was first released. *Two to Tangle* was ahead of its time. That's why we had to lose the penile implant scene. Broke my heart to cut it, but, hey, that's showbiz."

The men conferred in a huddle, deciding where next to attack their prey's defenses.

If I'd had a few hits, you'd be kissing my ring, thought Leonard as he watched them plot.

He was right. Hit films are the great Hollywood deodorants. Nobody notices the stink of an evaporating few million if there are hits happening at the same time. However, Leonard knew his recent slate had been nothing short of disastrous.

A Japanese man who had been standing silently to the side, staring intently at the view of the San Fernando Valley afforded by the conference room's picture window, now turned and interrupted Leonard's reverie.

"Mr. Felk, let us, as you say in your country, cut the shit."

"Who are you?" asked Leonard.

"Who I am is immaterial to you, Mr. Felk. Think of me as the umpire who is going to blow the final whistle on this episode of fiscal rape."

"I think that's a little—"

"Shut up!" screamed the man.

Leonard shut up.

"The numerous illegalities perpetrated by you on this company are all litigable. You know that. We know that."

Indeed, Leonard had spent the previous evening poring over hypothetical charges with Davis Elliot and had reached the inescapable conclusion that he was facing checkmate.

"Mr. Takashiri wishes to make an example of you. He profoundly desires to see you put behind bars for several years."

Leonard began to sweat. Hollywood executive thievery had been going on since the town's invention. Surely the Japs understood that?

"However, Mr. Takashiri has been persuaded, albeit temporarily, that the attendant poor publicity would have an adverse affect on both the parent company image and its stock price. Instead, you will sign this."

The man removed a document from his inside breast pocket and placed it in front of Leonard. The studio executive pulled out his glasses and scanned the document, turning over page after page carefully and deliberately.

Minutes went by. Particles of dust shimmied in the shafts of yellowing afternoon sunlight. The silence in the room, broken only by the merry chirping of the birds outside, became oppressive. Finally Leonard reached the end of the contract, took off his glasses, and looked up impassively at his oriental nemesis.

"Why don't you just tie me to the table and fuck me in the ass?" he asked matter-of-factly.

"Sign it!" the man ordered.

"I ain't signing shit," insisted Leonard. "Furthermore, I suggest you go tell Mr. Take-a-dumpy that he can go fuck himself."

The man clapped his hands and barked something in Japanese. The doors to the conference room burst open. Three uniformed Japanese policemen rushed into the room and roughly pulled Leonard out of his chair.

"What the fuck is going on?" demanded Leonard, clearly rattled. "Are we remaking *Bridge on the Fucking River Kwai*? Gonna change the ending, you little yellow bastard?"

"Ah. Racial epithets; I wondered when they would arrive." The man threw another bundle of documents onto the conference desk. "Since this a Japanese-controlled company, we have arranged for you to be extradited to Japan. You will be tried there. When you are found guilty, you will be jailed there too. So, you see, you will be able to tell Mr. Takashiri to go fuck himself in person."

"I want my lawyer."

"Mr. Elliot? Mr. Elliot now works for us. It was he who drew up the extradition papers."

Leonard glanced feverishly at the papers in front of him and recognized Davis Elliot's signature. He weighed his options. Surrender was his only course.

"Okay, Okay. I'll sign."

"Too late," spat the man, and clapped his hands once more.

Leonard was not proud of his behavior over the next few hours: the peeing himself in the car on the way to the airport, the plaintive begging on board the corporate jet as it sped over the Pacific, and then finally the groveling gratitude as his tormentor allowed him to sign an even more adverse termination agreement. Two hours later, the plane deposited a soiled, gibbering Leonard back at the Burbank airport.

"The greed I can tolerate," said the Japanese man in parting. "The lack of honor is unforgivable. Good-bye, Mr. Felk."

"Yeah. Yeah. Yeah. Good-bye. Try not to bomb Pearl Harbor on your way back."

The news hit the trades the next day: "Leonard Felk is ankling his studio post to start up a new production company, Quixote Films. 'I miss the nuts and bolts of production,' said Felk yesterday. 'I miss exercising my creative muscles. Quixote will allow me to conduct the orchestra once more.'"

Nobody in the industry believed the spin the PR firm Leonard had employed was putting on the news. *Spin,* incidentally, was a relatively new term for what Leonard used to call bullshit. Everyone in the know was aware the Japanese had canned

Leonard. However, in a town in which everyone eventually gets canned, there is no shame in being fired, providing you can stay in the game and avoid self-pity.

Leonard was actually enthused rather than deflated by his changed circumstances. A winner and survivor by nature, he decided it was healthier to view his current slide as an opportunity. When faced with lemons, Leonard Felk always attempted to make lemonade. Armed with this can-do attitude, almost immediately good things started to happen to him. First, Denise asked for a divorce. In Rome she had met an Italian with an even larger bank account than Leonard's and had decided to trade up.

Denise's departure needed to be spun as well, of course. Leonard knew he would look vulnerable if it appeared his wife had left him for another man. He needed to be seen at once with someone younger and better-looking than Denise. It was time to make Eva public and permanent.

"Why can't we live in the Bel Air house?" pouted Eva.

"Because I've sold it. That place is a shithole compared to the house Mitzi's gonna find us."

Leonard and Eva were driving to meet Mitzi Taylor, realtor to the stars.

"I still can't believe it. Mrs. Eva Felk," said Eva dreamily.

Leonard slammed on the brakes and pulled over to one side of Doheny Drive. "Let me set one thing straight. We can live together, but we're not getting married. I will never be married again. I've done married. It hurt."

"Me too, sweetie. We'll live together, like Goldie and Kurt."

Eva had done extensive research on the palimony laws of California. "Live-in lover" status suited her fine.

Mitzi Taylor—tight white suit, spiked heels, gold ankle bracelet, deep tan, sixty-three years old—leaned against the hood of her black Mercedes convertible, tapped her ruby talons on the car door, and tilted her face toward the California sun. The combination of sun-soaking and finger-tapping said heaps about Mitzi; she was permanently capable of being impatient and relaxed at the same time. On hearing Leonard's car pull up to the curb, Mitzi lowered her painted face and her scowling, lip-lined mouth curved into a beaming, fraudulent smile.

"Baby doll," she growled in a voice that sounded as if it had been run over by a train. "I've got some delicious properties to show you today. Are you ready to be wowed?"

Leonard and Eva slid into the backseat of the Mercedes.

"The first property I'm showing you is a delight. Very private. It has no view; it looks in on itself," reported Mitzi as she careened around the more dangerous bends of Mulholland Drive. "It boasts twelve bedrooms, a steam room you could have a party in, and an indoor racquetball court. The owner's an Arab and is very price-flexible. It's a pocket listing. Nobody knows about this little gem, and I think you might just fall in love."

Moments later Leonard and Eva were staring up at several pornographic images etched on the foyer ceiling.

"Paint can always be removed," Mitzi assured them.

The gold chandelier over the dining-room table also featured bare-breasted beauties. Indeed, lamps and statues celebrating the female form were stationed in almost every room.

"So what do you think?" Mitzi asked.

"It's a brothel," said Leonard.

"I can't fool you, can I?" Mitzi said, lighting an unfiltered cigarette. "He's a shrewdie," she cooed to Eva, slipping into compliment mode so as to extricate herself from made-a-mistake mode.

"Mitzi, you're letting me down," Leonard scolded after the sixth property had failed to impress him. "You know my last house. You sold it to me. I need one better than that."

"You should have said, baby doll."

Mitzi chauffeured Leonard and Eva to an estate she silently considered totally out of the price range of an unemployed studio executive.

"How's this for a great approach?" Mitzi asked as they drove nearly vertically up a cliff.

Perched high on a mountain in Pacific Palisades, the Mediterranean castle had magnificent views of the ocean from every oversized room. Two swimming pools, a canoeable lake, skeet shooting, a tennis court, a bowling alley, and an archery range were all featured on the vast property. Eva was in heaven.

"This property was spotlighted on *Entertainment Tonight.* Sixteen thousand square feet and everything top of the line. Floor's imported from Italy, roof's imported from China, kitchen's imported from France; you'll have the only house that has a passport."

"How much?" asked Leonard.

"They're asking nine."

"Asking's asking. How much?"

"They won't take anything that doesn't have an eight in front of it," Mitzi confided.

"You like it?" Leonard asked Eva.

Eva, who had liked every house they had seen so far, even the pornographic one, could only nod speechlessly. Words failed her as she pictured herself living in this palace.

"Seven-point-eight, offer good 'til one minute after nine tonight. Pending inspection, of course."

"He's a shrewdie," Mitzi repeated to Eva.

The deal closed at seven-point-nine at 9:07 that night. Eva and Leonard moved in later that week. Eva was left to decorate the new property while her new partner flew to Europe to stitch together the various investment and distribution packages necessary to put Quixote Films firmly on its feet.

Leonard Felk was back, and Eva Duran had arrived.

New York State of Mindy

Six months pregnant and on her way to New York, Mindy turned to Loretta and said, "I wish they made these plane seats bigger. I'm sitting for two now."

"That's how I feel all the time," Loretta commented, her ample girth pressing against the armrests.

For the entire three-hour flight Loretta fretted about temporarily deserting her loved ones for a career opportunity.

"Stevie had a fever and threw such a tantrum when I left."

"Your husband can take care of him."

"Stevie *is* my husband."

"Sorry. I get Stevie and Petey mixed up."

"Petey is six. He's the more mature one."

"Loretta, you don't have to feel guilty about leaving for a few days."

"Try telling them that."

Mindy could understand Loretta's dilemma. Although she still had three months to go, Mindy already felt the hefty, protective tug of maternal obligation. Indeed, the bond was so strong she was considering not having the umbilical cord cut right away, but leaving it intact so she could keep track of her child's whereabouts until he or she was at least twenty-one. She opened her notebook and wrote that down. That was a joke. Mindy liked it when the two parts of her brain came together like that.

More than her physical appearance had changed during her pregnancy. Though the minority of Mindy's brain was still concerned with writing jokes, the majority had been completely possessed by thoughts about her unborn child. Determined to give her baby a four-star womb, Mindy had committed to her pregnancy with the same intensity she had applied to dancing and comedy. The book she was currently reading, *The Unborn Guest,* gave her guidelines on what to eat, what to wear, how to sit, and when to breathe. It was one of the several self-help books concerned with pregnancy and parenting that Mindy had devoured as she attended every possible class and had every possible medical checkup on offer.

Her comedy act had been forced to adapt. The routine that had previously centered so firmly on being single was now primarily concerned with being pregnant and being married to the imaginary husband Mindy had chosen to create.

"I'm not sure if my husband is going to be there when I actually have the baby. He said the only way he's going to be in the room when there's a delivery is if there's a pizza involved."

Mindy knew confessing to single motherhood was probably a more empowering message to deliver, but she simply did not have the strength of will to carry it off. Besides, she reasoned, surely one of the joys of artistic fiction was the ability to create a pleasanter reality? Given her middle-class, bourgeois upbringing, a married, pregnant Mindy felt more acceptable to her than a single, pregnant Mindy, especially in New York, where people knew her and where, if necessary, she intended to perpetrate the fiction offstage as well as on.

Loretta had never been to New York. They landed on one of those cold, crisp East Coast November days, so clear it was as though the Manhattan skyline had been given the once-over with a household cleanser. As they drove in from JFK, Mindy pointed out the tall buildings jutting up in the distance, promising to take her new friend on a detailed tour of the cement play-

ground Mindy knew so well. Loretta seemed somehow dimin-
ished by these new surroundings, her natural bossiness muted,
replaced by timid awe generated by the sight of gigantic, fre-
netic New York City.

Irving Levine had arranged for his two clients to share a room
at the Plaza. When Mindy opened the curtains in their shabby,
cramped room, the view of the dark alley outside assaulted her.
Loretta, in contrast, was happy to make the best of it.

"It could be worse. We could have a room with no window at
all. And it *is* the Plaza. I've seen this place in movies."

Mindy marched over to the phone and picked up the receiver.
"Hello, I'd like to speak to the front desk."

"Mindy, what are you doing? It's a room at the Plaza, and
we're not paying," Loretta protested.

"Hello? This is Mindy Solomon. My associate and I are in
town filming a special for HBO, and you've mistakenly given us
an old, tiny room facing an alley. Do you think you could check
and see if there's anything newer and bigger with a park view
available? If not, I'd like to speak to the manager about checking
out. Sure, I'll hold."

"Color me impressed. Where did you get those balls?"

"My ex-friend Ursula taught me always to complain," Mindy
explained.

The front desk attendant came back on the line. "I'm sorry
about that, Ms. Solomon. I'll have a bellperson sent up immediately with keys to a room I'm sure you'll find much more to
your satisfaction."

"Thank you."

Mindy and Loretta transferred to a room that was twice the
size and overlooked the park. Thinking about Ursula again had
made Mindy confused. Her feelings about her erstwhile best
friend were being further complicated by the advertising cam-
paign for *Cindy,* due to debut the following Wednesday at 8:00
P.M. On the way in from the airport, Mindy had counted seven

billboards for the show and, as Mindy and Loretta hurried down a cold Fifth Avenue toward their rehearsal, Mindy was assailed by an enormous Ursula beaming at her from the side of a passing bus. Mindy sneered jealously at the caption: " 'A Mary Tyler Moore for the eighties,' says *Newsweek*."

The bus ran through a puddle and splashed dirty water up at Mindy, as if protecting its beautiful client.

Over the previous few months Mindy had tried erasing Ursula, Mitch, and Penelope from her mind. Nuggets of upsetting information had still managed to infiltrate, though, mainly while Mindy stood at the checkout lines of various Miami supermarkets, cursorily flicking through magazines. Mindy knew it was emotionally healthier for her to avoid such publications, but she was powerless to resist the urge to self-immolate.

Her hopes had soared in guilty delight when she learned from *Us* magazine that the original pilot had been scrapped, but they subsequently plummeted when fed the information via *TV Guide* that the new, improved pilot had tested so well that the show had been added to ABC's midseason schedule. Of course the news that would really have devastated Mindy would have been any inkling of a romance between Ursula and Mitch. Her worst fear was the nightmare image of the two of them locked in a limb-and-lip embrace. Each week Mindy scoured *People* magazine for the Hollywood photograph that would link the couple together. Her self-destructive impulse was almost satisfied when, in a photo from the premiere of *Leonard Part VI,* she spotted Ursula walking down the red carpet with Penelope. Ursula looked fabulous, whereas Penelope looked even more terrible than usual.

Mindy fantasized about how Mitch would feel when he saw the TV special. The idea of his witnessing her pregnant and talking about her happy marriage on prestigious HBO filled her with delight. He would probably have to check into a clinic for acute depression and would never recover. She wondered how often the "Mary Tyler Moore for the eighties" would visit him.

Probably often at first, but then as it became clearer that the old Mitch was never going to return and as the ongoing demands on Ursula's massive comedic talent grew even larger, nouveau MTM would gradually stop going to the clinic at all.

Huge lighting grids and speakers were being unloaded from trucks double-parked outside the nightclub that HBO had chosen as the TV special's location. Mindy and Loretta hurried into the sanctuary of the nightspot's interior. A temporary proscenium stage had been installed at one end of the space, behind which an Art Deco backdrop in the style of Erté was in the midst of being erected. Circular tables, each with a central miniature Tiffany lamp and surrounded by four Bauhaus-style straight-backed chairs, had been symmetrically distributed around the shiny black dance floor.

At various posts around the room were stationed six unwieldy-looking film cameras complete with headphoned operators. A seventh camera dangled at the end of a crane and was practicing swooping over the heads of the imaginary audience and below an enormous steel grid from which were suspended a myriad of lights. Technicians balanced on tall ladders, adjusting and readjusting the lighting apparatus aimed at the stage. It all looked very impressive, but Mindy had only one thought: *High ceilings. Bad for comedy.*

Mindy knew people packed together in a low-ceilinged room made the best audiences. The laughter bounced off the ceilings and back onto the audience, magnifying the cackles and encouraging the audience to laugh louder, which in turn encouraged the comedian to be funnier. Loretta, meanwhile, was not experienced enough to know to worry about a high ceiling. A television virgin, the technical equipment alone was more than enough to terrify her.

"There are so many cameras. Which one do I look at?"

"There'll be a red light. That's the camera on you at that particular time."

"I have to tell jokes *and* look for a red light?" Loretta panicked.

"No. You don't have to look for the light, but it's good to know where it is in case you want to use it on a punch line."

A sweating, harried man wearing headphones and a worried expression approached the two women. He had pronounced, protruding lips that when parted revealed polished, Chiclet teeth that monochromatically contrasted with his all-black ensemble, tight, curly black hair and full, dark mustache.

"If you're not in the show, you'll have to clear."

"Mindy Solomon and Loretta MacKenzie. We're two of the comedians."

"Oh. I'm Hank the stage manager. We've been looking for you two. Could you wait over there with Carmen and Sue?"

Hank pointed toward a closed bar, at each end of which sat two unsmiling young women on stools. Both were flanked by what at first sight appeared to be either two supervising adults or parents. Mindy recognized the young woman with the cropped blond hair on the left. She had seen Sue Newton on the *Tonight Show*. She was funny. The other dark-haired woman was unknown to her. Mindy and Loretta wandered over.

"Hi, I'm Carmen Herrara. This is Harvey Madden, my manager, and Marilyn Michaels, my agent," said Carmen, extending her hand. "Nice to be working with you."

The two underrepresented comedians shook Carmen's confident hand and said hello. Mindy turned toward Sue Newton, seated at the other end of the bar.

"Hi, Sue. Mindy Solomon."

"Hi," said Sue, and nodded dismissively.

"I saw you on *Letterman*," Carmen told Mindy. "What was wrong with him that night?"

Before Mindy could respond, Hank approached. "We're ready to start rehearsal," he said, pulling a piece of paper from his back pocket. "Mindy, you're up first."

Mindy was taken aback. "How did that get decided?" she asked.

"We had a meeting this morning, and the running order is you, Loretta, and then we're still deciding who'll close the show," Hank informed her.

The woman behind Sue clucked derisively. Harvey glared at her, then turned back to Hank.

"Carmen's contract specifically states she's the headliner," he insisted with a glacial smile.

Sue looked furious, and her two handlers both placed placating hands on her shoulders.

"Don't worry. We'll figure it out," Mindy heard the female handler whisper to Sue.

"Mindy?" prompted Hank, holding out his hand to assist the young pregnant woman to the stage.

It dawned on managerless Mindy that tomorrow night she was going to be placed in the unenviable position of coaxing a tight television audience into its first laugh.

Mindy began to go through her material, aiming it at empty chairs. A few sporadic chuckles from the stagehands helped her along. As her eyes grew accustomed to the lights, she noticed a phalanx of serious-looking, well-dressed people enter and cluster at the very rear of the club. Sue's and Carmen's representatives noticed them as well and rushed over. The debate grew more heated as Mindy tottered through her act. In the middle of the setup for her final joke, Mindy heard a raised, abrasive voice insist, "Get this straight. We're pulling Sue if she doesn't close." Mindy ignored the interruption and finished her joke.

"And that's the end of my act," she announced to nobody in particular. "Then I go back to my hotel room and cry."

Hank appeared below her.

"Don't be silly. That was great," he said enthusiastically. "All we need now is for you to show Tim what you're going to wear."

"Tim?"

"The designer," Hank explained. "Loretta. You're up."

Mindy took herself and her stomach off the stage and looked for Tim. A nervous Loretta replaced her but never made it to the center of the performing area. She positioned herself slightly to one side and began mumbling her act at great speed. It was all too much for her: New York, television, and strangers.

"They can't hear you," said Hank, relaying a message from the production truck.

Mindy jumped in. "She's just a little nervous. She'll be fine tomorrow. Loretta, slow down and speak up."

Loretta took Mindy's advice but still looked uncomfortable. She left the stage with a visible sense of relief.

"I'll be okay," she promised Mindy. "No audience and all the lights just threw me a little. I'll be okay tomorrow."

A man appeared in front of them. "Hi. I'm Tim. Can I see what you're planning to wear?"

"Carmen, you're up," Hank called out.

Nobody moved. The heated discussion at the rear of the room was still underway.

"Take ten, everyone," announced Hank wearily as Loretta and Mindy followed Tim back toward the makeshift dressing rooms.

"When I saw the space, I immediately thought thirties," Tim clucked. "That dance floor is so Fred and Ginger. When you due, hon?"

"End of March," said Mindy.

"Fabulous. You'll love it. I have four."

Mindy and Loretta exchanged looks of utter disbelief as they entered the dressing rooms.

"Two of each. My wife just pops 'em out."

Mindy held up the maternity evening dress she had found in a Miami store called Battle of the Bulge.

"Fabulous. That'll light like a dream. How 'bout you, hon?" he asked, turning to Loretta.

Loretta rummaged in her garment bag and pulled out a wrinkled denim dress.

"It needs a little ironing," she said apologetically.

"Do you do a character?" Tim asked, his nose flaring in distaste.

"What do you mean?"

"Farmyard Fanny. Pigpen Patty. Something like that?"

"No. I'm just me."

"Oh. Well, it *is* very thirties," he commented. "Just more *Grapes of Wrath* than *Flying Down to Rio.*"

Loretta look confused.

"Look, hon, I pulled a couple of things out, just in case, and I have a fuchsia, ostrich feather number that is simply out of this mundo."

"That sounds good," encouraged Mindy.

"Okay," agreed Loretta uncertainly, as Hank entered the room.

"Thank God you two haven't got managers and agents," Hank shared wearily. "Right. This is what's happening. You two have the rest of the day to yourselves. We're all gonna meet up at a try-out club at nine tonight so the four of you can run through your acts. That way we can make sure there's no material overlap, plus the head of HBO will be there to make the decision on the running order."

"Which club?" asked Mindy anxiously.

"Stars of Tomorrow. It's on Second Avenue."

Mindy grabbed the back of a chair for support.

"I can give you directions."

"Don't worry. I know where it is," said Mindy hollowly.

"Are you okay?" asked Hank solicitously.

"Yes," said Mindy, holding her stomach. "It's just my past kicking."

The thought of returning to Stars sent a tsunami of panic rushing up Mindy's spine. Would she be capable of peddling the lies about her personal life to her old friends with the same conviction she possessed when addressing an audience of strangers?

When they arrived back at the hotel, the women were given a message to phone Irving Levine.

"What's the matter with Loretta? I heard she was a mess," Irv inquired from his semiprivate room in Miami's Mercy Hospital. A heart murmur the week before had forced his doctor to admit the ancient agent for observation.

"She'll be fine. She just got a little nervous," Mindy said placatingly—and unconvincingly. "More importantly, how are you feeling?"

"I'm fine. Let me talk to 'Retta."

Mindy handed Loretta the phone.

"Loretta, listen to me, sweetie. Pretend you're on stage in Miami. You're not in New York. You're not doing the special. You're in your home club in Miami, and it's a normal Wednesday night. You got that?"

"Yes, Irv."

"Good girl. Let me speak to Mindy."

Mindy took her turn holding the receiver.

"Mindy, you gotta help her. I know I should be there with you two for this, but I can't. It kills me."

"We're fine, Irv. You just concentrate on resting up."

"You're a good kid. I'll be thinking of you. Break a leg."

Mindy hung up the phone. She had decided to relay to her agent neither the ongoing argument of who was to close the special nor her concern about going on first. The information that Loretta was about as funny as a blister was quite enough for him to cope with for the time being.

"Okay, Loretta. Stand there and do your act for me ten times," Mindy commanded.

Loretta performed her material until the occupant of the room next to them called and begged her to stop. In the taxi driving to Stars, Loretta silently rehearsed her act once more while Mindy silently rehearsed her lies about her imaginary husband Doug. No, not Doug. David. David sounded more intelligent. David was her childhood sweetheart with whom she had become reacquainted when she returned home to visit her father. He had proposed suddenly. Mindy fiddled with the cubic zirconia ring she had bought on the way back to the hotel. David wasn't in show business. He was normal. A doctor? A lawyer? No. Here, Mindy decided to invent a man who would be difficult to trace after the imaginary divorce she had planned for the near future. David's a marine biologist, she decided. Spends most of his time underwater. Mindy's father was not so much losing a daughter as gaining a marine mammal.

As they walked into the club, she took a deep pregnant, pre-lie breath.

As Loretta went to report in with Hank, Mindy approached Moe, still seated at his perennial place at the bar.

"Mindy! What the hell happened to you? Where have you been?"

"Busy," Mindy replied, pointing to her belly.

"I can see that!"

"Childhood sweetheart. A marine biologist," Mindy continued, a little too quickly.

"Congratulations!"

"Thanks."

Just then, Mindy heard a familiar voice admonish her from behind.

"A postcard? Something to let me know you were still alive?"

Mindy swiveled and saw an unsmiling Dan approaching.

"Dan. I'm sorry."

"Yeah, well, you should be. You just disappeared. Did you ever even think about your friends? That we might be worried about you?"

Mindy had not presumed her swift exit from the city would have any affect on other people.

"Sorry. I didn't think. I just had some personal things I had to take care of."

"You know, running away from your problems doesn't solve them. Can you tell I've been seeing a shrink?"

Mindy smiled. Dan smiled back.

"In fact, I'm so well adjusted I think I've already forgiven you." Dan bent forward and hugged Mindy awkwardly. "By the way, did you know you're pregnant?"

"Thank you. I've been made aware of that."

Mindy hated lying to Dan and tellingly slightly averted her eyes as she listened to herself recount the false fairy tale of marriage to her part man, part dolphin. What kind of friend was she? First she deserted Dan, then she deceived him. Mindy knew there was simply no alternative. The fact that Tommy Marsico was her baby's father was a secret kept firmly locked by Mindy inside a dark cage that resided beneath the trapdoor in the very bottom of her psyche.

"Do you hear from Penelope?" asked Mindy casually.

"She came through town about six weeks ago to have her hair cut, get her teeth cleaned, and visit her gynecologist. I can't imagine her in L.A. She's such a New Yorker. I can't wait to tell her I saw you."

"Could you not do that just yet?"

"Why?"

"Just because."

Mindy was saved from further explanation and introspection by her fellow comedians who, having heard she was in the bar, gathered around to welcome her back. To Mindy's enormous relief, their jealousy regarding her upcoming spot on HBO far outweighed their concern with her personal life.

"How did you get the special? How did you get an agent? Is your agent taking any new clients? Is he accepting tapes?"

These were the prying questions she should have prepared herself for, rather than any paternity queries. In the competitive world of comedy, Mindy was temporarily the envy of her colleagues. It was official. Mindy had become a senior statesperson in the club where she had started by checking coats.

By now Carmen and Sue had appeared in the bar area, flanked, as ever, by their people.

"We're just waiting for the boss," Hank explained to Mindy.

Mindy's eyes opened wide. "As if I'm not nervous enough, Bruce Springsteen is coming?"

"Rob Frasier. The HBO boss."

"Could you do me a big favor and never tell anyone I just said that?"

"Said what?" Hank smirked. "Ooh, there he is."

Rob Frasier was a hairy man with ironically very little hair. His overtaxed fleece had abandoned his upper summit some years ago to concentrate on covering his nether slopes. He marched into the club as though he already wanted to leave. A woman with hair as short as a freshly shaved schnauzer stood on one side of the HBO chief, and a man wearing a pageboy cut stood on his other. These two had perhaps confused beauty appointments and were now forced to face the world wearing each other's hairstyles. Carmen, Sue, and their commissioned representatives rushed toward the great white shark to plead their cases. Frasier raised an imperious arm, causing them to stop before they invaded his space.

"We'll talk later," he pronounced.

Frasier and his miscoiffed cohorts made their way to their reserved table in the showroom filling with actual ticket-buying customers.

"Can we get them on now?" Frasier requested. "I don't want to have to sit through a lot of shit."

"Of course," said schnauzer-head, scuttling away to get the show started prematurely.

Carmen was up first. Mindy was relieved to discover that Carmen portrayed characters, so their material would not tread on similar subjects. Carmen left the stage to enthusiastic applause while her manager, Harvey, visibly relieved, waited for her at the side of the room, his arms extended. Carmen collapsed into his bulky frame as he gave her a congratulatory hug.

"Great set. You nailed it," Mindy heard Harvey whisper conspiratorially in Carmen's ear.

Mindy was up next. As she ascended the stage, the familiarity of the setting immediately put her at ease. Mindy suddenly realized what an advantage choosing Stars as the tryout club had been. She had home-court advantage.

"I'm so glad I could be with you tonight," Mindy said. "I have to go home tomorrow. It's a family emergency. My parents are coming here."

Mindy approached her first joke with exactly the correct amount of sincerity and sneaked the punch line through the back door of the audience's expectation, thus surprising them into a rolling laugh.

A bleached-blond woman in the front row wearing red-rimmed glasses and a matching mouth found Mindy unbelievably funny. The more jokes Mindy told, the harder this woman laughed, infecting everyone around her.

"They're great. You'll have a blast," Mindy whispered to Loretta moments after her set. "There's a blond woman up front with a laugh so loud I want to tip her."

Loretta was already beginning to tense.

"I'm at the club in Miami," she told herself, as she stood at the side of the room, waiting for her introduction.

"And now, please welcome to the stage another star of tomorrow night's special . . . Loretta MacKenzie," Marty announced.

The applause died down, and there stood Loretta, as frozen as a TV dinner. Her hands choked the microphone stand as she looked down at the red-rimmed woman who had found her friend Mindy so hilarious. Loretta focused on the woman's wide smile and happy demeanor.

"What's your name? Right here in the front?" she asked.

"Shelley," the woman replied.

"Shelley," Loretta continued, "make sure you finish your drink. You know, there are comedy audiences in China who are completely sober."

Shelley's features rearranged themselves into a frown. "I'm an ex-alcoholic," she replied. "And this is just ginger ale. I no longer drink."

Loretta was off to a bad start. The members of the audience knew something had gone wrong, and they were beginning to feel embarrassed and worried. The Floridian attempted to win back their confidence.

"I've got kids. They don't need their own rooms. They're all very tiny. I sleep them in half an egg carton."

Mindy cringed. Loretta had forgotten to say "six." She had six kids. Half an egg carton. Six. That was the connection.

"I've never used a baby-sitting service. I'm an old-fashioned mom. I prefer shackles."

"That's so cruel," Mindy heard a member of the audience call out.

"Next," was the follow-up heckle.

Loretta left the stage prematurely, without even a "Thank you and good night."

Mindy followed a fraught Loretta through the bar and out onto the sidewalk in front of the club. Marty the emcee was enjoying a smoke outside. When he saw Loretta and realized the audience inside was staring at a bare stage, he quickly threw his cigarette down and streaked back inside faster than a grey-hound on fire.

"I don't know what happened," sobbed Loretta.

"It'll be okay."

"I was terrible."

"No, you weren't. You just got started on the wrong foot. They'll understand that."

When they returned, Sue was just completing her set. Five minutes later, Sue, Carmen, their handlers, Mindy, and Loretta all gathered at the far area of the bar to hear Rob Frasier's irre-vocable decision.

"Okay, this is what's gonna happen. Mindy Solomon closes the show."

They all stood in silence, attempting to process the wrench Rob Frasier had just thrown into their career paths.

"Then my client walks," Harriet, Sue's manager, threatened.

"Then she walks. We have time to find a replacement."

"Do we walk?" Harriet asked Sue.

Sue whispered something in Harriet's ear. Harriet reported back. "She doesn't walk as long as she doesn't open."

"She opens," Frasier stated.

Sue and Harriet conferred again.

"She doesn't walk as long as there's a warm-up act before she opens," Harriet announced.

"Fine. Carmen Herrera follows Sue Newton—"

"One second!" Harvey exclaimed, raising his arm in protest.

"That'll be fine," Carmen interrupted, lowering it.

"So I'm third?" said Loretta.

Rob Frasier paused. "Loretta, I'm going to do you a big favor. You're not ready to be on television yet. We'll look at you again for the next one. I'm sorry."

At first, Loretta could not take it in. "What? What are you saying?"

"We'll honor your fee."

"But I'm on the show. I'm booked to be on the show."

"I'm sorry."

As Loretta's non-waterproof mascara started the journey down her cheeks, Rob Frasier put his arm around her and took her to one side while Mindy looked on in sympathetic horror. Mindy knew the HBO executive was making the correct deci-sion. Loretta was a passable club comic, but her material would disintegrate under the scrutiny of TV cameras.

"These cable specials can be big opportunities. You're a great type and you have a strong presence. Don't blow it by not being ready. You have my word. Go back to Miami, and we'll find a spot for you in another special."

"But it's not fair," wailed Loretta. "I came all this way."

"It's business, Loretta," said Rob. "Believe me. I'm doing you a favor. Tell your agent to send us a tape when you have some more material."

Loretta had stopped listening. She was inconsolable.

"I have to go," announced Rob Frasier, looking at his wristwatch. "I'm late for drinks with Andrei Sakharov." And with that he turned and left.

Back in their room at the Plaza, Mindy tried to help her friend act rationally.

"It's one in the morning. We can't call Irv in the hospital."

"But it's not fair," Loretta wailed, pushing her belongings into her duffel bag.

"I know it's not fair. Lots of things aren't fair. There'll be another show. You heard him. It's not the end of the world," Mindy found herself saying.

"Not for you. You're closing."

"I had nothing to do with that decision. The guy liked me. Am I supposed to say, 'No, I won't do it?'"

"If you were really my friend, you would have said, 'I won't do the show unless Loretta does it too.'"

So there it was.

Mindy was suddenly in Ursula's position. Had she been this unreasonable in Los Angeles nine months ago? Mindy looked down at her belly. It was no use now: "Hi, Mitch. I still love you, but I'm pregnant with another man's child" was not something she could utter. *Well, you live and you learn,* thought Mindy. *Definitely a dyslexic way to go through life.*

"Loretta, what are you doing?" Mindy asked as her friend zipped up her luggage.

"I hate this place. I'm going out to the airport. There's an early flight," said Loretta.

"Loretta, stay and watch the show. It'll be good preparation for you. That way, you won't be so nervous next time."

Loretta slammed the door behind her. "Girls Just Wanna Have Fun" was filmed the following evening, with three girls wanting to have fun and one girl wanting to kill herself.

Santas and Mantras

M arc Mosley was getting fifteen percent of Ursula, but it was not the fifteen percent he wanted. He had always found Ursula attractive, and the higher she ascended in the Hollywood hierarchy, the stronger that attraction grew.

Dating a stunning woman in Los Angeles was a humdrum occurrence for someone like Marc Mosley. Extraordinary-looking women might be unusual in Peoria, but in L.A. they were everywhere. They were human weeds. Look to your left, and there was one in a Mustang. Look to your right, and another goddess roller-bladed past. Wasn't that your dream girl straight ahead jogging across the street? In fact, that was exactly how Marc had met his last girlfriend. He had honked and waved at Kiva from his convertible, and she had jumped right into his Mercedes 560SL on the corner of Melrose and Fairfax.

Ursula Duran was in a different class—an Aston Martin compared to a Corvette. Already a budding television star, Ursula was also independently wealthy, as well as the de facto daughter-in-law of a genuine Hollywood player. There was no arguing with it, Marc reasoned: Ursula Duran was prime casting for the part of his next girlfriend.

Cindy was not a hit, but neither was it a miss. It was a hiss. It narrowly won its time slot, achieving the same rating as the show it had replaced. That was enough for ABC to trumpet it a success in the trades and for those connected to the show to feel their cash cow would stay alive at least deep into the next season, if not further.

This was important to Marc Mosley. Ursula was now a guaranteed, sellable commodity for the next two or three years at least, which meant she was worthy of representation. Marc was careful about things like that. A manager sleeping with a client he no longer wanted to represent was like a jockey riding a dead horse. There was very little chance of a pretty finish.

Marc sped through a yellow traffic light on his way to Pacific Coast Highway. He was picking Ursula up at eight, and his fulfillment counselor's words were freshly chiseled on his mind: "You must live in the present, be conscious of the past, and not be more than thirty-five minutes late for the future."

Meanwhile in Malibu, as waves lapped leisurely against the broad wooden beams supporting Ursula's new house, Penelope coerced the zipper up the rear of her friend's Versace gown.

"Jesus, Ursula. This isn't a dress; it's a bandage. How do you breathe in this thing?"

"Marc picked it out. He says I can breathe after I'm more famous."

Penelope, who had been staying with Ursula, was not a Marc Mosley fan.

"I don't see him running around in a Speedo," she replied curtly.

Ursula, ignoring the remark, checked herself in the mirror for imperfections and found none.

"If you're coming to Mom's party, you'd better get ready."

"I *am* ready," Penelope insisted. "These clothes are clean."

"The invitation said 'black tie,'" Ursula reminded her friend.

"I'm a comedy writer. A renegade. And I've been sick. I can go to a party wearing a Hefty bag. Besides, I'm going with Zaundra, and everyone'll be looking at her anyway."

Penelope's date, whom she hoped might prove a potential

sex partner, was a multiply pierced young woman with a smoker's cough and a penchant for black leather. Penelope had met her when Zaundra had been visiting a relative in the hospital and had been instantly attracted.

It was 8:34 when Ursula's doorbell insisted someone answer it.

"You answer it," Ursula asked Penelope. "Tell him I'll be ten minutes."

"But you're ready," replied a confused Penelope.

"My mother taught me to always make them wait a little," Ursula responded with a smirk.

Penelope shook her head with incomprehension and left to answer the door. Ursula smiled as she thought of Eva's kooky, handed-down precepts of behavior toward the opposite sex. As crazy as her mother was, Ursula had to admit Eva had really landed on her feet, although *on her back* was probably the more appropriate phrase. Who could have imagined the woman who had shown up so bedraggled and lost in Ursula's room a few years ago was now a mogul's mistress presiding over a multi-million-dollar mansion? Ursula was both pleased and impressed by her mother's achievement. She had arrived in America pregnant and alone, with very little English, and, baby, look at her now. Wow.

Marc Mosley stood on the deck and gazed nervously out at the view. He disliked the sea. He disliked Malibu. He disliked that dyke writer Ursula let live with her. He had heard this entire area of exorbitantly priced real estate was just a sliver of land jutting out above the ocean. Submarines had apparently been able to sail directly beneath it. One good shake from an earthquake and billions of dollars could just drop into the sea. He shuddered at the thought. No doubt Ursula's pushy mother had talked her daughter into buying this place. Marc wondered again about the live-in writer. Maybe Ursula was into that scene. Hmmm. That could be fun.

"Sorry to keep you waiting," said Ursula, interrupting Marc's erotic reverie as she arrived down the stairs.

"Is that the dress I picked out for you?" Mosley asked, scrutinizing his client and future girlfriend.

"Yes."

"I thought I liked it."

Aside from the brief period in her life when she was living at the East Side Hotel for Women and had threatened to break free of her mother's clutches, Ursula continued to be attracted to destructive, dictatorial personalities. Tommy Marsico had been a carbon copy of Eva, first blaming his career demise on Ursula and then resenting her success. He had been followed by a pool guy who knew he was really a writer, who was followed by a surgeon who wanted to change the shape of Ursula's nose, who was followed by a professional tennis player who liked to paddle her ass with his racket. Ursula was stuck in a pattern of adverse familiarity. While most women were subconsciously looking for a man like their father, Ursula was subconsciously looking for a man like her mother. Marc Mosley was definitely in with a chance.

That is not to say Ursula's personality had not grown and expanded. It had. The experience of performing on television had undoubtedly improved Ursula's self-confidence. The reviewers of *Cindy* were, on the whole, kind to Ursula Duran, the cute ex-model turned sitcom actress, happy to point out all her apparent positives and equally content to ignore all her glaring negatives. Ursula deeply valued the opinions of these strangers who found her appealing. The fact that most of them were men simply did not occur to her. In her mind, this was the first time in her life she had been complimented about something other than the way she looked. Carefully clipping the reviews out of various papers and magazines and applying glue to only the outer corners in order to avoid any smudging, Ursula pasted the keepsake cutouts into an album, something she had never done with any of her modeling photographs.

The cause of Ursula's awkwardness was not the length of her arms and legs but rather the insecurity brought on by the feeling she had nothing to offer humanity other than her good looks. So as her self-esteem rose, her habit of knocking things over began to retreat in diametric balance.

Ursula was starting to worry that her alter ego's oft-demonstrated characteristic of klutziness was somehow demeaning. Feeling that both her character and the show should have more emotional depth, she had scheduled a meeting with the writers for the day after her mother's party. She intended to demand that future scripts concentrate more on the verbal and less on the physical.

Ursula's opinions about her character had joined a growing list of problems for Mitch. On the night of Eva and Leonard's party, alone in his Studio City apartment, he hung up his phone and dismantled the argumentative bow tie he had just succeeded in getting straight. His plan to attend the party had just been thwarted. The phone call had been from Perry Strauss. After viewing the eighth episode of *Cindy,* the network head had been vociferous in his opinion that Ursula's performances were regressing in quality.

"Beautiful girl goes boom-boom. That's comedy," explained Perry condescendingly. "Beautiful girl goes talk-talk. That's drama."

Perry went on to explain how he felt the season's remaining episodes should feature Meagan Nash, the sixteen-year-old actress playing Cindy's fourteen-year old sister to whom Perry had taken a shine. Meagan's smart-ass attitude and short shorts were testing better with the eighteen-to-thirty-four demographic than anything Ursula Duran was doing. The next three scripts would have to be torn apart and totally rewritten.

Mitch collapsed onto his bed and stared dizzily up at the ceiling. The overhead light appeared to yo-yo down toward his head, almost hitting him before retreating back up to the white stuccoed ceiling. Mitch closed his eyes. He opened them again. Now the light was stationary. Deep, purple circles had appeared beneath his eyes, and his formerly puckish cheeks now looked as though they had been hollowed out with an ice cream scooper. The admonition to be careful of what one wishes for certainly applied to Mitch Putnam. His overweening desire to make *Cindy* a hit and his readiness to twist his life and literary gift into pretzels all for the sake of the show were undoubtedly taking their toll.

The expensive, ambitious writers Mitch had hired with ABC's coin were no doubt eager to siphon part of the insanity onto their less-experienced comedic shoulders. However, Mitch knew that only Penelope's sensibility truly synchronized with his own, and she was only working part time now since her operation. Mitch also recognized the show had problems, or rather one problem, deep at its core. Accepting Ursula Duran as his lead had been a deal with the devil from the very beginning, and it had turned around and bitten him viciously in the ass. If only the network had liked Mindy Solomon.

His telephone rang. Mitch slowly rose from the bed and wandered into his office. Stopping in the doorway, he focused on the stacks of scripts surrounding his word processor. The trash can below his desk overflowed with different colored sheets of wrinkled paper, reminding him of the umpteen changes he had made to the *Cindy* scripts over the last few weeks. The telephone continued to ring, an electric drill boring a hole through his head. He tried to pick up the receiver, but his hand started to shake uncontrollably twelve inches away from the phone. He tried again. No luck.

"Hi, this is Mitch. I can't come to the phone right now. Leave a message, and I'll rewrite it and get back to you."

"Hello Mitch. Sidney Dole from Standards and Practices here. We have a problem with Ursula's misunderstanding of

Meagan's use of the word *pot* in this week's episode. Sorry, but we're going to have to insist you reshoot the scene tomorrow morning. Our sponsor has threatened to pull out, and with the show as fragile as it is, I'm sure you'll agree we don't need any negative publicity. I know what you're thinking, but we can't cut the scene. We need the time. Can you have the rewrite ready in the morning for our review? Thanks."

Mitch felt lightheaded. He braced himself with either arm in the doorway in an effort to stay vertical. Failing, he dropped to his knees.

The Christmas party was going to put a delightful exclamation point on Eva's fabulous year. When she looked back over 1986, she had no doubt as to its highlight. No, not the new house. Not the relationship with Leonard. The highlight was the unexpected phone call Eva had received over that summer.

"I didn't know how you'd feel about my calling," Brandon admitted.

"Don't be silly," said Eva, surveying her exquisite surroundings. "Come over to the house for tea."

Eva had spent a delicious afternoon rubbing her good fortune into her ex-lover's open-mouthed face.

"Leonard is a wonderful man. I couldn't be luckier. Moving west was the best decision I ever made. And I have you to thank for it. If it weren't for you, I would probably still be in Munich." Curling her legs up on the sofa, Eva noted with satisfaction that Brandon had not aged well. His wrinkles had matured into folds, and his suit, while sharp, sported a slight stain on the lapel.

"You do look fantastic," Brandon noted, wondering what she'd had done and whether he could afford it.

"Thank you," purred Eva. "I do Jane Fonda. With Jane. Are you still in advertising?"

"No. Personal management. That's why I wanted to see you."

"Uh-huh."

"I think our daughter should be a film star. She's—"

"Let me stop you there. I have nothing to do with the direction of Ursula's career, Brandon. I handle her money, but Marc Mosley is her day-to-day manager. Do you know Marc?"

"Only by reputation."

"As far as I know, she's very happy with Marc, but if the situation changes . . . Who else do you represent?"

"A couple of music acts. Three or four actors. The *Cosby Show*—"

"Bill Cosby?" said Eva. "I love him."

"Not Bill Cosby. I was going to say the *Cosby Show* has called about one of my actors."

"Oh."

"I just felt with Ursula, we could keep it in the family," said Brandon lamely.

"You know," said Eva, unable to resist. "If you'd married me all those years ago, we probably would have."

Eva had invited Brandon to the Christmas party but had not received a response. No doubt he couldn't handle her success. Revenge was more than sweet—it was positively diabetic, Eva concluded, as she stood alongside Henri, party planner to the stars, and watched refrigerator trucks dump snow all over her Pacific Palisades lawn.

"I think it needs a little more around the great oak," Eva suggested.

"Guys, yoohoo," Henri said, flailing. *"Grande* tree over there. More *nieve."*

As more last-minute snow was shoveled around the confused California oak, Eva turned back to look at the house. Twelve valet parkers, each attired in matching lederhosen, lined up in front of the fairy-lit mansion. "A Hollywood Winter in Heidelberg" was what Eva and Leonard's invitation promised, and Henri had not left a schnitzel unturned.

"Didn't Jeremy do a fabulous job?" Henri commented, referring to his lighting-designer boyfriend whom he had nepotistically subcontracted to decorate the house's exterior. "It's so *Sound of Music.*"

Inside the caterers were placing midget knockwurst into diminutive buns, topping each off with a pinch of sauerkraut and then placing them at uniform distances from each other onto polished silver trays. White-hatted cooks stirred potato dumplings that bobbed up and down in vats of fat. Leonard drifted into the kitchen, intending to grab a bottle of Evian but instead turning and exiting abruptly.

Leonard had at first queried, albeit mildly, his partner's choice of theme for their first public soiree, but in typical Eva fashion, she had remained adamant.

"I will not give one of those dull, piss-elegant parties that could be given by anyone," she insisted, stamping one of her Charles Jourdan–encased feet. "We need to establish ourselves in people's minds."

"Who are we? The Nazis? American Jews don't like German food. They like to drive German cars to Chinese restaurants."

Eva threw a punch at Leonard that fortunately missed most of him, then ran sobbing up to their three-thousand-square-foot bedroom suite. Leonard, realizing he had overstepped some sort of sarcasm boundary, followed her up the marble staircase. Actually, Eva was not that upset, merely experienced in getting her own way. Sure enough, Leonard quickly acquiesced to the Bavarian notion and concentrated instead on putting together the guest list to beat all guest lists.

A-list guests were not enough for Leonard. He had to put together an A+ list, consisting of a lethal people cocktail: current Hollywood royalty, a gaggle of legends, and a smattering of prominent politicians. Of course, Leonard understood his recent dismissal had deleteriously affected his position within the town and knew his party needed a hook, a gimmick, to ensure the maximum number of positive RSVPs. The day after the invitations were hand-delivered around town by snowmen wearing Ray-Bans, Leonard followed up each invitation with a phone call.

"I really hope you can come. I'd love you to meet Akira. Oh, didn't I tell you? He's staying with me for a few days. We're considering working together on something. I know. Can you believe it? Leonard Felk from Long Island producing an Akira Kurosawa flick."

Kurosawa was a magical name in Hollywood. The revered Japanese director did not make movies; he crafted masterpieces. *The Seventh Samurai, Rashomon,* and *Ran* were all tremendous pictures Leonard had been meaning to sit through. Kurosawa was a grade A, prime cut, top of the heap, living fucking legend, and Lenny Felk had him. The positive RSVPs flooded in.

Leonard looked at his Cartier tank watch—7:50, and the party was about to begin. Akira was upstairs getting dressed, his translator by his side. The roving accordion players stood in the foyer, awaiting the signal to begin their musical wander.

Henri had made the house look magical, no small feat, given what he had been given to work with. When she had moved in, Eva had not bothered with snobby decorators but instead had furnished her home herself in the style of one of the giant *schlosses* she had visited as a child on public holidays. As unacquainted with understatement as her ancestors, she had left few surfaces uncovered. Eight chandeliers hung from the floral painted ceiling. Eva liked chandeliers. Why have just one? She had continued this theme of repetition throughout the house. Discovering that a store on Robertson specializing in the medieval was going out of business, Eva had purchased five suits of armor at half price, scoring a sixth one free. These metallic offerings were duly scattered around the mansion.

Tonight, Henri had arranged for the suits of armor to be inhabited by live people who were told to begin slowly to move whenever approached by a partygoer. Henri had also installed a gypsy fortune-teller at one end of the living room, her wild eyes roaming, ready to lasso any important guests to whom she could explain she was really an actress in need of a break. At the other end of the room, a fireplace worthy of San Simeon housed a roaring blaze that roasted anyone who came too close.

Henri's most audacious party trick was the ice-skating rink. The French doors in the ballroom opened onto the Olympic-size pool. After a series of downright hazardous attempts involving a refrigeration unit and liquid nitrogen, the pool had finally been frozen over. The Manolis, a pairs skating team that had placed third in the nationals, spun, spiraled, and occasionally fell, all for the enjoyment of the party people nursing imported schnapps who looked on from the warmth and safety of the mansion's balconies.

About an hour into the evening, with whispers of "Where's Akira?" rippling through the house, the small, pleated Japanese director made an inscrutable entrance down the marble staircase. Guests applauded. Akira seemed embarrassed but appreciative of the deserved attention. Mingling among the enraptured crowd, he bowed and answered questions through his translator.

"Mr. Kurosawa, this is an honor."

"Mr. Kurosawa, it is such a privilege."

"Mr. Kurosawa, I'm blessed."

The lauded director was passed from admiring tongue to admiring tongue like a Japanese lollipop. Leonard and Eva hugged privately in the kitchen. It was two hours into the party, and not one guest had feigned an excuse to leave early. Their first team effort was an unqualified success.

Ursula, sitting next to Marc and enjoying her Schweinebraten dinner in the intimate dining room that sat eighty-six, suddenly thought she heard a skirmish occurring in the foyer.

"I'm late. Where is everybody? Is it over?" a male voice demanded.

"Wait here, sir. I'll find Mrs. Felk."

"You don't understand. I'm late. That's bad. Late's bad."

A disoriented Mitch appeared in the doorway of the dining room. He had awakened on his office floor, not remembering anything very much except the certainty that he was late for Ursula's mother's party. He had dressed quickly, sped over the hill and down Sunset, and now there he stood.

"I'm sorry I'm late," Mitch explained to the stunned onlookers.

Ursula and Penelope ran to his side.

"Mitch, come out in the hall," Penelope pleaded.

"Why? I'm here now."

"Mitch, you have to come with us," Ursula urged.

"No." Mitch shook off Ursula's grasp. "I'll just sit down and have dinner. I'm starving."

Ursula whispered into Mitch's ear. "Mitch, you have to come with me. You're . . . underdressed."

"What?" he demanded, affronted. He fingered his bow tie. It was definitely there. "What do you mean, 'underdressed'?"

"Mitch, you're not wearing any pants."

Mitch raised himself up to his maximum height. "Oh? I see. So now you want to rewrite my pants?"

The manic gleam in Mitch's eyes transfixed the room.

"Why not?" he continued. "Hey, let's rewrite my whole outfit. This jacket. Would you like it to be plaid? Maybe houndstooth? How about my shirt? Maybe a short-sleeved one would appeal better to a younger demographic?"

Mitch began ripping off his clothing and discarding it around the room. His jacket landed on a suit of armor. His tie landed on an ornate grandfather clock.

"You don't know what it's like," Mitch raved. "It's not enough that I have to write and write and write to please a million fuckers who can't do anything themselves. Now I can't even get dressed without somebody criticizing me. I can't take it anymore. Stop it. I just can't take it. You have to stop."

The unemployed actor in the suit of armor, who had been blinded when the jacket landed on his visor, started to lumber forward. Mitch looked up to see the armor moving toward him, an outstretched axe dangling dangerously from the chain-mailed left hand.

"Oh my God," screamed Mitch.

Just then the Bavarian accordionists rounded the corner playing "The German Clap Dance."

"No!" screamed Mitch. "No more . . . I can't take it . . . no more delusional visions!"

"Good evening. My name is Akira Kurosawa."

As the diminutive Japanese man extended a hand, the tormented screenwriter, wide-eyed with panic, collapsed in a naked heap.

Although many of the guests had caused nervous breakdowns in other people, few had ever witnessed one up close. The Heidelberg winter in Hollywood never really recovered its frivolous feel after paramedics placed the limp Mitch on the stretcher in the driveway. People began announcing the need to relieve their baby-sitters, early morning meetings were trotted out, and headaches began to race epidemically through the guest list.

Ursula and Penelope accompanied Mitch inside the ambulance, while Eva and Leonard were left alone with only Akira for company. Akira turned to Leonard and said in perfect English, "You owe me five hundred dollars."

"What? We agreed on three hundred for the night," Leonard objected.

"That's three hundred for impersonating Kurosawa and two hundred for the extra planting I'm going to have to do after this snow melts."

Leonard forked over five one-hundred-dollar bills. Given the party disaster, it seemed pointless to argue over two hundred dollars with his Japanese gardener.

Part IV

There's nothing worth the wear of winning,
But laughter and the love of friends.

—*Francis Bellamy*

And Baby Makes Two

The birth turned out to be relatively painless; it was only excruciating. Mindy abandoned her "natural" plan early into the experience and instead demanded a lobotomy. Luckily, her obstetrician knew she meant an epidural and duly administered one, together with a generous helping of Demerol. She might have wimped out by taking the drugs, but Mindy felt somewhat victorious defeating the need for forceps. Giant barbecue tongs floated around her nether regions, but their mere presence had acted as a pushing catalyst, and Rebecca popped out seconds before they were due to be used.

Rebecca Solomon came into the world on March 5, 1987, at 5:00 A.M., a pink baby, with a full head of thick black curly hair and a Roman nose just like her father's. Mindy had harbored hopes that her daughter would resemble her alone, but Rebecca was physically just as much a Marsico as a Solomon.

It didn't matter. Mindy was besotted. Her well-thumbed copy of *What to Expect When You're Expecting* had warned of postpartum blues, and Mindy had fully anticipated feeling ambivalent after the arrival of her accidental offspring. However, the clarity of the unconditional love she felt for this baby shocked her with its sharpness.

The experience made Mindy reevaluate her attitude toward her mother's death. She had always considered how devastating it had been for her to lose her mother; for the first time she contemplated how devastating it must have been for her mother to know she was going to lose Mindy. She also recognized how two people as deeply bound to each other as a mother and her daughter are never really separated, even by death. After Rebecca's birth, Mindy felt her mother's spirit more than ever before, and she became determined to pass on to her daughter the same quality of love she herself had received as a child.

Mindy enjoyed the hospital. She accepted that the hospital staff knew much more about babies than she did and so was perfectly happy to see Rebecca at regular intervals for feeding or cooing over. The remainder of the time she rested, secure in the knowledge that her loved one was receiving excellent, professional care. The first moment of terror came when she left and was standing outside the hospital with her father. Rebecca lay in her arms, and Mindy realized it was now her sole responsibility to keep this child alive. Arriving home, she gingerly placed her daughter in the room where she herself had grown up. During her last few weeks of pregnancy, Mindy had sewn a tiny, pink rose out of satin ribbon, and it now hung on the end of the crib, a symbol of Solomon continuity.

The first few weeks were madness. It was all Mindy could do to take a shower each day. Some days she never even got out of her bathrobe. However, slowly a schedule emerged. Mindy learned to nap when Rebecca napped. She and her father had their diaper regimen down to an army exercise.

When three-month-old Rebecca first lifted her torso with her arms while lying on her tummy, Mindy rushed for the camera and shot three rolls of film. When Rebecca first learned to swipe at her mobile to make it move, Mindy shot two more. Rebecca would have been the perfect baby, if only she would just stop crying. In her first three months of life, Rebecca Solomon stopped screaming only to nap, eat, and poop.

One night, Mindy dreamed of a cat being tortured. The pliers tightened around the cat's tail, causing the feline shrieks to intensify until they became unbearable. Mindy opened her eyes and reentered consciousness, or at least her new version of it. Across the room, Rebecca wailed hysterically at full car-alarm volume.

Mindy squinted at her illuminated alarm clock: 3:43. Surely Rebecca couldn't be hungry? Her last feeding had been twenty minutes ago, and Mindy had changed her then too. Should she go pick her up or should she take a stand?

"Pick her up," her father always commanded. "Your mother picked you up."

"If you pick her up once, she'll expect it and cry every night," Loretta had warned.

Mindy and Loretta had made up. The moment Mindy had returned from New York, Loretta had phoned and apologized for her overreaction.

"I know it wasn't your fault. I just needed to blame someone, and you were there."

Mindy was ashamed. Loretta was obviously a more mature human being than she was. Loretta knew better than to let a capricious career swing adversely affect a relationship.

So far, Loretta's prediction had been entirely accurate. Mindy had nightly given in to Rebecca's needs and was now unable to break the pattern. Surely it was impossible for someone so young, sweet, and helpless to be cunning enough to manipulate her own mother. Then how come Mindy felt manipulated as she lifted herself wearily out of bed and stumbled over to pick up her infant? Rebecca continued the wailing for a little while longer so as to register a complaint at the length of time it had taken to address her needs. Mindy rocked her baby in her arms and sang the lullaby her mother had sung to her when she was a child. Gradually the tears subsided.

Hush, little baby, don't say a word;
Mama's going to buy you a mockingbird.

And if that mockingbird don't sing,
Mama's going to buy you a diamond ring.
Ahwohwohwohwoh.

Mindy's father shuffled into the room to check on his girls
and to add an off-key harmony to the chorus. Hal was Rebecca's
baby slave. When Mindy was an infant, he had been too busy
traveling and earning a living to become fully involved with his
daughter's day-to-day care. His granddaughter was a completely different story. He was never happier than in those early
months, sitting in the den with Rebecca resting in his arms,
watching Jim Bakker's fall from grace unravel on his TV set.

Her father's rapture with his grandchild allowed Mindy a few
hours each week to visit the Comedy Outlet. She did not want
to be rusty when the HBO special began airing on television.
She had no idea whether opportunity might knock again, but if
it did, she wanted to be ready. The special's first showing would
be in June, and Irv had already heard that the advance word on
her performance was pretty positive.

Somehow, Rebecca knew not to cry between the hours of
9:00 and 10:00 on the evening of June 24. She was not even
sleeping but was staring up at her bunny mobile and giggling the
entire time her mother was on television telling jokes. Mindy
and her father sat on the twin recliners in the den and watched
the special together. Sue and Carmen did well, but Mindy was
the highlight. It was almost as nerve-racking for Mindy to watch
her performance as it had been for her to perform in the first
place. Even though she was aware that the audience reaction
had already been recorded and the jokes could not be reevaluated, she cringed in anticipation of each punch line's falling flat.
When the credits rolled, Mindy heaved a sigh of relief. Her
father heaved along with her.

"Why are *you* heaving?" Mindy asked.

"It's tough. I worry. You're my daughter; I want you to be
good."

"It was okay, wasn't it?" Mindy asked hesitantly, wanting a compliment.

Hal wiped his glasses with his handkerchief. "You know, honey, when you were a little girl, I could have predicted you would have been a lot of things. But that, never. That's totally out of left field. Congratulations. You were great."

Hal emptied the last drop of champagne into Mindy's glass.

"To you and to my granddaughter. Every father should be so lucky."

In the days after the special aired, Irv's phone began to ring with job offers. Mindy knew she was to about to face the ultimate single-mother dilemma. Hal volunteered to stay home with the baby and play nanny or, as he referred to himself, "manny." Mindy was grateful but turned him down. Rebecca was her priority now, not her career. When the offer came in to headline a club in Atlanta for a week, Mindy said no. The club increased the offer. She again refused. The club doubled the original offer, and Mindy, faced with the prospect of living for the rest of her daughter's formative years off her father's charity, wrestled with her conscience.

Finally Mindy rationalized that in the comedy business the demands on your time are exclusively at night. So why, then, did she have to leave her child behind? She accepted the job, phoned a service that specialized in qualified nannies, and began the interviewing process. Much to her father's alarm, Mindy chose a gay man or, as Hal referred to Brett, a "ganny."

Brett was an angular man in his early thirties with a pencil-thin nose, a pointed chin, and streaked blond highlights. His qualifications were exceptional. He had been a male nurse but had quit.

"I couldn't take it. People would die constantly. It was so depressing," he told Mindy, his hazel eyes welling up with tears. "I want to be around life."

When he picked Rebecca up, she smiled up at him and gave Brett her toothless stamp of approval.

Mindy's appearance at Just Kidding, Atlanta's premier comedy club, marked a sea change in her professional career. No longer was Mindy performing to people who happened to be at a comedy club that evening. Most of this audience consisted of people who had seen Mindy on television and now wanted to see her live. The reactions to her jokes were heightened by the recognition factor, as was the applause when she left the stage—and the check at the end of her engagement.

Another club had called Irv with a matching offer immediately following Atlanta, so the curious threesome flew off to the Funny Farm in Cincinnati. Mindy had never imagined herself as the mother of the screaming child on the plane, but there she was, covered in embarrassment and drool.

Hal phoned Mindy in Cincinnati with a message.

"Somebody named Penelope called," he said, trying to decipher the note he had made on the back of a magazine. "Is she the writer you told me about that took the job in California?"

"Maybe," said Mindy, anticipating her father's reaction.

"Don't call her."

"Did she say what she wanted?"

"No. Just forget about her. She doesn't exist. I'll throw away her number."

"No," Mindy said, grabbing a pen. "Give it to me."

Mindy could now recognize she had an unhealthy habit of cutting people out of her life without the possibility of reconciliation. The source of this characteristic had become clearly apparent to her since moving back home and witnessing her father's misanthropic behavior from an adult perspective. Mindy picked up the phone and dialed the L.A. number. A strange voice answered the phone.

"Cedars Sinai Hospital."

A hospital? What was Penelope doing in a hospital?

"Penelope Wexler, please."

"I'll ring her room and see if she's back yet."

The call was transferred and then picked up.

"Hello?" said Penelope.

Mindy hesitated.

"Hello?" Penelope repeated.

Still, Mindy failed to speak.

"I can't believe I'm getting a crank call in a hospital room. Whoever you are . . . have you no shame? I'm hanging up now."

"Penelope, it's me. Mindy."

"Mindy! It's Mindy! Oh, I'm so glad you called back. I wasn't sure if you would."

"What are you doing in a hospital?"

"Ehhhh, nothing," said Penelope dismissively. "I had a little bit of cancer."

Mindy could not believe what she was hearing. "What?!"

"It's okay. They got it all."

Mindy sat down heavily on her hotel room bed, completely shocked. "What happened?" she asked. "Tell me everything."

"It's very boring. I'll give you the abbreviated version. I had these incredible stomach pains and I knew something was weird. I went to my gyno back east, and it was hysterectomy time. Ovaries overboard. Luckily, I'm a lesbian who doesn't like children. This time I'm just in for some follow-up tests. No biggie."

"This is unbelievable. Do they know what caused it?"

"Well, my surgeon isn't sure, but he thinks it had something to do with my fighting with you."

"You're kidding?"

"Yes, I'm kidding. Jeez, you're still so gullible."

"You shouldn't joke about things like that," admonished Mindy.

"Why?" asked Penelope. "I'll get cancer? Too late."

Mindy laughed at her friend's gallows humor, realizing how much she had missed her.

"Enough about me," continued Penelope. "So I watched your HBO special. When are you due?"

"I filmed that in January. Rebecca's almost four months."

Now it was Penelope's turn to be shocked.

"You're kidding? You've *had* it? It's taken me almost two weeks to get used to your being married and pregnant. So what's its name?"

"Her name's Rebecca."

"Wow. Is she funny?"

"Very. She's here now, making faces and waving a plastic hammer."

"She's doing Gallagher's act? Does he know?"

"God, it's so good to hear your voice," said Mindy, meaning it. "I'm so sorry about the way I behaved. I think I had a point being angry, but I should have come around. I shouldn't have let it nuke our friendship."

"Hey, I didn't behave like Mother Teresa either, but I thought you'd get over it and everything would go back to normal."

"Yeah, well, I was a jerk. I overreacted."

"Yeah, well, I had cancer. It puts things in perspective. The minute I saw you on that special, I knew I had to try to talk to you again. I don't have a lot of friends, and you were a big one, Mindy. By the way, you weren't easy to find. Until you showed up on TV, it was like looking for a Nazi war criminal."

"How did you get my dad's number?"

"HBO gave it to me. I told them I had cancer, and they gave it to me. Cancer is very empowering. You just mention it, and people do what you want. Incidentally, your dad answers the phone like a parole officer."

"I know. You're sure you're all right now?"

"I'm fine. I'm just in this joint for a few tests and for the Jell-O."

"I hope they're not written tests, because I know you, and I know you didn't study."

"I really missed talking to you, Mindy."

"I missed you too."

The two women chatted for over an hour, Mindy asking all

the questions that had been floating around in her head for well over a year. Penelope was a fountain of information, and Mindy was a pile of superabsorbent paper towels. The item, of course, that floored Mindy was the news that Mitch had suffered a nervous breakdown and left the show.

"Where is he?"

"I heard he's in Italy somewhere."

"Really? Is he seeing someone?" Mindy could not resist the inquiry.

"What do you care? You're married to a big-shot marine biologist."

"It's not that I care. I just wondered."

"Sure. Well, he wasn't with anyone when he was here. The only thing fucking him in Hollywood was the network. But now, who knows? A neurotic comedy writer let loose among all those Italian girls? He could come back with a Coppola."

As sorry as she was to hear about Mitch's breakdown, Mindy felt vexed knowing he had not seen her triumphant television appearance. Plus, if she was being perfectly honest, she had to admit that a little glee at his failure was mixed in with her concern.

"How's Ursula?"

"Fine. Still N.F."

"I know. I've see the show."

"I can't say anything bad about her. She's been great to me. Took care of me after my operation. Let me stay with her all during my chemo. Oh, wait a second. I *can* say something bad about her. She still has terrible taste in men. She's seeing yet another asshole who tells her what to do and what to wear. Some things never change. Let me give you her number. I know she'd want to talk to you."

"Gee, Penelope. I'm not sure. It's all so complicated," said Mindy, looking over at Rebecca, who had just fallen asleep in her baby seat.

"Why?"

"I can't really explain. Okay, give me the number anyway."

"Five-five-five, sixty-oh-nine-two. Same area code as the hospital. It's my number too, until I move someplace on my own."

"Let's keep in touch," suggested Mindy.

"Absolutely."

"It was so great to talk to you."

"I know. I'm a little less cranky now that I don't get my period. Call Ursula. I really want you two to be friends again. Cancer."

"I'll come out there and see you when Rebecca's a little older."

"That'd be great."

"You're sure you're okay?"

"I'm fine."

"You take care of yourself, you hear?"

"Cancer," Penelope sang as Mindy replaced the receiver.

She would definitely go out to California in a few months, Mindy resolved. She would ask Irv to book her into one of those clubs on the shore.

"Sure, kid, whatever. The *Letterman* show wants you back, by the way. And there's a new show filming in New York. *Comedy Tonight.* You can knock them off both at once."

Mindy was visiting Irv in the assisted-care facility to which he had moved since his health had further deteriorated.

"I press a buzzer by my bed, and they come running and ask me what I want. I tell them, and they bring it to me. It's good. I feel like a very old king."

Mindy laughed.

"Sit down, kid. I need to talk to you."

Mindy sat, nervous about what might be coming.

"I'm too old to do this anymore, kid—"

"Don't be silly," interrupted Mindy.

"Hey, listen to Uncle Irving. He knows best. I had a talk with a hot young agent at ICM, William Richardson or Richard Williamson, one of those. Son of an old friend of mine, or maybe a grandson, or is it a son-in-law? Anyway, he's some-body's son, and he's expecting your call."

Mindy knew Irv was right, but it did not make the parting any less painful.

"Move back to New York, kid. It's time. You got hurt. You recovered. Now get back in the game."

"I can't, Irv. Rebecca—"

"What did you want to do the most when you were a kid liv-ing in Miami?" the old agent said, interrupting.

"Move to New York."

"Exactly. Florida's for old people. Bring the kid up in Manhattan."

Brett, who had been a cheerleader in college, literally leaped at the chance to move north.

"It's my dream," he exclaimed, touching his hand to his heart.

And so, on her trip to Manhattan to tape the two television appearances, Mindy rented a large, run-down, three-bedroom apartment at West End Avenue and 89th Street and signed with Richard Williamson at International Creative Management.

Having reconnected so strongly with her father, she now felt as if she was deserting him. She begged him to come with them.

"You like being different. You can be the only person who retired and moved *out* of Miami!" Mindy urged.

"I've lived in this house for forty years. That's not exactly a day. I'll visit, but only in the summer. You be careful with my granddaughter," Hal warned, shaking hands with Brett in an overly masculine fashion. He looked back at Mindy. His eyes grew red. "Remember honey, you can come home whenever you want. You can change your mind. Please be careful."

Mindy thought back to the first time she had left home nine

years before and remembered how her father had given the exact same speech. Somebody who was always there for her no matter what—that's what her father was for her. That's what she would always be for Rebecca.

"Thanks, Dad. Thanks for everything," Mindy said, hugging him.

Hal leaned down to Rebecca in her stroller.

"You take care of your mother. She's going to be a famous comedian."

Brett turned out to be more than just a nurse. On Mindy's meager budget he scoured the junk stores on Eighth Avenue for secondhand furniture and eclectic antiques and decorated the apartment better than Mindy could ever have thought possible. Rebecca made some friends in a play group in the park.

Mindy's new agent kept her busy with one-nighters as well as her first gig in Atlantic City, opening for Julio Iglesias. Hal made the trip up for the prestigious appearance, sitting in the front row in a group of Spanish women driven to the point of sexual frenzy.

"That's my daughter," he said proudly.

"Get her off. We want Julio," the women replied.

The one show Mindy was never able to get was NBC's prestigious *Tonight Show*. She auditioned twice at *Stars* for the show's comedy talent booker. He had passed on her both times. Charlie Moon felt Johnny would not appreciate her.

"Can you tell me something I should work on?" Mindy asked politely.

Charlie rubbed his receding chin and took another sip of his Scotch and soda.

"Maybe you should do more funny things in a row. And not do so many jokes about men. Do more jokes about women. Johnny likes jokes about women."

The third time Mindy auditioned for Charlie, she did more jokes about women.

"I still don't think you're right for the show," Charlie decided. "The jokes are better, but your timing! Johnny doesn't like that kind of timing. Work on your timing."

Mindy was hoping to get a booking, not only to benefit her career but also to use as an opportunity to visit Penelope. The two reacquainted friends had spoken once when Mindy was still in Florida, when Penelope had called to discuss baby Jessica down the well shaft. Mindy had tried to phone California a few times since the New York move but had always gotten an answering machine containing Ursula's voice. Mindy had a mental block about leaving a message and her new number. Ursula might call her, and that would open up that whole can of wriggling, emotional worms. Ursula had been on the *Tonight Show* twice, Mindy noted wryly. First guest both times.

Hal phoned one day just before Christmas to check on the sniffles Rebecca had caught at her play group.

"By the way, a friend of your friend Penelope called. Do you want the number?"

"Was it Ursula?"

"No. I know Ursula. It was someone named Zondie. Or Zoundy. Something like that."

Mindy knew something was wrong. Why would a friend of Penelope's call? Why wouldn't Penelope call? Mindy dialed the number.

"Hi," a strange, raspy voice answered.

"Hi. This is Mindy Solomon, returning your call."

"Oh, yeah. Listen, I'm Zaundra. I was a friend of Penelope Wexler's."

Was. That one word confirmed everything Mindy had been dreading. *Was.*

"We thought you'd want to know," the voice continued matter-of-factly. "Penelope died yesterday. . . . Hello, are you there?"

"Yes," said Mindy. "I'm here. I . . . I . . . thought she was okay."

Everything had suddenly taken on air of unreality. Surely this could not be happening.

"Oh no. She was in terrible shape. You know, they never got it all in the first place."

"I didn't know. She didn't tell me."

"They found a tumor the size of an orange. And it had spread so far."

Mindy felt her lower lip buckle. Her friend Penelope was gone, just like her mother.

"She tried everything. She had a stem-cell replacement treatment. The doctors thought it would work. Just made her sicker."

"But she said she was fine," sobbed Mindy. "She said they'd got it all and she was fine."

Zaundra caught Mindy's tears and began crying herself. Going through Penelope's address book was proving to be a tough job.

"Shit, here I go again," Zaundra said grabbing another Kleenex. "She never believed she was going to die. Right up until the end. Ursula and I were both there with her. Penny wanted to say something, and I bent down, and she asked me if I'd sneak her in a chocolate milk shake tomorrow. Today, I mean. Oh God!"

Mindy attempted to stop crying. "I'm sorry I wasn't there. If I'd known, I would have been."

"We know. We know you would. Look, Ursula's having a kind of memorial service for her on Tuesday. It's not a funeral or anything. Penelope's parents took her body back to Toledo."

"Toledo? I didn't know Penelope was from Toledo."

"Nobody did. Her parents never even knew she was gay. You know Penelope. She compartmentalized. Anyway, can you make it?"

Denial, grief, and then ultimately acceptance; those were the three stages a person went through upon losing a loved one. Mindy remembered reading that in a book once and recalled relaying the thought to Penelope. Her friend had considered the remark, then replied, "Denial, grief, and then ultimately acceptance . . . those are the three stages I go through whenever I get a haircut."

Remembering this, Mindy laughed aloud on the plane on the way to Los Angeles. Other passengers turned and looked at her, and she smiled unapologetically. It was impossible to think of Penelope and not recall something funny she had said. What a facility she had possessed for turning the ordinary into something unique. And now it was gone forever. Mindy thought of her last flight out to Hollywood, seated in first class with Penelope next to her in her khaki pants and jeans jacket, her feet up inappropriately on the seat in front of her.

"I don't believe in heaven and hell, but I do believe in first class and coach," Penelope had said to Mindy somewhere over the Midwest.

If there was an afterlife, Mindy had no doubt Penelope was making herself comfortable, her feet up on whatever furniture heaven's decorator had considered appropriate.

If only Mindy had known what Penelope was really going through when she had phoned, she would have flown out to help. Too late for that. What could Mindy do for Penelope now? Her final request had been for Mindy and Ursula to reignite their relationship. That was what Mindy had to do, in memory of her friend. Driving up Pacific Coast Highway from the airport, she rehearsed the speech she would have to make to Ursula.

"I slept with him once. It meant nothing to me and even less to him, and out of it came the most precious little girl."

Mindy handed the valet parker the key to her rented Ford Escort, then walked through the open gate at the side of the house and into the side door. She quickly scanned the guests milling about the oak-beamed living room in search of the beautiful blonde.

No Ursula yet. Instead she found unfamiliar faces, chattering to one another as if at a cocktail party. Only the muted volume and wilted facial expressions betrayed the sad circumstance that brought them all together. It was an eclectic group drawn from the various corners of Penelope's life that she had clearly felt the need to keep separate. There was the TV showbiz contingent, the comedy club showbiz contingent, the heterosexual contingent, the gay male contingent, and the gay female contingent.

Mindy wandered out onto the deck to gaze at the ocean, appropriately gray as though in mourning too. A couple stood alone on the deck, holding glasses of white wine and gazing into the distance. The man turned, and his somber face broke into a wide smile.

"Mindy," said Dan. The wine poured out of the glass Dan held in his right hand as he hugged his old friend.

"Dan, it's so good to see you," said Mindy enthusiastically. "I thought you were on the road somewhere."

"No. I sold a movie script. I'm out here now."

Mindy looked Dan over. He looked wealthier and older. He introduced the young woman at his side.

"This is Dinah. She's a comedian too."

"Hi," Dinah drawled in a southern accent. "Ah'm juhst new at it. Ah've seen yew though on television, and yew're soo funny."

"Thank you. That's nice of you. You knew Penelope?"

"No, Ah didn't. But Dayen told me he was comin' to the service and Penelope was a comedian too, and Ah thought Ah should. Oh look, Dayen, yew spilled yer wiyne. Ah'll git yew some more."

Dinah took Dan's glass and vanished back into the palatial living room. Mindy smiled at Dan.

"Good to see you again. That's so great about the script."

"I think Penelope would have approved of my bringing a date," said Dan. "She knew how hard it was for me to get one."

"I can't believe it, can you?" Mindy said wistfully.

"That I got a date?"

"No, stupid. Penelope."

"I know. Have you seen Ursula?"

"Not yet."

"She's right over there."

Dan pointed into the room. Mindy turned to see the back of a tall, slim blonde with bare feet wearing a black, flowing, gauze sundress. As if feeling Mindy's stare, Ursula slowly turned and met her friend's tensely smiling face. Ursula immediately excused herself from the group of people she was talking to and moved toward Mindy. Aside from her California tan, she was exactly the way Mindy remembered her.

"It's good you came."

"I should have come sooner. I didn't know."

The two women hugged.

"You look great, Mindy."

"So do you."

"We have to talk, but not now. Stay here tonight. I've got the guest room all ready for you."

"Well, I . . ." began Mindy, searching for an excuse.

A caterer tapped Ursula on the shoulder. "Miss Ursula, emergency in the kitchen. Bad shrimp."

"I'll just be a second," said Ursula, turning back to Mindy and looking beseechingly at her.

"I'd love to stay," lied Mindy. "You go and discipline the shrimp."

As Ursula retreated to the kitchen, Mindy spotted Alvin, the skinny comedian from Stars whom she remembered being one of the first of the bunch to move out west.

"Alvin, how are you?"

"I'm on *Out of the Blue,*" he replied, referring to a new sitcom that had just begun airing. "I'm testing very well. Michael J. Fox, in the *Family Ties* pilot, scored a twenty-eight. In our pilot, I got a forty."

"That's not really what I meant."

"Oh, you mean how am I personally? My analyst says I'm fine."

Mindy smiled. Comedians. Just then, Ursula put *Beatles for Sale* on the stereo at low volume. Mindy recognized it as Penelope's favorite album.

"I thought we might go out on the deck," announced Ursula. "And anyone who wants to tell a story about Penelope can just get up and tell it."

They all shuffled out awkwardly and stood overlooking the ocean. Dan spoke first.

"I was over at Penelope's apartment one day. . . . We were trying to write sketches, which eventually would be rejected by everyone, and, may I say, we were very successful at that particular endeavor . . . when she mentioned there had been a rash of burglaries in her building. People were putting bars on their windows. She said that was too expensive. She'd bought a jar of axle grease. 'I'm just going to cover my window sill with this,' she said. 'Since this is the sixth floor, when the burglar tries to climb in my window, he'll just fall to his death.' I said, 'Do you think you want to hear someone scream his lungs out and fall to his death from your window in the middle of the night?' She put the jar away and said, 'You know, you're right. That'll wake me up.'"

Zaundra stepped forward next. "I first met Penelope when I was visiting my sister in the hospital after she had to have her stomach pumped . . . again. And Penny . . . she said I was the only one she let shorten her name because she always hated being compared to the least valuable coin on earth . . . anyway, she was just leaving after a treatment, and I had just shaved my head that morning because my hair was just wretched. She was bald because of the chemo, and we just looked at each other, and Penny said, 'Chemo?' and I said, 'No, razor.' And she said, 'I've tried both, and I recommend chemo. It keeps your head smoother longer.' . . . It's not fair. She was the only woman I ever really loved." Zaundra sobbed and ran into the arms of a comforting Ursula.

A well-dressed woman of about thirty-five who appeared far more conservative than the rest of the group in the room intro-duced herself. "I don't know most of you here today, but I'm Julia Burnhard, Penelope's doctor. I've never been to a service like this, but when Ursula told me about it, I had to come." The woman's voice caught slightly in the back of her throat. "I just wanted to tell you all that . . . that I really, really did my best." She struggled to continue as she looked around at the collection of people staring at her. "I feel I let you all down."

A chorus of sympathetic denials reached out to her as she blew her nose loudly on a tissue.

"Everyone knew how funny Penelope was. But she was really, really brave as well, and I wanted to come here to tell you all that. I've never had a patient who wanted to live more than she did. I did everything I could, and doctors aren't supposed to say this, but I'm so sorry I couldn't save her. She was really spe-cial. And I feel really, really shitty that I couldn't do more. That's all."

Mindy felt for the woman. She must have been only about ten years older than Mindy and yet had responsibility for other people's lives resting on her shoulders. As she passed by, Mindy grabbed the stranger's arm and squeezed it sympathetically. The woman attempted a smile and moved on as Ursula began speak-ing from where she stood, trying to lighten the mood.

"I loved Penelope, but she wasn't the easiest cancer house-guest in the world. I invited her to stay with me after her opera-tion. I put flowers in her room, and I said good night and turned out the lights. I'm in bed and I hear, 'Ursula? Come here, I have to ask you something.' I get up and I go into her room and she says, 'Ursula, this room is so noisy. Is there any way you can stop that ocean?'"

Everyone laughed, recognizing the truth of the anecdote.

"And I know a lot of you weren't aware of just how sick she was and you're feeling guilty that you didn't do more, but don't. She didn't want you to know. She told me the one thing she hated more than anything else was people staring at her like she was going to die. And she never thought she would. I came home one day last week and she was lying in bed, too weak to move. She could barely open her eyes. I had her paycheck from the show and she asked me to open it. I did, and I showed it to her, and she said, 'Next year I renegotiate.'"

Marc Mosley had decided to attend the service not for Penelope, but for Ursula, his girlfriend. Stepping forward and telling a story was a risk, but his new psychiatrist had encouraged risk, so Marc stepped forward.

"Penelope was the most honest woman I've ever met. If she didn't like you, she let you know it. She didn't like me. Whenever she'd answer the phone, I'd say, 'Hi, Penelope,' and she'd say, 'I don't like you.'"

Marc stepped back. That was the end of his story. He thought it had gone well. Mindy moved to the front of the crowd.

"Hi. I'm Mindy Solomon from New York, and I was Penelope's writing partner when we were at Stars together. One day, we were sitting in my apartment and she was eating a muffin. She was the sloppiest eater. The amount of food she left around her always exceeded the amount she actually got in her mouth. We couldn't think of anything funny, and we sat there in total silence for—I don't know—it seemed like forever, and finally she looked at me and said, 'Mindy, how do Japanese people know when their babies start to talk?' And we must've laughed for an hour. There'll never be anyone who could think of things like that again, and if she were here today, she'd be in the living room watching football because, as Ursula mentioned, she hated the ocean, or, as she called it, the fish toilet. And I just want to say Penelope, wherever you are, I'll always miss you. You left the party way too early."

The group on the deck dabbed and sniffed their way through numerous tissues as each person related their personal Penelope story. As the sun began to dip below the horizon, the mourners threw flowers into the rising ocean in memory of their friend.

After the last few stragglers headed home, Mindy and Ursula sat on the deck with their feet up on the railing, finishing the leftover hors d'oeuvres and wine.

"The good thing about being the hostess is you don't have to drive home. Let's get drunk," said Ursula, filling Mindy's glass. "I cannot believe you're a mommy."

"Well, not just a mommy . . ."

"No. Of course not. I didn't say 'just,' did I?"

"No," admitted Mindy.

"Well, then. Don't get defensive. I watched your special. It was really great."

"Thank you."

"Made me think back to your telling all those jokes into a broom."

Mindy decided to plunge into an apology. "Ursula, I'm so sorry. I behaved like a complete idiot over that television show. It all seems so stupid now, but at the time it was the biggest thing in the world to me."

"I'm sorry too," said Ursula, relieved that her friend took the initiative. "I knew how much it meant to you. I didn't even want to take the job, but after I left all those messages for you and you didn't even call me back, I thought, *Why not?*"

"Messages?"

"We thought you'd call at least one of us back. Mitch was really upset."

"What messages? I didn't get any messages."

"Oh, c'mon, Mindy. Between us, we must have left about twenty."

Mindy thought back to her return from L.A., remembering

that her answering machine had been stolen from her apartment.

"Ursula, when I got back from that nightmare trip, I'd been robbed. I never got any of those messages."

Ursula was not sure whether to believe Mindy but decided to give her the benefit of the doubt. "You know, the important thing is, it's over now. I knew we'd get together again, and so did Penelope."

"You're right," said Mindy, not sure whether Ursula believed her about the robbery. "Penelope's death puts everything into perspective. It's nuts to ruin a friendship over a silly television show."

Ursula slowly poured herself another glass of wine. "Well, I don't think it's a *silly* show."

"No, I didn't mean that. I meant a silly circumstance concerning a show," Mindy added quickly.

"Have you seen *Cindy*?" asked Ursula casually.

Cindy. Even hearing the title made Mindy's nostrils flare involuntarily.

"Uh-huh. I've seen it a few times. Not every week. I'm kind of busy, between Rebecca and my career, but yes, it's good," lied Mindy.

"Well, it's getting better, I think. It took me some time to feel comfortable with the comedy, but now that we're in our second season, I think it's coming along."

"I'll try to watch it again next week."

An awkward silence descended. Ursula decided to break it.

"So tell me about your husband. You haven't even mentioned him. What's he like?"

Mindy knew that this was the point at which she should reveal the truth. "Oh, I guess you haven't heard. We're separated." Knowing and doing. Two very different things.

"Separated? For good?"

"Yup."

"Oh, Mindy, I'm so sorry. What happened?"

"Oh, you know. Those childhood sweetheart things sound great, but they never work out. He wanted me to move to Alaska. He was doing some research, and I didn't think the Comedy Igloo was a good next career move, so I moved back to New York with Rebecca."

Mindy was now completely embroiled in her fricassee of lies.

"But your daughter. Surely . . . ?"

"He sees her in the summer. It's better this way, really."

"Wow. Who'd have thunk it? We're both divorcees before thirty! I would expect it of me, but not of you! Not Miss Goody Two-Shoes."

Mindy felt defensive. Ursula had always said things like that to her in the past, and Mindy had always laughed. Why was she offended now?

"I'm not really like that anymore," Mindy replied. "I've changed a lot, you know."

"Of course. I didn't mean anything bad by it. I was only joking. How old is Rebecca now?"

"Eight and a half months."

"Pictures, please."

Mindy opened her handbag and pulled out a recent photograph of Rebecca. Maybe this would lead her into the confession. She kicked herself for not coming clean immediately and for making up the bullshit story about Alaska. The photo of Rebecca chewing on her favorite stuffed toy was one of her cutest.

"Oh, is she adorable?" Ursula gushed. "Look at that little cutie. Will you mail me one? I'll do a portrait of her."

"Sure," Mindy replied, taking back the picture and replacing it in her wallet. A baby can look like a lot of people, but to Mindy's eyes this photo of Rebecca might as well have had PROPERTY OF TOMMY MARSICO stamped across its center. As if catching her guilty vibration, Ursula dropped a bombshell.

"Oh, I have to tell you this gossip. I just heard. Tommy Marsico got married again. Can you believe it?"

Mindy froze. "What?"

"Dan told me. One of his friends who was working a club in Birmingham told him. Tommy was sleeping with a waitress at the club—now, there's a surprise—and she got pregnant, and they got married. Can you imagine having that loser's baby? I'd have to kill myself."

"Yes. I mean no."

Mindy didn't know what she meant. As well as being slightly drunk and completely overtired, she was now thoroughly confused. Was this the same woman who had sobbed over this man for month after month? Certainly there was no way Mindy could now confess the truth. Perhaps Ursula was just covering up her true feelings for Tommy with her venomous comments? The only true sign that a person is over a relationship is indifference, and that was certainly not the emotion Mindy's antenna was picking up.

"How's your mother?" asked Mindy, eager to change the subject.

The story of Eva living in a castle with a millionaire producer was a good one. It kept Mindy awake for another twenty minutes, but then she officially declared herself the loser in the battle of the eyelids.

"Ursula, I have to go to bed. I've got to leave at six. I have a seven-thirty flight back."

"Why so early?"

"Rebecca has a doctor's appointment tomorrow afternoon, and she has to get a shot, and I have to make sure the doctor does it right. Do you think I'm too hands-on?"

Ursula laughed. "You were always the perfectionist."

"Don't get up when I leave in the morning. Honestly, I'll let myself out. I'll call you from New York. I know I'll be out here again. I'm auditioning for the *Tonight Show* for the third time next month, and one of these times I know I'm going to get it."

"Of course you will. I've done it a few times. Do you want me to talk to somebody for you? Maybe Marc could make a call?"

"No, but thanks."

They hugged and wished each other well and apologized again, professing delight at being back in each other's lives.

Mindy lay down in the white-sheeted guest bed and set her portable alarm clock for 5:30 A.M. She wondered whether she and Ursula would keep in touch and what Penelope would have thought of their strained conversation. Before Mindy turned off the light on her end table, she noticed a portrait of Penelope, painted by Ursula, hanging on the far wall. It was a Penelope that Mindy had never known: a bald woman, smiling hard and hoping. Mindy could see how much the woman in the painting wanted to get better, and it made her feel sad. She was pleased that Ursula had really captured the intensity Penelope possessed in her dark, rich eyes. As Mindy lay awake, listening to the waves slapping themselves continuously against the beach, she couldn't help but agree with her funny dead friend. The ocean *was* very noisy.

Let's Party Like
It's 1989

Rebecca began walking and talking before any of her playmates. Mindy took this as a sign of the fierce independence she herself had shown as a child. One day she came into the living room and saw her two-year-old daughter, whom she had believed to be taking a nap, dressed in a sweater and diaper and trying to push open the front door.

"Rebecca, what are you doing? Mindy asked.

"Becca go park," Rebecca announced.

"Do you want me to take you to the park?" Mindy asked.

"No. Me go."

Loretta stayed with Brett and Mindy when she came to New York to appear on the next all-female HBO special and; after four more auditions, Charlie Moon finally deemed Mindy ready for the *Tonight Show*.

"Now that's a set Johnny'll like," he proclaimed.

Mindy decided against informing him it was the same set she had originally performed at her very first audition almost four years earlier.

Mindy's several *Letterman* appearances had prepared her excellently for the increased pressure of the L.A.-based show. Indeed, Mindy's set went so well, Johnny called her over to the famous couch. Looking across at the face she had seen for so many years on television, all she could say was, "You know, you're Johnny Carson."

"And you know, you're Mindy Solomon," was Johnny's reply.

She met up with Ursula for lunch at Spago's, just as Ursula arranged to see Mindy when she was in New York filming promotional spots for her show, and they always phoned each other on birthdays and holidays. However hard they tried, though, they could never rekindle the intimacy they had shared as teenagers at the East Side Hotel for Women. Maybe that was just gone forever. Mindy had a new circle of friends, mostly mothers of two-year-olds, and Ursula was engaged to Marc Mosley and ran with the Hollywood in-crowd.

The show that had changed the course of their friendship was never a hit. It languished in the ratings, never low enough to cancel, never high enough to make an impact. Mindy watched the program from time to time and noticed that Ursula was no longer the focus of the show. Cindy's younger sister had all the tight clothes and main storylines. In the middle of its third season the network even changed the name of the show to *Samantha and Cindy*. To Ursula's credit, she genuinely didn't seem to care. When Mindy phoned to wish her a happy birthday, Ursula seemed happy to have less to learn each week and shorter rehearsals.

Mindy was currently in like with a kidney doctor she had met while jogging in the park. Barry Summerland was a thirty-five-year-old divorcé with two young children who visited him one weekend a month. Mindy never felt a rush when she saw him, but he was nice and normal and knew lots of cures for cystitis. Brett, on the other hand, was massively in love with Kyle, who worked at a chic art gallery on Wooster Street in SoHo.

One Sunday in June, Mindy was at the park, watching Rebecca play on the swings and plowing through the Sunday *New York Times*. Suddenly an ad in the book section caught her eye.

"Meeting Florence (A Neurotic's Italian Adventure), by Mitch Putnam," it read.

A small picture of her old boyfriend lurked in the bottom corner of the announcement of a book signing being held at noon the following day at the Barnes & Noble store on Fifth Avenue.

Over breakfast the next morning, Brett, the only person on earth to whom Mindy had confessed the entire, gory story, had an immediate reaction to the breaking news.

"Get dressed up and get down there."

"It's been over three years! He's probably married to a beautiful Italian girl."

"Listen, you might see him and feel nothing, but if you don't find out, you'll just build this thing up in your head."

It was a clear spring day in Manhattan. Mindy wore a bright pink dress that she felt made her look happy and flattering high-heeled sandals that had the potential to cause her feet to bleed. Paula Abdul was singing "Forever Your Girl" in the taxi on the way into midtown. Maybe that was an omen.

The book signing was on the second floor of the store. When a trepidatious Mindy stepped off the escalator, her ex-boyfriend radar immediately detected Mitch in the back corner of the store. He didn't spot her. Ex-girlfriend radar isn't as strong, Mindy knew. Mitch was seated behind a small table. His arms were folded, and on either side of him were stacks of books. Mindy looked at her watch. Five to twelve. She was early. Maybe that's why there was no one there. Mindy was in a quandary. She didn't want to be the first person in line and look too eager. She ducked behind a bookcase and began perusing titles, pretending to be a customer.

Mindy looked at her watch. It was ten minutes after twelve and still nobody was there. She didn't want Mitch to know that she knew there was no one at his book signing. She noticed a man was threatening to walk over to Mitch. Mindy attempted mental telepathy. *Go over. Go over to Mitch.* It worked! The man walked over. He shook hands with Mitch. He picked up a copy of his book and examined it. *Buy the book. Buy the book.* The man put the book down and walked away. Mindy had to switch tactics.

Two more people were searching for books in Mindy's aisle. She opened her purse and took out some money. She turned to the woman next to her.

"If I give you twenty-five dollars to go and buy a book from that man and have him sign it, will you do it?"

"Why don't you go buy the book yourself?"

"I'm going to. I just don't want to be the first one. I'm in therapy for it."

"Weird." But the woman took the money and walked over to Mitch's table.

As if by magic, people milling around the store began to gravitate toward Mitch's table. Everybody wants something someone else wants.

Why do people even say "hello"? thought Mindy. *Why don't they just say "baaaa"?*

A line began to form, and Mindy took her place in it.

"Just make it out to 'Stupid Mindy,'" she said before Mitch looked up to see who was speaking.

As Mitch raised his eyes from the book his pen hovered over, his look of surprise swiftly changed to joy and a broad smile creased his tanned face.

"Mindy!"

"That's me."

Mindy was pleased to see that Mitch looked almost exactly like Mitch, only, bizarrely, a little Italian.

"It's so great to see you," he said as he stood up awkwardly, knocking a few books off the table.

"That's a relief. I wasn't sure you'd talk to me," said Mindy.

As they both squatted to recover the spilled books, Mitch brushed her cheek with his fingers. "Mindy! Mindy Solomon."

Mindy felt a rush of electricity surge through her body at the touch of him.

"Can you wait around for a few minutes?" he asked her. "This won't take long. I'm not very well known."

One hour later, Mindy and Mitch sat in the Oak Bar at the Plaza Hotel, overlooking Central Park and each other.

"So, who's going to begin the necessary inquiries?" Mitch asked.

Mindy shrugged. "We've got so much baggage. I don't know where to start putting it all down."

"You go first. I saw you on the *Tonight Show* and I know you're divorced and have a little girl."

"That was my baggage. You opened my baggage. I was going to tell you both of those things, and now they're already out on the floor."

"Okay, I'll go—"

"You had a nervous breakdown, moved to Italy, wrote a book about it, and now you're back," Mindy interrupted.

"Boy, talk about baggage theft."

"Don't worry. There's a lot left. Are you married?"

"No. I had a girlfriend in Italy, and it was going really well until I learned to speak Italian. Are you seeing anyone?"

"Well, I live with a guy."

"Oh." Mitch's face fell.

"But he's gay, and he's Rebecca's nanny."

"Ah."

Mindy chose not to even mention the kidney doctor. Seeing Mitch again made her feel things that undoubtedly relegated her current semiboyfriend to future ex-semiboyfriend status.

"You know about Penelope, don't you?"

"Yes."

Neither had to say more.

"I saw Ursula at the memorial service. We've kept in touch," said Mindy. "She says the show—"

"Let me stop you there," said Mitch. "I want to hear nothing about the show. The show no longer exists for me. I no longer write for television. I write books for people who don't drive me crazy."

"Sorry. I think I tripped over some ripped baggage."

"That's okay. I'm slowly sewing it back together."

Mitch was on a three-week book tour that shuttled him to a new city daily. When Mitch kissed her good-bye, it was on the corner and on the cheek.

"I'll call you when I get back to the city," he said, stuffing Mindy's number in his pocket.

She had heard that before from men, she thought to herself in the back of the taxi. "I'll call you." Maybe the fact that she had a daughter now was too big a negative for him to overcome. Well, that's the way it was. Rebecca was more important to her than anything.

"Fuck him," Mindy accidentally said aloud in the cab.

"Yeah, fuck him," the cab driver agreed.

When a scowling Mindy walked back into her apartment, Brett was waiting.

"What's the matter with you? I hear it went well."

"What do you mean?"

Brett read from a piece of his leopard notepaper. "Mitch called and left his number. He's changed his flight to tomorrow morning and wondered if you are you free tonight. When can he meet your daughter?"

Mindy smiled.

Leonard Felk's first film under his Quixote banner was a spectacular failure. A thirty-million-dollar action adventure called *The Ticker,* the story concerned a bomb that was placed somewhere in America and the two mismatched cops from the LAPD special unit who had to find it. The review from the *Los Angeles Times* began, "Look for the bomb no more. It's in the theaters."

Leonard wasn't worried. He had followed his own showbiz adage and already had two more films in production. He was confident one of them would hit.

A few months later, Leonard watched a rough-cut of *The Cursed Mask* and had a horrible feeling that the chances of having a hit had just been reduced to one. When he flicked the lights on in his projection room, he turned to Eva, hoping she had seen a better movie.

"Well, what did you think?"

"It's such a fuck-up. How did it become such a fuck-up? I read the script, and it was scary. Why is this funny?"

"Maybe it's a comedy," Leonard suggested hopefully.

"No. It's not funny enough to be a comedy. It's not frightening enough to be scary, and it's not boring enough to win an award."

"What is it, then?"

"It's a fuck-up."

"It doesn't matter. That's the good thing. It doesn't matter," Leonard told Eva, as well as himself. "I've seen the dailies of *A Tale to Tell,* and it's a flat out winner. I am here to tell you—and I am never wrong—that Jeffrey Stone is a major star—a clean-cut, all-American star. He's going to wipe Tom Cruise off the map."

Leonard and Eva were dining on their patio overlooking the pool when the phone call came in.

"What do you mean, 'Jeffrey's dead'?" Leonard croaked into the portable receiver. "Wake him up. He can't be dead. We've shot only half the picture. What happened?"

Leonard prided himself on being a man who could wiggle out of anything. He was a man who could manipulate the weather if he had to. However, Leonard Felk knew deep in his gut that now he was officially in trouble. He was already sixty million down and had received phone calls and faxes from around the world threatening to pull the financial plug. If this last movie was not released, he was going to have to dissolve

Quixote Films and find all new money. It was one thing to find money when you had recently been the head of a Hollywood studio. It was another thing entirely to try the same thing after you had personally driven a variety of highly visible money sources straight down the shitter. Eva had never witnessed Leonard's features express this particular degree of panic.

"Lenny?"

"Jeffrey Stone killed himself last night. The selfish fuck."

"How did he do it?"

"You don't want to know."

Leonard packed his bags and took the 6:00 A.M. flight to San Antonio, where the movie was being filmed. He called a meeting with his director and his line producer.

"First things first. How much more of the film do we have to shoot?"

"Approximately half," Suzanne Patrillo, the line producer, told him. "Let me give you the alternatives. Number one—we start from the beginning with a new actor."

"How much will that cost?" Leonard asked.

"Well, apart from the cost of the reshoot, we'd have to rebuild the plane we've already disassembled and call back the stunt people. . . ."

"How much?" Leonard barked.

"At least five mil."

"Don't have it. Next."

"That's it," Suzanne said. "That's our alternative."

Leonard was puzzled. Surely the whole idea of alternatives was that there was more than one?

"What about we shoot the rest of the movie on another actor's back, and we have a guy imitate his voice?" Leonard suggested. "That's how they finished that Natalie Wood movie."

"Half the movie on the star of the film's back? Get real, Leonard," said the director. "You *have* to get more money. This is a good movie. No, I take that back. It's not a good movie. It's a summer blockbuster. We'll get another actor and we'll start from scratch. We already have the sets. We already have the locations. If we do it quickly, we can still meet our release date."

Leonard thought for a minute. Who was he if he couldn't talk people into another five million for a potential blockbuster?

"Okay," he said, suddenly resolved. "Find me an actor who won't accidentally hang himself in a motel room while jerking off, and we'll start the reshoot Monday. Frame by fucking frame."

The fiscal consortium Leonard had stitched together, however, had lost faith in its Hollywood leader. It's members were not prepared to throw good money after bad, preferring instead to take their losses and write them off. The word on the street about Leonard and *A Tale to Tell* was that they were both DOA. In a town ruled by perception, Leonard smelled of formaldehyde.

Eva had never seen her partner beaten up to this degree. It upset her. He had no interest in her or the pump. He just lay in bed, staring up at the ceiling, knowing the closing of production on his one potential hit was now inevitable.

"Leonard. How sure are you that this movie is a hit?" asked Eva, considering something dangerous.

"Absolutely one hundred percent. I've seen the dailies. You've seen the dailies. Losing Stone turned out to be a blessing. The new guy Suzanne found is sensational. Steven Winner. He's even got winner in his name. This guy is so good-looking even *I* want to fuck him. Eva, I'd bet my balls, and you know how I feel about my balls."

"Why don't you put in your own money?"

"Don't you think I would? Every last cent I had went into Quixote as seed money."

"How about putting this house up as collateral?"

"The house is mortgaged up the kazoo. So are the cars. I'm beaten, Eva. It had to happen eventually. Hollywood fucked me. I've tried everywhere. I can't raise a dime."

"Okay, now listen. You know I'm in charge of Ursula's finances. I've been investing her money for years. I have total power of attorney. Ursula has about five million dollars on deposit."

Leonard hugged Eva. Maybe it was his imagination, but just for just a second, he felt he had a natural erection.

"Thank you, Eva. Thank you."

A Tale to Tell was once again half finished when the unthinkable happened. A stunt man fell on top of Steven Winner, crushing his pelvis and separating his spine. He wasn't dead, but he would not be allowed to move for at least a year, maybe longer. When Leonard got the phone call, he didn't tell Eva right away. First he proposed.

Leonard's tactic was a good one. The high of the proposal cushioned the low of the financial disaster. Eva thought quickly. Ursula still was pulling down a good income on her TV show and never asked her mother for a financial breakdown. Eva would begin reinvesting, begin building the portfolio back up. And when Leonard finally had a hit, he could return the five million. Her daughter need never know the cardinal sin her mother had committed. The most important thing in her life was her new title: Mrs. Leonard Felk.

Ursula was in a meeting two weeks later with Marc Mosley's newly formed financial team. Marc had recently opened up another branch of his management company. His inspiration had in fact come from his fiancée and her complete lack of understanding concerning her finances. One day, while attempting to meditate and clear his mind of all things work related, a brilliant business idea had popped into his brain.

"There are all these talented people out there who not only can't manage their own careers, they can't manage their own money. Why am I letting ninety percent of the money I make for them walk out the door for other people to take a percentage of?"

Marc Mosley's financial services department was born. After head-hunting top investment strategists from highly regarded firms, Marc put together a team of advisors, printed stationery, and set up a series of meetings to introduce the new team to his clients.

"What kind of return are you getting at the moment?" Stewart Lymen asked Ursula.

"I don't know."

Stewart gave his cohort James a "she needs us" look.

"What percentage do you have invested in stocks and what percentage in bonds?"

"I'm going to have to stop you here," Ursula said. "I know nothing about my money. My mother manages everything. My checks go directly to her, and she pays my mortgage and my bills. I live on an allowance, unless I need more; then I ask her and she gives it to me."

"And you're happy with that arrangement?" Stewart probed.

"Yes. Why shouldn't I be?"

"Look. Let us just take a look at your statements. If we think your mother is doing a good job, we'll leave it the way it is. If we think we could do a better job, we'll tell you and we'll show you a detailed plan of our investment strategy. We want to involve you," Stewart said.

He stood up and stretched his suspenders with his thumbs. He had just seen *Wall Street* and it had dramatically affected his wardrobe.

"You're an adult," double-teamed James. "You should be informed of every decision we make and have input. Let us take a look. You have nothing to lose."

Ursula had to admit these guys had a point. Why was she still giving her mother carte blanche with her hard-earned money? They had made that arrangement six years ago because Ursula felt sorry for her then-penniless parent. Now, Eva was living with a millionaire in a house ten times as expensive as Ursula's. It was time to break away. She phoned her mother that evening.

"Why do you need to see everything right this minute?" Eva asked, trying to stay calm.

Urusla knew that flattery was the way to get what she wanted out of her mother.

"I just want to show the statements to Marc's new investment team so they can see what a good job you're doing."

"Let them call me tomorrow. You don't have to worry yourself with this."

"Mother, I'm not a little girl anymore. It's my money. I'm driving over now and picking up this month's statements. I'll probably leave things the way they are, but I owe it to myself to consider all the possibilities."

"This is a bad time for me. Leonard's film's in trouble."

"I heard. He lost another actor. I'm sorry. I really am. But you can't use that as an excuse, because that has nothing to do with me."

"Well . . ." Eva had no choice but to tell her daughter about the money.

"You *what?!*"

"It's only a temporary cash-flow problem. I'll begin investing your salary again, and it will build right up in no time. And Leonard will restore everything. With interest."

"I'm coming over."

"Ursula, there is no need for you to come over. You don't need the money right now. You're overreacting."

Ursula was livid. "I trusted you. I trusted you with everything I had. I want all my papers out of your house. I never want to see you again. You're out of my life for good this time."

Ursula slammed down the phone and jumped into her Mercedes.

Pulling out of her drive and onto Pacific Coast Highway was

always a tricky maneuver, and this time, Ursula forgot to look both ways. The truck swerved and tried to go around her, but clumsy Ursula stepped on the accelerator instead of the brake, putting herself right in the path of the oncoming vehicle.

The Mercedes was pushed fifty feet, despite the trucker's slamming on his air brakes. Surprisingly, Ursula was still okay. It was only when the car disengaged from the truck and hurtled toward a telephone pole that Ursula was thrown forward. As the Mercedes crunched sickeningly against the wooden pole, the head that had graced so many magazine covers hit first the side door and then the windshield, at approximately thirty-five miles an hour.

The truck driver pulled over, jumped out, and ran back to the accordioned metal. He pulled open the passenger door.

"Oh Jesus," he said, seeing the mess inside. "Oh Jesus Christ."

Mitch gently moved Mindy sideways in the bed as she lay dozing in his arms. He found the remote control and turned on the TV to watch CNN's report on the atrocities just committed by the Chinese army in Tiananmen Square. He found instead a photograph of Ursula. He quickly turned up the volume to hear the news anchor.

"Actress Ursula Duran was critically injured in a Los Angeles car crash earlier today. . . ."

Mindy sat bolt upright. An hour later she was at Kennedy Airport. Six hours later, she was in a taxi in Los Angeles, hurrying toward her friend. The first person she saw as she entered the intensive care unit was a pale and forlorn-looking Eva, sitting in the waiting room, twisting a bunch of shredded tissues in her fingers as she rocked backward and forward on a plastic bucket chair.

"Eva, what happened?"

"It's all my fault. I did it. It's all my fault."

"How is she? Tell me what happened," Mindy demanded.

"It's all my fault," Eva repeated.

Leonard Felk entered the waiting room carrying a glass of water and a pill for Eva.

"Eva, here."

Leonard tried handing his partner the sedative, but she brushed him away.

"I don't know what to do. What can I do? My baby. What have I done to my baby?"

"Eva, please take this," implored Leonard. Eva took the sedative and the glass of water from Leonard's shaking hand.

"You must be Leonard. I'm Mindy. I'm Ursula's best friend," said Mindy, suddenly secure in the knowledge that best friend was indeed and always would be her role in Ursula's life, just as it was Ursula's role in hers.

Leonard guided Mindy away from the malfunctioning Eva.

"The doctor said he'll come by and give us an update in a second," Leonard explained to Mindy, trying to keep his voice on an even keel. "Poor Eva. She feels so responsible."

"Fuck Eva," said Mindy sharply. "Eva's been a disaster for Ursula from the minute she was born."

Leonard was taken aback.

"If Eva's saying it was all her fault, it probably was. That's her problem, and it's immaterial. I'm here for Ursula."

Leonard had no more fight left. He felt old. He nodded acquiescently to Mindy.

"I'm glad you came," he said.

Just then the chief neurosurgeon arrived.

"Who's in charge?" he asked.

"She is," said Leonard, gesturing to Mindy.

"My name's Mark Santos," he said.

"Mindy Solomon."

"Okay," he said, all business. "Ursula's suffered a head injury, which has caused her brain to swell. Because the brain is encased within the skull, it doesn't have room to swell, and so part of Ursula's brain has compressed. This compression has decreased the blood flow and oxygen to parts of her brain, and that has caused more swelling. I've removed some blood clots and repaired some damaged blood vessels, which has stopped any further bleeding. That's given her brain more room and stopped that cycle of compression."

"Is she conscious?"

The doctor hesitated. "I thought you knew. She's in a coma."

Mindy felt all the air leave her lungs.

"Every brain injury is unique," the doctor continued. "We can't predict the rate a patient will progress or where a patient's recovery will plateau."

"Can I see her?" Mindy asked.

"She's in postop right now. She'll be down shortly. I'll come back to see you then."

He attempted to cheer up the despondent Mindy. "Hey, your friend's a fighter. I saw what was left of her car on the news. It's a miracle she even survived. I'm cautiously optimistic."

As he left, Eva started to moan.

"What *is* her problem?" asked Mindy impatiently.

Leonard explained the full circumstances of the crash, and why Ursula had been hurrying over to see Eva.

"Take her home," said Mindy. "She can't do anyone any good here."

"Okay," said Leonard.

"And where's this wonderful fiancé-manager?" asked Mindy.

"He was here earlier," Leonard told her. "He has a psychological problem with hospitals. I have his mobile number if you'd like it."

"Don't bother," said Mindy, disgusted.

Leonard took the distraught Eva home to the palace that was no longer theirs, while Mindy sat waiting to hear whether her friend would live or die. After an hour or so, Mark Santos reappeared.

"They're bringing her down now. Let me explain some things to you about her condition. A coma isn't a state of complete unconsciousness. Even though Ursula doesn't react, it doesn't mean she can't hear what's happening around her. The most important thing to do when you're with her is to speak positively. A lot of patients very distinctly recall events that happen when they're in a coma. Always speak about her as if she's going to get better, and never speak about her as if she's not there. These first twenty-four hours are the most critical."

"I understand."

"And I'd better warn you. She's looked better."

Mindy hovered by the door as Ursula was wheeled into a room by a team of efficient nurses. A catheter and a feeding tube were reinserted into Ursula's body. A humidifying machine compressor was switched on and began a relentless, rhythmic squeak.

As the nurses moved away, Mindy edged slowly toward the hospital bed, adjusting to the sight of her friend's swollen, black-and-blue face, her bandaged, shaved head, and her sealed eyelids.

Only react positively, she told herself. *She can hear.*

"Hi, Urs. It's Mindy. I've just been talking to the doctor, and guess what? You're going to be fine."

Having a conversation with someone who didn't answer was an odd sensation. At first Mindy felt self-conscious, but after a few minutes, she pulled up a chair and really began to talk. Boy, did she talk. She told Ursula everything. She told her how important Ursula had been to her in her life and how she had been her first real friend. She told her how lost and alone she had felt when she had checked into the East Side Hotel for Women and how she considered meeting Ursula to be one of the luckiest things that had ever happened to her. She told her nobody had ever paid any attention to her before that; she told her how friendless she had been back in Florida and how the fact that someone like Ursula would be friends with her had given her more confidence in herself. She told her how having someone to share things with had made every day of those difficult but exciting times special. Mindy told her how much she had missed her these past few years and how, when Ursula woke up, it was all going to be different.

"I know we've had some difficult times, but that all goes in the friendship pot. If we have differences, or even fights, it doesn't matter. It just makes the pot fuller because we're always going to come out the other side. There'll never be another you and me who went through the things we went through. The only thing that matters is that someday we'll be two old ladies, drinking tea on a porch, remembering the mattress commercial and the topless audition and talking into a broom and being hit on by your father and dating Ed the married piano player and paddle—for God's sake, let's not forget paddle. Nobody else in the world will ever know what we're talking about or what it was all really like except you and me, Ursula. Except you and me."

Mindy arranged to sleep in a cot by Ursula's bed and took a shower in the maternity ward. She phoned home to check on Rebecca, who was having a great time monopolizing both Brett and Mitch.

On the second day, while Mindy was telling Ursula all about giving birth to Rebecca, Ursula's eyelids began to flutter. Mindy called in a nurse. When the nurse pinched Ursula's foot, she recoiled.

"I'll call Dr. Santos," the nurse said.

Dr. Santos came quickly.

"Maybe she's coming out of it," Mindy offered.

"Perhaps," he said, not particularly hopeful. "Sometimes these actions suggest recovery, but in actual fact they're just involuntary movements."

As he left, Mindy started talking again.

"Ursula, there's one thing I have to tell you to clear the air once and for all. So that when you wake up, it's going to be the way it was. We're not going to have secrets anymore, you see. We're going to be able to tell each other everything just like we used to. Okay, here goes."

Mindy took a deep breath. "I was never married. I made it up. I got so angry with you when you took that television show that I slept with Tommy Marsico. And I accidentally got pregnant, and Rebecca is his baby."

Ursula remained perfectly still. There was no movement whatsoever.

"How is she?" said a voice from the doorway.

Mindy looked up. "Come in and see," she offered.

"I can't," said the voice. "I can't come in there."

"Then you're a disgrace," Mindy growled.

"Yes," said Marc Mosley. "I am. Can I do anything? Can I pay for anything?"

"You can just be here for her."

"I really wish I could do that," he said plaintively.

Suddenly something started beeping. Mindy hurriedly scanned the machines, fearing something had gone wrong.

"Marc Mosley speaking."

The noise had come from Mosley's mobile phone. He stood in the hospital doorway of the woman he professed to care for and discussed a deal point in a contract.

"Look, let's discuss this further tonight, Michelle. Bistro Garden? Seven? Okay, see you then," said Marc. *"Ciao."*

He put the phone away. "Sorry about that," he murmured.

Mindy threw him a withering glance.

"Look, if she wakes up . . . could you just tell her I'm sorry?"

Mindy sighed. "A fair-weather fiancé," she said loudly. "Jeez, Ursula, you sure can pick 'em." She looked up, expecting a reaction, but Marc Mosley was already gone.

Leonard came by later that day. It was his second visit. He had returned the day before to check on Ursula's progress and to see whether Mindy needed anything. This time he brought Mindy magazines. He stroked Ursula's hand.

"Hello, beautiful," he said. "How ya' doin'?"

Mindy was beginning to grow fond of this physically unattractive man. He had character and reminded her of a younger Irv.

"Eva's heavily sedated," he told her. "Or else she'd come by."

He gave Mindy his number. "You call me any hour of the day or night if there's anything you want or anything I can do," he urged.

"Thanks, Leonard."

"No, thank *you*. Having you here has made all the difference. Ursula's very lucky. If I'd ever had a friend like you, I could have owned this town."

"From what I hear, you did own it for a while," Mindy said.

"Not 'for a while,'" said Leonard. "Maybe for a long weekend."

He paused, reflecting on past glories. He shook his head, dismissing the thoughts. "I'll see you tomorrow."

"See you tomorrow, Leonard."

By the third day, Mindy was beginning to feel engulfed by hopelessness. It had been almost thirty hours since Ursula's eyelids had fluttered. Since then, there had been no movement whatsoever. Mindy was tired, and she ached, and she didn't know what else to do or say. She pulled her chair up close to her friend's bed and whispered urgently in her ear.

"Now listen, Ursula. They've told me I have to be upbeat and positive and all that shit, but I'm going to have to lay it on the line for you here. I can't lose you. It's as simple as that. I lost my mother. I lost Penelope. I can't lose you too. I couldn't bear it. You have to wake up now, you hear? I need you to wake up."

She stared at her friend, lying supine and bruised on the hospital bed, and willed her to wake. Nothing happened. Mindy dropped her head and began to weep. Her shoulders heaved as she cried great sobs of misery.

"Mindy?"

She looked up. Ursula was staring at her.

"Ursula!" she gulped.

"Are you going to talk all night?"

Ursula jumped at the idea of convalescing in New York under Mindy's care. While she concentrated on getting well enough to travel, Mindy packed up the house in Malibu that was about to be taken over by the bank. Even after putting some of the clothes in storage, Mindy still filled four large suitcases. She had Ursula's paintings freighted back to New York, advising Brett to have Kyle hang them in the apartment to help Ursula feel at home.

Two weeks later, Ursula's orientation had returned, her bruises were fading, and her hair was growing back, starting to conceal the scar left by the craniotomy incision. She and Mindy boarded a plane bound for New York. Marc Mosley had paid to fly them first class in return for the ring. Ursula had let him go as both her manager and her fiancé, and Marc had been secretly relieved, especially once he learned ABC had decided not to renew *Samantha and Cindy* for the next season.

"I'm so excited you're going to meet Rebecca," Mindy told Ursula as their flight taxied down the runway. "You know what she said to me on the phone this morning?"

"'I can't believe Tommy Marsico is my daddy'?" Ursula teased.

Mindy turned beet red. She had not talked about her coma conversations with Ursula and hadn't known whether her hospital-room confession had registered.

"You remember, then?"

"Hey, I heard a lot of mumbling from you in that hospital room, but *that* message came in loud and clear."

"I'm so sorry."

"Mindy, why would you think I'd care?"

"I was ashamed. It was such a stupid, spiteful thing to do. I thought better of me than that."

"Oh, cut yourself some slack. Did he do the 'naked except for the socks' trick?"

"Yes!"

"Creep. Look, just think of sleeping with him as like going to a sperm bank, only slightly more impersonal."

Mindy giggled.

"Did you ever tell him about Rebecca?" Ursula asked.

"No."

"Good. Did you tell Mitch?"

"Not yet."

"Don't tell him now. Wait until he's in a coma."

Rebecca, Mitch, and Brett met the women at Kennedy Airport. Mindy wrapped herself around her daughter and wallowed in the smell, the touch, the feel of her.

"Mommy, we missed you. We missed you bad."

During Mindy's absence, some domestic alterations had taken place. Mitch had moved in, and Brett had moved out to live with Kyle.

"I hope that's okay." said Brett anxiously, as they drove in to the city. "I'm still available twenty-four/seven."

"Sounds fine to me," said Mindy, surreptitiously squeezing Mitch's hand.

"Kyle is very interested in your work," Brett told Ursula. "We showed your paintings to his boss, Simon, and he really wants to meet you. We didn't tell him you were Ursula Duran. We just said you were a friend of Mindy's."

Simon Ball phoned a few days after that and offered to include a selection of Ursula's paintings in his annual exhibition of new artists. They met up, and she was delighted to find he looked like James Taylor when he'd had hair. He was delighted to find she looked like Ursula Duran.

To Ursula's astonishment, she discovered the approbation she had always been looking for lay in the talent she had always dismissed. She sold three paintings in that first exhibition, although she kept her portrait of Penelope, despite a handsome offer for it. With her anemic finances suddenly healthier, Ursula moved into an apartment on the same block of Gramercy Park as Simon, whom she had started dating.

The first few times Eva phoned, Ursula refused to take the call. Eventually, though, she relented and spoke to her manic mother. Eva and Leonard had lost the Pacific Palisades mansion and had moved into a one-bedroom apartment somewhere in West Hollywood. They were working on a new project together. They had optioned a script Eva had found years before called *A Girl's Best Friend* and, against all odds, had interested Bette Midler and Disney in it. Eva apologized profusely about everything and vowed she and Leonard would repay Ursula every last cent of the money they owed her.

"The money is just a fraction of what's wrong with us, Mother. It's always been you first. I've never known what it was like to be important to someone. I watch other mothers, I watch Mindy and Rebecca, and Rebecca's needs always come first. That's what a child's supposed to be—someone who matters to you more than you matter to yourself. I don't think you'll ever be capable of that feeling."

"One more chance. Just one more?" Eva whispered. "I know I was a bad mother, but Ursula, when I sat in that hospital and thought you might die, it hurt so much, I went a little crazy. You're my baby. As long as I've got you, I'm wealthy and I'm pretty and I'm happy and all those things I was always chasing that were really there all of the time. Without you, I've got nothing. Just one more chance."

This particular door once again refused to shut. "Maybe just one more," Ursula replied, looking up to the sky and regretting it already.

Not only was Rebecca walking and talking but she was also becoming so bossy she was practically directing traffic.

"Mommy sits over there," she said one day at dinner.

"Daddy sits over there," she continued, pointing at Mitch.

"Rebecca, Mitch is mommy's boyfriend. He's not your daddy," Mindy said.

"Yes, I am," Mitch said. "Rebecca, ask your mommy to marry me."

"Mommy, will you marry me?" Rebecca asked.

Mindy was speechless.

"Now come over here and give your mommy this ring."

Rebecca obeyed and carefully brought the tiny diamond ring over to her mother.

"It's small now," Mitch said, "but the guy at the magic store says if you put it in water, it gets bigger."

"I love it just the way it is," said Mindy tearfully, as her daughter and future husband hugged her tightly.

Toward the end of the year, Mindy received an offer to headline at a special New Year's Eve, end-of-the-decade show at Stars.

"The club has a new owner, and he wants to call you. Is it okay if I give him your number?" asked Richard, Mindy's agent. "He wants to open for you and wonders if that's okay."

"Sure," said Mindy. "Tell him to give me a call."

Mindy realized she didn't even know who the old owner of the club was, never mind the new. The phone rang five minutes later, and she picked it up.

"Hello?" she said.

"Hi, Mindy. This is Ronnie. Ronnie Braverman."

Mindy felt a flood of nostalgia at the sound of the voice of the comedian who had been such an influence on her when she was first starting out.

"Ronnie! I don't believe it!"

True to his word, Ronnie had given up comedy and gone to

work for his father. However, after his father died, Ronnie had sold the family's medical supply business and reinvested the money in Manhattan real estate. One of the properties he had chosen to buy had been Stars of Tomorrow.

"Moe was happy to sell it to me."

"Moe? Moe the ex-con owned Stars?"

"Of course. Why did you think he was there every night?"

And so, on December 31, 1989, before they all headed over to Mindy's show to say good-bye to the '80s and hello to the '90s, Mindy, Mitch, Rebecca, Ursula, Simon, Brett, and Kyle gathered together in Ursula's apartment.

"I've got a present for you," Ursula told Mindy. "It's in my bedroom."

Mindy followed her friend down the hallway.

"I hope you like it," said Ursula.

Standing in the middle of the room on an easel was a finished canvas. It depicted two women in a boat on a river.

"It's you and me in a shit storm," said Ursula.

"Oh, Ursula, I love it. But we still don't have a paddle," laughed Mindy.

"Yes, we do, Mindy. Don't you see? We're each other's paddles."

And so they were.

And so they would continue to be, right through the SadaamO.J.GingrichTailhookMicrosoftDahmerLAquakeIPO BobbittJerrySpringerBillaryRoseanneNancy'n'TonyaTiger CD-ROMButtafucoBeLikeMike*Heaven'sGate*KatoMillion ManMarchPerotSeinfeldwww.comKenStarre-mailMonica *Titanic*DVDMilosevicInternet'90s.

As Rebecca liked to say, "Fish banana."

Acknowledgments

There are many people should I have to thank. That's how I would have written a sentence had I not had considerable help. I'd like to thank my editor Kathy Bowers for gently pointing out that many things I wrote were not very good; my agent Alan Nevins for having the skin of a rhinoceros and for not giving up; my friends Morwenna Banks and David Baddiel for reading and recommending my efforts; Sarah Shrubb and Alan Sampson at Little Brown and Mitchell Ivers at Pocket Books for publishing those efforts; Chris Albrecht and everyone at HBO for helping me become a comedian; and my husband, collaborator, and parole officer, Martin Bergman, who worked even harder on this book than I did.